Advance

"Brilliant and captivating, r... ...nd's Feet on High Places."

I'm not typically drawn to fiction, even historically based fiction, but I loved this adventure. This beautiful book brings humanity to the characters—fear, panic, anger and doubt. As a mother, seeing her grit to find her child was gut-wrenching.

—Sandra Carr, Artist and Interior Designer

"Twists, turns and the 'OMG!' moments you expect."

As a young girl attending Sunday School, I heard about Abraham and Sarah (and Hagar). The stories felt like felt-board caricatures. *Sarah's Song* is a page-turning, don't-want-to-put-down book that both thrilled me, frightened me and opened my eyes and heart.

—Kelli Dingmann, Administrative Professional, Creative, Missionary.

"This book is a healing balm."

This transformative work helped me explore how I am part of God's story of redemption. Walking alongside Sarah was like taking a flashlight to dig deeper into the depth of my own grief, loss, rejection, abandonment, abuse, betrayal, and trauma.

—Nicoleta Koha, Preschool Teacher

"Every woman's story—her fears, regrets, sorrows and unfulfilled dreams."

As Sarah travels dangerous mountain paths searching for Abraham and Isaac, you'll discover her song—a sweet melody coming from the deepest longings of her heart. God's gentle care surprises Sarah, and as I read, I experienced God's grace redeeming my struggle with infertility."

—Diane Marie Mitchell, Senior Developer, Business Intelligence

"So many parallels between her journey and mine."

Reading *Sarah's Song* was enlightening. As I traveled with Sarah, I watched her face and overcome her demons, deepen her commitment to Yahweh, and transform her relationships with her family.

—Janice Wright, Educator

"Has changed my relationship with God in a profound way."

I traveled back in time, laughed, cried and saw the dark recesses of my own heart. Not for the faint of heart, *Sarah's Song* is filled with adventure, and suspense.

—Jermiah Jones, Museum Educator Media Specialist, Teacher Librarian

"Heart-changing biblical principles fill the pages!"

Reminded me of the critical nature of walking in openness with the women God places in my life, to strengthen my soul for the battles that will inevitably come. I loved learning about this historical period through Robin's scholarly in-depth studies and creativity.

—Mary Freeman, IT Admin, Nuclear Technologies and National Security

"His plans are always good…even when it's painful."

Sarah's trust in Yahweh grew throughout her journey to Mount Moriah. At the end, she knew her true purpose in life because she surrendered to his plans. Like Sarah, as Yahweh's beloved daughter, I am most effective when I see how Yahweh sees me.

—Chrep Meitner, Certified Life Coach, educator and mother

"I want to follow in the path that brave women have carved before me."

The wonderfully descriptive text transported me to her world. I was living her life with her and thinking about the story during the day. Especially inspiring for me was the realistic depiction of Sarah as an older woman.

—Robin Wadsworth, Performing Arts Teacher for 29 years

"Will leave readers with a sense of longing…"

A deep dive into the life of a female warrior and pillar of faith. Robin's exquisite talent of storytelling comes alive in these pages. It is an epic journey of love, faith, healing and strength that will leave readers longing for a deeper connection with their creator and others.

—Jordan Brilhante, Enrollment Representative at the University of Phoenix

Sarah's Song

AN ALLEGORY

ROBIN WEIDNER

Personal Study Guide and Book Group Guide Included

Robin Weidner

Author of *Secure in Heart, Eve's Song, Grace Calls* and *Pure the Journey* (with David Weidner)

ISBN: 978-1-953623-67-6

Cover features background artwork by **Erin Hanson**. "Combining the emotional resonance of 19th-century Impressionists with the lavish color palette of Expressionism, Erin Hanson's unique style has come to be known as 'Open Impressionism.' Her paintings appear in art school curriculums around the world, and with millions of followers online, Hanson is inspiring a new love for Impressionism in the contemporary art world." https://www.erinhanson.com/

Cover layout by Jason Gonzales, Miah Graphics and inside layout by Illumination Publishers. Published by Illumination Publishers International.

Why the Voice? "The Voice distinguishes the unique perspective of each author. The heart of the project is retelling the story of the Bible in a form as fluid as modern literary works while remaining painstakingly true to the original Greek, Hebrew, and Aramaic texts. Accomplished writers and biblical scholars have been teamed up to create an English rendering that, while of great artistic value, is carefully aligned with the meaning inherent in the original language. https://www.biblegateway.com/versions/The-Voice-Bible/

To the women of old whose stories
are only known in part, but whose
perseverance and love still light up
the dark corners of dim times.

"For now, we can only see a dim and blurry picture of things, as when we stare into polished metal. I realize that everything I know is only part of the big picture."
1 Corinthians 13:12a

Allegory

A poem, play, picture, etc., in which the apparent meaning of the characters and events is used to symbolize a deeper moral or spiritual meaning.

A story that has a deeper or more general meaning, in addition to its surface meaning.

Source: dictionary.com

Note from the Author:

This book is a unique blend of fiction, scripture, Jewish midrash, and personal experience. These words are *not* an attempt to accurately explain all that the Bible is silent on, but rather to illuminate the way we see God, our relationships, and our own healing journeys.

Scriptures are noted at the bottom of each page to make them accessible. Due to space limitations, scriptures are sometimes shared in part. See the references for the full text.

Table of Contents

And not to have is the beginning of desire.
To have what is not is its ancient cycle.
It is desire at the end of winter, when....
It knows that what it has is what is not.
And throws it away like a thing of another time
As morning throws off stale moonlight and shabby sleep.

—Wallace Stevens, "Notes toward a Supreme Fiction"

To sing is to mourn.
To mourn is to accept.
But redemption comes
From Yahweh alone.

Born of idol worship.
Seeker of one God,
Singer of Eve's song,
Ezer to my husband.

As I sing, I wonder
Is it my song or yours?
Or so one, we cannot
Tell the difference.

This I do know.
Abraham sang to me,
Sarai the seeker,
Bearer of prophecy.

Yet I became to him
Unable to deliver,
Barren of a child,
Denying his blessing.

All that remains is
A song of Yahweh.
Only I can sing,
Only he can witness.

Then I wonder,
Is it my song or yours?
Or so one, we cannot
Tell the difference.

Despair brought chaos
My handmaid birthing
The son of unrequited
desires and unbelief.

Now my true son
Of a revived womb
Carries me forward,
Into my hidden fears.

How do I obey
When Yahweh asks
Me to sing a song
Without an ending?

How can a husband
Be called my lord
Who risks the gift,
For an unlikely faith?

Then I understood.
It is my song and yours.
Now so one, we cannot
Tell the difference.

INTRODUCTION
Prayer Song

MY HUSBAND IS PRAYING IN THE NIGHT I am terrified. Within decades of marriage, I have borne witness to many of his prayers. Petitions for our family. Pleas for deliverance from cruel rulers. Requests for protection from wayside robbers. Supplication for diminishing water supplies. Intercession for our ailing camels. Thanksgiving for God's goodness. But none like this. Hunched over with his forehead pressed to the ground, close to a fire he built with his own hands, Abraham is on his knees crying out to the God he knows as Yahweh. His muffled cries are a smoky mist that rises from the ground. Creeping through the entrance of our tent, the mist pushes its way into every hidden crevice in my spirit. Although I can only hear some of his words, I strain for more, as any devoted wife would do.

What concerns him so? Is trouble simmering that he hasn't yet divulged?

His soul is at war, but this time not with a trio of kings like the ones who abducted his nephew Lot. I sigh as the heaviness of his prayer weighs on my shoulders. This invocation shows no signs of subsiding. Like a song, his prayer must find its crescendo before resolution may come. Impulsively, I take one step beyond the door of our tent, towards him. Will the darkness hide me from view? Feeling like an intruder, I quickly move back into the tent and lower myself onto the mat at our tent's entrance. *He desires this time alone with Yahweh. Tomorrow is soon enough.*

On most nights I would already be in a dreamless slumber. As Abraham would say (or Abram, as I sometimes call him affectionately), a whole tribe of bandits could come through our camp and I would not even stir. Yet, just as a mother awakens at the first cry of her babe, a wife intuits her husband's distress. From times of old, it has been called the eye that sees the danger. Yes, the ezer, a gift of Yahweh, yet also a burden in Abraham's estimation. As much as my weary legs want to move me towards him, I imagine him raising his bushy gray eyebrows and saying dismissively, *Meddling is not from Yahweh, Sarai...my ezer.*

"This is not meddling, Abraham," I whisper. "You need an ezer more than you know."

And so, if my husband will pray in secret, I will watch in secret. A man's ways aren't nearly as apparent as a woman's. They claim women are wily, deliberately difficult to decipher. But a man who doesn't want to talk is an impenetrable wall, his face a slab of stone. But just as giant desert boulders eventually crack, I must watch for the moments where he drops his guard.

Our story testifies that this intercession will most likely affect me.

Whenever Abraham has received a calling to prayer, then other summons followed. *Leave your household, your possessions, your wealth, your security and become a nomad traversing the desert to some unknown destination.* Abraham always replies *hinini,* meaning, "I am here to do your will. You can count on me." And at other times, he discerns a calling where there is none. *Yes, you can form an alliance with Egypt by telling them your wife is your sister. This is a wise plan.* I exhale loudly to push away the memory before it ushers in nightmares of a wicked king determined to seduce me.

Suddenly a loud wail escapes Abraham's lips just as a popping noise sends a flurry of ash and spark into the air and, no doubt, dusts his head. He speaks louder. This allows me to make out a few anguished words…*sacrifice, blessing, hinini, Isaac, Ishmael.* Hearing the word Ishmael, I am suddenly done with listening to my husband's pleas. I gently close the flap of our tent. Then I carefully feel my way through the darkness back to our bed. The beat of my heart pulses in my forehead. Ishmael is the source of all this passion. Yes, this explains why he prays without me. Ishmael is a muddy bog Abram and I cannot navigate without getting sucked in up to our necks. Abraham knows that pleasing me means Ishmael must be far away. Perhaps that's why my husband has been preoccupied lately.

Yes, Abraham's faith, fasting and intercession often includes the son I have sought to forget. I can't be sure of the last time I prayed for Ishmael, the son of my handmaid Hagar. Legally and emotionally, he was my son for seventeen years. Tired of Hagar's abuse, I gave him back to her and dismissed them to find their own way. Secretly, I hope that Ishmael is still alive. If he is alive, I wonder if Abraham visits him without my knowledge.

I take a deep breath, willing my heart and head to quiet. My hips ache, the curse of 105 years of living. Sleep will not come back to me easily. So, I do what offers refuge. I push away the uncomfortable to make room for other thoughts. My husband's seeking of his God through prayer moves me. For Abraham, faith and prayer can no more be separated than the wheat stalk from the mother kernel that surrendered her life to bear it.

I shiver, shaking my shoulders like a deer dispelling the rain. With a chill in the air, bedcovers cannot replace the warmth of another body. Nor can they banish the chilly disquiet that remains in my soul, a trepidation Abraham's prayer fanned into flame. Once chilled, my bones simply refuse to let it go.

My thoughts slide to my son. I am well past the nights when Isaac would crawl into bed with me. As a young boy, he liked to hide on the other side of me under the bed coverings and surprise his father when he arrived. He knew that a day's labor about our camp meant we would be too tired to take him to his nursemaid's tent. Now, sprinting towards his fifteenth year, he has his own tent. Although Isaac boasts of his increased status, I purposely have a maid's tent near his. Help is nearby if he were to need it. Her watchful eyes are more tolerable to him than having "my mother Sarah hovering over me like a pesky dragonfly" as Isaac sometimes jests, relishing the use of my proper name.

A rush of warmth runs down my spine all the way to my toes, pushing out the chill. If I am the mother tree rooting our family, my child is the sap that runs through my veins. Isaac is more than I prayed for, all that I yearned for, worth the fifty years of waiting, despairing and even despising my childlessness. My son is strong in body and fluent in mind. Having been spared from the soul deadening influence of idol worship[1] that Abraham and I knew in our upbringings, his spirit thrives. Am I too protective? Protectiveness (and even a little pandering) is proper for the guardian of the child of Yahweh's promise. It comforts me to know that Isaac will carry Yahweh, *and* the family name, to another generation. One day his people will be as vast as the stars in the heavens.[2]

Oh Abram, please come to lie with me and whisper in my ear...*my sweet Sarah, let me tell you about my petition for Ishmael tonight.* I would even welcome your gray-flecked beard teasing the ticklish part of my neck, an affection you know I don't

[1] But whoever does make an idol is not *improved* or enriched. On the contrary, their passing fancies contribute nothing to power or *purpose*. Those who look on *at such misplaced attention* don't understand what they're seeing, and the idol-makers will end up embarrassed *at best*. Isaiah 44:9

[2] Genesis 15:5

usually allow—especially when your beard *is* full of smoky ash.

I take another breath to quiet my mind, allowing me to hear the faint echo of words drifting inside my tent. Silence comes at last, and with it the crunch of footsteps and crackle of sticks being broken. My husband is rekindling the fire.

Abraham has no intention to come to me anytime soon. He cannot give up the starry night. The stars bring him perspective.

After sixty-five years of marriage, I know one of his enduring pleasures to be building his own fires. He begins by slowly making a nest of tinder—dry grass, leaves and bark—and then stacking a pyramid over it of the smallest of twigs. His eyes dance with anticipation as a spark from his fire flint and knife ignites the tinder, then works its way through the bramble, to seize the log he has waiting. Now I hear the crackle of the fire, but I also hear my husband's voice, singing softly. He has found peace. Just as he has let go of fear, I know I can as well. I let my shoulders relax. Sleep wraps its tender arms around me and with it the faint memory of another word Abraham uttered in his prayer vigil...*hinini.* Too tired to reach for its implications, exhaustion overtakes me.

In the morning hours, before sleep has lost its grip on me, a dream slithers its way into my tent, under my covers, into the deepest reaches of my being where loss resides.

Sing, barren woman, who has never had a baby. Fill the air with song, you who've never experienced childbirth. You're ending up with far more children than all those childbearing women. God says so!

Isaiah 54:1

[1] The Message.

CHAPTER ONE
Barren Song

I *AM WALKING IN THE DESERT NEAR OUR CAMP in mid-morning, full of years, struggling to accept that I may never bear a child. I recount all the signs that my childbearing years are gone. The sure indications that my womb no longer prepares for a little one. There is sadness in me, but also contentment, fullness in my love for Abraham, but also loss. I look around confused as the camp suddenly seems deserted. Wait...I do have a babe...through Hagar. I gave my Egyptian maidservant to Abraham so that I could have a son. As her belly swelled, I imagined that it was really my belly—the baby growing within my womb. Isn't Hagar just an extension of me, my property as surely as my own body? Memories swirl around me like dust.*

How I waited at the birth stool so that I could be the one to catch him, my offspring, a baby boy with a lusty cry that Yahweh instructed us to name Ishmael. How relief washed over me that a boy meant that Hagar would need no more conjugal visits with my husband in order to extend our lineage. How I believed that Yahweh would miraculously give me milk for the child. Suddenly, my heart stops.

Where is Ishmael? Have I fed him lately?

I touch my chest. I do not remember nursing Ishmael. But surely, I must have. I start running into the desert, not sure where to search. I have no water with me. I have made no preparations, yet I must find him. As I run, I urge my breasts to make the milk he will surely need. By the time the sun is high overhead, when I can barely put one foot in front of the other, I see something ahead. But it isn't a babe. It is a young man stretched out under a bush. Motionless. Filthy. I call out, "Ishmael, it's your mother. I am coming."

When I arrive, I almost faint with relief. His chest moves up and down. He looks to be 17 years old. Why can't I remember anything from his childhood? I begin to shake violently. How could I have forgotten Ishmael? With a surge of adrenaline, I kneel beside him and nestle his head in my lap. "Wake up Ishmael, I am here. Your mother is here. Please, please wake up."

As he begins to stir, I see Abraham and Hagar approaching me with Isaac, only three years of age. "My son of the promise," I say, confused. "My husband." Then it all floods back. I gave Hagar to Abraham, but then, spurned by his tenderness toward her, I struggled to love their child. How I birthed Isaac in my old age, loved him, but lost sight of Ishmael. How I sent Hagar and Ishmael into the desert…away from us. Yet something is terribly wrong. Hagar is dressed in my clothing. Does she seek to steal my very identity?

As Abraham fondly runs his fingers through Isaac's hair, he says, "My son Isaac." Glancing at Hagar, he adds, "And my beautiful wife Sarah. Wait here." Coming up to me, he says, "I am sorry Hagar, but you and Ishmael must go."

My heart squeezes like a fist as Ishmael sits up and looks at his father confused and hurt. "No please!" I cry out. "You are mistaken. I am not Hagar! I am Sarah, mother of Isaac."

Abraham is kind but firm. He motions to Ishmael, "Is this not our son Ishmael? He needs you Hagar. I entrust both of you to the care of Yahweh."

I reach for Isaac, the one I just weaned from my breast. "No, don't leave me son."

Isaac smiles up at Hagar, "Can we go now mother?"

Desperation descends. I plead with her, "Tell them Hagar. Tell Abraham and Isaac who I am."

Instead she protectively throws an arm around Isaac.

"My son!" I wail, as Abraham, Hagar and Isaac walk away, leaving me and Ishmael alone.

I wake up from the dream terrified, burst out of bed, and stumble outside into the courtyard surrounding my sleeping tent. My handmaid, the one who replaced Hagar, approaches, "Can I help you Mistress?"

"Abraham. Where is he?" I wipe at the sleep still remaining in my eyes, unable to find my bearings.

"Today, Abraham and Isaac left for sacrifice. Abraham came for Isaac several hours before sunrise. He let me know that you were not to be disturbed."

"Yes, of course." I smile, trying to convince my handmaid that I am not upset. "They will be gone for seven days to worship Yahweh. Just a bad dream. It is nothing." Still, my mind is reeling. *His prayer last night...was it about this sacrifice?* Confusion is quickly replaced by indignation. *Why didn't you wake me Abraham?*

"May I help you to prepare for the day?"

"Thank you, Amah,[2] but I will take care of myself this morning. I am fine." Although in truth I am grateful for her concern, thank you has come to mean something more. *That is enough. You may leave now. Please do not question me any further.*

I see in her eyes that she is worried but has no choice but to concede. Part of me longs for her to push back for once. That she might say, "No, you are *not* fine, and I will sit here with you so another woman may listen." And then perhaps she would tell

[2] Handmaid in Hebrew is *Amah*.

me of similar losses that she has suffered. Or, I would call out to her as she leaves my tent and ask her to sit with me as a believer in the one God. Or even end up laughing with me at my fears.

But then, where would I begin? Tell Amah about being put in harems twice with two kings who lusted after me, leaving me with an emotional limp that still endures? Abraham's insistence that everything he did was to honor Yahweh? If Abram, a man who loves me well, cannot leave space for the way pain lingers, how can I safely entrust myself to others?

If it were even possible for Amah and myself to bridge the gaping canyon of life circumstance that stands between us, a mistress and her handmaid, perhaps then I could ask the questions that expose my fears. *What was Isaac's countenance? What kind of provisions did you see on Abraham's donkey? Did Abraham give a reason he did not want to wake me?* Even if we *could* speak with this frankness, I might discredit Abraham by declaring my hurt that he showed me disrespect by not waking me.

Seven days ago, Abraham came to me. One glance at him told me that yet another calling had come from Yahweh. Before he could speak, my mind was already racing. *Will we travel to another place? Sacrifice security for yet another calling? Is there a battle to be fought that only you can fight?*

"Sarah, Yahweh came to me in a vision. He wants me and Isaac to go and offer a sacrifice, a burnt offering." He added, "A burnt offering is most precious to Yahweh since we devote the entire animal to God instead of eating the meat."

I smiled. Abraham does love the taste of smoked meat. "Then I will prepare to go with you."

"No, my love, Yahweh was clear. This sacrifice is to come from me and from the boy alone. It is time to commit Isaac to the Lord."

"Wasn't he given to the Lord as an infant when you circumcised him? Haven't you daily taught him of Yahweh?" And then sensing the futility of my arguments I added, "Abram, couldn't you ask Yahweh if I could sacrifice as well?"

"We will go alone. He has given us time to prepare for a seven-day journey."

"When will you depart? How long will you be gone?"

"With Yahweh, he could call us tomorrow, it could be forty days from now. He doesn't see time as we do.[3] When he calls, we will go. We will be gone for at least seven days." Abraham sighed, "Trust me. At fourteen years, the boy is old enough to offer his own sacrifices. Our journey will be a rite of consecration where we show our love through obeying his bidding."[4]

"Will you take some men with you?"

I told myself that I was only thinking of Abraham and his age, but something did not bode well about this journey. Perhaps the long sojourn to an unknown place. Then I remembered a way I might speak Abraham's language. I touched his arm. "Abram, even you were bold enough to plead with God to change his plans for Sodom."[5]

"Very well," he sighed. "I will take two men, but no more."

I pursed my lips, holding back the words I wanted very much to say.

Abraham arched his gray eyebrows as he raised his hazel eyes to the heavens. "Sarah, please."

Although he didn't say so, I know from many conversations what my husband thinks. *Will you ever trust me to lead this household? Am I not trustworthy with our son of promise? Will you dishonor Yahweh?*

And now, having risen this morning to hear from my handmaid that my husband and son are hours down a path to

[3] Don't imagine, dear friends, *that God's timetable is the same as ours; as the psalm says,* for with the Lord, one day is like a thousand years, and a thousand years is like one day. 2 Peter 3:8

[4] Keep quiet now! *You are standing* before the Eternal Lord because the day of the Eternal One is near; *His judgment is coming.* He has prepared the sacrifice, and He has chosen His guests *with* care. Zephaniah 1:7

[5] Genesis 18:16-33

offer a sacrifice, one that I don't understand, I only find regret. How I wish I had negotiated more with him.

"Only if you let me know the moment the Lord tells you to come, even in the night."

"Only if you let me pack provisions for the trip."

"Only if you make it clear what paths you will take."

He wouldn't have been pleased, but perhaps Abraham would have compromised. Or I could have gone outside after his prayer, when he was singing. Stayed with him into the night or playfully teased him to come lie beside me. I sigh, heavy with regret.

Abraham's uncompromising God would choose this morning. Often, I wake in the early hours as age has lessened my need for sleep. But, having sat up last night listening to my husband pray, I've slept until the sun is already halfway up the sky.

Then the truth rises within me. He already knew what I would want. Abraham chose for me, even if Yahweh came in the night. Then I hear Yahweh, almost as if he is speaking to me as well.

Arise and come.

Yes, Abraham could have roused me. He left under the cover of darkness so that I couldn't interfere. My husband would not question his God. Nor would he let me.

But one mystery from his prayer remains. What does this have to do with Ishmael?

My eyes go to the carved olivewood chest Abraham built for me as a wedding gift. To honor me, he had a trained craftsman carve a terebinth tree that extends from the front of the treasured box onto its lid. Above the tree, two birds are carved as if they are dancing for joy. When he gave it to me, he said simply, "My promise to always cherish you."

Abraham, have you forgotten your promise?

Within the chest are my most precious possessions, including one from each of the boys—the silk garment Isaac wore at his weaning celebration and Ishmael's childhood bow that he and Abraham made together.

My other woman servant Ruchama[6] appears with a comb to brush out my hair, and then uses a soft cloth to freshen my skin. Afterwards she brings me boiled quail eggs and the soft yeasty bread Amah knows I prefer. Although she does not tell me this, I guess that Amah prepared this and sent Ruchama for my sake. Ah, us women. We leave our insecurities unexplored until like rising waters they divide us. Our self-accusations—our regrets, our secrets, our fears—become stones that sink to the bottom.[7] I learned from my experience with Hagar, that if those stones lie unturned for too long, we are tempted to fling them at each other.

After Ruchama leaves, I open the terebinth tree chest and rummage until I find Isaac's silk garment. I pull it out, hugging it as if it could bring Isaac back. Laying it tenderly aside, I then pull out Ishmael's bow from the bottom where I hid it, fingering its smooth wood. A memory rushes back, the day of Isaac's weaning celebration, fresh as if it is happening in the moment.

Isaac was three years of age and it was time to let go of the nighttime feedings. We called this becoming independent of the stalk, an important milestone. Throughout the day, dignitaries arrived from near and far, as food appeared and drink began to flow. Isaac's rosy cheeks shone with health as he ate, and then attempted to dance with the adults. At sunset, just when I was thinking of putting Isaac to bed without letting him suckle, my husband called me over.

"Sarah, you need to nurse the boy one last time."

[6] Ruchama means comforted.

[7] The deep waters covered them; they sank to the muddy depths like a stone…the waves stood up like a wall…. Exodus 15:5-8

"I don't understand," I said.

"Rumors have been circulating that you did not give birth to Isaac…at your age," he whispered. His voice sounded slightly frantic.

"There will always be rumors as long as stories exist," I said. Suddenly what he really wanted came to me. "You want me to nurse in front of everyone?"

"Some are saying that perhaps Isaac came through Hagar. Like Ishmael." He looked at me with determined eyes. "My Sarai, please. I don't want it either. But seeing the miracle may help them understand that this pregnancy was from Yahweh."

I shrugged, saddened and embarrassed that our story has brought us to this indignity. I went to get Isaac and brought him to his father.

Abraham stood up, walked to the front of the crowd and motioned for all to sit. Then he announced, "To mark Isaac becoming independent of the stalk, Sarah will nurse the boy one more time."

The look in his eyes told me that this had to be done.

I took Isaac onto my lap and whispered in his ear that he could drink one last time. Thank Yahweh, he smiled and nodded his approval. When he latched on, some looked away in respect, but others stared. They were surprised, even amused. Abraham had shrewdly proven my maternity. Yes, he defended Yahweh as well as us. But I also intuited that this indignity would long linger. Another consequence from my actions with Hagar.

The next morning, before Isaac stirred, I heard a commotion outside our tent from the children playing. As I stepped outside and stretched, I heard Ishmael, Abraham's son through my handmaid Hagar taking aim at my son.

"Here I am, soft little Isaac in my silk tunic. See how pretty I am. How protected I am. Don't come close to me or you might break me!"

All the children laughed.

Incensed, I quickly moved around the corner of the tent to witness Ishmael taunting, "God boy Isaac will never ride a camel into battle like the rest of us. He will never get his hands rough from the hard work of being a man."

Seeing me, all the children froze and then ran away, except Ishmael, who turned to face me with his hands on his hips and his eyes laughing at me.

"How dare you, son of my handmaid!" Feeling his insolence, I made my voice firm. "I know you care about your brother."

"I am the firstborn son of Abraham," he boasted as he boldly met my eyes. "One day Isaac will bow to me."

At that very moment, Hagar came from around the corner. She lifted her chin and declared, "He is Abraham's first-born son and though you will never fully acknowledge this, I am his wife." Hagar's dark eyes flashed, and her nostrils flared like those of an angry bull. Even in her rage she was beautiful.

When I sighed and put my hands on my hips, she added, "I heard last night that some came wondering whether Isaac is Abraham's son or perhaps even a token of your time in a harem. A few even asked me if I gave birth to him. No wonder Abraham needed all the dignitaries here last night."

Her words enraged me. She was poking once more at my pain. It took every bit of control I had not to slap her face. Actually, she would have liked nothing more. An abuse she could run to Abraham with. Instead I turned and walked away.

That night I went to Abraham saying, "Cast out that slave woman with her son, for the son of this slave woman shall not be an heir with my son Isaac."[8]

[8] Genesis 21:10 (ESV)

Abraham was shocked by my strong language. Hurt by my insistence that they leave. But I stood my ground. Was he blind to how Hagar threw sharp stones carefully aimed to tear open my longtime wounds? Her insinuations and disrespect, always behind Abraham's back, had gone on for far too long.

Hagar's abuse started after she had Ishmael. She now resented submitting to me as her mistress. I corrected her often, and then, following Abram's advice, finally sought to ignore her. When I became pregnant, Abraham said that Isaac's birth would bring clarity.

When Isaac was an infant, I let Hagar hold him in her arms and even sing songs over him. Ishmael was proud to have a baby brother and treated him with great tenderness. By the time Isaac was two, he knew by heart the little bedtime song I taught him for Hagar and my other maids...

Lord bless the women
Who use their hands
To bring the food
That graces our table

Lord hold the women
Who gather the water
To wash our feet
Weary from journey

Lord lead the women
Who make our beds
To warm our hearts
And hasten our sleep

Lord hold the women
Who will wake before us
To prepare our camp
For a day to enjoy

And then I would tickle his feet, until he would beg me to stop. Before he would doze off, Isaac would look up at me, his eyes shining with purity and say, "Mama takes care of me." And I would reply, "With the help of the women and Yahweh, my son."

If only my appreciation had been enough for Hagar. If only, I could have humbled myself, and admitted that we put her in a difficult position. Perhaps she could have stayed.

We told Hagar to take whatever she wanted including their tents. As a token of peace, I offered the she-camel Ishmael named Gamal,[9] but despite her son's begging eyes, she refused. Abraham gave her a large sum of silver. When he offered for some of our men to escort them through the wilderness, she shook her long hair in disgust. Watching the two of them step onto the path that leads to the desert, alone and unprotected, I saw Ishmael's anger. He didn't even glance back at his father.

I prayed silently, "Yahweh, please spare their lives. Establish a new life for them. Forgive me if I have sinned against you in sending them away."

For days afterwards, Abraham avoided me. All that could have been discussed wasn't, and when I tried, Abram found reasons why it was never a good time. I knew he only consented to banishment because Yahweh himself urged him to listen to me.

And now, the morning where my husband has taken my son and left without waking me, the morning after he warred and wept in urgent prayer, I think I understand a little better how Abraham

[9] Hebrew for camel, meaning to be independent.

must have felt. My husband and son are moving through the wilderness on the path to a sacrifice I don't understand. And then the dream. Am I the slave woman who is being cast out of Isaac's life?

I begin to speak out loud, "Abraham, I know I have never said this, but I also miss Ishmael. I feel your persistent longing for the son of Hagar, so clearly your son—from his dimpled chin to the wildness in his eyes."

Why have I kept this small bow Ishmael carried around as a boy? A flush of recognition blooms on my cheeks...*Abraham doesn't know I kept it. The secret-keeping travels in two directions.*

As I stroke the bow's smooth wood, I remember Abraham telling Ishmael that a bow had two limbs, upper and lower divided by a leather grip, just as he had two arms. How the string formed a window that could be stretched open wide. Hagar would be surprised to know that I still sometimes yearn for this wild donkey-boy of a child, Ishmael. Perhaps Ishmael could have been redeemed from the godless ways of Hagar and the godless superstitions of Egypt.

Long before I knew I was pregnant I had made peace that Ishmael would carry the promise, and I had convinced Abraham of the same. Hagar talked to her son about this often. At the same time Abraham was preparing Ishmael to walk in his steps. Imagine Ishmael's shock when he learned that I was giving birth to another son, and that his promise was being handed to another. How do you explain this to a boy going back and forth between being a boy and a man? After Hagar and Ishmael were gone, Abraham told me that before the weaning party Ishmael came to him with tears asking, "What blessing will be left for me Father?"

But what was I to do? Hand the inheritance to a boy and

his mother who return hatred and disrespect? Let the boys' relationship creep toward tragedy like Cain and Abel? Without a persecutor, Isaac could be raised to fulfill his legacy. Peace would return.

From the day they left, Isaac had questions which only grew more complex as he aged. *Where did they go Mama? When are they coming back? Why is Abba sad? I miss Ishmael.*

Around the time Isaac reached eight years of age, he began to take more interest in the camels as if he had to fill Ishmael's place. And my answers to my son's questions were as lame as one of our donkeys that fell into a ditch and never lost his limp.

When Isaac asked where Ishmael was, I would answer, "Only Yahweh knows where they went," to which he would say, "Why doesn't he tell us then?"

Or I would say, "They cannot come back, my son. We had to send them away because they no longer belonged here," to which Isaac would respond, "Do I belong here? Will you send me away?"

Just recently, coming into his own as a young man, Isaac has had new, harder questions like, "Mother, why does Ishmael have a different mother and the same father?" To explain this to Isaac I would have to delve into my long barrenness. Can a boy even understand the shame of being unable to show one's womanhood through a belly full of child? And Hagar? Didn't I actually do her a favor? Staying with us, she could never have Abraham again, nor could she remarry. That position would force her to only have one child. Surely, by now she has remarried and has a whole bevy of children to comfort her.

My throbbing head once again brings me back to the present, a husband and son gone, the headache a testimony to my endless rehearsing of all that has come before and all I fear could come. I am still holding Ishmael's bow when Amah enters the tent holding hands with her little girl, Nomi,[10] her first child. I quickly lay it aside to be put up later. Seeing me, the child's face lights up and she runs and throws herself into my arms, "Dodah[11] Sarah, can you tell me a story?"

I offer a weak smile, comforted by her sparkling eyes and loving nature. Although she is not mine, Nomi is the closest I will ever have to a daughter.

"Dodah Sarah has a headache right now. My precious one, if you return another time, I am sure there will be a story waiting just for you."

After Nomi runs off to play, Amah prepares a remedy for my headache. First, she takes a goat hair headband, douses it with cool water and ties it around my head. This is said to have come from goddess worship. After tying the headband with seven knots, the worshipper said an incantation to the goddess allowing the pain to ascend into the Heavens. Although I have no such superstition, the coolness comforts me. Then she brings me a feverfew tea of dried leaves, flowers and stems. I drift into a sudden, deep sleep, and with it comes a new dream.

It is time for our burnt offering. Yahweh has told Abraham to bring a strange assortment of sacrificial creatures to make an offering by the Terebinth tree. These include a three-year old cow, female goat and ram, as well as a turtledove and a young pigeon.[12] *I am confused about the wild array. I cringe as Abraham takes a sharp knife and kills each of the animals with a clean cut of the knife. Then he carefully slices the cow, goat and ram in half, dividing bone and flesh, his hands and the rock platform on which he works quickly bloodied. He keeps wiping his hands on his robe until he too appears covered in blood.*

[10] Nomi in Hebrew means beautiful.
[11] Hebrew for aunt, pronounced do-daw'.
[12] See Genesis 15:9-18.

Abraham carefully arranges the carcasses into two rows of halves. His precision is unnerving, but I dare not question him. Although my stomach turns, my eyes will not allow me to turn away. Then he lays the dead turtledove on one side with the halves, and the young pigeon on the other. Two vultures circle overhead and then close enough that Abraham has to take a stick and scare them off.

We sit quietly until it is dark, waiting for Yahweh to attend to our burnt offering. Did we forget the fire? Abraham snores lightly, but I cannot rest. The slaughter of animals distresses me. As the night continues, the darkness becomes so deep I cannot see my hand in front of my face. Suddenly, my vision clears, and Abraham sits up and looks upward intently, as if he hears the voice of Yahweh.

Abram repeats random words, as if he wants to make sure he hears correctly. "Oppressed for 400 years. Four generations. Sin of the Amorites. Everlasting covenant." A flaming torch appears, but no hand seems to hold it. It passes between the halves of the carcasses. Suddenly my eyes are lifted upward by a falling star streaking across the heavens.

When I look back, I gasp. The fire is gone. In place of the animals and birds, Isaac lies on the altar and Abraham stands over him with a knife.

I flail and then sit up, as if a hand has reached into my chest and jerked me upward. I sharply draw in shallow breaths. It is just a dream. Relief quickly turns to rage. It feels like there are balls bouncing to and fro against the inside of my ribs, like the linen, string and rag ball that Isaac and Ishmael tossed back and forth. The ball that Ishmael taunted Isaac with, teasing him that he would never learn to catch. Anger, fear, helplessness, sadness and fury lift the hairs on the back of my neck. I picture myself beating Abraham just below his ribs with my fists to force him to notice my pain.

How dare Abraham take Isaac into the wilderness with no

word of where he is going? Is he taking my son away to give him back to Yahweh? Is Abraham delusional in his great faith? Does he take advantage of me deferring to him?

I begin pulling travel clothing out of a different trunk and start throwing it into a pile with as much force as my weary arms allow. Then I kick the small pile of clothing with my foot again and again, scattering the items across the tent. I look around my normally neat abode. I would tear it all into bits if I had the strength.

"Enough," I say to Abram and his god. "Enough. Enough. Enough!"

I pick up Ishmael's bow, lower myself to the floor and begin weeping the wail of a spurned mother, a mute swan's dirge. A memory arises. When he was nine years of age, Ishmael hid in the bulrushes and shot a mute swan with this bow and arrow, killing it instantly. Isaac witnessed it and ran to tell me and his father. I was astounded at Ishmael's cruelty. Abraham and I sat down with Ishmael afterwards.

Abraham looked his firstborn in the eyes and said, "Ishmael, you are fortunate the mute swan didn't have an offspring. She likely would have attacked you first by using the bones in her wings. It is known that a swan can break the legs of a grown man!"

Ishmael rolled his eyes and whispered, "All this over a stupid swan."

Hoping he might respond to a motherly voice, I spoke up, "Ishmael, Yahweh allows the killing of animals for food. But never for sport or to test your skills."

Ishmael refused me the dignity of eye contact, his face rigid.

Abraham added, "A righteous man is known for his kindness

to animals."

As a consequence, Abram took away the bow for a time, finally giving it back to Ishmael after he made penance, one that was never specified to me.

I stuff the bow back into its hiding place inside the terebinth tree chest, now unsure whether to keep it or cast it away. A wild energy fills my bones. Thinking of the mute swan I say out loud, "I will break your legs, Abraham, if you let any harm come to my son!" Then an irrational thought comes. *So, this is what Noah's wife must have felt when he neglected his own children on behalf of all those animals.* I begin laughing, wildly, while wondering if I am losing my sanity.

Amah speaks from outside my tent. "Mistress, is there anything you need?"

I wipe away the remaining tears and take a deep breath. "How long have I slept?"

"For some hours, my lady. It is well into the afternoon."

"You may come in." I have slept the day away and every moment of slumber has allowed my husband and son to move further away from me.

Amah politely ignores the clothing strewn around the tent. If she heard my outburst, she makes no admission. "My mistress, I knew you were concerned about Abraham and Isaac, so I took the liberty to ask some of the men."

How well she knows me. "What did you learn, Amah?"

"There were a few of the men who saw him preparing to leave with Isaac and two other men. Abraham's donkey was loaded with wood and provisions, but there was no animal for the burnt offering. One of the men said he questioned Abraham and reported that the Master said the strangest thing."

"What did he say?" I lift my chin to show I am only mildly curious.

"He pulled the man aside, where Isaac could not hear, and said that Yahweh, our Jehovah-Jireh, would provide the burnt offering."

My fingers begin to tremble. I put my hands together like I sometimes do when I pray and wedge them between my knees. I bite the corner of my lip lest I once again burst into tears. I gather myself, knowing every bit of my strength will be needed.

"Amah, what I am really hungry for is dried meat, cheese and bread. Yes, I am ravenous. Can you bring me enough to eat now and later on? Bring me an abundance. And then please bring me several skins full of water. I thirst."

I see her thoughts turn. She knows I am planning something. She may even have already guessed that I will follow Abraham into the wilderness to chase after my son, my only son. Knowing Amah, she will discreetly gather whatever she thinks I need.

"Would my mistress like some extra blankets for tonight as well?"

I nod, relieved that she knows what I will do and is ready to help me. When I return from my journey, I promise myself to find something new in this relationship. Perhaps allow her to use my name, Sarah.

Isaac will soon be fifteen years old and an idea has taken root in my heart—a secret I haven't even told Abraham. We lost Ishmael at a tender seventeen years due to my own jealousy and fear. Now I fear I will also lose Isaac before the start of his fifteenth year. That fate in its cruelty will circle back around. Consequences will come forward to testify to the dark day when shame stole some of the light from my eyes.[13] Has Yahweh been waiting until I understood better before he demands restitution?

[13] Disgrace follows me everywhere I go; *I am constantly embarrassed.* Shame is written across my face. Psalm 44:15

I have long been a sojourner. Abraham has trained me well. There may be danger, but there is a bigger threat that makes thieves, robbers and predators seem like petty annoyances. Yahweh himself. Will his wings crush me or comfort me? As surely as he spun together the heart of a mother, Yahweh knows I will follow after my son. He will either protect me or I will become the burnt offering he desires.

"Their offspring grow to their full strength in the open field; then they leave and do not return. Who set the wild donkey free? Who cut it loose from its bonds?"

Job 39:4-5

CHAPTER TWO
Donkey's Song

BEFORE THE SUN DROPS BELOW THE HORIZON, Amah brings abundant provisions including items I would have overlooked. She even carries camel skin coverings for my sandals in case it is cold in the mountains. As she stands by waiting for my direction, my thoughts skitter around like the spiny mice with scaled tails we sometimes find around camp. *How will I travel quickly enough to catch up to them? Who will protect me?* A saying comes back that we heard from a traveler to our camp, "He who sings songs to a heavy heart is like one who steals another's cloak in cold weather." *Abraham, I may have coverings for the cold, but you've left me with a heavy heart and a song of distress.*[1] I shake my head, my shoulders and my hands in exasperation, and then remember Amah. I know I cannot tangle her within whatever decision I make.

"Mistress Sarah, is there anything I can help you with?"

There are tasks she could help me with, but I smile to reassure her. "Thank you for your thoughtfulness."

Once Amah leaves, I roll up one of the scarlet wool rugs by the entrance to our tent, to make a place for the donkey to stand. These luxuries, brought from our stone home in Ur, make our

[1] Like a man who undresses in winter or *a woman who pours* vinegar on a wound, So is anyone who tries to sing *happy* songs to a sorrowful heart. Proverbs 25:20

tent a home. Then I go outside to bring Ayarim,[2] my she-donkey, into my tent. It seems right for her to travel with me. I have favored her ever since she pushed out of her mother's womb with her head between her forelegs. Sadly, her mother died soon afterwards, and so I became a surrogate mother, feeding her goat's milk from a dappled leather wineskin Abraham fashioned. When she was old enough to wean, I gave her our best grain winnowed with a shovel and fork,[3] and entrusted her to the herd as a guard donkey for our other livestock. Do I risk Ayarim by taking her on the mountain trails? Although I am seeking to protect my son, I wouldn't want to risk anything precious to him, like this donkey.

The first time I introduced Isaac to Ayarim, he was barely walking. Isaac held out his pudgy arms to her and she trotted over. As I lowered him to her level, she put her scruffy head on his shoulder and gave a lick to his cheek with her pink tongue, signaling that he was hers and she was his. She only wanted Isaac. Unable to pronounce the donkey's name, Isaac called her Maya. The name stuck for all of us.

Maya the she-donkey was fiercely protective of Isaac. By the time Isaac was four, he would ride on her back with me keeping a protective grip on both of them. Sometimes Abraham joked that the silly beast would bite him if he had a harsh word with the boy. One evening, Isaac wandered outside his tent in the night. The donkey alerted us by her sharp brays, and Abraham ran outside to find that Isaac had rolled under the fence and was clinging to Maya. Later, he found scat nearby from a mountain lion. After that, we didn't fence her, and she never wandered. Not too long afterwards, I overhead Isaac telling the donkey, "You are mine, Maya."

Tears gather at the brims of my eyes. "Maya," I say, stroking

[2] The Hebrew word ayarim can mean both "ass colts" and "cities."

[3] Also if the oxen and donkeys that work that ground *for you* are well fed with good grain that is carefully winnowed with shovel and fork, *then they will be content.* Isaiah 30:24

her ear. "We are going on a long journey, perhaps all the way to Mount Moriah or even Hebron to find Isaac. You know the way. I know you are still strong. If I take you to Isaac, can you be my guard? Remember how you have driven off coyotes with your cries, stomps and bites? How you once rescued Isaac from a mountain lion? You will protect me, won't you my friend? Or... do you just love me because I feed you?"[4]

She nudges me with her nose then shakes her head.

"I know you also belong to Isaac, but I think he would give his permission."

As I sort through the provisions Amah gathered, I continue pondering this creature who has become a valued companion. Before Isaac was conceived, Maya comforted me in many ways. Seeing her beautiful golden coloring, unique markings, and a favorable temperament, Abraham wanted to breed her. We tried on numerous occasions. While the copulation was successful—despite Maya's cries of displeasure—she never became pregnant. I insisted that we stop the breeding and let her be. And to my surprise, Abraham agreed.

I look at my loyal steed, who stands in my tent patiently waiting for instruction. *Is this what Abraham expects of me? To patiently wait?* To be fair to myself, waiting is not always Abram's best quality either. I shudder, remembering his words of frustration after the attempted breeding and after I insisted that Maya is valuable in other ways, "The animal is just a donkey and a barren one at that!" When he saw my distress, he tried to vanquish his insensitivity, "Sarai, you are not barren. Otherwise Yahweh would not have promised you a son. As Yahweh witnesses, I would never compare a princess to a lowly animal!"

But his words had already rooted into my soul, a dry weed of unfulfilled promises and the taunts of rain clouds that never

[4] Oxen know their owners; even donkeys know where their master feeds them, But Israel is ignorant. My very own, they ignore Me. Isaiah 1:3

provide water.[5] Then Abraham used my new name, the one I had asked him to refrain from using until there was a sure sign of its fulfillment. "Sarah…if you cannot trust Yahweh, then trust me."

I stop and slowly lower myself onto one of the floor pillows, tufted in softened flax by Amah, not only a maidservant but also a talented seamstress. Winded by the burst of effort and the thought of what is ahead, my mind is now circling, gathering tidbits of the last hours. From the late-night prayer, to Abraham and Isaac's disappearance, to my recognition of loss.

In my old age, I have learned to ward off fear or sadness by finding meaning. This is no small task when your skin is naturally thinner and your tolerance often feels like brittle ice over a mountain pond, likely to give way at any moment. Tears start streaming from my eyes, using my wrinkles as passageways to wet the sides of my ears. I lay my hand upon my rising and falling chest. My anger comes from helplessness, but my pain is real. I love my husband. But I am hurt and terrified because of the preciousness of the gift of Isaac. I was born for this calling and Isaac was born to fulfill it. In comparison to my son, the vanity of maintaining our tribe's customs seems frivolous. *No, I will not be passive.*

Bearing a child is anything but passive. I often explain to our women who have just married, how pregnancy strips away the self. The promise required offering myself to my husband in the lunacy of hope. When I was about to say *no more,* Isaac appeared as a small flutter in my womb. When the nausea kept me up through the night as I heaved only to expel nothing, I sang to him of the stars. When late-pregnancy brought an unrelenting burning in my chest, and a lone white hair grew out of the

[5] Like clouds and wind that bring no rain, so is one who boasts of gifts *promised but* never delivered. Proverbs 25:14

middle of my forehead, I stroked my belly and talked to Isaac about what it meant to be a bearer of the covenant.

Yes, as Hagar liked to remind me, an old woman with a huge swollen belly was a humorous sight. After I gave birth, I looked in the mirror that Abraham fashioned for me out of polished obsidian and thanked Yahweh for the hardships that, now, only highlighted the joy.

Isaac emerged into the world fully aware. I sought to swaddle him in the soft blankets my maids had prepared but he refused them. He would work for hours to wriggle his way out of my swaddling until his arms and legs were free. I had seen many newborns come into our clan, but never one so attentive. Within two weeks of his exit from my womb, he was pursing his lips and cooing at me in response to my words. Whereas Ishmael was up on his knees rocking and then crawling by three months, Isaac was content at that age to lay back and take in the world around him with his wise, perceptive eyes. By four months, he had the start of his own language made of a wide range of noises, coos, songlike cries and sometimes surprisingly loud noises made with amusing facial expressions. Hagar laughed that Isaac would likely be a lazy child, but I was grateful that, like me, Isaac was more cerebral. He drank in the world around him.

Before Isaac was born, Hagar had the gall to suggest that if I couldn't nurse the new babe, she would no doubt be able to find a way. I still remember her exact words, "Fourteen years past birthing a child, I am more likely to create milk than you."

When my milk came, it felt almost as miraculous as childbirth. Abraham loved to watch his son nurse, saying, "Like a newborn craves milk, so we feed on Yahweh's promises."

The years have passed too quickly. Isaac is now fourteen years old, full of vigor and strong faith in Yahweh and in us. *Please understand, my husband. Isaac still needs me, and I will come to him.*

Maya stamps her foot heavily and tosses her head back and forth, spewing spit my way, and breaking the tension in my heart. Then she lets loose a stream of gas that smells like rotten food. Coughing and wiping away a dribble of spit from my left cheek, I say, "Maya, you may be a bit pampered to endure this journey, but I cannot take a younger donkey from the herd without being sighted." I scratch her ears. "The keepers know that I sometimes take you for long walks when Abraham and Isaac are gone."

Maya's disappearance is unlikely to be noticed, at least until it is too late for anyone to easily find me. Her sharp sense of smell will help me track Isaac. She can easily wedge between trees and tromp down any wicked thorns in the thickets that might consume me.[6] She can navigate off of the path to help me avoid other travelers.

As I stroke her coarse fur, I give thanks that she is prepared for rain or cold. She looks at me with trusting eyes. I shiver a little. I pick up the camel skin cloak that Abraham had commissioned an area craftswoman to make for me after I told him I was pregnant. He was especially proud that he tanned the skin himself to offset the exorbitant cost of such a luxury.

The first time Hagar saw the cloak, her reaction was predictable. With eyes like daggers, she clucked her tongue as her lips curved upward, and then spewed, "Ah, Abraham finds yet one more way to show Ishmael his birth is of less significance."

"Ishmael trusts his father's choices," I said under my breath. As much as I struggled with Ishmael, when I allowed the softness to come, love was there.

Hagar moved closer to me and whined in my ear with the insistence of a strong-willed child in an adult body, "If you have

[6] Every mouth utters foolishness like a wildfire, *out of control;* wickedness rages, leveling and clearing briars and thorns; Forests and thickets burn, leaving the whole a smoking heap. Isaiah 9:18

something to say, speak."

"These are adult matters, not the concern of a boy." I made my voice stern as a warning, but Hagar's haughtiness knew no limits.

"He needs to know," Hagar said. "Like his mother he will always have to fight for his rightful position." She smiled and feigned speaking to herself, "As if a camel hair coat is the mark of anything except this...migrant lifestyle. Ishmael is a prince of Egypt and Abraham's firstborn seed. If we hadn't left Egypt, he would be living in a palace with garments spun with pure gold thread."

Of course, I would never say the obvious. That her mother was a harlot of the king of Egypt, not a true wife...Hagar's claim to esteem but also her curse. As much as I took pity on her, is it not me who made her into a used woman like her mother? Did my desperation for a child push Abraham to value her in ways I could never accept? The root of this conflict is barbed and nestled deep into the soil. *The King of Egypt chose me as a wife above Hagar's mother. A foreigner.* And as badly as Hagar's mother yearned for that status, being the wife of a Pharaoh was something I could never accept even at the cost of my life.

I clumsily pull on the camel cloak and feel its familiar heft on my shoulders. Abram's camel cloak is irreplaceable. At night in the desert darkness, it would be a way for him to embrace me. Perhaps, the cloak would act as a talisman, or even ensure the protection of Abraham's God, the God I struggle to call my own right now.

But if I am honest with myself, Abraham would have no such thing, this trusting in the leading of a donkey and the skin of a camel. He would be worried about robbers and predators. I must minimize the risk. Where do I start? I stroke the cloak, musing that it represents all that we have fought for.

I expect that Yahweh will protect me, but I can't fathom the thought of losing this cloak.

I tuck away the cloak into the Terebinth tree chest Abraham fashioned from olivewood and hide it under some older things. Instead, I will carry with me several worn, yet warm coverings I can layer for the retreat of hot desert sun and the onslaught of cold.

"Lord, protect me...*please*," My heart bangs against my chest as I set my face for what is ahead. Questions circle like pesky moths hungry to devour freshly-woven clothing.

Will I back out when faced with the prospect of venturing into the darkness?

Will this choice determine what happens to Isaac?

Will he be lost because I am not brave enough to pursue them and turn back?

Maya senses my hesitation and fusses at me with her spasmodic song, exhaling with off-tune hoarse yowls, and then inhaling with high pitched squeaks, like she can't catch her breath. Does she reprimand me for my folly? Abraham, as usual, is right. Our entire camp knows that a woman venturing into the wilderness by herself is foolhardy. I can only imagine the words Abraham would have for me, "Have you misplaced your mind, woman?" I begin to construct the conversation, irked by the very thought of him calling me "woman." It is his way of reminding me that since Eve came from Adam's flesh and bone, I only live through him. As he has been known to say in the heat of a disagreement, "Man will always be part of woman but woman would not exist without man."[7] I have even heard others pronounce that man is the head of woman, to which I cringe inwardly.[8] Women are the only ones who keep their heads when men set their course

[7] Man, *you remember,* was not fashioned from the body of a woman. But woman, *though she was sculpted by the hands of God,* was fashioned from the *bones and flesh of* man. 1 Corinthians 11:8

[8] But *it is important* that you understand this *about headship*: the Anointed One is the head of every man, the husband is the head of his wife, and God is the head of the Anointed. 1 Corinthians 11:3

straight into danger.

I start speaking, keeping my voice low.... "I might ask you the same thing Abraham Terah Shem. Did you think I wouldn't know what you plan to do? Is it not enough that we have risked everything on the call of *hinini?* We've changed from city dwellers to wandering people of the land. From mentoring students in the natural order of this world, to spiritual seekers intent on convincing the world that there is only one unseen God. In doing so, we have gained so much, including our beloved son. Isaac has been worth the loss of all things. But now, this impossible promise depends on this one young man."

I sit down, exhausted by my thoughts and the deepening darkness, yet determined to stay awake. Surely God will not change his mind, and divert the promise to Ishmael, emboldening Hagar to believe she is a full wife. Another memory rises from the ground, circling around me, stalling me from completing my preparation.

About a year after I cast Hagar and her son out, we heard that stories were circulating of a handmaid cast into the desert. But we could not know whether they were about her. I liked to think that I wasn't the only jealous mistress who had to let go of a persecuting handmaid and insolent child. Surely, my story was not unique.

Not too long afterwards, a traveler was ushered in by one of Abraham's men. He had come asking for water, and, as was our custom, Abraham invited him to share a meal and sleep near our tents. Abraham savored such opportunities. Emboldened by the promises Yahweh had made to him, Abraham yearned for others to know God Most High and be freed from false gods with their demeaning practices of supposed worship. Abraham welcomed me at such gatherings knowing I also craved conversation from outside our clan. Having just one traveler this night promised the opportunity for more intimate conversation.

As we sat around the fire eating a meal of spiced lamb stew, the men began to talk. The conversation was lively, circling from trading routes, to dangerous encounters with beasts to the threats of safely negotiating peace with people of different cultures and clans. Abraham wasn't like other clan leaders who expected their women to be without opinion on matters of religion. He valued my mind and spirit.

As was his habit, Abraham waited for his opening to talk about the one true God.

"If you are willing, I would enjoy hearing what you have learned in your wanderings," the traveler offered. To this day, I cannot remember the man's name, only his long, matted hair and equally scraggly beard, along with tattered clothing that needed the care of a woman.

Abraham smiled. "A man of your experience surely has found that each place you visit has unique ways of seeking divinity."

Many times, I would excuse myself at this point, knowing the conversation that would ensue. But on this night, stirring in the wind that whipped around my feet and pushed the loose hairs around my face into my eyes, I felt something compelling me to stay.

"Yes, I have seen many kinds of worship. It seems that anything at all can be a reason to build an altar.[9] I suppose we all fear that if we don't worship the right god, we will find our worst fears fulfilled. Some of the ways of honoring so-called gods have appalled my own sensibilities…offering flocks and crops is one thing but drinking yourself into a stupor so you can offer a child?[10] Inexcusable."

[9] You truly are a religious people. I have stopped again and again to examine carefully the religious statues and inscriptions that fill your city. On one such altar, I read this inscription: "TO AN UNKNOWN GOD." Acts 17:22-23

[10] "Do not give any of your children to be sacrificed to Molek, for you must not profane the name of your God. I am the LORD." Leviticus 18:21 (NIV)

Abraham sat back, shook his head and crossed his arms in shared indignation.

I longed for Abraham to tell him the truth, that child offerings are an abomination to the people of Yahweh. But time has taught me my husband's wisdom in pacing these discussions.

Abraham nods his encouragement for the traveler to continue.

"And the godless ones...to be honest, they frighten me the most. Do they refuse to learn the lessons of Noah?" He paused and stroked his unkempt beard, suddenly self-conscious. "Perhaps none of us can truly know. We have to question why we think we know anything at all."

Abraham caught my eyes for an instance. His tender glance was like a secret kiss on the lips. "I have had the same thoughts. The more questions arose, the more I studied. It was only when I was called away from the affluence of city living to become a wandering nomad like yourself, that I began to see differently."

"What did you see?" the man asked.

"I don't think it was as much what I saw, as what I heard."

"And that was?"

It has always been our tradition that each time the teller of a tale pauses, the other gives an indication he still wants to hear.

"A calling."

"Your calling?"

"Yes, by then everything I had learned pointed to the idea of there only being one god. So, still being a city dweller, I began to inquire of this God."

"By offering sacrifices?"

"No, by walking outdoors in the early morning or at the end of day, outside of the city limits, even out into the hills. Asking, listening for a confirmation of what I thought I knew. I longed for a god with a specific plan for me and my own." Abraham's face glowed in the firelight and the passion of speaking his truth.

"Most people believe that the gods only care to the extent we prostrate ourselves to them," the traveler added.

Abraham nodded. "Idols can never give what the spirit longs for most."

"And what would that be?"

Abraham paused for a time, thinking. Then with a soft voice he finally replied, "Mercy and steadfast love."[11]

Our servants entered with more lamb and more wine. Our visitor had quite an appetite. We considered hospitality to be among the highest declarations of righteousness. As my husband had been known to say, "Feed the belly and you can feed the soul."

As we sat in silence, each now with our own thoughts, I discreetly glanced at the man. Somehow, I knew that the gods he spoke of had stolen from him, leaving him restless and eager to keep the ground moving below his feet.[12] I was moved with compassion. Just as he wanted some truth to grasp on to for security, so did I. Moving slightly behind Abraham, I deferred the conversation to the two men.

"I heard a story of your God," he said, nodding at Abraham for permission to continue. As he dipped the bread into the lamb gravy, his half-full mouth giving me an excuse not to look at his face, he told the tale. "There was a young woman from Egypt who came from the palace of one of the Pharaohs. She became a handmaid to a family who were said to be from the lineage of Shem."

"Do continue," Abraham offered.

"When the master's wife could not conceive, she invoked our law, and legally gave this handmaid to her husband to bear a child for them." His eyes twinkled. "Now we all know the

[11] Those who worship worthless idols *turn their backs on God and* renounce their loyal love. Jonah 2:8

[12] *From now on,* when you till the ground, it will no longer yield for you its strength *and nourishment.* You will be a fugitive and a wanderer on the earth. Genesis 4:12

stresses of these situations. My wife would never survive such a thing. Having a child through a handmaid appears to offer hope but complicates matters deeply."

My mouth twitched. I shook off a chill and I pulled the wrap around my shoulders tighter. The smell of lamb was gone, replaced by smoke. My racing mind told me to excuse myself, but my feet, my hands, my legs had no strength. Cold dread crept up my spine. Was he about to tell me that I committed murder by casting off Hagar?

Abraham offered him some more wine, which the man gladly received. I held up my vessel to the maid to fill it as well and drank it quickly to calm myself. Since I sat slightly behind Abraham to his left, I was not in the direct view of our visitor.

"The woman's son thrived, but never bonded to the man's first wife. And so enmity arose between the son and his father. The son, feeling his father's warring loyalties, found ways to create tension. And the handmaid grew bolder, hoping she would be recognized as a true wife." He paused and scratched his mangled beard. "I hear that those who follow the God of Shem sometimes practice a ceremony that gives a handmaid in this situation a higher status of wifehood?"

Abraham nodded as if he had heard of such a thing. If he did, it had never been discussed, never even offered as a possibility. My thoughts picked up speed. *Had Abraham considered this secretly?* Our legal contract was for Hagar to give us a child. The child's status would come from his father, but Hagar's would remain the same.

Abram waved his hand, inviting more. I felt faint. Sweat was gathering under my arms and at my hairline. Amah's husband Joshua entered to add kindling and then more wood to the fire, urging the coals to reignite. Sparks drifted upwards, suspending the moment.

With darkness dancing across his face, the man finally continued. "As fate would have it, the wife, the wholly legitimate one, however you God-fearers say it...." The man glanced at Abraham with half veiled eyes fearing he had overstepped.

"You say it well." Abraham smiled and nodded, prompting him to continue the story.

"The wife of nobility became pregnant in her old age. Some whispered her pregnancy was from the Pharaoh, from some unfortunate situation on their travels. At the boy's weaning, the master held a huge feast to quiet such rumblings and affirm his fatherhood." The man sighed and then smiled, enjoying his own riddle. "So now he has two sons. Which will gain his father's blessing? The first born from his wife offering his seed to a foreign handmaid? Or the second born, given under suspicious circumstances, to the only woman he fully loved as his wife?"

"And what would you say?"

The man chuckled, oblivious that he spoke to the characters in his wayfarer's tale. "It would take the wisdom of a sage to decipher this one."

"Ah, yes," Abraham said. Both men sat silently with their own thoughts until Abraham spoke once more. "I see the great dilemma. Tell us more."

"Then the first-born son of the handmaid began to persecute the second-born son of the lady," the traveler continued. "And the lady finally cast her maid and son moving toward manhood, into the desert, with only meager food and water."

I gulped, almost choking. My face flushed. Then it occurred to me... *There would be no story without someone to tell it.*

"Do you know if this story is true?" Abraham asked, finally touching the heart of what I needed to hear.

"One can never be sure, after the passing from one person to the next. But in the telling, one could hope to find out."

Suddenly I blurted out, "What happens to her, the woman and her son?"

I had finally asked the question I knew Abraham would not ask, the question that had caused me so much agony.

"Ah. The women always want to know the same thing." His face shone with delight that I had joined the conversation. "Here is the amazing part, my lady. When the handmaid and her son run out of provisions, she finally gives up on life for her and her son. Although she resigns herself that they will die soon, an angel visits her, a representative of the gods."

Then turning to my husband, he offered, "Or the one God as Abraham believes. He tells her that he has seen her and that she should not despair because her son will become a mighty nation. When she looks up, meat and water are nearby...provisions she knew were not there before. And the mysterious visitor is gone without a trace."[13]

Abraham nodded and smiled. "Now that is a story worth telling. And does the young man go on to fulfill the vision of the mysterious visitor?"

"This I do not know. But may I tell you what I discern?"

"Of course," Abraham said.

"If this story did come from the handmaid who suffered all this, and if it has been passed from weary traveler to weary traveler accurately, then she surely saw your one God." Then glancing up into the heavens and laying his rugged hand on his chest, he says the words Abraham longs to hear. "And then your god is different from any other god."

"How is that?" Abraham asked with a smile.

"None of our gods see the individual. Oh, we like to think

[13] Genesis 21:8-21

they do, with all our mad dancing and, what some call, immoral pursuit of them. But the gods I know demand much for the gifts they supposedly give us. Any conversation with them is one-sided. They never come to us to bless us despite supposed promises. We go to their temples never knowing what they want. The very next day, even after some random good omen comes, we begin the same frantic game of trying to appease them. One never knows where they stand."[14] He stopped and again stroked his beard. Finally, he spoke again. "If this tale of the handmaid is true, then that angel must have come from your one god."

A rush of love passed over me, recognizing this man as a possible seeker of Yahweh.

"If I may be so bold as to ask...." Abraham paused. He would not continue without the man's permission.

The stranger nodded.

"Will you continue to serve these random, impersonal gods who ask much but give little?" Abraham asked kindly. "Or will you seek the God who provides? The God who has a voice that speaks, hands that touch and eyes that see?"[15]

I took note that there was no condescension in my husband's tone, only respect.

"Me?" the man sputtered. "A crusty old skeptic? I would have to see such a providing for myself, not just stories that are the fodder of lonely men around campfires."

I rose to announce my departure. My head pounded with the sure knowledge that Hagar and Ishmael survived the casting out. I could hear no more. I had to leave before Abraham told this traveler anything else.

"My lady," the man stood up quickly. "I hope my story didn't exhaust your fine hospitality."

[14] Those nations worship idols of silver and gold, crafted by human hands: They have *given their gods* mouths, but they cannot speak; eyes, but they cannot see. They have *provided their idols with* ears, but they cannot hear; noses, but they cannot smell. They have *fashioned* hands, but the idols cannot reach out and touch; feet, but they cannot walk. Psalm 115:4-7 (NIV)

I offered my hand silently and allowed him to raise it to his lips. Although he did not understand, I owed him much. Did Yahweh bring an answer to my pleas for knowledge?

With a sigh, Maya plops down on the floor of my tent, curling her head into her chest to fully rest, jolting me into the present. No sooner than her head is down, her noisy breathing alerts me that she is sleeping. Does she sense the journey ahead and signal that we should both rest?

Leaving in the night holds too much risk, including being discovered by our camp's nightly patrol of the perimeter of our camp. Before dawn, there will be an hour between when the patrol ends, and the sun rises. I will leave then. As I relax into the comfortable, yet portable bed Abraham had fashioned for me by a local craftsman, my thoughts are with Isaac…and Ishmael. I know now Ishmael survived his and Hagar's travails in the wilderness. They established a new life. Still I long to see Ishmael in the flesh, hear his words, feel his calloused hands, notice how age has deepened the lines in his face and sharpened his sense of betrayal. *Oh Ishmael, how I would gather you under my wings like a hen sheltering her chicks if you would have let me.*[16] *And Isaac, you are the chick snatched from under my wings into the wilderness for consecration without a mother hen around to brood and cluck her displeasure.* I will find you.

Long before dawn, I wake up. A fleeting moment of peace flits by, until reality shoos it away. My husband and son have now been gone for a full day. I think about eating some of the food I prepared the night before for nourishment, but my nervous stomach will not allow it. I stroke the woolen gathers of my tent,

[15] If you're called upon to talk, speak as though God put the words in your mouth; if you're called upon to serve others, serve as though you had the strength of God behind you. 1 Peter 4:11

[16] O Jerusalem, Jerusalem. You kill the prophets *whom God gives you;* you stone those God sends you. I have longed to gather your children the way a hen gathers her chicks under her wings, but you refuse to be gathered. Matthew 23:37

knowing I will miss the security it offers. I open the Terebinth tree chest to rub the camel cloak I am leaving behind. I say a silent prayer to Yahweh... "Lord and Provider, you remembered me in my old age with a son. As you supported my cause then, please uphold it once more."

I will travel until the noon hour. Then I will find a place to rest during the most common hours for travel. At twilight I will set out again. Night risks me being tracked by an animal. That I will put in Yahweh's hands since daytime could mean meeting men on the trail that might take advantage of a woman, even in her old age. My plan is full of risks. If I were to be abducted, who would know? Abraham would deduce that I followed him. The missing donkey would be discovered. Amah would be compelled to break her oath of silence.

I quickly load my donkey with the minimum provisions I think I could need. I cannot let being overloaded slow us down. I lead Maya outside the tent, praying for her silent compliance as we step into the darkness to wait and watch. Our perimeter guard has a torch, and I know from sleepless nights he passes every thirty minutes, stopping an hour before sunrise. We call this hour the sacred hour. Abraham has taught me to identify this time by glancing at the stars. As the stars blaze before their retreat, the crickets sing louder. A short time after the light passes, we pick our way carefully past Isaac's tent, past my maid's tents, then past Abraham's summoning tent where the men meet to strategize, on to the edge of camp. As we step past the perimeter onto a trail I sometimes walk on in the early morning, I am startled by a stranger. A tall man.

I grasp Maya's mane for protection, but she seems undaunted, as if she instinctively knows the man. He smiles and takes a step forward. He looks familiar in the darkness, as if I know him but don't comprehend him. In the light of his torch, his eyes dance, while his stance projects strength.

How did he appear with a torch without the guard seeing him?

It may be that my quest has emboldened me, but suddenly I am not afraid. Close to our encampment, I can easily call for help and Abraham's men will be here. Yet I cannot, because they might prevent me from going or, even worse, follow me.

I keep my voice low, expecting him to do the same, "Who are you?"

"I am Zerubim." He tilts his head in deference. With kind eyes, he speaks softly with a lilt I cannot discern, "On behalf of Abraham, may I ask where you are going?"

Hear my prayer, O Lord, and listen to my cry; Do not be silent at my tears; For I am Your temporary guest, A sojourner like all my fathers.

Psalm 39:12[1]

[1] Amplified Version

CHAPTER THREE
Song of Sojourn

I REPEAT HIS NAME TO MYSELF SOFTLY, AS MY aged mind can so easily lose a name. *Zerubim.* He surprises me with both his boldness and his invoking of my husband's name. Although the impetuous part of me wants to dismiss him outright, I surprise myself with my curiosity. By what turn of circumstance did his coming exactly coincide with my going?[2] Did Abraham know I would try to come after him? If not, what is this man seeking? In our custom, a strange man would never come into another's camp without the permission of the clan's patriarch. Likewise, in our custom, a married woman would not be outside in the darkness before the light of day, testing herself to make sure she can locate the path without a torch. Despite these reservations, I pick up no threat.

"May I apologize that I startled you with my abrupt question. You must be wondering where I came from. Although you haven't told me yet, I think I know who you are...Sarah the wife of Abraham. Your beauty and spirit are just as your husband boasts."

"Flattering an old woman? Every woman is beautiful by torch light." I say with a small chuckle, despite myself. "You must

[2] The Eternal will keep you safe from all of life's evils, From your first breath to the last breath you breathe, from this day and forever. Psalm 121:7-8

be wondering why I am outside before the light of day." I draw in a deep breath, my throat catching. "I am preparing to join my husband and son. I sense that Isaac, my son, needs me. It is imperative that I find them."

I lift my chin slightly. Even though he only knows me through my husband, Zerubim must understand. This is *my* decision not his. Scanning his appearance, he appears to be a cross between an Egyptian and a Mesopotamian. The silver streaks in his brown hair and crinkles around his eyes suggest a full life, but his strength is that of a much younger man. Generations separate us. Did Yahweh send him?

He speaks again, "May I inquire … how do you propose to find them?"

He is bold, yet I am not offended. At my age, forthrightness wins the heart as much as a kiss on the lips.[3] This is a question I have wrestled with all night long. "I think they are headed towards Moriah, or perhaps even to Hebron with two of our servants. Abraham said he wouldn't be sure until he arrived."

"If they stop in Hebron, Moriah could be a three-day journey from here."

"Yes, Abraham did say they would be gone for at least seven days."[4] That would allow three days to travel to wherever Yahweh leads him. Holding Zerubim's eyes, I add, "There are many reasons I believe this, more than I have time to discuss. He left a day ahead of me, so I must go. I will travel day and night to catch him."

"These roads are dangerous for an unaccompanied woman. Even your husband and son didn't travel alone. Abraham is a day's journey ahead of you. Even if you were to journey through the night, you will move more slowly than him. And what of predators?"

[3] A straight answer is as precious as a kiss on the lips. Proverbs 24:26
[4] Genesis 22:1-4

"I couldn't ask my maids to take the risk. And the men wouldn't be willing to risk their standing with Abraham … my husband. They might try to prevent my leaving…or follow me." Inwardly I curse myself for my candor. "How do you know Abraham? And why do you ask?"

"Like your husband, I follow Yahweh. We learned of your husband when we were seeking out Melchizedek, priest of God most high.[5] It seems that our experience as guides would be a help to your own travels. Those who know me well call me Zerah."

"Our?" I say.

"I traveled with my sister, Yasmine. She is at the well getting water. I felt sure since Abraham invited us, he would want us to replenish our supply."

I know that Zerah means follower of righteousness. Have Abraham's prayers from the other night afforded me this protection of a righteous man and his sister, even without his knowledge?

"We had determined to travel until we knew what Abraham's desire might be for us. No one will know if we accompany you. Yasmine can help meet your needs. I have traveled these paths often. To go without the protection of a man who fears God is to take a great risk." He pauses, raises his eyebrows in curiosity and adds, "More of a risk than Abraham would wish?"

More than Abraham would wish, I repeat to myself. Inwardly, laughter bubbles up, the same laughter that came when an angel reported that I would have a child in my womb within a year's time.[6] *Isaac, my son of laughter.* I hold my hand over my mouth and bow my head, seeking to hide my amusement. *So much more risk than Abraham would ever wish.*

Maya stomps her foot and snorts, protesting that she is being

[5] See Genesis 14:17-18

[6] So Sarah laughed to herself, saying *under her breath,* "At my age—old *and decrepit,* as is my husband—both of us long past having any desire to *engage in lovemaking?*" Genesis 18:12

disregarded as my protector for this trip.

"My donkey has been known to ward off jackals and other wild beasts." Maya tosses her head and then shakes her body, mimicking my boldness.

Although Zerah doesn't laugh with me or at me, his eyes betray his amusement. He undoubtedly sees my trust in an animal for protection as naive.

He glances towards the north, even though it is still quite dark. "Since we just arrived last night, we are prepared to go. We have more than enough provisions for the three of us to travel for seven days…or more." Nodding at Maya, he adds, "And our donkey is young and strong, used to navigating steep trails."

Does Zerah expect me to leave Maya behind, my only comfort?

Looking at their donkey, I see that he is midnight black with a white ring around his snout, an exceptionally fine animal with large ears, some thirteen hand spans tall, just a little taller than me.[7] I remember Abraham has told me of seeing donkeys that their keepers call giants, or jokingly, Nephilim donks. Although Maya is at least four hand spans shorter than his donkey, she is sturdy.

"My donkey…Maya…she knows the scent of Isaac."

His kind eyes search my face. Does he read the conflict within? Have I become double-minded? I leave in faith, yet I am full of doubt.[8]

"None of the other men need to know," he reiterates. "We are here on behalf of Abraham and obviously he is not here." He bows slightly, and adds, "Isn't it reasonable for us to accompany you? Is it possible we came here for this very purpose? I have run these paths day and night. Surely, your travel will be less taxing with company."

I am surprised that he uses the word run. Does he really mean

[7] 5 foot, 8 inches tall.

[8] Father (*crying in desperation*): I believe, Lord. Help me to believe! Mark 9:24

to walk? When he lifts his head, his eyes draw me in, as if he knows something that I do not. I feel lighter in his presence.

"I need to leave now," I say and then regret the whole conversation. Am I really considering traveling with a man and his sister, who I have just met? Would Abraham want this? Then I remember. Abraham did not want me to go in the first place. Whatever I do, I am stepping past his will. But I will go. Nothing will stop me, even this man standing tall before me in the semi-blackness of the approaching dawn with his midnight black donkey. When I assume this kind of bold position with Abraham, he likes to say teasingly, "Ah, she has her face set like flint."[9] What he doesn't always realize is that I wield my strength to prevent disgrace, like the taunting of an ambitious handmaid or an overzealous husband who needs protection from his own self.

"If it would please you, let me get my sister Yasmine and our provisions. We will be ready to leave before the sun breaks the horizon." Seeing my hesitation, he adds, "Perhaps Yahweh brought us here to protect you on your long journey and help you find peace about your son Isaac. After all, we are just temporary guests on this earth, sojourners."[10]

I pause, noting that he does not tell me to stay. Then Zerah says the words I need to hear, "He gives wisdom to the wise and knowledge to the discerning. He reveals deep and hidden things; he knows what lies in darkness and light dwells with him."[11]

I take in a quick breath. These are the words that the faithful descendants of Noah use to identify each other. These phrases identify the seekers of the One God. This man knows Melchizedek. I will accept his help. He reaches out both hands and I lay mine on his, the greeting of the followers of Shem.

"How will we catch up to them, when they are a day ahead of us?" In this question I give my final assent. In doing so, I

[9] Because the Lord, the Eternal, helps me I will not be disgraced; so, I set my face like a rock, confident that I will not be ashamed. Isaiah 50:7

[10] Hear me, O Eternal One; listen to my pleading, and don't ignore my tears Because I am estranged from You—a wanderer like my fathers before me. Psalm 39:12

[11] Daniel 2:21b-22 (NIV)

have crossed a threshold. I have committed to the journey and whatever danger it may bring, including any lasting consequences with my husband and son.

"With Yahweh, a path always appears. Since you don't want to be seen, should we meet at the Northern edge of the camp, by the old dry well?" We can still be on our way before sunrise."

All at once it occurs to me that I didn't feed Maya this morning. This small delay will provide for her needs. Just as I turn towards my tent with my packed donkey, I see he is smiling. Is he pleased?

A short time later, after I feed and water Maya, I wake my maids and once more swear them to secrecy. Then I take my loyal donkey, laden with provisions and go to the dry well.

As I see the mysterious brother and sister in the distance, they appear to glow in the predawn changing of light. Their donkey is fully loaded with goods, including what appear to be several tents, provisions that I had been unable to secure without suspicion. Where would I have slept? If God can provide a tent, perhaps he will also reveal the deep and hidden things Abraham holds close to his chest.

Yasmine and Zerah keep their backs turned to me, watching the sky until I say, "I am here."

As they turn to face me, I draw in a breath. Although they are dressed in the simple apparel of wilderness guides, they both project strength. Yasmine's eyes are a piercing hazel-green and her reddish-brown hair is bound behind her in a braid. She and Zerah share the same spirit, but otherwise I wouldn't discern they are brother and sister. I guess that she is half my years and I wonder at her story. Was she ever married? Is she a widow?

"Sarah, this is my sister Yasmine."

"It is my honor to minister to you for these next days, Sarah."

Her voice skips like water dancing over stones. She is plain yet her countenance speaks of dignity. Just as I did with her brother, I cipher genuine concern.

"Yasmine, thank you. Is this as strange to you, as to me? After all, we have only just met each other."

"Oh no, my mistress. Undoubtedly Yahweh brought us here to accompany you on this quest. I have anticipated meeting you. May we find what you seek, and in doing so, may every path open before you. May your descendants be numerous and inherit a good land."[12]

She invokes a blessing, hinting at *the* blessing. Is she reassuring me that Isaac will live? Or does she unknowingly point to Yahweh's ability to choose his own way to fulfill a promise? Like Ishmael.

"Thank you, Yasmine." I nod at Zerah. "Shall we go?"

Zerah points his torch towards the path and leads the way away from camp into the brush and nearby trees. I see that he also has a walking staff, tied to his donkey. I hear roosters crowing and know soon the camp will wake up. Do they also herald my knowing betrayal of my husband's will? Zerah sets a pace considerate of my age. I keep a good distance between us but close enough I can see where he turns.

We walk the first several hours in silence, each attending to our own thoughts. Yasmine walks behind me, waiting for me to invite her closer. If I were her, I would be brimming with questions about the exact nature of this sojourn. I am grateful for her silence, even though I also have questions. But for the moment I am distrustful of questions, weary of memories. Perhaps if I take time just to be present, to look, to listen.

A deep breath of the clean air brings the aromatic smell of cedar, the wood Abraham prefers for sacrifice and undoubtedly

[12] Your descendants will be exceedingly fruitful. Nations and kings will descend from you. Genesis 17:6

the wood he will use in two days. My feet crunch as they land on the soft pine needles lining the path. I straighten my back and relax my shoulders, willing my aging body to accept the stress this journey will bring. Dread but also comfort if I can only push past my deep anxiety to allow it. As my vision widens, I hear the song of birds, not just by flock but as individuals. Listening carefully I hear dark-throated thrush, desert larks and scrub warblers.

When we resided in the city, I never knew nature's soothing touch. The same walls and courtyards that seemed a protection in our old life also kept me from learning—not the kind of information absorbed from teachers, but the kind that comes from personal experience and tumult. Like how we quickly realized that our provisions were not limitless, that we would have to learn to find our sustenance from the land. With this in mind, Abraham asked Eliezer to accompany us on our journeys.[13]

Having been a wilderness guide before he lived in the city, Eliezer patiently taught us all the ways the land could supplement our small herds. How nuts, berries, mushrooms and even trout from the streams we crossed could provide savory meals. Wild herbs and edible wild plants could teach us new tastes and new ways of thinking. Abraham was an eager student, unable to hide his pride in conquering the world around him with his bare hands. Eliezer enjoyed talking about Adam, the first man made from the dust by Yahweh, his naming of the animals. He conjectured how Adam's intimate, yet guarded experience with different creatures prepared him and Eve for life outside the garden. Abram added his knowledge of Noah, another naturalist, who spent 100 years studying the animals while he built the boat that would give his descendants a chance to live under the promise of the rainbow.[14]

[13] See Genesis 15:2

[14] See Genesis 9:13 (NIV)

Abraham said that Noah spent many nights on the deck on the ship after the rain ceased, studying the stars to understand where he was and when the flood might recede. I remember him saying, "Sarai, if we never had left our home, I would have never understood how invaluable the stars are and all the functions they perform. The stars declare their creator and humble me that God would single me out, as if a single star had a song to sing."

As we traveled and sometimes struggled to find our bearings in this new life, Abraham learned to shoot a bow, build fires, put up and take down unwieldy tents, manage a herd of camels, or even stay up all night to assist animals in birth. He trained men for battle in case of attack and negotiated treaties with potential hostile sovereigns. Our group grew from twenty to one hundred, and then over a twenty-year span to over 500 of us traveling together including the babes and children. As our numbers grew, he recruited more men to assume leadership. As his hands hardened and his courage swelled, Abraham did his share of the wearisome tasks of survival. All this took a toll on my husband, but mostly for the good.

Now Abraham has a wilder look in his eyes and a ruggedness about him. His heart naturally seeks dominion over whatever is around him,[15] whether it is wood to be built with, unruly camels to tame, or hostile kings to conquer. And now Yahweh has promised his legacy will extend throughout generations to the edges of the earth.[16] As his wife, I never lost my womanly softness, but yet have grown more wilderness-prepared over time.

My eyes lift to the sky above just in time to see a golden eagle soar over the path. How did I know to look up?

My husband seems to know his own song well, trusting its dark and bright strains. And now, I can't help but wonder…as a single star in the vast expanse of the heavens, do I have a song

[15] See Genesis 1:26 (ESV)

[16] Your kingdom will never end; Your rule will endure forever. [You are faithful to Your promise, and Your acts are marked with grace.] Psalm 145:13

to sing?

After some time of silent traversing, my stomach begins to rumble a little. I notice Zerah ahead waiting for us to catch up.

"I know another way which may be shorter. Are you comfortable with taking a less well-trod path? Do you need refreshment or rest before we continue?"

Glancing up, I see the sun is now overhead. Somehow, we traveled for half a day. Yasmine steps in to prevent me from embarrassment. "I have an urgent need."

Zerah nods, "I will be just ahead."

Once he is out of sight, Yasmine whispers, "Mistress, let me find a place where we can relieve ourselves."

I hadn't yet thought about these intimacies, but now that she speaks, I recognize my need. Yahweh created women to freely use their intuition to help others attend to their souls and bodies. Thank you, Yahweh, for this gift of friendship.

We tromp up a hill, and finding a log leaning over a path, we each take our turn. Of course, I know the physical demands of catering to a woman's body while traveling. I am also accustomed to having several maids who always find new ways to make these demands less cumbersome. At least monthly bleeding won't be an issue. I bled for weeks after Isaac's birth and then my womb returned to its mature state. Yes, Yasmine will protect me in ways I don't yet understand.

When we come back, Zerah hands me a flask of water, and the cool liquid revives me.

"You are so kind, but I prefer to keep moving."

"If you sit on your donkey, you can eat while we travel."

I nod my assent. Although I don't want to press Maya too hard, I know she will gladly bear my weight. To protect Maya,

Zerah takes all my provisions off of her and puts them on his donkey. Then he expertly puts a folded blanket on her back and ropes her so that I have a handhold.

"If Maya wearies, our donkey can also carry you."

Our journeys have taught me how to tie up my garments in order to mount an animal. As I climb onto Maya, I silently thank Zerah for the dignity of riding on my own beast. After I am positioned, Yasmine hands me a packet of dried meats, nuts and a small loaf of seeded barley bread. In my nervousness, I didn't eat earlier and am now ravenous.

"Zerah, I trust you to lead us. You lead and we will follow."

Once again, our procession finds its rhythm. While we head uphill, I sit on Maya's back slowly consuming the nourishment Zerah and Yasmine gave me to protect my nervous stomach. On the flat land, I dismount in order to let Maya walk without my added weight. Occasionally we stop for rest and relief. Strangely enough, Maya seems to be enjoying the company of the other donkey. When we stop, Maya nudges up next to their donkey, in the protective way she does with Isaac. Although the Nephilim donkey towers over her, Maya is mothering her new friend.

Later, as the evening shadows begin to fall, Zerah stops and turns to me. "We have found our place to stay for the night. Yasmine will cook for us."

Although I am weary and my feet are punishing me, I know this is not possible. If we stop now, we may be as far behind Abraham and Isaac as we were when we started.

"No, we can't stop," I say. "Not now. We must walk into the watches of the night...all night if we need to. We knew this starting out. Abraham and Isaac are almost two days into their journey. We cannot let them arrive at Moriah without us."

"Look at your donkey," Zerah says kindly. "She is winded and so are you. Besides, our donkey should rest as well."

"Please…try to understand." My voice cracks in exhaustion. I want to cry. *Will my own body betray me?*

He reaches out and touches my arm. His voice is low and respectful, "Sarah, we don't know that Abram is heading towards Moriah. You also mentioned the wilderness around Hebron."

My head spins. Have I come this far, a day's travel away from our camp for nothing? Did I forget in my zeal that finding Abraham would take a miracle in itself?

"I know these paths and can run them under the cover of darkness. I will search for Abraham in the night, and then return in the morning light."

Did I hear Zerah right? Does he plan on running the paths in the darkness until he locates my husband? Will he run a two-day journey in one night?

"First, I will run the path towards Hebron to see if he has stopped there. If I don't find him, tomorrow night I will run the path to Moriah. Surely Yahweh will not bring us this far without helping us accomplish his purpose."[17]

His purpose. That is what will determine my path. Zerah, like Abraham, exalts the will of Yahweh above his own, even above my own. But I am only a day away from Isaac. Tonight, I will sit under the same stars as my beloved son and yearn for their meaning just as he and his father will do. That is all I have, and so I will accept the small comfort.

As Yasmine unpacks and sorts our provisions, Zerah builds a fire and then sets up two tents, while feeding the donkeys. Yasmine hands me a container of barley beer to sip on while she cooks. The alcohol lulls me into a short nap, while the scents of sage and cinnamon circle around me.

I awake to a dish prepared with figs, lentils and broad beans

[17] People go about making their plans, but the Eternal has the final word. Proverbs 16:1

simmered in aromatic spices. Abraham likes to quip that we eat with our eyes and nose before food ever touches our lips. In some unknown place in the wilderness of Judea, we are partaking of the food of the gods, or of the one true God. How I wish Abraham and Isaac could taste this. Before we finish eating, we mop up any remaining stew with malted bread. For a brief time, my heaviness lifts.

After dinner, Zerah disappears into his tent to rest and his sister Yasmine insists on cleaning up while I rest. Afterwards, she strings up the meat high in a tree so wolves, bears or wild pigs won't be lured to us. Zerah's snores soothe me. *He is human.* When darkness falls, Zerah wakes. We watch silently as he uses leather straps to attach strange thick-soled sandals to his feet and ties a white cape around his neck. He uses another strap to tie a wineskin full of water and dried beef to his waist. After his warning about the danger of being in the wilderness at night, he is leaving two women alone. Then he jumps to his feet, glugs down a vessel of beer, flashes a boyish grin and springs onto the trail, disappearing except for his cape billowing behind him. As we watch him effortlessly bypass the trail to clamor up the side of a steep hill, he appears to be a cloud. *Will he return or run straight into the heavens?*[18]

Since we have two tents, Yasmine and I will sleep separately, leaving the donkeys outside to stand guard. But even after the day's exertion, neither of us is quite ready for sleep. We stir the fire back to life and will sit until it burns down. Looking at Yasmine closer in the firelight, I see she has unbraided her tresses. Her red hair flames like a sunset after a storm blows through, while her cheeks flush with warmth. The woman who I thought plain now exudes radiance.

"My lady, may I rub some healing balm into your feet?"

[18] The strength of the Eternal filled Elijah. The prophet pulled up his garment around his thighs and sprinted ahead of Ahab *the entire way* to Jezreel. 1 Kings 18:46

Yasmine asks.

"You are tired too. I couldn't think…"

"It will be my honor to minister to you."

I smile and hold out my sore feet. She removes my goat-skin coverings and my sandals, exposing several blisters. Now I understand where the pain came from.

"What is your balm made of?"

"The women sages say it was first discovered by Eve after being cast out of the garden. Like her, I harvest it from the balsam trees that grow around springs."[19]

Ah, the ancient wisdom of women…I think to myself.

After Yasmine gently applies medicine to my blisters, she uses her thumbs to push the salve into my arches. Glancing up at me with fire dancing in her eyes she says softly, "I discern that you are a prophetess."

I look at Yasmine surprised. It is time to allow her to minister to the places that I fear letting anyone into, even Abraham. "Abram sometimes calls me Yiskah, meaning seer, because he says I can see into the future. I am never sure if he teases or if he believes this to be true. I do see what no one else sees. These visions can inspire or terrify me." I smile. "He also calls me his princess."

"A princess and a prophetess. A high calling indeed. Either can be a great blessing, but also may appear to be a curse."

I nod in agreement and then groan in pleasure as she rubs my ankles, with alternating strokes of her warm hands. "Physical beauty may fade but fear of the Lord endures…at least Abraham believes this to be so."[20]

"If I may be so bold to ask, does the gift of prophecy bring you here?" She takes one of my hands to continue the healing touch. With each stroke I feel my vigor returning.

[19] Robin Weidner, *Eve's Song*, p. 39.

[20] Charm *can* be deceptive and *physical* beauty will not last, but a woman who reveres the Eternal should be praised **above all others.** Proverbs 31:30

"What brings me here?" I glance upwards through the trees at a sky bursting with stars. "I have long been barren...until 15 years ago. Then Yahweh appeared to my husband promising that generations as vast as the stars above would come from our son. When the son never came, I asked my handmaid Hagar to become my child's surrogate mother and gave her to Abram. A son, Ishmael, was born. When he was thirteen, a messenger of Yahweh came and announced the time had now come for me to bear a child. I laughed, and then ashamed, I lied about it."

"Laughter can signal many things. I like to think that God enjoys laughter." Yasmine has an uncanny knack of addressing what I haven't quite said.

"Having a child as an old woman...how can I describe the wild joy? Isaac, we called him, since we both laughed. Then Hagar turned against me. When she incited her son against Isaac after his third birthday, I felt compelled to cast her and her son, also now considered my son, into the desert." Feeling the familiar guilt, I add, "We would have let her take anything she wanted, but she scorned our offers."

"I see the difficulty. I think any woman would have felt the same conflict."

"Since then my premonitions, often appearing in the form of dreams, terrify me. Ishmael killing Isaac. Hagar becoming me and me becoming Hagar. Isaac paying the price for my sin. Are they prophecies, or just what I fear could happen?"

"Are these dreams always of Isaac, Ishmael, Hagar and Abraham?"

"No, there is more. Whenever I take a step towards Yahweh, it feels like there is a counter force pulling me away. Sometimes I think I hear the one who came to Eve in the Garden." My voice catches. "He comes in dreams but also when I am awake...at least it seems so. This evil one offers me the gods of my youth and opposes each step I take forward. I saw him in the lustful eyes of foreign kings who wanted me for their own. Could this be my fear speaking or could it be what they call the holy breathing, the very spirit of God?"[21]

"A prophetess is one who senses what others don't usually see, as the breath of God fills her and moves her along. To hold the promise means that you become a threat to those who oppose it. Your fear is part of your gift. Without it, the gift would be of little significance."

"Do you think we are safe here alone tonight? Will Zerah return?"

"If Zerah believed we were in danger he wouldn't have left. We will be protected until he returns. The distance to Hebron and back is not a long distance for him. I've known him to run for two days straight. It is his gift."

The embers of the fire pop and sizzle, as the fire dies down to a red bed of coals. *A man who can run for two days? A woman moved towards her fate by the breath of God?*

"Have you heard of the ezer? The eye that sees the danger?" I ask.

"Yes, since the days of Eve, wise women have known this great gift and sought its power. Yahweh is an ezer, our very great helper."

"I am here because I see danger. Abraham took my son, the son of the promise, far away for a sacrifice on a day I did not expect. When my maid asked his men what Abram took, they said he brought no animal for a sacrifice. I cannot think of any way to understand this, unless it is a conclusion that terrifies me."

"So, to be an ezer, you must intervene?"

"How will an old man protect a boy on the cusp of manhood

[21] Prophecy has never been a product of human initiative, but it comes when men *and women* are moved to speak on behalf of God by the Holy Spirit. 2 Peter 1:21

who is still innocent in the ways of the world? And how will an old woman find her way to them in time to intervene?"

"Does Abraham love Isaac?"

"More than himself."

"And Isaac, he feels the same way about his father?"

"Isaac is fiercely devoted. He will not stray from the path his father leads."

"Abraham trusts you as his Yiskah. He left, trusting you would find your own way." And, then lowering her eyes in deference to my position, she adds, "And so my mistress, here we are."

"Here we are. May I ask one last question?"

"But of course."

"Why does your brother wear a white cape? So that the animals see him as a white cloud passing by?"

Yasmine puts her hand over her mouth. Have I shocked her by my boldness? But then her shoulders begin to shake and suddenly I see myself in her. *The woman who laughed.* I begin chuckling as well and the mirth between us runs deep, until tears run down our faces. Even more than the healing balm, this amusement soothes my creaky back and weary bones, releasing my shoulders to resume their natural position. Maya, always responsive to my emotions, stamps her foot and begins her own kind of snickering.

Afterwards, we sit quietly, bonded by our moment of wild joy, the kind that sees hilarity in the impossible, the dangerous and sometimes even the tragic.

"Thank you for letting me minister to you tonight, my lady."

With her words, I remember Zerah's promise that Yasmine would be my handmaid. Sure enough, she has done all the tasks my maids would have done if they had been here, and perhaps more. But her service is different, prompted by a different motivation. My responses have been unconstrained by the sense of unequal power. Perhaps, she could help me understand all that evolved with Hagar.

"Being a handmaid gives me pleasure," she says as she stands to do the last tasks of the day. *Does she read my thoughts? Is she a handmaid or a prophetess?*

Before the fire dies down, Yasmine preserves some of the coals in case we need them in the night.

Her actions suggest that I should sleep. Although, reenergized by the laughter, I could imagine talking deep into the night. I wrap my cloak around me and stand to test my feet. They slide into my walking sandals without pain. Yasmine nods towards the larger tent, obviously intended for me. As I turn towards my tent, she whispers with a smile, "Zerah's cloak is made of the hide of an albino deer."

I nod and pull open the door to my tent and then secure it. Within the tent it is strangely warm. *Ah, the fire was built near the tent's opening. They warmed it for me.* Conviction quickly follows. How many times have I thanked Yahweh that I am not a lowly handmaid?[22] How many times have I neglected showing gratitude for the thankless tasks a handmaid is expected to perform?

My premonition tells me that Yasmine won't retire until Zerah returns. That she will sit watch outside with the donkeys. She is not a woman of fear. *Thank you, Yahweh.* As I pull the covers around me, I groan aloud, my bones burning like glowing embers. Will the rest of my days vanish like smoke?[23] Then I hear a song softly drifting from the campfire. In the silence of the night, Yasmine's voice swaddles me like a newborn babe.[24]

[22] See Luke 18:11

[23] For my *days come and go,* vanishing like smoke, and my bones are charred like *bricks of* a hearth. Psalm 102:3

[24] Look here. I have *made you a part of Me,* written you on the palms of My hands. Your *city* walls are always on My mind, *always My concern.* Isaiah 49:16

SONG OF SOJOURN

A song of sojourn
Unsure yet friends
Daily we ascend
Each turn and bend

A verse of sojourn
The end unknown
Walking in trust
We're never alone

A prayer of sojourn
To father and friend
Asking to follow
To journey's end

A shout of sojourn
Trusting the Lord
Surrender the going
With one accord

A whisper of sojourn
As darkness descends
Held in his hands
We calmly ascend.

A song of sojourn
Resting in peace
Counting each favor
Then finding release

Owls of all sorts will take up habitation there, nesting and laying their eggs. They will hatch their young and cover them beneath their wings....

Isaiah 34:15

CHAPTER FOUR
Owl's Song

I ROUSE BEFORE SUNRISE AND VENTURE OUTside, wondering whether Yasmine is asleep under a tree or Zerah has returned from his long run. The door is drawn to the second tent and so I must hold my curiosity in check. I glance at the sky, trying to discern the hour, asking myself what knowledge I could bring to bear. I do remember Abraham saying that it is coldest right before dawn. Dawn could be approaching as it is markedly cooler than yesterday morning. The stars still glimmer but are circled by clouds. At this time of year, these hills are known for violent downpours accompanied by thunder. Because rain comes so seldom, it can be violent, the clouds shaking out all the moisture they have accumulated for many long months. Even the sky has fits of rage, like my outburst in our tent the day I found my husband and son gone.

I pull my cloak tighter. Even in the twilight, I can see that Maya has her legs curled underneath her body deep in sleep, while Zerah's donkey stands tall, watching. I note that neither is tied up and wonder whether this is wise. The Nephilim donk shakes his head at me. I cautiously edge my way over to let him sniff my hand.

"Good morning loyal watchman," I whisper to the donkey, as I pat his side. "Did Maya take the first shift, or did she leave you to do all the watching?"

He stamps one foot in reply.

"The traveling life suits you. And what donkey wouldn't be happy to have masters such as Zerah and Yasmine?"

I walk over to my donkey and give her rein a tug. Her signal to get up. Maya sighs, not ready to rise and likely protesting this journey not of her choosing. She turns her nose away from me, asserting her control. I have to give her three tugs before she reluctantly stands, shakes her head at me, and then puts her head down and shoves me. Surprised, I do what I've learned from my husband, I shove her back as hard as I can. She seems surprised and takes a few steps back from me, as if we haven't done this numerous other times. She nods her head at me. I approach once more and stroke her nose to comfort her. I whisper, "Maya, I know you see Isaac as your most beloved pack leader. But to find him I will need your help." As I move Maya right beside Zerah's donkey, my mind quickly finds commonality. *Ah, Abraham, you had no trouble thrusting your wife out of the way to accomplish your calling.*

Hearing a branch crack behind me, I wonder about wild animals. But the donkeys seem unfazed, so I put one hand on Maya and one on the Nephilim donk. As we breathe each other's musky scents, my eyes begin to adjust to the darkness.

"His name is Hamor."[1]

Startled, I hastily let go of Maya and almost lose my balance. A strong hand catches my elbow. I turn and find Zerah behind me, his albino cloak still around his shoulders.

"When he was a young jack, he was quite a noisy animal, and his cries sounded very much like his name...Hay-more, Hay-

[1] Hamor is the most common Hebrew word for a donkey in the Bible, used some 100 times.

more." His eyes twinkle in the quickly departing darkness, "I apologize for startling you. I just returned and was thinking of building a fire."

"You just returned?" It seems that someone who walked through the day and then ran through the night would be winded. He looks invigorated and his eyes are bright.

"I didn't expect to see you up before dawn. But perhaps I should have known… considering our first meeting. Is there a way that I can serve you?"

"Thank you. No…just anticipation I suppose. Do you have news of my husband and son? I prayed late into the night that Yahweh would guide you to them."

In answer, he takes the walking stick by his side and extends it across his palms.

"I came to a fork in the path, where Abraham could have gone one of two ways. I followed the first for quite a while and found no signs of other travelers. So, I circled back to try the other. Just a few steps further, this walking stick stood next to an oak tree, as if it had found its mate."

I take the weighty stick into my hands and turn it in the approaching dawn. "Red oak with carvings down the side. A project Abraham worked on when he stayed up into the night." I glance at Zerah and smile. I point to the top of the staff where two white and golden-brown tail feathers are bound by twine and resin. "He bore this hole just recently so his stick could hold these two golden eagle feathers he found outside our camp."

"Yahweh saw to it that it would reach your hands."

"Abraham told me that the carvings were of my hair. When he would hold it by the fire, the burnished wood would remind him of our first meeting…the sun-kissed mahogany streaks in my hair shining in the sunlight."

"Could he have left it as a marker?"

"I would think not. This walking stick has been with Abraham many years. It is precious to him…" I smile shyly, "and to me."

As I rub my fingers over the carvings, I decide it is more likely a testimony to Abraham's forgetfulness. Did he lay it aside while he relieved himself? Did he discover far down the trail he had left it, but felt Yahweh would have him press on?

"I only saw it because of the white feathers. But I thought you would want it for safekeeping and to carry your husband with you."

Zerah surprises me in his understanding of a woman. But he still hasn't touched on what I really need to know. "Is this all you saw of Abraham?"

"Actually, the walking stick told me enough. I had conjectured he might head to Hebron, perhaps for a meeting with Melchizedek. But when I took the path moving towards Hebron, I found nothing. I came back and turned onto the path to Moriah. There was the walking stick and a little further down the trail, I found a moist spot where there were clearly footprints from four travelers and a donkey. Startling their party in the night didn't seem wise. And I knew you would desire me back before dawn."

Despair washes over me. "But how could you be sure it was them? Silently, I now wish I had given Zerah instructions since he was now employed by us. *Run ahead but be sure to see them in person. Do not leave until you know without doubt it is them.*

"You never explained why you suspect he is going to Moriah."

"The day before he received the final call to leave, I overheard him talking with some of the men about Moriah. The beauty of the mountain and the trails to the peak. Although his voice gave away nothing, his shoulders were hunched over. The way they are when Abraham is deeply troubled, weighed down."

"I can see why that would concern you."

"When I asked him about it, he said he would like to take me back there sometime. He didn't want further questioning. But that night, I woke to a noise outside our tent. Abraham was outside nurturing a fire, but instead of carving, he was on his knees praying. Listening from the door of our tent, I could only discern a few anguished words.... Isaac, Ishmael, surrender, sacrifice." I sigh. "And, yes, he said the word *hinini,* the same word he replied with when Yahweh called us to a nomadic lifestyle."

Zerah leans over and nods. His lips move faintly like he converses with himself.

I sigh and decide to continue. "Then Abram began to rock back and forth on his knees, putting his head to the ground again and again. I surmised he was mourning the loss of Ishmael, who was seventeen when he left." I brush away a tear, surprised at the well of emotion that lies underneath. "I thought I should not interfere with such a moment."

"Did you hear the word Moriah in his supplication?"

"No, but a wife knows her husband's anguish. Now that I think of it, his distress was as if he had already lost another son. The next day, I had a dream where Abraham was standing over Isaac with a knife. What if Isaac is the sacrifice Yahweh wants? What would that even mean? Only the pagans offer their children in sacrifice."

Zerah sighs deeply. When he looks up his eyes are full of compassion. "It is not my place to stand between Abraham and his calling. Only to lead you as you desire. Do you believe Yahweh goes before him?"[2] A wind suddenly kicks up around us, pushing my hair into my face. I am chilled, tired, hungry

[2] He is ever present with me; *at all times He goes before me.* I will not live in fear or *abandon my calling* because He stands at my right hand. Psalm 16:8

and out of words. Although Zerah, the running wilderness guide with the white cape of an albino deer, scaled mountains and blazed down trails in half a night, it will require another day's travel on a donkey to follow the path marked by a carved staff.

"Will you rest while Yasmine prepares for the day? I will need some time to rest myself. Not too long. Shall we leave after the sun lifts over the hills?"

I nod my agreement. As if on cue, Yasmine emerges out of her tent. With a small smile revealing a dimple in her right cheek, she brings out the fire pouch made of two shells holding the hot coals from last night's fire and sets to work. Her hair is bound in a braid for travel.

Zerah is right. I was up too late and arose too early. My eyes are heavy and at this moment a few more moments of rest under warm blankets sounds blissful. Yasmine brings her own blanket to add to mine and assists me in getting comfortable. "Don't worry Mistress. I will make sure you do not delay our departure."

"Yasmine," I whisper. "Could you bring me my husband's walking stick? Your brother found it in the night."

She nods and quickly returns with the stick. She folds back my blanket so that the stick can be next to me, then whispers. "I hope you find strength for your journey. The One God sees you and hears the pleas of your inner being."[3]

"I heard you singing last night," I whisper, before I drift back to sleep. "Can you teach me the sojourn song today?"

She nods and slips outside, closing my tent behind her. At that moment, I feel like a child being mothered.[4] How does it happen that as I become older, time is reversing? Yasmine has stirred my embers of yearning for the one who gave birth to me. It's been sixty years since I've seen her, known her, but the passage of time has only made the bite more bitter, the burn

[3] O Eternal One, You have heard the longings of the poor and lowly. You will strengthen them; You *who are of heaven* will hear them. Psalm 10:17

[4] Instead, we proved to be gentle among you, like a nursing mother caring for her own children. 1 Thessalonians 2:7

more searing, the desert winds more scorching.[5] How could I have known that following Abraham would mean missing my mother's sudden illness and passing to the next life? *Yahweh, how long will it be before I am with her again?*

It seems like I have barely drifted into sleep when Yasmine touches my shoulder. "It is time, Mistress. And there is something I desire to show you."

I whisper sleepily. "Sarah. You may call me Sarah."

Yasmine waits as I rise, gather my cloak around me and step outside the tent. Maya is up on her feet and shakes her head at me in greeting. Yasmine extends her hand. "Cardamom seeds to chew…to freshen your mouth." Then putting a finger in front of lips signaling silence, Yasmine leads me into the forest. As I chew the zesty seeds that taste of cinnamon, nutmeg and ginger, we pass ferns and ever-thickening trees—pistachio, oak and pine—the small strip of gnarled trees sprouting growth in every direction. Suddenly she stops and I step beside her. Cupping her hands around her mouth she intones, "Buo, buo, hu-huhoooh." The return call comes quickly from below us. I know immediately it is an owl. We climb slightly downhill and then wait near a single elm tree. Finally, Yasmine points. It takes a moment for me to locate the creature since its pale face is turned away, and its blotchy brown spotted wings blend with the tree. It is sitting on a high branch close to the trunk. I only see it when it adjusts its wing.[6]

"It is a Pharaoh owl." Yasmine whispers and then pulls a live mouse from a pocket in her cloak. I start to mouth, "Where did you …?"

Again, she puts her finger in front of her lips. She slowly walks up to the tree, places the mouse on a low branch and backs a few steps away. A few minutes later, the Pharaoh owl drops

[5] *Wherever they are,* they will be *fine,* never hungry nor thirsty. They will be protected from oppressive heat and the burning sun Because the One who loves them—*as a mother loves her child*—will be their guide. God will lead them to *restful places, rejuvenating* springs of water. Isaiah 49:10

[6] See Craig Childs' description of owls in *The Animal Dialogues.*

silently from the heights straight down to the mouse, his pale brown and black feathers stretched wide, and extends his talons to snatch the mouse from the branch with a crunch and then lifts straight to the top of another tree. He comes so close I can see his fierce bright orange eyes. I shudder, remembering a time Pharaoh snatched me from our camp in Egypt.

"No doubt the female owl awaits this meal from her mate. I wouldn't be surprised if she is either preparing to lay eggs or sitting with young fledglings."

Of course, Yasmine is a student of nature…like my husband and my son. "Isaac encountered a similar owl just last year."

Yasmine nods her interest.

"The owl was sitting in a tree near where we were camped. Isaac was the only one to see him. When he tried to move closer, the owl stared at him with wild agitated orange eyes. He immediately sensed the threat and slowly backed away. He sat down as a show of submission and spent time watching the owl turn his head."

"He sounds like a bold young man."

"When he ran home to tell us about it, his father said that sighting an owl meant a change was coming. He said something poetic like… 'In the wilds, we learn the freedom to let go and embrace what is ahead. We then leap like wild goats toward the mountains to see new vistas and take on new adventures.'"[7] I smile. "Abraham pretended to be a wild goat and had us both in tears by his wild jumping to and fro trying to mimic their movements."

Yasmine laughed. "Only my brother has met your husband. But he sounds like a good traveling companion. I would like to see his dance of the wild goats."

"Where did you find a live mouse?"

[7] Only desert animals will occupy the deserted city; owls will nest in their *formerly swept-clean* houses. *Mangy* jackals and wild goats will roam *among the rubble* and romp *among the ruins.* Hyenas will *prowl around* and howl among its towers; jackals will haunt its *formerly* palatial palaces; Babylon's time *of destruction* is coming; her days are numbered. Isaiah 13:21b–22

"First the owl was right above our camp...perhaps a night of lean hunting. When a mouse scurried right by our feet, we knew what the owl sought. My brother caught him with a piece of dried meat and suggested that we give him to the owl. It seems cruel, but it is the way of nature."

I touch Yasmine's arm. I don't want to arrive back at camp just yet. "What do you think it means Yasmine? Does Yahweh pursue me? This whole ludicrous journey is because of this, this...wild, moody God who falls out of the sky to terrorize us with his callings."[8]

She smiles, clearly not offended by my irreverence. "Yahweh does have a wildness about him. We cannot domesticate him or remake him in our own image. I suppose each of us has to decide whether to look at his wildness as a threat or as a calling."

Yasmine has just described my relationship with my husband. I see the wildness as a threat. He sees it as a calling.

"Yahweh doesn't withhold this part of himself, so we can trust him in his fullness."

Her words stir me. Do I seek to protect Isaac from a wild God? Have I kept him in the nest so long that Abraham and Yahweh needed to take Isaac away lest he never learn to fly? When we step back into camp, I am surprised to see Yasmine's tent down and packed. While I eat, Zerah puts out the fire and covers the area with dirt.

"What do you need now, mistress Sarah? How can I serve you?"

"Please give me a moment in my tent and I will be ready."

I come out of the tent feeling filthy, covered with the grime of travel. Wild God or not, all that matters is finding Abraham and Isaac. As I drink some of the camel's milk Amah provided, Zerah and Yasmine water the donkeys, then load the rest of my

[8] You can no more predict the path of the wind than you can explain how *a child's* bones are formed in a mother's womb. Even more, you will never understand the workings of the God who made all things. Ecclesiastes 11:5

provisions and take down my tent. They move with such speed and ease. No doubt, if it weren't for me, they would leap like goats up and down the hills leading to Moriah.[9] Although Zerah didn't see Abraham and Isaac in the flesh, it comforts me that he has already mapped the day's walk with his quick feet.

As we start walking on the trail, Zerah leading Hamor and Yasmine leading Maya, I remember the song Yasmine sang the night before. She makes good on her promise to teach me and we repeat the song until it becomes the melody that moves our feet from place to place. Even when we start uphill, I still don't need the donkey to carry me, with the song lightening my steps.

A song of sojourn
Unsure yet friends
Daily we ascend
Each turn and bend

A verse of sojourn
The end unknown
Walking in trust
We're never alone

A prayer of sojourn
To father and friend
Asking to follow
To journey's end

A shout of sojourn
Trusting the Lord
Surrender the going
With one accord

[9] He made me sure-footed as a deer and placed me high up where I am safe. Psalm 18:33

A whisper of sojourn
As darkness descends
Held in his hands
We calmly ascend.

A song of sojourn
Resting in peace
Counting each favor
Then finding release

The lyrics fill me with desire, good desires, and for a time, curiosity overcomes my fear for Isaac. I ask Yasmine, "When the song says, unsure but friends, to what does it refer?"

"Walking with Yahweh. We are unsure, but we ask him to establish our steps like a friend would." She points in front of us, where Zerah has left his donkey to walk ahead. "Cracks in a path near the edge of a cliff could mean unstable ground, a signal to test it before you lead a fully loaded donkey across."

Thinking again of my husband I blurt, "Have you ever been married?" I don't know if this topic is forbidden, but I get the feeling that she might know of another kind of traversing—the kind between a man and woman who walk in covenant.

"No, I haven't. At a young age, I knew my life would be devoted to God. Both Zerah and I made the same commitment. We have found fulfillment in this service."

"Please know that I don't mean to offend, but surely many men would be blessed with you as a companion."

"No blessing comes without a cost." Yasmine smiles. "And I am not offended. I see the gifts marriage could offer." She smiles and her eyes are dreamy, like a woman smitten with a man. "You have your gift, Abraham. And I have mine…my desire is for Yahweh.[10] To be sure, there are times when I am intensely curious about marriage. Yet, Yahweh has given me my own flame to tend, one that burns brightly. My walk has become its own kind of covenant, one holy to me and to Yahweh."[11]

"Have you ever been tested in your resolve to be devoted to the Lord alone…drawn by the attention of a man?

"Yahweh put the desire into woman for a man, a partner, by creating Eve with part of Adam's rib. But since Yahweh breathed himself into women, our desire for him is even stronger."

Yahweh, are you stirring in me a stronger desire for you?

As if in response, a call comes from the forest. Hoy-poo. Hoy-poo. When Abraham and I heard this call, we would stealthily try to find the quail before they flew off. It is the separation call of a quail. Both male and female quail give a three to four note call when separated from their covey. I softly imitate the call three times. One for Isaac. One for Abraham. And yes, one for Yahweh, in case he has lost sight of me. Or is it I who has lost sight of him? I smile, remembering Isaac's joy at my ability to mimic birds.

Zerah motions that all is well and gives the donkey a signal to follow. I am surprised to see how high we ascended so quickly and glad to have guides who help us sojourn safely. I am also grateful I put on the camel skin covers for my sandals.

Yasmine touches my elbow, "Listen. Do you hear that?"

A different bird cry echoes around us…the same call Yasmine did earlier?

"Is that the call of the Pharaoh owl?"

"Perhaps the owl now thinks we are carriers of mice? He will track us until we leave his territory. Although he usually only hunts in the night, we have proven to provide the type of food he needs."

Again, all I can think of is Pharaoh who randomly claimed

[10] I wish that all of you could live as I do, *unmarried*. But the truth is all people are different, each gifted by God in various and dissimilar ways. 1 Corinthians 7:7

[11] Because you, too, have heard the word of truth—the good news of your salvation—and because you believed *in the One who is truth*, your lives are marked with His seal. Ephesians 1:13

women from traveling bands to be concubines and a husband who used me to buy safety for our band. *Yes, she is available. She is my sister.* Yahweh rescued me, but an unseen jagged wound lingers—hidden under the skin closest to my heart.

From the top of the pass we can see the descent into a desert canyon. There are high rocks with swirls of purple, and a dry riverbed meandering through the wasteland surrounding it. Although it is stark, it is beautiful. Now I am glad I walked uphill, because the downhill walk could test my knees. Seeing my discomfort, Zerah stops and rearranges his donkey's load, revealing a type of seat I've never seen with a handle of sorts for me to hang on to. He helps me up and I give the donkey's neck a pat. It pains me to give up riding Maya, my son's companion. But now, only I can protect her, by putting my desires below her needs. "Hamor, I am trusting you to bring me down this winding trail."

Maya makes a noise I recognize as displeasure. "Maya, I should think you would be happy about this. You will thank me later."

As we wind toward the bottom, scruffy trees and shrubbery along with the rising canyon walls take away our sightline. We call this type of canyon a wadi. On top of the donkey, my back begins to spasm with a protest of its own from sleeping on the hard ground and being jostled by a Nephilim donkey. Thankfully, the going is slow on the looping trail. A fall off of here might be disastrous, causing me to slide down a steep hill through brush and rocks. My stomach twists realizing I might not even survive such a fall.

Then a whisper comes, circling around my head like a vulture, and I feel the hot breath of evil on my neck.

Sweet barren one. The all-knowing one leads to you a destiny he knows will destroy you. He has rejected your pleas just like your husband.

Without warning, the Pharaoh owl we saw earlier drops from the sky and swoops over us, his wing almost brushing my head. Hamor whinnies and then rears up, causing rocks to slide over the edge and almost throwing me. "Whoa, boy!" I yell. I see something disappear into the brush on my right. A snake?

Pure fear washes over me. I sense a brooding evil nearby. Am I drifting into a dream? Was the whisper from my own thoughts? Did I sense the owl preparing to attack? Or could this be the evil one who visited Eve in the garden?

Zerah, who is on foot, turns around and takes the donkey's reins, saying words softly into his ear in a language I don't recognize. His words are melodic like water skipping on the rocks. The donkey relaxes, shakes his head to affirm his master's instruction.

Zerah touches my arm to remind me that I am safe. "Hamor only rears this way when danger is near. The owl startled him. Did you see or hear anything else?"

"I saw something move into the brush. Perhaps a rodent that the owl is chasing? Or a snake?"

Zerah takes a deep breath and I feel a call to breathe with him. "You are safe," he says simply.

"I am safe," I say, and then surprise myself by adding, "wherever Yahweh leads."

The rest of our downward journey, I quietly sing the song of sojourn, never wearying of the beauty of its words. I sigh in relief when we turn the last switchback and descend into what appears to be a dry riverbed with stony cliffs on either side.

Zerah glances overhead. "It appears we have plenty of time to make it to the other side. We will traverse this quickly, so we will keep you on the donkey for a time."

Yasmine takes Maya's rein and leads us toward a bend in the path ahead where the wadi's walls almost come in to touch one another. As soon as we turn the corner, there are a series of large rocks leading upwards, as well as a passage that now slightly expands into yet another curve.

The air feels heavy, like it mimics my soul. Seeing darkness on the horizon, my apprehension grows. I cannot stop looking upwards. Keeping my left hand on the reins, I put my right hand on my chest, right where I feel the jagged tear of all that has passed. When Zerah climbs up a few tall rocks to survey the sky, the donkey shakes his head and rump, making my heart pound.

"Enough of you," I say under my breath.

Glancing over my shoulder and seeing that Yasmine has lingered behind to inspect a plant, I swing my left foot over him, and then slide off on the donkey. The drop makes me land awkwardly on my left foot, twisting it with a cry of pain. I hobble over to Maya, who I would trust with my life, and prepare to try to get on her, but I can barely put weight on the ankle. I untie Abraham's walking stick from her side to use as leverage.

"Mistress Sarah, wait," Yasmine calls out, running to catch up to me.

I try to mount Maya on my own and then tumble to the ground.

Yasmine kneels beside me, reading the pain on my face.

"If you help me, I can get on," I say, my voice now husky. "We should move on." I'm not sure whether it was the whispers, the owl or Zerah's checking of the sky, but I am unnerved.

Zerah nods at Yasmine, some sign I cannot interpret.

"We need to make sure you aren't hurt first."

Letting loose of his donkey, Zerah walks over and swoops me and Abraham's staff up in his arms, as if I am a child. "I will take you up higher where it is safe." He lifts me above him onto a rock, and then hoists me on to the next, repeating the procedure several times until we have a better vantage point. Yasmine quickly gathers a couple of blankets, her fire packet, some food and water along with healing herbs and salves and then follows us up the rocks. She slowly begins to check my joints, my skinned elbow, my hip…slowly testing each part for movement and noting what brings pain.

When she finally allows me to sit up, I gasp in alarm. Dark clouds have moved in and are circling the sky. I smell rain.

"There is a cave above us. We will take shelter."

"What about Maya and Hamor?"

Drops start to fall out of the sky. We hear a strange roar, and it seems like the very rocks beneath us are shaking. Thunder booms somewhere nearby.

Zerah picks me up once again and hoists me up another series of steps into a rock shelter. As fleet of foot as a rock badger, Yasmine swiftly descends the rocks to move the donkeys, then realizes the rocks are too steep to get them all the way up the cliff.

"Maya, my donkey," I cry.

"Yah, Yah," Yasmine yells as she slaps the donkey's haunches, causing them to startle and then run. As she easily scales the rocks, the noise turns into a deep rumble and muddy water appears pushing itself down the riverbank, full of sticks, logs and the noise of rocks hitting each other. The donkeys are barely ahead of the muddy water. Quickly, Yasmine is back beside us.

As Zerah and Yasmine gently urge me into the cave, I cry, "No, no, no! Maya! Hamor!"

The heavens break loose with a downfall of water, which quickly forms a waterfall over the entrance to the rocky shelter.

We hunch together in the opening plenty large to keep the three of us dry and safe.

As quickly as it started, the rain finally stops, but the running water has only gained momentum. Water is wildly making its way into every crevice.

"Our donkeys, our provisions! If I hadn't slowed us down, we would have already passed. If I had stayed on Hamor, we could have run the donkeys ahead of the flood." My chest squeezes like a fist, my shoulders move toward my ears, and my heart beats wildly.

Zerah looks at me with kind eyes. "Fear can only be conquered with truth. Getting off of Hamor and twisting your ankle brought us high on the rocks, saving us." He lays a hand softly on my shoulder, and, as if commanded, my shoulders return to where they usually live. Is he able to share the burden of another with a simple touch?

"The donkeys…their chances?"

"Small, I'm afraid. But thank Yahweh, they weren't tied up. Hamor knows how to swim, but the power of the water is great."

Now tears run down my face in a torrent, full of unseen sticks and stones. "Maya has never seen anything like this. Even if Hamor makes it, Maya won't."

"Sarah," Zerah says, his voice tender. "Maya or Hamor would gladly give their lives for you. It is their gift and calling."

Glancing in Zerah's eyes, I suddenly believe that *he* would lay down his life for me. Isaac and the mountain lion come to mind, and I know he is correct about the donkeys, but I am brokenhearted. Suddenly, I feel faint and the cave begins to move around me.

Yasmine turns her body, so we are back to back, with me resting against her. As I lean my head on her shoulder, strength flows from her body to mine. Zerah brings the skin of milk to my lips and I drink. "I will survive." I repeat it in an attempt to convince myself, "We will survive."

As the water continues to move, I hear boulders rolling along the bottom. I clutch my chest. I push away the thought of Maya being pulled under the water, knowing it is more than I can bear. I want no more conversation, even though my ankle is throbbing, and I should ask for assistance. Then I remember. Perhaps there is still a chance for Isaac if I can only keep moving forward. I hear my husband's tender voice in my head, "Sarah, the most daunting tasks are achieved by one simple action followed by another."

I sit up on my own and extend my ankle. It is now swollen, and I know it will no longer support me.

"Is it possible that Hamor...and Maya...will circle back after the waters recede?" My eyes beg the two of them for just a small measure of hope.

Zerah's silence is the answer I dread.

Yasmine now attends to my ankle, as I wipe my wet cheeks with my sleeve. Her features are soft, yet she doesn't speak a word. She lightly rubs some healing balm into my ankle and my skinned elbow, then tears off the edge of the blanket to make a wrap. Laying out the remaining provisions, she begins to assemble food for us. Food is a blessing, although our tents, extra clothing and cooking utensils are gone. Perhaps Abraham was right all along about his journey with Isaac. It is just a simple burnt offering. But of course, that would mean that I embarked on this perilous journey and lost my precious donkey all for nothing except for a mother's fearful imaginings.

As quickly as the flood came, it is gone, leaving mud, sticks and rocks strewn throughout the riverbed. Zerah stands up and calls for the donkeys. His voice echoes off of the rocks that would be beautiful in any other circumstance.

"I will climb to the top of this cliff to look for Maya and Hamor."

As Zerah hoists himself from rock to rock with ease, I have no words for Yasmine and certainly no words for Yahweh.

Doesn't he understand this is more than I can bear?

After a time, when Zerah returns, Yasmine raises her eyebrows in question, and he frowns in answer. The donkeys have disappeared. They could have been swept out for a long distance.

"We will wait the rest of the afternoon, until we regain some firm footing. Then I will carry you on to Hebron. Yasmine can carry our provisions. I know of a cave there that belongs to an acquaintance. We can spend the night there and attend to finding a donkey in the morning."

At Yasmine's prompts, I force myself to take some nourishment. Then she helps me find a way to lie down and elevate my foot. Surprisingly, the ground inside the rock shelter is soft. As my soul urges my body to slumber, melancholy replaces panic. Drifting off, I hear the cry of the Pharaoh owl, ever desirous of another mouse. Am I the mouse or am I a desert owl lying among the ruins of her journey?[12]

When I finally wake, the light has started to shift. Yasmine again has food and water laid out for me. Everything else is tied up in the blanket into a sling to go around her shoulders. Abraham's walking stick lies near me, my only token of hope. Thank Yahweh for this small sign of his presence.

"Yasmine will carry your husband's stick and use it to support herself." Seeing my sad eyes, Zerah adds, "You can rest in my carrying.[13] I once carried a person for a full day and according to Yasmine, I am as sure footed as a mountain goat.... You may

[12] I am like a *solitary* owl in the wilderness; I am a *lost and lonely* screech owl *at home* in the rubble. Psalm 102:6

[13] And here in this wilderness, all along the route you've traveled until you reached this place, haven't you seen the Eternal, your True God, carrying you the way a parent carries a child? But you still don't trust the Eternal your God. Deuteronomy 1:31-32

even be able to rest against my chest."

"How far do we have to go?"

"It will take us a bit into the night, but the cave will give us a good resting place."

"Will you then run after Abraham in the night?"

Zerah looks into my eyes as if he were reading me. "Even if I did locate them, I would still need to go into Hebron the next day to secure a donkey." He pulls his right ear, thinking aloud. " If Abraham arrives back at your home camp before us, he will suffer great worry."

I sigh, deeply distressed. "How will you pay for the animal?" Gold was among my lost possessions now buried in mud.

"I always carry some shekels in my clothing for times like this."

Of course, I know what all this means. Abraham and Isaac are headed towards Moriah by now. Zerah will not go to them with my message. As much as I want to pretend, I am on the brink of losing Isaac…and myself.

"Prayer could be a way to intervene,"Yasmine offers.

"I prayed on the hills and look what happened," I intone softly, mostly to myself, partly to her and partly to *her* god, Yahweh.

Now ready, we take off into the sunset—a fleet-footed man carrying a heartsick older woman like a baby, with his warrior-like sister carrying provisions on her back and my husband's walking stick as her only aid. Zerah is right. The rocking motion of his smooth movement lulls me into a deep state of relaxation and I only fully wake up when we arrive in the night at our destination.

Yasmine has somehow arrived ahead of us and prepared a fire in the mouth of a large cave. When Zerah gently lowers me to a blanket, sorrow rushes over me, full of mud, sticks and rocks, ready to batter me and push into crevices where I do not want to go.[14]

[14] *I'm no good to You dead!* What benefits come from my rotting corpse? My body in the grave *will not praise You.* No songs will rise up from the *dust of my bones.* From dust comes no proclamation of Your faithfulness. Psalm 30:9

Truth will spring from the earth like a plant, and justice will look down from the sky.

Psalm 85:11

CHAPTER FIVE
Spring Song

MY SOUL IS DOWNCAST WITHIN ME. YOUR calling has swept over me. For the first time since I set out for Moriah, prayer is my first thought. I open my eyes, roll over and sit up. Yasmine nods at me, forever knowing my mind before I do, and holds out her hand to hoist me up. With the fire throwing dancing lights against the dark cave walls, I wonder if I am in a sanctuary or a burial site? I test my ankle and find that it is ready to bear a little weight. It is only a small sprain. Yasmine hands me Abraham's staff. I finger the white and brown eagle feathers remembering Isaac's joy in finding them and gifting them to his father. Abraham's words, "One for my beautiful wife and the other for my son." Then loss flashed across his face as he added quietly, "Ishmael, I will find a feather for you as well my son."

Isaac surprised me by adding, "And one for his mother Hagar?"

In that sacred moment, Yahweh gave me the strength to smile and nod. Isaac glanced at me with relief. Although weeds of anger and fear still remain, a new seed of empathy is ready to vie for its place.

Yes Lord, allow me to find the feather for Ishmael.

Using the staff, I make my way carefully out of the cave into the dark night. Yasmine and Zerah respectfully allow me this time alone. I sit down on a flat rock in front of the entrance, grateful for the smooth layer of stone surrounding the mouth of the cave. A natural bench. A place to seek peace. Abraham has told me often that if you lack perspective you should sit under the stars. Although I would prefer a bounty of wildflowers fluttering in a field, tonight I will seek solace from Abraham's way of seeing. As I breathe in the night air and read the stars for meaning, I hear the soft rumble of Yasmine and Zerah speaking deep within the cave. I am grateful that I cannot discern their words.

I think back through the events of the day, still shaken. A joyous song of sojourn. Whispers brimming with evil threats. Being brushed by a Pharaoh owl's wing. Almost being tossed off of Hamor's back. A painted canyon. A muddy flood. The loss of two beloved donkeys. Being carried toward my fate by a mysterious man of God. All at once a prayer born of both loss and comfort comes to me, so beautiful I wonder if the words are given….

My soul is downcast within me.[1]
Your calling has swept over me.
Do I forget your promise?

My soul is downcast within me.
Is a twisted ankle your preparation?
My aching back your discipline?

Vindicate me and plead my cause.[2]
Invite me to come to your altar.
To find relief from the accuser.

[1] Why am I so overwrought? Why am I so disturbed? Why can't I just hope in God? *Despite all my emotions,* I will *believe and* praise the One who saves me *and is my life.* Psalm 42:5

[2] Pass Your judgment, Eternal One, my True God; do it by the standards of Your righteousness. Do not allow my enemies to boast over me. Psalm 35:24

Vindicate me and plead my cause.
Do not let my enemy gloat over me.
Lead me in your righteousness.

Guard those dear to my heart.
Lest, I wither like dry grass.
My bones burn like glowing embers.

Guard those dear to my heart.
Lest my drink is mingled with tears.
My days wither like the evening shadow.[3]

My soul is downcast within me.
Yet I know your integrity, Lord.
Trusting in you, I will not falter.

To the prayer, I add the words of Yasmine's song.
A whisper of sojourn.
As darkness descends.
Carried in his arms.
We calmly ascend.

Looking to the stars, I realize that darkness serves a purpose. By hiding what we would usually see, our eyes are drawn to the light above…the Father of Light as Abraham would say.[4]

Abram's words come to me, "And if he can hold the stars in the sky, surely he can sustain us."

A single beacon bursts from its spot in the sky and thrusts itself downward before it fizzles out. When Isaac was small, he would chant over and over, "One falling star brings another. One falling star brings another." Isaac's favorite nights were those

[3] See Psalm 102:1-8

[4] Every good gift bestowed, every perfect gift received comes *to us* from above, courtesy of the Father of lights. He *is consistent*. He won't change His mind or play tricks in the shadows. James 1:17

when numerous celestial bodies blazed downward. If Abraham happened to witness the beginning of such a display, he would wake Isaac and take him outside to watch with him. With time, Isaac came to thirst for the planets just as his father.

Did my husband and son also see this star fall, this night of all nights? Does Isaac behold the illuminated firmament and remember Yahweh's promise that generations will come from his seed? Yahweh was specific about this. This blessing will not come through Ishmael, only through Isaac. Isn't the blessing Yahweh's way of guaranteeing Isaac will enjoy both marriage and parenthood? That he will see his sons have sons? Or does Yahweh look for another path, when the one that he promised falls out of the sky due to a stargazer's frailty?

I whisper, "Isaac, I would fall out of the heavens rather than risk you, my beloved son." By faith, I hear him whisper back, "I know Mother. I know."

I remember the three of us sitting beneath the stars one night and Abraham saying, "He who created all the starry hosts has given each a name. So it shall be with the generations that come from your seed, Isaac. Because of Yahweh's great power, each individual will help fulfill his plan to bring a blessing to the earth. Each will matter."[5]

Isaac in his childlike way asked, "How do you know this Abba?"

And Abraham replied, "Yahweh is incapable of telling a lie my son. What he promised is as good as done."

I know without doubt that Abram believes this. So how can he reconcile all that has transpired? This I cannot understand.

But for the moment, another question looms in front of me demanding my consideration. Zerah said he will not stand between Abraham and his calling. Still I want him to go. Yet, I

[5] Look at the myriad of stars *and constellations* above you. Who set them to burning, *each in its place?* Who knows those countless lights each by name? *They obediently shine*, each in its place, because God has the great strength and strong power to make it so. Isaiah 40:26

must think of Zerah's endurance. Twice within one turn of the day, he has run into the night, this evening with a woman in his arms. I cannot ask more.

Is this the path to trusting Yahweh? First, we stubbornly act on our own instincts and follow our own path until it disappears before us. Or a wadi storm appears that swallows us whole, leaving us unsure whether deliverance will happen. We use all of our energy to try to clamor up the cavern walls, only to injure ourselves further. Only then, when our bodies and spirits are wasted, or a crushing loss takes place, do we turn to Yahweh's path ready to consider his direction.

Abraham has told me that listening is better than sacrifice.[6] Thinking of the Pharaoh owl and the quail, I would now tell Abraham that Yahweh speaks in the hope I will listen. But he will only silently drop out of the sky to grasp what is his, if it is offered up.

Still, I whisper with all the passion within me, "Please, please don't offer our son, Abraham."

I stand up and use the walking stick to hobble in a straight path away from the cave. As long as I can see the lighted entrance, I am not at risk. I then lift my arms to the sky, one holding a cane, and one by faith offering my stubborn will.... "Yahweh, I do believe you are the One God. I promise to never again seek a God other than you."

Am I offering an exchange? Do I seek to bargain with the Almighty? My faithfulness for his deliverance? *Yahweh, remember that you allowed Abram to bargain for the souls of Sodom.* Whatever it is, it still seems like a small step. Yet, the part of me that yearns for a life beyond this life offers comfort...*this small step is more than you understand.*

When I turn around to make my way back to the camp,

[6] Samuel replied, "Has the Lord as much pleasure in your burnt offerings and sacrifices as in your obedience? Obedience is far better than sacrifice. He is much more interested in your listening to him than in your offering the fat of rams to him. 1 Samuel 15:22 (TLB)

Zerah is standing in the entrance waiting with a blanket draped over one arm. My cheeks warm, wondering if he saw my gesture. When I make it back to the rock bench, I motion for him to sit beside me. He takes the blanket and loosely throws it around my shoulders. My words with Zerah have been few compared to the words I have shared with his sister. He is still an enigma to me.

"The cave, it is surprisingly warm...warmer than the heat that a fire provides." I reach over and touch the rock between us. "Even the wall is warmer than the outside air."

"It is said that the cave sits over hot springs that emerge not too far from here. If you were to walk into the back of the cave as far as it goes, you might even find a pool. There are likely other pools nearby as well."

"And I thought our tents being gone meant a cold night."

We both sit with our own thoughts until he pushes into the silence, "I am sorry about Maya. It is a sign of righteousness to care for an animal.[7] To lose her was to lose a friend." A tear rolls down his cheek and drops on to his garment.

"And Hamor," I add. Sharing this sorrow brings wetness to my eyes. I blink away the tears and take a deep breath. "Zerah, please help me decide how to proceed." My chest seizes with the fear of allowing another into this vulnerable place. "In your following of the One God that is," I add, as if he would make the decision out of a whim.

He nods. My mind circles back to the morning when he showed up on the edges of our camp, just as I prepared to set out on my own. How he showed me the sign of Shem, and with it, gave a silent pledge to honor both Yahweh and me. Yasmine spoke of me being a prophetess. Does Zerah see me in the same way?

"I will run into the Moriah region. And then, I will search

[7] Those who are righteous treat their animals humanely, but the compassion of the wicked is really inhumane. Proverbs 12:10

however long it takes to locate them. I can leave before dawn. Yasmine will travel the rest of the way to Hebron to secure provisions and search for a donkey before other travelers are on the road."

I nod, thinking that if I shouldn't travel alone, neither should she, no matter how bold and brave. "Is Yasmine also able to run?" Then I laugh, thinking my question foolish.

"Yasmine is a runner as well," Zerah says with a smile. "Although she is modest about such pursuits, she could run through the night if she had a reason."

I should not be surprised that a woman who commands Pharaoh owls and infuses comfort into barren wilderness camps has yet another gift, but I am. I can picture a man laughing, "A woman running? Her garments testify to her need for a slower pace." Suddenly, it dawns on me that they are both couriers.

Before I can censor her, the prophetess within me speaks. "Are you here to proclaim peace between me and Yahweh?"

His eyes twinkle with what I would call mischief, like he has a secret yet to be revealed. He says solemnly, "You could think of us as couriers." I am momentarily stunned that he uses the same word I just intuited. Does he read my thoughts? Before I can ask, he continues, "Yahweh will protect Yasmine's short journey. Once the markets open, she will accumulate what we need for the journey. Securing a donkey will undoubtedly take more time. I will circle into Hebron to meet her by the afternoon and we should be back here well before the fall of evening."

I nod, surprised. A day alone?

"Are you comfortable with this?" His eyes search for my face, seeking the truths I might hesitate to reveal.

"Yes, I think so," I offer haltingly. Helplessly doing nothing for a day is not what I imagined, but my body longs for a respite, time alone. Now invited, exhaustion creeps from my head to my chest, downward to my hips, finally weighing down my legs. Aches chime in from all over my body. I blink my eyes to hold back tears. "There is enough food and water. And I long for a change of clothing."

"Yasmine can secure that for you."

"And when we return to our camp, we will reimburse her…"

Zerah reaches over and squeezes my hand in a way that is chaste, like a son with his mother. "Yours to decide. I honor your free will, the good gift of Yahweh."

My heart starts beating faster. "What will you do if you find Abraham?"

"Only Yahweh knows."

This is not the answer I desire.

With that he stands and yawns. I stay seated, unwilling to leave my perch just yet.

"Do you want us to wake you before we leave?"

"It is not necessary." I surprise myself with this choice.

"As long as you stay in the cave, you will be safe. Yasmine and I have entreated Yahweh's protection over it. You are important to the Almighty."

I whisper, "A star with a song to sing." Then it occurs to me that the mysterious murmuring that came from within the cave earlier was Zerah and Yasmine praying. "Are you also a prophet like my husband?" I ask. "One who hears the voice of the One God?"[8]

He smiles and then continues as if I didn't ask. "The cave belongs to a man named Ephron. He is not yet a follower of Yahweh, although he moves toward him. Yasmine will let him know you are here when she arrives in Hebron. He has offered the cave before, so you need not worry." With that, he quietly retreats

[8] Now *do the right thing*. Return the man's wife. He is one of My prophets. He will pray *and intercede* for you, and you will live. But if you do not give her back, I assure you, you will die—you and everyone associated with you. Genesis 20:7

into the cave. The few words he will use tonight are expired.

I lay down with my back against the rock. I urge this warmth, to enter my toes, make its way up my legs and into my sore hips, then creep along my back to circle my shoulders and finally cradle my neck and release the tension in my forehead. Although I am deeply relaxed, there is no sleep in me. Remembering their promise of safety within the cave, I stroke the outside wall, believing their prayers are enough.

Without invitation, the terror of the flood in the wadi rushes back. I picture the muddy water sweeping me off my feet, tossing me among stones and branches along with Maya. I see the snake laughing at me in my loss, then finding me tossed aside and biting me for good measure. Losing my donkey has ripped a hole in the garment of our family, one that won't be easily repaired. But there is surviving to do now. The loss will need to be tucked away in a place that can be accessed later. But first there are words to be spoken out loud…

Maya, I will remember you.
Honor you for your sway.
Trudging into the wilds.
Trust me to find our way.

Maya, I will remember you.
When Abraham leaves town,
When I see the little children
Chase the animals all around.

Maya, I will remember you.
When rain becomes dense
In a time of muddy floods

Look for your presence.

Maya I will remember you
When I hear a donkey laugh
I will scoff at my foolishness
Shake my head on your behalf.

How I wish I could write down these words for Isaac. But perhaps Yahweh will give Isaac his own words to remember Maya. Before I leave the wilderness, I promise myself a return to the canyon of the flood. I will gather wildflowers to throw in the creek bed. And I will step in the path of the torrent of destruction with Yahweh and without fear.[9]

I gather my blanket and go into the cave. The fire is smoldering and Zerah and Yasmine rest. I take a deep breath and say the words Zerah gave me, "I am safe," and then add, like I did before the wadi's flood, "wherever I go." I find a soft spot and a curved rock to hold my head.[10] Memories sweep through my mind like waves. Our wedding. My first home with Abraham. Our early years of traveling. How Abraham fought three kings in the Valley of Siddim. The devastation of Sodom. The loss of Lot's wife. The harems of Pharaoh and Abimelech. All that took place with Hagar. Ishmael and Isaac.

I cover my feet with the blanket in case a chill comes, musing that my many years have brought both blessing and trouble. For this moment, I choose not to dwell on the trouble. Lord, surely you still have a blessing for us. In the depths of the night, a dream finally rolls over me like a deep mist coming down from the mountains to water the earth.

I am in a canyon. There are rocks piled upon each other, like the ones we scaled to escape the flood, only smaller, neater, and leading ever

[9] This is how people from east to west will come to respect the name and honor the glory of the Eternal. For He will come on like a torrential flood driven by the Eternal's winds. Isaiah 59:19

[10] As dusk approached one day, he came to a place where he could stay for the night. He saw stones scattered all around and put one of them under his head; then he lay down to sleep. Genesis 28:11b

higher. Ascending and descending into a large cave high up the side of a mountain are what I think to be priests of the Most High. They look common, like ordinary people, yet they almost seem to float up and down the rocky stairs. They sing songs and as I listen, I can hear some of the strains. A female with hair cascading down her back intones with a voice clear and pure, "Sing, O barren one, you who did not bear; break forth into singing and cry aloud, you who did not travail with child! For the children of the desolate one will be more than the children of the married wife."[11]

Another man, old and wrinkled but with a shining face replies, "His purpose is worthy of 100 years of waiting."

A man with hair as bright as the sun sings in a low voice, "Blessed be Yahweh who gives the barren woman a son in her old age. Through him will come the very son of God."

Marveling that their songs bear my story, I see that they carry various offerings—fruits, vegetables, and a pair of doves. I smell a fragrant aroma of cardamom, myrrh, cinnamon and mint.

Then a loud voice resounds from within the cave, "I am the LORD, the God of Abraham, and the God of Isaac. Your descendants will be as numerous as the dust of the earth! They will spread out in all directions—to the west and the east, to the north and the south. And all the families of the earth will be blessed through you and your descendants. What's more, I am with you, and I will protect you wherever you go. I will not leave you until I have finished giving you all I have promised you."[12]

As the mist lifts from the ground, I notice that Abraham and Isaac are sleeping near the bottom of the rocky stairs, in a riverbed, as the stars blaze around them. The voice then proclaims, "Bring me Isaac."

Abraham stirs, wakes and walks to the bottom of the stairs. He tries to make his way up the stones alone, but a man beaming with light refuses him passage. Determined, he continues to try until finally the man of God pushes him to the ground. There they wrestle, using all their

[11] Isaiah 54:1 (AMPC)
[12] Genesis 28:13-15 (NLT)

strength to try to pin the other to the ground. Finally, the man whispers something in Abraham's ear, and Abraham ceases his battle. They lie there for a moment spent, and then both stand and embrace, Abraham weeping into the warrior's shoulder.

Abraham goes and picks up Isaac, still sleeping, and begins to carry him up the stones toward the mouth of the cave, as thunder rumbles.

I wake disoriented and shaken by the dream's possible meanings. "Abraham? Isaac?" I call out. Seeing the unattended fire, I know that Zerah is already searching for Abraham, and Yasmine may be in Hebron by now. The food and skin of water are laid neatly by the fire, along with a stack of firewood. As they promised, there is no fear in the cave, only peace. I want to stay up and seek an interpretation for the dream, but my lack of sleep has left my eyes heavy. Just a little longer.

By the time I once again awaken, light is streaming into the mouth of the cave, calling me outside. I know I can make my way into the back of the cave to relieve myself, but I would have to fashion a torch to be safe. And my body craves the caress of light. But there is something more I yearn for...the hot springs that are supposed to be nearby. Finding them outside in the light seems more promising than walking into the depths of a dark cave where bats or snakes might dwell. To satisfy my nagging stomach, I decide first to eat some dried meat, goat's cheese and a piece of flatbread. With a jolt, I realize that as far as I know, today is the day of sacrifice for Abraham and Isaac. *Yahweh, grant Zerah success in his search for my husband and son.*

After I eat and drink and knowing that if I give anxiety a foothold it will overwhelm me, I decide to seek the hot springs in order to bathe. Remembering Zerah's urging to stay in the cave, I find a sharp stone and use it to tear a strip from the blanket, and then tear it into smaller strips. The small strips tied to branches will be my guides back to the cave if I venture too far. The rest of the blanket will dry me after I dip in the spring. I can then hang it on a tree to dry. I pick up Abraham's walking stick and ask Yahweh to bless it. *Lord Yahweh, allow me to carry the protection from the cave with me to the spring.*

By the time I step outside with my torn blanket and strips, the sun has ducked under the cloud. It is quite nippy, and I feel water in the air, a remnant of yesterday's storm. A hot spring creates tendrils of fog from the sharp difference in the heat of the water and the coolness of the air. They are easiest to find in the early morning. They also have the stench of sulfur, burping up from the earth's mouth. My intuition tells me to walk in a straight line out of the cave. Although they call this hilly area a field, it is overgrown with every manner of tree and vegetation. I may need to get higher to see. As I move forward, I tie strips in occasional branches to establish my way back. My ankle is sore but allows most of my weight. I do seem to be following a path, perhaps one that Ephron has used.

When I reach the top of the first hill, I lean on the staff and gasp in joy. I see a plume of mist a short walk away. The gentle slope has steps carved in it, no doubt leading to the springs. Next to a rocky outcropping I find a small pool of hot water, just wide and deep enough to use. I take off all my clothing and shiver. Carefully testing my footing and the temperature of the water, I ease myself into the water. The pleasure is beyond belief. Although I have passed 100 years, and have a few aches that chase me, I am known for being unusually strong of body. This journey is revealing my frailty. Heated springs are said to be rich with minerals, a healing elixir. *Restore me Yahweh. Prepare me for what lies ahead.*

Remembering my dream of the stairs, I pray...*send angels to intercede.*

If Yahweh provides hot springs to soothe my travel-weary body, won't he also provide deliverance for a son of the promise? Realizing my lack of control, I begin to weep in the cleansing waters. Will I dance again in pure joy upon being reunited with Isaac? Or will I perish from losing him? Although this has been a time to cast away all semblance of safety, will there also be a time to gather my family next to me?[13]

Suddenly feeling exposed, I get out of the warm liquid, dry myself off, and put on my clothing. Still longing for the warmth, I tie up my garment like I do when I ride a donkey, and then immerse just my feet into the water, leaning against a large rock rimming the pool. I close my eyes for a moment, but then a memory comes unbidden, falling out of the sky to brush my head with its wings and startle me in its clarity.

It is the thirtieth day of my stay in Pharaoh's palace. I am sixty-five years of age and I have been with Abraham longer than I was without him. Hagar, as my assigned handmaid, knows my schedule before I do, as if she is the mistress and I am the slave. "Today is the day," Hagar murmurs. "Pharaoh expects you tonight." Panic washes over me, but I control my face in front of her. This is not a place where it is wise to show fear. In the other women's eyes, I am a threat to be managed in order to find their place in this demented reality.

When we arrive at the pools, Hagar waves her hand impatiently. I am always slow to undress. She stares at my most intimate parts with such brazenness. Getting in quickly, I try to keep up to my neck in the water, to avoid the sense of utter rawness, pretending I am somewhere else than a harem. After the

[13] Ecclesiastes 3:1-8

pool, there are worse indignities. I am toweled off by an Egyptian eunuch and then led to a bed, where mud is slathered over my whole body and face. A eunuch massages my hair with musky oil and then twists it in a towel. Beauty treatments, they call this. Instead of an indulgence this is an indignity. Even after a moon's turn of treatments, I've never grown used to all the nudity, the herding of women as if we were livestock to be inspected. I dare not try to find common ground with these women, because their eyes tell me they would use anything I told them to slay me.

After I am rinsed off and my hair is washed, I am led into a sunny garden where there are beds to recline on, where my hair can dry. A brief respite and a time to pray for deliverance. *Yahweh, please intervene. Hear my cries. Deliver me lest all that is sacred is stolen from me.* Although my eyes are closed, wetness gathers underneath my lids, a few tears leaking out to be kissed by the sun. After my hair dries, I am led into another room, one I have yet to enter in my stay here, to be dressed and made up for the Pharaoh. First oils are rubbed into every pore of my skin. My hair is styled in the Egyptian manner with a comb holding part of it high upon my head. The rest is left to trail my shoulder, since Pharaoh has drawn attention to the beauty of my hair. They rub color into my cheeks. The garments they put on me are gauzy, teasing, hugging my curves to accent them. Finally, they proclaim me ready for the Pharaoh.

My hands sweat as I am led down the corridors, an oxen led to her slaughter. When I arrive, I keep my eyes downcast until he extends his scepter giving me permission to look around. I note that his appearance is pleasant and his body trim, but his eyes are arrogant. His court sits around him watching with amusement. The lights are dim, but their eyes glow with the fire of the many golden torches lighting the room, making me think of the snake in the Garden of Eden that taunted Eve, and still seems to be taunting me. Six women sit on thrones, three on each side of him. His queens. The queen on his right is first in rank. Although each is covered with silk and jewels circle their throats, wrists and headpieces, their beauty is only outward. Their eyes bore through me like swords drawn in battle.

The Pharaoh nods again, my cue to kneel before him turned sideways to his throne. I kneel but refuse to bow to him like a God. With one motion, he takes the comb from my hair to release it. Even that gesture seems more intimate than I can bear. I look for a way out, but there is none. Guards are posted at every exit.

Beauty is a curse... I think to myself. I am only valued here for how I might please. And if I don't please, I've been told I will become a harlot, a whore. *Yahweh, where are you? Abraham, if you could rescue Lot and his whole clan from three violent kings, why haven't you come for me?*

The king uses his hand to lift my chin, commanding my eyes to once again look at his. I see pure lust. He motions for me to stand again and turn around slowly, so that he and his entire court may inspect me, the garment revealing far too much. The people around me murmur in pleasure. Will he assault me in front of them? He stands and puts his arm around my waist, his hand grasping my waist to turn me toward them, and nods to the onlookers.

They applaud with glee, and I feel relief, and then shame that I would want their approval. Abram hasn't touched me in this way for so long. I feel oh so vulnerable, like I won't have the power to resist if Pharaoh steals all that belongs to Abram alone. I am given a golden flute full of liquid and instructed to drink all of it. I take a sip and then seek to hand it back. My handmaid

Hagar whispers, "It will be an insult to Pharaoh if you do not drink." I drain the goblet and give it back to the steward.

Then a man sitting just a step away, his bald head decorated with black designs and his eyes lined with the same, removes the lid of a large woven basket, and begins to play a melody with a flute. Enticed by the music, a snake slowly lifts its head and then rises in a swaying dance. Terrified, I latch my arms around Pharaoh. He laughs, having achieved the desired effect. Music begins and a troupe of barely dressed women enter and begin a seductive dance, thrusting their hips in rhythm to the music of flutes, lyres and drums. Every eye in the room is fastened on me. My knees go limp, and Pharaoh pulls me tighter, taking the chance to caress my hip. He leans into me, his lips seeking out the curve of my neck. I shudder sensing wickedness around me. *You need him*...the serpent seems to say, somehow communicating with me. *You want him. He will make you his queen.* One of the dancers eyes me as she thrusts her hips. *She will show you the way to have him.*

Pharaoh whispers in my ear, "I will give you anything you desire. All that I have can be yours. But only if you give me all that is yours. An exchange." His hand wanders up my side toward my chest, and I push it down.

Hagar glares at me but he laughs, amused, savoring the thought of conquest. He leans over and whispers in my ear, "Do remember I have already rewarded your brother richly for you, more than for any other woman." Seeing the shock on my face, he adds, "Oh yes, oxen, camels, donkeys, male and female servants, material goods...wedding gifts."[14]

My heart starts to hammer. Abram accepted a...bribe? He took payment for me in the guise of being my brother to wed me to Pharaoh.

[14] And when Pharaoh's officials saw her, they told Pharaoh just how beautiful she was. So Sarai was taken into Pharaoh's house *and made part of his harem.* She pleased the Pharaoh, so he treated Abram very well, giving him gifts of sheep, oxen, male donkeys, male and female servants, female donkeys, and camels. Genesis 12:15-16

Seeing my displeasure, Hagar digs a sharp elbow into my side. It is not only my fate that lies in my hands. If I fail, Hagar will have failed in her preparation of me. She could be at risk as well. This is why I requested that another maid accompany me into his private quarters. I have heard rumors of women being seduced and then humiliated in front of his whole court. Better to take my chances with him alone.

Abandoned by my husband, I gather all my courage to look Pharaoh right in the eyes and raise one eyebrow, nodding toward the exit. I pray that he reads this as eagerness for him, rather than an attempt to escape. He leans over and makes a show of kissing his first queen. Does he mock me? Then, gripping my arm so tightly it hurts, he leads me out toward my fate, two eunuchs following close behind. Will he be too strong for me, or will I fight him to the death? Or frozen in terror, will I pretend he is Abraham and bear the gross indignity? I pray I have the courage to resist.

A rustling in the bushes brings me back to my senses and pure fear washes over me. I lean over away from the spring and lose the contents of my stomach. I then use the warm water to wash out my mouth. Even though I've been cleansed, now I feel dirty. I am tempted to take off my clothes again and wash once more, but I dare not show my garmentless body again. *The memory was worse than a dream yet the truth of my life. I must get back to the safety of the cave.*

As I rise, I hear movement, like something or someone is moving toward me. A wild animal? I reach for Abraham's staff, my only defense. I dare not run, because if it is an animal, I might incite it to chase me. I move a few steps away from the pool and slowly turn in a circle. If it is a mountain lion, I need to face it eye to eye and will myself to stand my ground, show no fear. I suddenly fight the urge to laugh, thinking that the same skills are needed for facing a mountain lion as in facing a Pharaoh. If a lion attacks, I will fight back with all my might. I urge my shoulders to release. I see nothing but must be vigilant.

In the harem, I didn't have to fight either. Abram didn't arrive with armed men to demand his wife back. Instead, Yahweh fought for me. After I was led into Pharaoh's private chambers, a eunuch began to undress me before him. As the garment began to fall away from my chest, Pharaoh fell desperately ill and went running from the room. That night everyone in Pharaoh's household, young and old was stricken with a plague, except for me and Hagar. Seeing the possibility of being blamed, Hagar ran to the Pharaoh's officials to tell them that Abraham wasn't my brother. He was my husband. Two days later, I was called to the Pharaoh and Abram was there. Glancing at my husband, relief washed over me. Pharaoh was slumped over in his throne, looking pale, gaunt, his eyes reddened from the force of his illness.

"How could you have lied to me?" he choked out, barely able to talk in his great weakness. "You are her husband! By telling me you were her brother, you put my entire household at risk. Take her, and all that I gave you, and leave!"[15]

"May we take Hagar as well?" I willed my hands not to shake. It was dangerous to confront the ruler of Egypt, but I didn't want Hagar to be mistreated after we left.

Pharaoh glared at me for a long moment, rage burning in his reddened eyes. He glanced at Hagar, then huffed and waved his hand, eager to have all of us out of his presence and out of his land.

Now I am alone in the wilderness by the springs where I

[15] So Pharaoh summoned Abram *to come before him.* Pharaoh: What have you done to me? Why didn't you tell me this woman was your wife? Why did you say she was *only* your sister, so that I *felt free* to take her to be one of my wives? Here she is—take your wife and get out of here! Genesis 12:18-19

ventured from a cave, the property of someone I have not met. All this lest Abraham disobeys Yahweh and loses his status with the Almighty. Shaken by the memory, I am afraid to stay by the heated springs, but also afraid to walk back to the cave.

I make myself take deep measured breaths, calming myself.

"I hope you enjoyed the warm springs," I hear a husky male voice say.

To Him was given authority, honor, and a kingdom so that all people of every heritage, nationality, and language might serve Him. His dominion will last forever, His throne will never pass away, and His kingdom will never be destroyed.

Daniel 7:14

CHAPTER SIX
Ephron's Song

I TURN TO SEE A STRANGER STANDING AT THE top of the rise, looking down at me. I put Abraham's staff in front of me. If I can defend myself from a Pharaoh and a mountain lion, I can stand my ground once again. As he silently moves closer, I wonder how long he has been there, what he has seen. My cheeks warm and my skin flushes at the possibility that he saw me in the springs. He stops a respectful distance away.

"I am Ephron. I own this field and the cave in it." Seeing my embarrassment, he adds, "I only just arrived. I made some noise as I walked along, to give you some notice that someone was near. Your torn strips of cloth gave me confidence I would find you. You must have experience navigating in the wilderness."

My mind races for a way to explain all that brought me to be in his cave, alone. I find no words. Something about Ephron stirs my memory of Pharaoh, only his eyes are kind instead of arrogant, and he is of smaller stature. His presence is that of a larger man.

"I have seen a mountain lion near this spring," he says, looking around and stroking his grey streaked beard. He smiles. "The cave might be a safer place."

"I thought you were a mountain lion, so I am greatly relieved to meet you instead. I am Sarah, wife of Abraham."

"Yes, I have heard of Abraham, the great clan leader, masterful in military and economic pursuits...and of you. Yes, many believe his powers come from his god, Yahweh. I wanted to welcome you and see if I could make you more comfortable or offer protection."

"Thank you for allowing me to sojourn in your cave." I cover my mouth with my hand. It seems laughable to thank a man I've never met for his cave, which I stayed in without his permission. "Did you know I was here? Did Yasmine come to you?"

"My wife Lilah had a dream last night that a highly esteemed woman was resting in our cave and that we should go to her with provisions. Although I wondered if it was just her imagination, the dream hovered around her like a mist waiting to be heeded."

I sigh in relief that Ephron is not alone. I use the walking stick to move a step closer and wince when my ankle catches.

"Can I help you up the rise? You've been hurt?"

"I fell off of a Nephilim donkey while we were traveling through a wadi. While I was being tended to in a rock shelter higher up, he and my donkey Maya were washed away by a sudden flood."

"I heard rumors of such a flood on the canyon path yesterday. You were there?" I am thankful he doesn't offer well-trodden words that minimize pain like...you should be grateful you only lost your donkeys.

"Yes, we were caught by the flood, but it is too painful to discuss." As I wipe away a lone tear, I add, "As it has been said, it is better not to plow a wet field. Sorrow needs time to be ready to speak." When he hangs his head in empathy, I add, "Your warm cave is comfort enough."

"May I take a look at your ankle?"

I sit down on a nearby boulder and surrender the ankle to yet another person.

"Can I apply some pressure? I've been known to help with cranky ankles."

His hands feel warm and comforting as they lightly circle my ankle, stroke my instep and rub the top of my foot. He talks as he administers this touch. "My wife Lilah came with me, knowing you would be more comfortable with a woman. And we brought provisions including a portable bed I built for just such occasions. Lilah waits at the cave, along with my personal donkey, Azaz."[1]

I am overwhelmed with gratitude. A portable bed in a cave? A woman with a dream from Yahweh? A donkey whose name means strong?

Catching me by surprise, he uses two thumbs to press into my big toe. Pain shoots through my leg and I almost jump off of the rock.

"Ah, we've found part of the problem," he says, unfazed by my response.

He gives the toe a yank, and then repeats the pressure, this time without pain. Once more he takes his hands and lightly strokes the foot and ankle, moving his hands quickly. "Ankle pain also comes from the hip. Lilah could administer some healing balm later."

"Thank you for your kindness." Already my words seem inadequate to communicate how Yahweh once again has used a stranger to rescue me. I silently pray, *Yahweh please richly reward him.*[2] I smile. "Could we go ahead to the cave? If you could just support my elbow."

The strange but kind owner of a field helps me up the rise and then toward the cave. We walk slowly, my left elbow steadied by

[1] Strong in Hebrew.

[2] *You shall be richly rewarded,* for when I was hungry, you fed Me. And when I was thirsty, you gave Me something to drink. I was alone as a stranger, and you welcomed Me *into your homes and into your lives.* Matthew 25:35

his hand, and my right hand steadied by Abram's staff. Although I am grateful for the help, my ankle feels sturdier after his healing touch and the long soak in the hot springs.

"We noticed your fire had died, so we took the liberty of bringing it back to life."

"My companions had left me a fire, but I neglected it for the hot springs. They have gone into Hebron and should return by sunset." I want him to know I am not so foolish as to travel by myself, and then almost laugh. *That was exactly my intention.* Longing for my husband, I ask, "Are you a believer in Yahweh?"

"Ah, you must be from the camp of Melchizedek? Your faith, I mean. Those who consider themselves in the lineage of Seth and who, because of this, refuse the thought of multiple gods. What do you call them? Idols?"

"I've never met Melchizedek, but my husband speaks highly of him. We believe he is a priest of the Most High, of the one true God." This is my first attempt at testing my convictions, after Abraham's betrayal, to see if they will still hold my weight. Even in my awkwardness, I picture my words floating upwards as a fragrant offering to Yahweh. It is easy for a wife to receive warmth from her husband's faith, while secretly nurturing embers of her own way of believing.

"I enjoy hearing of your God. Many in Hebron talk of teachings originating with Melchizedek. The rumor is that he speaks about mysterious times and circumstances that could illuminate faith and events yet to come.[3] Such lofty intentions. He is known as a peculiar priest and rarely appears. I've heard he looks for peace to come…deliverance from ourselves?"[4]

"You are a physician?

[3] The prophets who spoke of this *outpouring of grace* upon you diligently searched and inquired *of the Lord* about this salvation: to whom and to what time was the indwelling Spirit of the Anointed referring when He told them about the suffering of the Anointed and the honor that would follow it? 1 Peter 1:10-11

[4] See Hebrews 7:2

"No, but I use my hands to provide healing touch to those with aches and pains. I apprenticed with a master healer. It takes a lifetime to understand the workings of the body."

As the cave entrance comes into view, I see Ephron's wife, Lilah, leaning against the rocky entrance. She has long wavy hair with streaks of grey and white, deep brown eyes, and dark grey eyebrows that rival those of her husband. Her garments are simple, but her smile is contagious. Although she appears to be older than her husband, she exudes joy.

"Sarah, this is my wife, Lilah."

She dips her head in respect and then holds out a hand to grasp mine. "Sarah," she says, using my name without my urging.

The women who've served me faithfully in more recent times pass through my mind—Hagar, Amah and Yasmine. One legally bound to my husband and then dismissed, one married with a child, and one never married. Lilah isn't a handmaid, yet she has come to serve…with dignity. Her eyes twinkle with intelligence. I intuit she is a woman who knows her own mind. Her gentle authority makes me think of Yasmine. *Even now, is she searching for garments for me?*

"May I cook for you?"

My stomach rumbles. I thank Yahweh for the rations that Lilah and Ephron have laid out to prepare a small feast, including the meat of a calf prepared for roasting. My mouth waters in anticipation seeing the wild mushrooms, rosemary and a loaf of bread that smells of yeast. A meal, but also an offer of friendship. This is one way women show their dominion over creation and over matters of the heart. They pour their affection into the meat they prepare, the bread they knead, the vegetables gathered from the ground and the healing herbs they add to stoke the senses.[5] Before Lilah begins to cook, she offers me some roasted pistachio

[5] **Abraham** (to Sarah): Sarah, *we have guests.* Quickly prepare three measures of our best flour, knead it, and make cakes." Genesis 18:6. Note: Sarah used 28 cups of flour to quickly prepare bread for the strangers (which came to announce her upcoming pregnancy). Some Jewish midrash suggest that her doing so was miraculous.

nuts, nodding at her husband with pride. "Ephron grows and roasts these."

I sigh in pleasure, tasting honey, smoky sea salt and cumin in the pistachios. "Delightful," I say nodding to Ephron. Regret comes that I have nothing to offer in return, except my stories. I sigh. Even though I see myself as strong, in our culture the elderly are freely given what they need in gratitude for a long life of service. I am humbled, yet it is a sign of respect to receive what is given in love.

Pleased, he speaks up, "I came for a second reason, to inspect the field. Our olive and pistachio trees do better with tending. And there are always thorns seeking to choke what good the soil would bring up. It is important to stay on the paths around here, lest a nasty thorn spring up and burrow itself into your skin. How I despise thorns."

"I could imagine Adam saying that to Eve," I say, glancing at Lilah. Then I remember that Ephron doesn't share my faith. He may not know our stories from the beginning.

"Ah, yes, the curse on the ground. Yes, I do know that tale." He smiles and casts a loving glance at Lilah. "My wife believes in Yahweh. And you, Sarah, must see it as fact, not myth? Personally, I wonder whether Adam and Eve were real people, or their story was a morality tale."

"I fully expect to meet them in the next life," I say. "And whoever Eve was, I feel her Spirit in me. Yahweh, our God, made a promise to my husband of generations coming from our seed.[6] How can that be since I have mothered only one son, and that in my old age? I think Eve must have wrestled with the same question after one of her sons killed the other. How could a mother of one son multiply and fill the earth?[7] Although I know

[6] No longer will she be known as Sarai; her new name will be Sarah. She will receive My *special* blessing, and she will conceive a son by you. With My blessing on her, she will become the founding *princess* of nations to come. Genesis 17:15-16

[7] "Even my name cries out against me. Eve means living.... Couldn't a real mother save her sons?" Robin Weidner, *Eve's Song,* p. 15

her existence through the stories handed down, she has come to comfort me. I believe I will see her."

Lilah smiles as she grinds peppercorns harvested from drupe plants. The twinkle in her eyes tells me she is grateful for someone else to tell her husband these things. She softly intones, clearly meaning for me to hear and her husband to overhear, "Sarah, a foundling princess of nations to come."

Ephron turns to face me. "Are you always so quick to reveal your innermost thoughts with those you just met? What brings you to our cave, Sarah?"

I look at Lilah, thinking it might be more proper to discuss this with her privately, but she nods her encouragement. "My husband and son. A sacrifice on a mountain. Two mysterious guides. A mother's quest." I laugh. "You must think I am talking nonsense. Sometimes I wonder whether I have any idea why I am here."

Lilah finally speaks up, "Not at all. I hear stories to be told." She smiles and winks at me, "Perhaps, your offering to our feast?"

She seeks to protect my dignity. I smile in return, remembering the traveler who came and told us stories of our own household, yet stories that released me from some of the guilt of Hagar and Ishmael. "It would be my honor."

"I will leave you women to talk and will return in time for the meal."

As he strides off, he reminds me of my husband, so confident that his every contribution to this earth holds the possibility of redemption.[8] Then my chest tightens. *Zerah. Where is he now? Has he found Abraham and Isaac?* How can I share lighthearted banter with a stranger when my son has not been safely returned to me? I am not sure why, but I very much want to accompany him. I call out to him just before he disappears, and he turns and

[8] So every plot of ground you possess carries a "right of redemption." Leviticus 25:24

strides back quickly.

"What is it Sarah? How can I help you?"

"I'd like to see your field, know about all it means to you." After I say the words, I feel a little self-conscious, like an older sister wanting to accompany her younger brother.

He glances at my ankle and frowns, "It would be my honor, but should you rest your foot?"

Now I feel foolish, perhaps even a little senile in my agedness. I must be some forty years older than Ephron, enough to be his mother, or even his grandmother.

Lilah wipes her hands on a rag and stands to face her husband. "If you think it wise, Sarah could ride Azaz up to the overlook. She could observe your work from there. Azaz could stand guard and I'd be able to hear her call if she needs me."

Her respectful touch with her husband impresses me. Ephron nods his affirmation and then reaches over and lets his fingertips graze his wife's cheek as their eyes meet. Although she is a hand's breadth taller than him, I sense mutuality in their respect.

"Perhaps you could join me when your preparation is done?" I say to Lilah.

"I would love to," she says with anticipation in her eyes.

Ephron lays a blanket over Azaz's back and in response the donkey makes a bold bray that I think might explain his name. After I am loaded, Ephron leads me and the donkey around the side of the cave, following the curves of the hill it is carved into. A tear pauses at the corner of my left eye. *Maya and Hamor, I haven't forgotten you.* Suddenly, a dirt path appears winding its way up the hill. Azaz is sure footed as he plods up the steep rise. Quickly, we are at the top of the hill where there are flat rocks and a view over Ephron's property. Learning from what I've suffered, I allow him to steady me as I slide off of the donkey's back onto my new perch. Even at the higher elevation, the smell of seared meat has come with us.

"Here, we can sit and chat before I go to inspect the property." Ephron says, standing with his feet spread wide, hands on his hips. I tell myself that he is reluctant to sit because standing speaks to the dominion of man over what he tills and cares for.[9]

"How far does your property extend?" I ask, using the language of man.

"Not so far" he replies modestly. "Do you see the pine that is taller than the rest?"

"The one two birds are circling over?"

"Yes. A pair of golden eagles see my field as part of their hunting ground."

A thought circles overhead and then rests within my mind.... *I might find golden eagle feathers here.*

"Now look to the left for the peculiar tree that appears to be crossing its legs and then holding two arms upwards. Another type of pine tree."

"I see," I say, thinking to myself that the tree has a pregnant belly. "Unique indeed."

"On the right, there is a gray tree whose branches spread like a canopy. A pistachio tree. Those three trees, with the cave as the fourth point, line my property."

"How did you come across the cave?"

"Actually, it was my grandfather who discovered it. When the light shines in at just the right angle, it is flooded with light, perhaps like a place of worship. There are circular openings up high in the sides."

It almost seems as if Ephron describes a different cave from the one in which I spent the night. All I could see was a fire, a few meager provisions, a single blanket and a curved rock

[9] The Eternal God placed the *newly made* man in the garden of Eden in order to work the ground and care for it. Genesis 2:15

for my head. Blinded by my grief, I failed to see the light and beauty Yahweh had woven into the shelter Zerah carried me to. I remember Abraham's words, tender after a young child wandered away from our camp during a sudden sandstorm, and to our horror, never recovered.... *Even the afflicted have a song to sing.*[10] Forgetting Ephron for a moment, I nod and say quietly, "A place to sing songs of comfort."

He glances sideways and I feel his sympathy. He continues, "My grandfather purchased the field to obtain the cave, then later discovered the springs, the trees, all the beauty within. On his deathbed he gave it to me. And to Lilah."

"Could I ask you something personal?" I venture, a little unsure.

Surprise crosses his face. He pauses, then concedes, "But of course."

"Have you ever hurt Lilah by a decision you felt compelled to make? One you felt was yours alone, but that cut her to the core? To the point where she struggled to submit?"

Ephron pulls on his beard as if making it longer would give him more wisdom and then sits on a nearby rock. "Undoubtedly. For all of our talk of faith, Lilah longs for a type of communion I cannot give her. When she first decided there was just one God, she expected I would make the same decision."

Overhead the eagles are circling nearer as if they would like to hear my reply. "Abram knew the God Most High long before me. I longed for him as a young woman but did not know how to find him. Abram introduced me to him."

He nods. "Perhaps Lilah had been moving toward this decision for a time, like you. But it was like lightning struck our home, and suddenly we were different. She insisted that we have nothing in our home that represented what she called idol worship."

[10] For he has not despised my cries of deep despair. He's my first responder to my sufferings, and he didn't look the other way when I was in pain. He was there all the time, listening to the song of the afflicted." Psalm 22:24 (TPT)

"Sometimes, I tell myself, 'When lightning strikes a tree, it will not burn if it is full of water.'" Realizing he may not know this proverb, I continue. "When I already feel empty, I am more likely to be burned."

"Yes, the lightning burned me, frayed me to the core. I could not accept it. Lilah had already planted and watered her faith, and its appearance was soothing, confirming to her."

"But you had to find your own faith." I am no longer talking about Ephron and Lilah. I am talking about Abraham and me.

"Yes, but it hurt her. Once I came upon her praying on her knees. I was stunned to hear her ask for me to come to faith in her one God." He shakes his head sadly and shrugs. "But I cannot do it for her. To follow such a god would require wholehearted devotion. Idols allow us to dole out bits of devotion as we see fit. Lilah sees it differently. I've heard her say that divided devotion becomes no devotion at all."

Suddenly, Abraham's prayer at the fire comes rushing back. Hot coals pop, flinging burning ashes into the dark night. Smoke fills my nostrils. Words once again circle. *Moriah, Isaac, Ishmael.* My husband's voice rises and falls, agonized, and then peaceful. *Did he also pray for me to accept where Yahweh was leading him?* The tear from my left eye finally makes its way down my cheek. Instead of wiping it away, I let it linger. Time slows down. Looking up, I see that the eagles are now overhead. Their circling, together and then apart, reminds me of my own journey—sometimes closer to Abraham's way of seeing, other times venturing out to where I can test the edges of my own convictions. And in the painful moments, I am tempted to simply fly away.

As my thoughts turn back to Ephron, I finally ask, "May I share?"

He nods.

"That is why I am here alone. Abraham followed Yahweh in a calling I couldn't accept, forging ahead of me. I feel abandoned, even disrespected. So here I am. Riding on a donkey into the wilderness after him. And my only son. Until I lost her, Maya. She is my donkey, but also my son's donkey." My stomach seizes, ready for a bout of weeping which I refuse to indulge. I look upward, letting the sun warm my cheeks and my hair. At once, I hear birds all around me, chattering, singing and calling. The air smells fresh and clean, like the trees recently cleaned it.

His face softens in empathy. "I hear your pain." We both sit quietly, each with our own thoughts. Then he speaks up again, "But I can't help but wonder, can you follow this god if you cannot accept his calling?"

I nod, telling myself that believers in Yahweh aren't the only wise ones, and then utter a silent prayer: *Lord, how do I begin to explain?* Just when I think there are no words, I realize that truth is the best gift I have to give.

"After the flood stole my precious donkey and many of our provisions, I remembered a saying I once heard from a traveler who passed our way."

Ephron smiles. "The sayings of travelers are the desert's currency. Please share."

"Don't run until your feet are bare and your throat is dry."[11]

We both sit in silence as he ponders this.

"I have been running from Yahweh, fearing his calling, but the running stole my donkey and our provisions."

"May I ask a question then?"

Since he allowed my question, I should allow his. But I am frightened that he will expose the obvious—that I am not enough for this. Finally, I find the strength to nod.

"In going after Abraham do you run toward or away from

[11] *I warn you again:* stop running after these *rituals* till your feet are bare and your throat is dried out. You said, "I can't help myself, for I love these strange gods I am chasing after." Jeremiah 2:25

your one God?"

I sigh deeply, feeling exposed but grateful that he called Yahweh my God. "I cannot be sure," is all I can manage. I lean down and pick up a pale pink rock. On one side, the stone is dry and drab. But on the other, where it has been cracked open, the rock is pink with tiny flecks of gold. When I turn it toward the sun, the gold sparkles in the light.

Glancing at him, I think I see the glint of a lonely tear in his left eye. After a moment of respectful silence, Ephron scratches his beard and then shakes his head a little like a donkey. I wonder if he will stamp his foot next. "Is it possible that Abraham seeks the same thing as you—to prove his faith?"

I smile and nod. Ephron may be closer to faith than he knows. I am not the only person who struggles to process faith. Ephron and I have found common ground. As we sit quietly, the clouds shift causing one tree to light up and then another.

I hold up the stone to show Ephron, offering it to him. "Sometimes, life has a way of breaking us open."

"Yes, I see what you mean," Ephron says as he turns it in his hand and then holds the cut side to the light. "Closed but yet fully open. But the light can only fully reach the cut side." Handing it back to me, he smiles. "The rock found its way to you. Please keep it."

"Thank you," I say, thrilling a little. A simple gift, but full of meaning.

Ephron puts his hands on his hips and looks out toward his property. "If we could see all the animals, insects and birds hidden on this small plot of land, we might see that one must sit still to find all which is moving." He smiles at me, his eyes full of laughter and then surprises me by beginning to softly sing, as if I am no longer present.

Song of crickets, chirping loud.
See our handiwork!
Green and proud.

Trill of songbirds, singing sweet
Welcome to morning.
And time to eat.

Laugh of cuckoos, loud yet meek
Mock the stilt birds
Wading in creeks.

Roar of lions, warning call
Claim their hunting ground
With this sound.

Song of donkeys, loyal steed
Always complaining
Until they feed.

"I could listen to this song again and again." I say.

I glance at Ephron. Do I see tears forming in his eyes? My heart is full of questions but sense he has already given much. If there is a story, it is his to tell. I stand up and yawn. "My ankle is ever so much better."

"Let it rest. Remember not to plow the wet ground." We laugh in unison.

"Thank you for bringing me up here. I pray your work is successful."

"I have pistachio trees that need to be pruned since they are in their non-bearing year. Every two years they follow this pattern. A year of bursting with fruit and then a year of rest. But even in their rest years they will bear some fruit."

Not having visible fruit doesn't mean a tree has forgotten their purpose, I muse. *Lord may this friendship with Ephron and Lilah endure.*

Ephron gives his donkey a pat on the rump and secures him to a fallen tree, so he will not follow after him. "You keep a watch over Sarah," he tells Azaz. Then Ephron bounds down the path like a gazelle, reminding me of Zerah, the running man with the white albino deer cape.

Now alone, fear and anger suddenly flare, shoving away all of my talk of faith. *Isaac, how could I forget you even for a short time?* I walk over to Ephron's donkey Azaz and begin to stroke him in the same way I liked to rub down Maya. I am surprised that he allows my touch, even nuzzles my neck.

Suddenly I remember my son, walking toward his fate. Angry tears begin to stream down my cheeks, making dusty trails down my neck and even finding their way beneath my cloak. I imagine my skin sizzling like hot coals being touched by droplets from the sky. I lay the side of my face on the donkey's back, exhausted.

Then I hear Lilah's voice behind me, "Sarah, I don't mean to interrupt. Do you need some time alone?"

When I turn to look at her, she stands lower on the path looking upward. So bold, yet undoubtedly feminine. She doesn't appear winded from her climb up the hill.

"It is good to see you," I say. I want to escape somewhere, anywhere, by myself. But, the chance to be with another woman of faith is sacred, even if I have no words to give.[12]

"Would you prefer to sit here longer, or should we sit by the fire?"

I shiver, reminded of the chill in the air. "The fire sounds lovely."

[12] He was accompanied by a group called "the twelve," and also by a larger group including some women who had been rescued from evil spirits and healed of diseases. There was Mary, called Magdalene, who had been released from seven demons. There were others like Susanna and Joanna, who was married to Chuza, a steward of King Herod. And there were many others too. *These women played an important role in Jesus' ministry...* Luke 8:1b-3

She walks over, unties the donk, and then leads it beside a rock that can help us mount. She easily swings a leg over, and then nods. I am flattered that she allows me to mount on my own. She leans over to murmur into the donkey's ear, like Zerah did with his Nephilim donk. I put my arms lightly around her waist.

"Hang on as tight as you need," she says cheerfully.

The path downward seems so much more treacherous, but Azaz seems unphased. I breathe easily seeing Lilah's sure touch with the animal. When we arrive, she again finds a natural spot to dismount. As I walk into the cave, the aroma of roasted meat wakes up my senses and makes my jaw ache in anticipation. Perhaps, I can find words.

We each make ourselves comfortable. Lilah smiles, an invitation to begin or to just be silent. She tests the meat and seeing it nearly done, she moves it further back from the coals.

"In my old age, Yahweh gave me a promised child that would be the father of nations." I smile. This is the only way I know. To jump off the cliff into the depths. "My husband is solely consecrated to the Eternal One. I too follow him, but my zeal differs. And now circumstances have made me doubt Abraham, and perhaps even Yahweh, as he knows him. Where he sees faith, I see danger. And now his faith is taking him to a place I cannot follow, because I fear he will risk our son for his faith. Yet, I must." I catch myself in my ramblings. *Do I disclose too much?*

"Ah, yes." Lilah runs her finger through her wavy grey tresses. "The burden of all wives. *Especially* worshippers of Yahweh."

Her quick empathy catches me off guard. I take a deep breath and motion for her to continue.

"Ephron is also a man of zeal, although his zeal hasn't yet found a resting place in Yahweh. In my nature I push back, sometimes with all my might." She pauses then continues, "You hold great strength within you. No doubt, Abraham needs a woman who sees danger."

"And no doubt Ephron is doubly blessed to have you. His words.... He doesn't seem so far from faith." My left hip suddenly catches, causing me to wince in pain. "Ephron said you might have some healing balm?"

"Indeed, I do. Ephron says that pain sets up a tent right above the hip bones, then builds a fire to warm itself." She laughs. "In his way of seeing, every pain calls for a proverb. Can you show me where it hurts?"

Glancing around, I see a turquoise and orange woven bed cushion on a soft spot in the dirt. Not as elaborate as my portable bed, but still inviting. As if we know each other's minds, we both stand and make our way over.

"Ephron won't come until I signal that dinner is ready. I can either work on the area clothed or can rub the balm into your skin."

"Please do use the balm."

Lilah brings a soft blanket from her bag, and then works quickly to move aside my garments in a way that preserves my dignity, tucking the blanket under me to just expose my lower back. After warming the ointment in her hands, she gently presses it into the ache.

"Do you think I displease Yahweh? By fleeing into the wilderness with two guides I barely know, thinking I alone can intervene?"

"Sarah, your courage is worthy of imitation." Her hands continue to circle, bringing heat, warmth and the comfort of touch. It seems she not only releases the tension in my back, she also massages my weary spirit, shouldering a burden too great for me to bear.[13] Finally, smoothing my garments back into place, she removes my sandals, and massages my feet, again reminding me of Yasmine. First the warmth of the hot springs. Then Ephron's knowing work on my ankle. And now this pleasure.

"Is it possible that Yahweh sent you guides to invite you to follow?"

I sigh, both with the joy of being ministered to so intimately, but also with the ease of talking to someone who understands. "I'm not sure. But I do know he ministers to me through you."

Yet, I cannot deny that Lilah has opened up a possible new way of thinking. My heart beats a little faster. Did Yahweh bring Zerah and Yasmine to invite me to go after Abraham? Or to go after him, the Most High God?

Lilah finishes by covering my feet with a blanket, and then running her hands lightly up and down my back, as if she is kneading bread. "Rest, my new friend," she whispers. "I will finish our meal."

Although our words have been few, the meaning runs deep. As I rest, I picture roots springing all around me to press me into the dark earth below. The roots move downward until they reach a spring beneath the cave floor. *Ah, men accuse us of having too many words, but the truth is we have many ways of talking, far beyond the limitations of language.* Her presence is the healing balm I need.

I fall into a deep trance, somewhere between sleep and being awake, until the sound of Lilah talking with Ephron nudges me fully awake. The feast is laid out on a blanket, lamb with wild mint, bread with thyme and wild greens with olive oil. As we partake, my mouth tingles and shivers go down my spine, as the spices dance in my mouth.

After we eat, I now have the opportunity to entertain them. I get up and pace, waving my arms, as I tell them stories of a mute

[13] Shoulder each other's burdens, and then you will live as the law of the Anointed teaches us. Galatians 6:2

swan's rage, even adding how I kicked things around my tent, a persistent owl, a guide with a white cape who runs like the wind, and the flood that carried away two valued donkeys. The fluctuating emotions are now the salt that binds us together.[14] We shed a few tears, as in return they reverently offer me the story of a lost child, barely born before it went back to its creator, and Lilah's resulting barrenness, as if her womb couldn't bear the thought of another wound so terrible.

I glance at Ephron and he nods. He wrote the song for a child to come. Lilah reads our faces and looks at her husband with a question in her eyes. "Later," he says simply.

Ephron and Lilah finally excuse themselves, intuitively knowing that I long for time alone. They offer their donkey, but I insist that Yasmine will return with a new donk for our travels. Before they leave, Lilah and I embrace and hold each other for a tender moment, bound by our shared losses. Before they leave, she surprises me by handing me her lamb's wool cape. "This is for you to keep," she says. "For whatever your journey may bring." I cannot turn them down twice. And undoubtedly, it is warmer than the cloak I brought.

Through my new friends, Yahweh has shown himself present. I could walk outside to see them off, but instead stay near the fire, not wanting the letting go of new friends to be yet another loss.

Now alone, the desire for my son rushes over me, like the flash flood that stole two donkeys. I think back over my conversation with Ephron and a truth comes to me. Children are another way a woman seeks dominion.[15] Is this a way we seek the eternal? Why my long years of barrenness became a lingering wound? Is this why I still struggle to trust Yahweh to the same degree that Abraham professes?

[14] Don't be like salt that has lost its taste. How can its saltiness be restored? *Flavorless salt is absolutely worthless.* Luke 14:34

[15] Her children rise up and bless her. Her husband, too, joins in the praise, saying: "There are *some—indeed* many—women who do well *in every way*, but of all of them only you are truly excellent." Proverbs 31:28-29

"Oh Isaac, I will yet find my way to you," words accompanied by the soft crackle of the wood in the fire. And then thinking of Ephron and Lilah, I pray, "Lord, there is still time for them. Please Yahweh, intervene in your inexhaustible mercy to give them the miracle of a child.[16] A son to hear Ephron's song of crickets, lions and donkeys." I picture myself laying a hand on Lilah's belly as I pray, just as she used her hands to minister to me.

I walk outside to ponder my next step, and find that despite my protests, Ephron and Lilah left their donkey for me. A wool cape and a donkey. Is this permission to continue on my own toward my son?

I walk over to Azaz and stroke his cheek, "Azaz, should we stay or go ahead of Yasmine and Zerah?"

I am torn. I long for Zerah's protection and Yasmine's companionship. Yes, I want to respect their wishes and Yasmine's efforts to get me clothing and a new donkey.

Then I glance at Azaz's feet, and suddenly notice a miracle or perhaps even a sign. Close to his feet, there are two golden eagle feathers.

[16] Some how Your mercy is inexhaustible. Once more You listened to them when they cried to You in heaven *for help*. Over and over and over You intervened and saved Your people. Nehemiah 9:28b

The Eternal has sworn an oath and cannot change his mind: "You are a priest forever—in the *honored* order of Melchizedek."

Psalm 110:4

CHAPTER SEVEN
Melchizedek's Song

AFTER THE DIFFICULT DECISION TO PRESS on along, Azaz carries me with a sure but quick gait, trotting up the path, through the woods towards Moriah. In addition to me, he carries the provisions left by Ephron and Lilah, as well as the two additional golden eagle feathers that I have tied onto the end of my husband's walking staff. As Isaac said, "We still need one feather for Ishmael and another for Hagar." In the wilderness, now alone, I understand a little better the injustice Hagar must have felt. *These feathers testify that I still think of you Hagar...you and Ishmael.* A wave of regret swirls around me, its salty brine stinging my eyes. Being alone on the path, away from the protection of the cave leaves me more vulnerable than I would wish. For Isaac.

I lean over and lace my arms around the donkey's neck and begin to weep. He stops in his tracks, respectfully it seems, as my sorrow drips and then glistens on his strong neck. I offer the little prayer I have in me, "Most High God, I am overwhelmed with sorrow. How much can one old woman's soul endure?[1] Just as you appeared to Hagar and Ishmael in the desert, do you see me, alone, afraid?" Then realizing my prayer is more complaint than

[1] My soul is overwhelmed with grief, to the point of death. Stay here and keep watch with Me. Matthew 26:38

surrender, I add what I have heard Abram say before, "Yahweh, please lead me tenderly like an ewe who tends her young."[2]

As suddenly as the regret came, it pulls back, leaving its damp trail and the musty smell of donkey mane on my cheeks. With effort, I carefully push myself back into a sitting position, and give Azaz a nudge with my feet. *Such a noble name for a donkey.* He brays softly over and over, a nasal intake of air followed by a high-pitched whistle. Then he whinnies. Strangely enough, in his soft whinny I hear the word that propels me forward... *Hinini, Hinini. I am here. I understand the call. I am enough for it. I will not desert you.* The same word I heard Abraham utter in his prayer at the fireside the night before he left camp with Isaac headed for Moriah. I reach over and pat Azaz's neck. *Yes, I hear you. You are here. You are enough. You will not desert me.*

Thankfully, Abram and I traveled this path before. As a precaution, I also brought the remnants of the blanket I tore up. If confusion comes, I will mark the way back to the cave with discreet strips of cloth.

A guttural hiss comes from above me, startling me. I grip Azaz's mane tightly. My eyes reach above and beyond Azaz the noble, over the edge of the canyon, where I see three vultures circling. Could their raspy, drawn-out hisses have traveled so far? Are they couriers of death? Unbidden, the memory of Pharaoh that haunted me while I was at the hot springs once more circles around me like a bird of prey. With that, I remember what I swore to forget. A second memory of being given to an evil king. For years, whenever his name has come to mind, I have pushed it down, like Azaz uses his hooves to stomp the ground beneath us. *No, I will not remember your sickening advances.* My defenses must have weakened because his name rises from the path and circles around me. *King Abimelech.*

[2] He will feed His fold like a shepherd; He will gather together His lambs—the weak and the wobbly ones—into His arms. He will carry them close to His bosom, and tenderly lead like a shepherd the mother of her lambs. Isaiah 40:11

My body decides to tell its own story of pushed-down pain. My stomach sickens. My head suddenly seems full of cobwebs. But then I remember something new I have learned from Yasmine and Zerah, Ephron and Lilah. Stories of heartache soften in the telling. Although Azaz the donkey knows nothing of lustful rulers, I decide to entrust it to him. A herdsman's proverb comes to mind: *the best kept secrets are entrusted only to animals.*

"Azaz," I say, stroking his neck. "I have a story to tell you. Yes, it is true. It is about my son Isaac, a wicked king and a husband caught in a terrible quandary. When we moved into the southern region of Gerar, angels appeared to Abraham to announce that in a year's time, I would be pregnant with a child of promise." I sigh, finding the telling difficult without another person speaking. "Where was I? I was hiding nearby to hear the conversation that I was not asked to join. Yes, I burst into laughter, no longer caring if they heard."

Azaz shakes his head, as if he understands.

I also laugh at the absurdity of an old woman talking to a male donkey, one who barely knows her. I decide instead to rehearse for the day I tell Isaac these things. Yes, I want him to follow in his father's footsteps. But every parent prays this does not include their mistakes. A child can only avoid what they know.

Picturing Isaac sitting by me at the fire, I continue, now talking to my son. "We have told you about the angels of the Most High that came to predict that in a year's time I would be pregnant with you. From that time on, a change came. Wrinkles began to disappear. My skin firmed up and the skin of my neck tightened, and my cheeks spoke of renewed youth. My handmaids were the first to notice and told me that Hagar was inquiring about my beauty treatments. One day your father said, 'My wife, the promise suits you. You are radiant and your hair and eyes are shining.'"

Enough, my soul says. But a story that needs to be told will linger like a stream waiting deep beneath the ground for the spring. Again, I picture Isaac, his eyes full of interest, urging me to tell more.

"My son, not too long afterwards, some of Abimelech's men saw me and reported my reverse aging and growing beauty to King Abimelech, who set out to have me. Yes, wicked kings often keep a large number of women, to use as they would please. They call this a harem."

"A harem," Isaac repeats, his voice full of disgust.

"From the beginning, Yahweh intended for a man and a woman's covenant of marriage to be between them and them alone. When the King sent men to take me to him, my eyes begged your father, *No. You couldn't. Remember the covenant.* But if he kept me from Abimelech, the King might kill him to get to me. Feeling he had no other choice, your father said, 'Yes, of course. *My sister* is honored.'"

I imagine Isaac's eyes widening in the firelight, stunned. He blurts out, "How could he, mother? He put you in a King's harem?"

I reach over and squeeze his arm, to comfort him. He nods his permission for me to continue, and in that small motion, I see his father's son. The son I adore.

Enraptured by the vision and softly rocked by the surefootedness of Azaz, I continue talking to Isaac. "As I gathered a few things, your father whispered that just as Yahweh intervened with Pharaoh, he would again. Yes, God did send a warning to Abimelech in a dream, telling him he was as good as dead if he defiled me.[3] But not before I had been subjected to beauty treatments to prepare me for him. I spoke to the king boldly

[3] See Genesis 20:7

about my faith in Yahweh and he feigned interest. Although the king never touched me, a single look from him made me feel filthy. For the two months I spent in his household, Abimelech paid your father 1,000 shekels of silver."

Again, I imagine Isaac shaking his head, suddenly in awe of the great price, not understanding the terror of a woman who has been abducted by a man's lust. I imagine myself reassuring Isaac, lest he feel responsible, "You were more than worth any price I had to pay."

Suddenly, Azaz steps into a dip in the path, jolting me and causing my hip to protest. This story is too terrible for even a donkey to hear, and certainly for a son of a scant fifteen years who might in some way feel responsible. But my mind will not let go so easily. The events continue to tumble into my thoughts, one after the other like rocks in a landslide.

We take our leave of Abimelech with flocks and gold.

Two weeks after I leave Abimelech's court, my bleeding returns.

Abraham celebrates this sign of fertility.

Tormented by nightmares of seduction, I avoid intimacy with my husband.

Has Abraham negated the promise through calling me his sister?

Don't covenants require both sides to keep faith?[4]

Will Yahweh bless us with a child?

I sleep with my husband.

Like an oasis in the desert the signs of pregnancy appear.

Azaz sneezes, jolting me out of my memories. But another thought lingers, one that offers renewed hope. *Does Yahweh's faithfulness depend more on his character than our feeble faith?*[5]

I whisper to my husband, "Abraham, you will never again leave me with a king who mistakes me for your sister. I would rather die."

[4] When Abram was 99 years old, the Eternal One appeared to him again, assuring him of the promise of a child yet to come. Eternal One: I am the God-All-Powerful. Walk before Me. Continue to trust and serve Me faithfully. Be blameless and true. Genesis 17:1

[5] If we are unfaithful, He remains faithful, For He is not able to deny Himself. 2 Timothy 2:13

But then I remember that it was miraculous youth that attracted Abimelech. Surely, no king would want me now, well over 100 years of age. But tiny twigs of anger have now been kindled, and the coal they lit has burst into flame.

Abraham sneaking off with Isaac without confirming to me that the calling had come.

How I threw my clothing and kicked it around my tent like a madwoman.

Would Yahweh say that all this turmoil is a call to forgive? To make an allowance for the faults of others, as he bears with my flaws?[6] My unbelief? My laughter at his promise?

Azaz carries me up and down the hills, and then steadily up again. Being silent allows me to listen to the forest, to hear the chirps, trills, lisps and raspy zzits made by the insects and birds. Time is only marked by the shadows changing on the rocks and trees. From time to time, I pray that Yahweh reveals the right path since my memory of the way is foggy.

It seems we have already been traveling too long. I eagerly watch for the two roads where Abraham left the staff, which is loosely strapped to my back as a weapon ready for me to spring into action....if an old woman can do such a thing.

I wonder about Yasmine and Zerah. Are they still running, gathering, providing? In their mysterious way, do they already know I went on towards Moriah? My thoughts betray me. Doesn't their tender care matter? And what of the savory meal of figs, lentils and broad beans with aromatic herbs? The mysterious prayer Zerah uttered over me after the owl and the snake almost threw me off the side of a cliff? No, my behavior couldn't be called fair, but the soothing affirmation of *hinini, here I am, I am coming,* calls me onward.

[6] Put up with one another. Forgive. Pardon any offenses against one another, as the Lord has pardoned you, because you should act in kind. Colossians 3:13

I pause and then say aloud with a strong voice, "Yasmine and Zerah, please understand. Zerah, didn't you say that you cannot intervene in what Abraham does or what Yahweh has ordained? You cannot, but I will."

No sooner than I think these words, my faithful donkey Azaz comes to a stop. We have come to the division in the trail. I remember Zerah's description of finding Abraham's walking stick, how he went just a short way towards Moriah and found the stick there, to the left. I give Azaz a quick yank on the left side of his mane, and he shuffles onto the trail leading to Moriah. I strain to remember what Zerah said about Abraham's walking stick. Did he say what kind of tree it leaned against? It may be silly of an aged woman, but I want to pause in the exact place to see what the tree can tell me. Seeing a rock that will help me dismount, I decide to let the donkey rest for a time. I gingerly hoist myself off and tie the donkey to the tree, keeping an eye for other travelers or animals. I stretch my weary back and drink greedily.

Remembering how Yasmine helped me early in the journey, I locate a safe place to relieve myself. I come back and stroke the tree. *Are you where my husband left his staff?* I touch the tree longingly, hoping my husband's presence still somehow remains.

When we finally start again, the path is winding. We navigate bend after bend as the path inclines slightly upwards. Finally, Azaz slows. My skin tingles as I instinctively reach up with my left hand to clasp my throat.

There are two men standing a good bit ahead in the early evening shadows beside the path, one in front of the other, both looking towards me but neither engaging the other. As we move towards them, I keep my face expressionless until I decide whether they are friends or foes. As we get closer, I draw in a breath. The man standing a ways behind the other is Zerah, but without his white cape or his sister Yasmine. He nods to acknowledge me, turns and noiselessly runs away from me towards Moriah, leaving the other man, a stranger, by himself.

Momentarily stunned, I pull Azaz to a stop and take a closer look at the remaining man. Although the light is beginning to fade, his full white and grey tipped beard glows as if it has a story to tell of its own. His dark, slightly wavy grey hair with tendrils of white caresses his shoulders. His deep brown eyes hold a question I cannot discern, and he wears a turban that could be a resting place for a crown. His garments are a weathered deep orange and scarlet linen, the work of a skilled craftsman. His ears are small and close to his head, and his nose is long and regal. When he finally smiles in welcome, his eyes crinkle with warmth. I slowly lower my chin and my eyes as a sign of respect.

"Sarah, wife of Abraham."

Suddenly, I know this man to be a friend of Abraham, a man my husband described to me. "Are you Melchizedek? King of Salem?"

He nods, standing straight and solid as a tree and holding his own walking staff, a curvy white uncarved stick that appears to have the same waves as his beard. *Where did he find this unusual piece of wood?* Backlit by the golden hue around us, he stands within a ring of light. The embroidered sash he wears makes me think of one who serves Yahweh day and night.[7] His presence reminds me I am considered a prophetess. Despite all of my fear, anger, regret and willfulness, I still follow the One God.

I offer him the greeting of Shem, the same one that Zerah offered me at the edge of our camp, "He gives wisdom to the wise and knowledge to the discerning. He reveals deep and hidden things; he knows what lies in darkness and light dwells with him."[8]

[7] Eternal One: The tunic is to be made of finely woven checkered linen. Make the turban out of fine linen as well, and have skilled workers embroider the sash. Exodus 28:39

[8] He reveals deep truths and hidden secrets; He knows what lies veiled in the darkness; pure light radiates from within Him. Daniel 2:21b-22

Eyes glowing with an inner fire, he walks closer and extends his hands and I lay mine on his for a moment. He steps back; can he sense my need for space? "I am camped nearby.

May I offer you refreshment from your travels?" Melchizedek strokes Azaz's back and looks into his eyes, "And your donkey needs food and water?"

Guilt perches on my weary shoulders like a small vulture hissing in my ear. I was so distraught over Isaac, I overlooked the companion who carried me all this way. "Yes, I would be so grateful for you to minister to…Azaz."

My stomach rumbles reminding me that the dried meat I ate early in the morning is gone. I have a small amount of food and water with me and don't yet know where this path will lead. Thinking back to Zerah's nod, before he ran on to Moriah, I see now he was entrusting me to Melchizedek. When my stubbornness insists on the foolish, Yahweh provides another way.[9]

"As you say," I offer, pushing against my motherly instinct to move forward. I am still hours from the peak of Moriah. I clumsily swing a leg over the donkey, and Melchizedek catches me like I am a small child. His strength is obvious. My back is stiff from the ride, my hips sing a song of abuse and my head thuds in dull pain. So, when Melchizedek offers an arm, I take it. Azaz obediently follows as we meander to the left, through the woods until we reach a clearing where there is a fire and a tent. I pull Lilah's earth-colored lamb's wool cloak snugly around my shoulders, as the chill of early evening rises up from the ground, into my sandaled feet, up my legs, up through my hips, into my chest where a shiver overtakes me. I watch as a king ministers to a donkey with water and food. Azaz laps up a bucketful of water, then sloppily begins eating his grains and straw.

Satisfied, Melchizedek turns his attention to me, "You are

[9] Any temptation you face will be nothing new. But God is faithful, and He will not let you be tempted beyond what you can handle. But He always provides a way of escape so that you will be able to endure *and keep moving forward*. 1 Corinthians 10:13

chilled?" His protectiveness reminds me of my husband who captured my heart with his tender care and his wild stories about Noah, Shem and the flood.

"You expected me?" I say, cutting right to the heart of the matter.

"Ah, yes," he says softly. "When the intersection of Heaven and earth occurs, Yahweh draws together all that are his." He looks up, "Yes, even the stars shimmer in anticipation."

His words are mysterious, but I am somehow comforted that he knows the language of the heavens, like Abraham. *Perhaps this star still has a song to sing.*

He pulls at his beard as learned men like to do. "Unfortunately, it also draws the forces of evil. Perhaps you have experienced the pushback of the one who fell from the Heavens…but nothing to fear. Hinini."

I grasp Abraham's staff tighter like a talisman. *Did Zerah mention the snake and the owl? Is he involved in all that is playing out within our family?*

He helps me sit down on an albino deerskin. Again, I am surprised. Zerah gave him his cape for me. Then the thought traces through my mind unbidden…*Zerah knows that the covenant isn't just for you, Abraham or Isaac, it is for all who Yahweh loves.*[10] *The covenant is as much for Melchizedek as it is for us.*

The King of Salem motions towards the soup simmering over the fire in a black pot. "For now, rest and nourishment are the best protections."

"Many years back Abraham met you and gave you a tithe.[11] I have nothing to give in return."

"Allowing me to minister to you is a great gift in itself," he utters. "In doing so, you allow me to walk in the path of the Almighty."

[10] I want you to know that the Eternal your God is the only true God. He's the faithful God who keeps His covenants and shows loyal love for a thousand generations to those who in return love Him and keep His commands. Deuteronomy 7:9

[11] See Hebrews 7:1-2

Suddenly, I realize that I am the weary traveler with stories to share but little faith, and Melchizedek is the host who will talk to me of Yahweh, if I assent.

"Of course, it is up to you," Melchizedek offers, as if he reads my thoughts. "Whether you continue on tonight or rest here, the decision is yours." He then begins ladling soup into a bowl, and the aroma pushes away any other thought, as pungent and earthy spices fill the air.

"You prepared this?"

"My mother taught me to use what the Creator gives to prepare a feast…so that all to come may eat and drink at the Heavenly table."[12]

I put my hand over my mouth to stifle a laugh. He speaks in riddles. But it is good to know that cooking isn't just for women or maidservants, but a gift a man could boast about. As I sip the soup it warms my throat, then my chest and belly.

While I eat, Melchizedek gives new life to the fire. He repeats the rituals I've seen Abraham do, but also those of Yasmine…a woman. A yearning to build fires circles around me, like a hovering orange butterfly that has just learned it can fly.

After dinner Melchizedek warms water over the fire. "May I attend to your weary feet?"

"Isn't this the work of handmaids, rather than a king? I should wash your feet."

He smiles and waits.

In this moment, to refuse the washing would be to refuse the companionship of a king and the ministering of Yahweh.[13] I muse how I allowed Ephron to work on my ankle and Lilah, my hip, bringing blessed relief. I nod and remove my sandals with the lamb's wool covering, a luxury my handmaid Amah thoughtfully provided.

[12] And I confer on you a kingdom, just as my Father conferred one on me, so that you may eat and drink at my table in my kingdom and sit on thrones, judging the twelve tribes of Israel. Luke 22:29–30 (NIV)

[13] Peter: You will not wash my feet, now or ever! Jesus: If I don't wash you, you will have nothing to do with Me.
John 13:8

"May I?" As if this is ordinary, the King of Salem uses a soft cloth dipped in the warm water to clean off the dust on my sandals. Then he attends to my feet. As his strong hands gently remove the dust kicked up by Azaz, I feel like a young girl with her abba.

When he is finished, he takes a towel and gently rubs my toes as if they warrant special attention, and then pulls out what looks to be the same healing balm that Lilah used on my hips.

"Yes, a similar balm to the one Eve was rumored to use in the garden, the one created from the sticky sap of the cottonwood tree. I harvested this and made it myself."

He is a man of the trees and the forest...I think to myself. *A king I can trust. Perhaps the only man Abraham would approve of ministering to me in this way.* As he applies the healing balm to my feet, his strong hands have a different touch than Ephron's, yet I see that he has used this ointment often. His hands speak of love. I feel wetness lingering around the edges of my eyes, seeking permission to be released from their holding place. I bite my lip...not now.

"Sarah, with all respect, this tent is set up with warm clean linens and a soft mat. I would be honored for you to use it to rest or to sleep."

I note that he honors what is important to a woman, privacy and cleanliness. He wipes my feet dry and then offers the warm water and balm for me to use for my hands and face, while he takes a walk up the path to pray. How I long for the change of clothing Yasmine promised, but Lilah's cloak gives me a sense that whatever is needed will be provided. The clothing is wanted, but not needed.

After I wash, I go into the tent, sit on the mat, hold Abraham's staff and finger where he has carved...*Hinini.* I picture my husband saying to Yahweh... *I am here. I hear your call. I will act.*

This is my fear but is also Abraham's gift. So, I begin to sing in the way of a woman full of years, searching for a place to stand, a direction to go.

Lord of my coming and going
You know the path ahead
All I have you have given
But one child I have to bless

Does my husband see as you see?
Will he go beyond your call?
Have I come this far, to fail?
Too frail for what lies ahead?

Provider through Zerah and Yasmine
Healer through Lilah and Ephron
Carrier through Maya and Azaz
Guide through King Melchizedek

Hear my desire to go to Moriah
Protect Isaac from far above
Carry the gifts you have given
Through your own heart of love

If I were more faithful, I might promise faithfulness in return for Isaac's safety. But at this moment, I cannot. I'm not convinced that Yahweh trades in the currency of those he created. Abraham has said that Yahweh gave the promise because he takes pleasure in his people.[14] Yahweh, do you somehow cherish me, even now?

I take the king's tin of healing ointment that he made himself

[14] For the Eternal *is listening*, and nothing pleases Him more than His people; He raises up the poor and endows them with His salvation. Psalm 149:4

and apply it to my aching legs. I would feel safe to lie down or sleep, but I am not ready. I stretch my back and legs and then venture outside. Melchizedek is back and the fire is inviting. He has arranged a few logs around the fire to make the sitting easy on my bony hips.

"What story do you bring to the fire tonight?" He keeps his eyes on the fire, knowing I will not only be talking with him, but with the surrounding trees now shrouded in darkness, the birds saving their songs for the dawn, and perhaps even Yahweh himself.

I take a deep breath, willing myself to allow my story to be told, my song to be sung.

"I grew up among the Mamre trees near Hebron. As I splashed in the brook and ran through the groves, all that was created embraced me. I was happy."

"Those trees are magnificent indeed. I like to walk and pray there."

"My parents believed in goddess worship. I cannot call forth a name, since there were many. It seemed they sought social status instead of a deity."

I glance at Melchizedek to gauge his interest. He nods his encouragement.

"When they attended the feasts, my mother would adorn her body with shimmering fabrics and precious materials, like silver coins. They would come home late in the night, after cavorting with other worshippers. Yet it never seemed enough."

I notice Melchizedek completely attends to my words. A rare gift for a man.

"When others called out my ability to predict circumstances or speak of spirituality in precocious ways, it caught their attention. As my body began to mature, my mother sought ways to make me more attractive to men, which I endured." I smile, "Although I preferred to climb a tree or make my own adornments from leaves and flowers."

"A tree is a better object of affection than a goddess, if I may be so bold."

He does not judge me. Sitting at the fire, his appearance is regal, his back straight, his hands relaxed. "Did they let you find your own way?"

"One morning, they told me they had offered me to the goddess, to serve in her courts. They considered this a high honor or even a path to becoming a priestess. Yes, I still remember my mother's words, 'Ah, you would be so powerful as a priestess, my darling. Your beauty would draw worshippers from far and wide.' The way they looked at me was nothing like how a mother nurtures a daughter—at least from what I've seen from my handmaid Amah and her daughter. I was their possession to be bartered on the market for more status."

"I'm sorry," Melchizedek says. In his eyes I see my losses reflected. He feels with me. "My parents also desired for me to worship idols. A story for another time."

"And one I very much would like to hear."

I want to stop talking, insist that we start moving. Or divert to his story. But my story now has a mind of its own. It insists on being finished. I take a deep breath.

"One day, they arranged for me to meet with another girl who served in the temple. The things she told me horrified me. The way the priests freely used her body. The hardness of her gaze and boldness to inspect my body. She even showed me...a dance of seduction."

"You are so courageous," he says. I don't know if he speaks to the past or present, or both, but it doesn't matter in the sacredness of the moment. He must understand how stubborn of a hold an untold story has in the heart. How it weaves itself into the deepest recesses of the soul. His calling out of my courage is an invitation.

"She asked me to remove my clothing, allow her to touch me. She threatened me that if I refused, she would bring the high priest who would demand even more. I had no choice." I suck in my breath, realizing I have gone too far. Shared something much too intimate with a man other than my husband.

Melchizedek takes a deep long breath. In his eyes I see Yahweh drawing me out, taking the poison out of the wound. I know he wants me to breathe with him. I take several deep breaths and then, like my son Isaac, I begin talking faster, lest I neglect to say what has to be said. "Afterwards, I was humiliated and angry. When I told my parents what happened, they told me I made too much of it. It was just child's play. I was devastated."

Melchizedek's eyes flash with anger. He wishes he could right these injustices.[15]

"I said that I had no ambition to serve in a temple but would find my own way of serving the gods. By this time, I had heard echoes of truth…in the trees, the brook, the birds. I told my parents, 'I will find the real god. That will be my life's devotion.' My father said, 'You will do as we tell you foolish girl. You will not waste the prophetic gift the goddess has given you. By the turn of the next season, you will be in her service.'"

Although I am conscious that Melchizedek still listens, I am no longer 105 years old. It is ninety years earlier, and the girl who was never comforted desires mercy. "That night we fought violently. My mother sought to protect me, but my father shoved her into the wall and then struck me on the cheek with all his might. I ran into the trees sobbing. Finding my most beloved

[15] As a result of their injustice, the poor cried out to Him And as *you ought to know well,* He *always* hears the cries of the needy, *of the oppressed peoples.* Job 34:28

terrapin tree, I threw my arms around its trunk. 'You are my father,' I whispered. 'You would never give me to the goddess.'"

Now tears roll freely down my cheeks. "The small mercy was that my father's handprint remained on my face for many weeks. They made me hide, giving me time to devise my escape."

Pausing my story, I stand up and the outstretched arms of the forest trees point me to the night sky above us, but dark clouds cover the stars. By faith, I know the stars I do not see are still there proclaiming Yahweh's glory. Forgetting Melchizedek, I momentarily lift my arms towards the sky in an embrace. Then I turn back towards the king. "My mother was a good woman before goddess worship. I adored her." I sigh. "Finally, I fled. This is how I came to live with Terah, my father's brother, and eventually came to marry his son Abraham. And together we turned towards the following of Yahweh."

Melchizedek is silent, yet the softness of his stance radiates compassion. I should be embarrassed, even humiliated, but I am not. Suddenly, I feel younger. Will Yahweh allow me strength beyond my age one last time? I am ready to go to my fate.

Melchizedek stands. Surrounded by darkness, he almost appears to be one with the trees, as if this is his true kingdom. "I sense you know your path?"

"His curly hair," I say in a daze. "It was always so unruly, and I chided him to brush it. Now, I only want to touch his hair again. Put my fingers through it... He isn't even fifteen yet."

"Your son?" He respectfully looks down, rubbing his hands together to warm them.

"Yes, my son Isaac. My only son was born as a miracle in my old age. Yahweh called Abraham to take Isaac to give a burnt offering, I think on Moriah. But circumstances, dreams, prayers, words said and unsaid point to the possibility that Isaac is the offering." My voice chokes with anguish, "My husband said you are not only a king, but also Priest of the Most High. Can you intercede? Should I?"

He squats down, with his elbows on his knees before the fire, as if it holds the answer to my pleas. His white beard looks red in the glow of the coals.

Knowing there is no answer to my question, I say, "Yes, I want to go to Moriah tonight."

"Hinini," Melchizedek says. "So be it."

He will not hide himself from you, for your eyes will constantly see him as your Teacher. When you turn to the right or turn to the left, you will hear his voice behind you to guide you, saying, "This is the right path; follow it."

Isaiah 30:20b-21[1]

[1] The Passion Translation

CHAPTER EIGHT
Wayfaring Song

MELCHIZEDEK STIRS THE FIRE, GIVING just enough light to prepare for us to travel. He stockpiles food for our sojourn, gathering dried meat and cheese, even water and oats for my noble donkey. The King of Salem, as Abraham called him, then offers the rest of the stew to Azaz who whinnies for joy. In the presence of a man of God, his slurping accompanied by droning insects, the song of an owl, the crackle of the fire and the howl of a wolf all join as a hymn to Yahweh. Inhaling the piney smell of the trees around me, I stroke the soft deerskin underneath me and shiver.

There is a deepening, damp chill in the air, the kind that settles into an old woman's bones. I turn my head and my neck catches, sending searing pain down my left shoulder. My left hip joins the chorus, with an ache that sometimes jolts me awake in the night. Oh, that Lilah was here to use her strong hands to rub soothing ointment into my aches. Yearning for home settles into the pangs, which squeeze my forehead. I slowly stand up, throw Lilah's cloak around my shoulders and then utter a silent...no!

No to the yearning for safety.

No to temptation to turn back.

No to those who would criticize an elderly sage seeking safety for her only son.

It seems that Melchizedek means to leave the tent up for our return. We might need it high on the trail but showing that I trust his lead is more pressing. Before we leave camp, the king-priest prepares a fire-starter carried in a purse made of animal skin. The weather is unpredictable on Mount Moriah and the dark sky is ominous. He also wraps wood for the fire to keep it dry. He puts Zerah's albino skin over the noble Azaz for me to straddle, and then helps me up. As I stroke Azaz's neck in gratitude for receiving my tears, I whisper in his ear, "You are now clothed in the hide of an albino deer. I pray it protects you as we trudge through the dark of night."

When I look up again, Melchizedek emerges with his own donkey, lanky and pure white. "Resting behind the tent," he chuckles, answering my inquiry before I pose it, his eyes a dwelling place for the stars. "At her age, she usually ignores any other donkey who comes nearby. But she is surefooted for traveling. Her name is Yoorie, the pure one."

Instead of ignoring Azaz, Yoorie walks up and gives his rear left haunch a lick which he notes with a stomp of his rear left hoof. *He is pleased.* Melchizedek hoists himself upon Yoorie and motions for me to follow as he leads us out of the woods back to the path to Moriah. My heart beats in tempo with the donkey's sure feet.

"How long will it take to reach the top?" I ask, my voice cracking in exhaustion. As twilight enters, the wind picks up and it begins to drizzle lightly. Lilah's cape has a hood that I slide over my head, tucking in my long hair.

"The going may be slow and treacherous if this storm gains strength," he says.

"The donkey's large eyes help them see in the night and through the storm," I chime in, as if Melchizedek does not know this. Thinking of Maya, saltwater trickles down my face, joining freshwater dripping from the heavens. Droplets wiggle their way down my neck, chilling me. With cleansed eyes, I see dark, sharp edges to the foliage surrounding us. Does pain slice me open to the mystery of Yahweh's moving? Does the quickness of my breath alert me that a crucible is ahead?

When the path widens, the King of Salem motions for me to bring my steed alongside his so that we can talk—also a way to keep wild animals at bay. The sudden shower lets up as quickly as it came. Even in the darkness I feel the path is rocky, no doubt slippery. An uninvited shiver races down my spine. Do I risk the high priest of God by my determination to intervene?

"Abraham says he is blessed above all men to have you. Now, I see he speaks the truth."

Although talk isn't my first desire, my tongue loosens itself. "Strange as it sounds, I did not meet Abram until he was forty-eight, since he spent his first ten years living in a cave with his mother and nursemaid hidden away from an evil king...a story of its own...and then thirty-eight years living with his forefathers Noah and Shem, learning all he could from those who rode out the great flood in an ark.[2] Although his father Terah told me I would marry his son one day, by the time Abram returned, I wasn't sure if he would consider me a sister or a potential wife. By this time, I had already been called out as possibly barren. But I hoped against all hope."[3]

Our words insert easily between the rhythm of the donk's steps. I pause, my thoughts swirling around me like the pesky insects Maya used to flick away with her tail in the heat of the day. "Soon after he arrived, Abram announced we would marry.

[2] Chabad.org, "Abraham's Early Life." Retrieved from https://www.chabad.org/library/article_cdo/aid/112063/jewish/Abrahams-Early-Life.htm

[3] Against the odds, Abraham's hope grew into full-fledged faith that he would turn out to be the father of many nations, just as God had promised when He said, "That's how *many* your descendants will be." Romans 4:18

The dimple in his left cheek also announced this, and the way his dark bushy eyebrows lifted in amusement. 'So, you are the one,' he said, more of a statement than a question. And then, 'Father, I am hungry from my travels.'"

Talking about my husband sends warmth through my veins.

"With all you suffered as a young girl, the One God saw and intervened."

"Perhaps the One God urged me to use my cooking of tasty meals to woo Abram," I laugh. "Having created man, Yahweh knew that men are enticed by aroma, texture and taste. From the way Abraham eagerly tore into my food…yes, food spoke to him of love."

"Any man would enjoy being wooed with food," he laughs.

Laughing with him seems natural, yet altogether absurd. *A man of such great stature before God, yet he laughs so easily and well.* His laughter loosens the reins on my tongue. "Abram, as I first knew him, tapped into my desire for pure love. Our covenant began as a seedling from the mighty cedar of Yahweh's goodness."

"Ah yes, I have heard of Yahweh changing his name, with the promise?"

"Yes, from Abram to Abraham. And mine from Sarai to Sarah. We still use these names in private, Abram and Sarai, as tokens of our history and our affection. Usually only between the two of us." I grip the reins tighter. *Will Melchizedek take this as disrespect for Yahweh?*

He nods. "I feel certain Yahweh delights in your closeness. Just as he delights in us and calls us beloved, even a crusty Canaanite by birth, like me. Your words are like a coming dawn that pushes away darkness as it draws the light.[4] Yahweh loves without favoritism." He adds, "Did you marry quickly?"

"Before we wed, Abram desired us to commit to the one

[4] Yet the way of those who do right is like the early morning sun that shines brighter and brighter until noon. Proverbs 4:18

God of Noah and Shem. His father Terah had long earned his living from building idols and selling them in the marketplace, a craft he intended to hand down to his son."

"Ah yes. That is the way of families. The son has no choice but to follow in the trade of his father and clan leader."

"Abraham lasted exactly one day selling idols. At the end of his first day of labor, seeking to show the difference between an idol and God Most High, he crushed the head of an idol before a wealthy buyer. Abram quickly decided to breed livestock instead—goats, sheep and camels. Being in the fields meant he could work and walk with Yahweh. Terah was indignant, threatening to cast his son out. Yet, within four years his herding became wildly lucrative."

"Ah, yes. Success is a certain way to get a father's blessing."

"A turn of the moon later, we were wed before our parents and Abram's two brothers under the oaks of Mamre, with twelve white silk canopies scented with rose oil and lavender billowing in the terebinth trees. Our shared faith was the warm sunlight that nourished our sapling of love."

"And now it rises as a mighty oak," he offers, glancing over at me. "Surely Yahweh chose your husband because he was willing to abandon his father's idolatry, his faith, and his clan. Many fathers would disown a son who had such gall." He lifts his sparkling eyes upwards. "Praise be to God on High for setting son against father and daughter against mother."[5]

Such a strange benediction. I think of how distressed my parents were that their child shunned their worship practices. I whisper what I know to be true. "Yes, Yahweh alone is worthy."

He nods, as Yoorie shakes her head. "You have both fought valiantly for your own faith. It does not require a prophetic gift to discern why you move both toward each other and away."

[5] I have come to turn men against their fathers, daughters against their mothers, and daughters-in-law against their mothers-in-law. You will find you have enemies even in your own household. Matthew 10:35-36

Does Melchizedek seek permission to thrust his hands in the dark soil of our conflict?

I dig deep into the tangled ball of desires that dwell under my left rib. "I desire to please Yahweh and Abram, yet I don't always trust his way of seeing. Is he driven by true faith or fleshly desire?" I stop myself and whisper, "Does he ever seek to see as I see? Does he care for me more as he cares for our tribe? His standing?"[6]

He stops his donkey, musing, "The air smells of more rain." Motioning for me to wait, he dismounts. "I will walk a little further ahead while you wait here." Suddenly, the sky rumbles and then lightning momentarily breaks through the darkness.

Azaz rears up and I barely hold onto his rope. "Whoa boy!" I cry.

"Move back," Melchizedek cries out.

As I turn Azaz away, another bolt strikes, so close the hairs on my neck stand straight up. I hear the distinctive creaking noise that predicts a falling tree. "Run Azaz, move!" I yell, yanking on his reins. Cracking and wheezing, the tree tumbles through branches and lands with a loud thud, causing the ground to tremble. With that the heavens release their full storehouse of water, while Azaz gallops into the black wet night. He moves us past where we camped, back past where Abraham's staff was found, twisting and turning on the slippery path with me barely hanging on. Finally, the rain slows and then is gone. At my pull, he finally halts and then turns.

Of course, in the darkness, there is no sign of Melchizedek and Yoorie. I hear Abram in my ear, *"Do you think the King of Salem, high priest of the Most High should follow you?"* Filling my chest with air, I try to calm my banging heart. I take the sleeve of my cloak and wipe the rain off of my face. I am terrified to

[6] So husbands should care for their wives *as if their lives depended on it,* the same way they care for their own bodies. As you love her, you ultimately are loving *part of* yourself (*remember, you are one flesh*). Ephesians 5:28

go forward, reluctant to try to go back on my own. Time slows down. The forest sounds are ominous. The whispers, whines and whirls of wind and forest close in around me. Sitting still, I feel more at risk and most foolish for acting like a King should follow me. Like a two-headed serpent rising out of a basket, fear taunts me. Branches crackle nearby. The hairs raise on my arms remembering my fear of facing a mountain lion at the springs.

What if Melchizedek was injured by the falling tree?

I give Azaz a nudge with my feet and he plants his hooves in protest. After I dig my heels into his haunches, he reluctantly forges back toward Moriah until we once again reach the convergence of the two paths. *Does Yahweh drive me to this place of decision again and again?* Suddenly, I feel the presence of evil pressing on me, looking for an entrance into my innermost being. A vision appears like an emissary.

A strong man tears me violently off of the donkey, slamming my body on the wet ground and drags me into the forest by my hair like a bear dragging its prey. As I am stabbed by branches and brambles, he projects into my mind the murderous intentions he has for me.

I clasp the reins tighter, astonished at the vision. "No, you are not real!" I scream, shaken…evil seems intent on destroying me.[7]

Even as we continue moving, a whisper comes sizzling within the spattering rain. "Yahweh will ssseize your ssson, sssstealing eeeeverythingggggg. Only youuuu can sssstop himmm."

Blood courses through my veins, making my head pound to the same beat. I take a deep breath, allowing the air to find its way all the way into my hips. Am I the stumbling block to Yahweh's great plan? Is my fear of death driving me forward? Or am I the savior for my son that my actions profess me to be?[8] Shame scurries throughout my body seeking a resting place. I pull my seized-up shoulders backwards, away from my ears

[7] See Mark 3:27

[8] Since we, the children, are all creatures of flesh and blood, Jesus took on flesh and blood, so that by dying He could destroy the one who held power over death—the devil—and destroy the fear of death that has always held people captive. Hebrews 2:14-15

where they abide too often. Sensing my fear, Azaz stamps his hoof twice in warning, and then moves us quickly ahead.

"Yahweh, I need you," I pray. "Protect us as invited guests to your sacrifice." My spirits lift at the thought of being invited to the sacrifice. Reality follows quickly. *Have I just uttered the truth? Or do I project on Yahweh my own insecurity?*

My neck is tight as we make our way back past where my husband likely left his carved walking stick, then finally past where Melchizedek washed my feet and fed me a savory stew. The darkness has only become blacker. I lift one hand from the rein and barely see it. Finally, I see the shape of a man shrouded in fog and misty rain. Again fear clutches my chest—the dread of Pharaohs and Pharaoh owls, the lustful eyes of a greedy king and the most insidious enemy, the evil one, the snake, who met Eve in the garden and who chases me.

Thank Yahweh, it is Melchizedek, facing away from us. Even in the night, his white and grey hair appears to glow. His garments are wet, and his orange cloak glistens with water, even with no light. Yoorie is gone. He stands before an enormous tree straddling the path. He turns and notes my sudden appearance, as if I never ran away…with my only thought being to protect myself. *He is faithful when I am faithless.*[9] I restrain myself from sliding off of the donkey and jumping into his arms.

"Yoorie was spooked and took off into the wilderness. She has yet to heed my calls."

Azaz picks his way through scattered branches up to the tree now lying across the path. A wayfarer could go under the log on their hands and knees but getting a donkey past in the darkness and rain would not be possible.

Abraham once told me that a donkey could hear the call of a potential suitor some sixty miles away. I urge my donk as if he

[9] If we are unfaithful, He remains faithful, For He is not able to deny Himself. 2 Timothy 2:13

were human, "Azaz, call her!"

"Ah, the prophetess commands donkeys through the storm," he quips, his voice lyrical. He waves his large but graceful hand in the direction his donk ran.

Azaz bellows with a loud wheezy inhale and exhale. Unrequited, he does it again. I smile. *Azaz the noble summons Yoorie the pure one.* Again, thunder vibrates the heavens like a wind harp, pounding on my already frayed nerves. Just when I wonder whether both of us could ride Azaz, we hear a faint bellow in return.

Melchizedek throws his arms open to the misty night and yells at the top of his lungs, "Yahweh created the donkey's song to pierce through darkness and distance." Then he bends over and begins to chuckle until laughter pours out of him like a spring emerging from a rock wall after a rain. His amusement charms me to join him, the light rain our accompaniment. Minutes later, Yoorie appears from the woods, half slides down the embankments and trots up to Azaz, giving his head a quick lick. Lightning cracks and the light rainfall turns to a full rain. For a few sacred moments, our faces glisten with joy. The nasty attack in the woods shimmies away in defeat.

"Is there a way to move forward?" I ask, pushing my voice to be louder than the water falling around us. I am grateful that the wool of Lilah's cape only gets wet on the surface.

"We can backtrack and use a trail I know through the woods to find the path to Moriah again. Once we are back on the trail, there is a cave we can travel to where we can dry off." He looks upward into the darkness, "Yahweh leads those who fear him in the way they should choose."[10]

Going through the forest single file in the wet blackness, it seems every branch wants to touch us, pull at our clothing, and

[10] "MAY anyone who fears the Eternal be shown the path he should choose." Psalm 25:12

chase us for entering. The sizzle of the rain mimics the voice of the snake. I lean forward and pray silently, lest I panic, or a branch gouges my feeble eyes. We enter what feels like a ravine. Finally, we emerge out of the trees onto what I assume is once again the narrow path toward Moriah. I breathe easier and time slows down. The donkeys pick their way step by step up the rock-littered path in the dark. The path turns and begins to lead sharply up the mountain. I thank Yahweh for the darkness hiding the edge of the cliff. Yoorie moves easily. Azaz seems more unsure, more spooked. Pausing at points, whinnying, his anxiety leaves me dizzy…like I could tumble off. My feet and ears are freezing. I long for warmth.

"It is here." Melchizedek raises his staff to point out a wide-mouthed grotto, but it is barely discernible in the darkness and storm. When we are inside, Azaz flicks his head and I feel his haunches relax. He is relieved to leave this slippery path. It is pitch black, and I am grateful that I am still mounted, but out of reach of the rain falling from the cave's entrance in ropes.

Snapping, cracking and thudding informs me that Melchizedek is unbundling the firewood, splitting the kindling with his knife, building a pyramid on a rock, and finally using the flint to spark the wood. Does the King of Salem see in the dark?

Damp wood does not catch easily. Smoke teases my nostrils; my sneeze echoes and my nose begins to drip. I can sit at a campfire in the open air, but in a closed place smoke sometimes makes me sneeze. My eyes slowly begin to adjust to the darkness. Soon, the spark catches, and a small fire starts, which he carefully tends, the damp wood protesting with pops. Once satisfied, he comes over, saying, "Let me help you dismount."

When my foot touches the ground, I wince. Melchizedek lifts the albino skin from the donkey's back and lays it on the cave floor by the fire. After I take off the wet cape, I gingerly find my way down to a sitting position, leaning on the rocks behind me. Suddenly it strikes me that he prepares the cave for me, not for himself. Once I begin this narrative, the story begins to weave with scarlet threads into a cord.

The fire he builds is to warm and protect *me.*

The doeskin he lays is for *one person* to rest.

The food he carefully places near the fire is to nourish *me alone.*

A dancing desert dervish spins in my head, picking up all of my convictions, hopes and prayers and whirling them to and from. I am left dazed, with no coherent arguments. My ankle throbs but thanks me for the warmth. The musty, damp cave air gathers in my chest. In a wavering voice that betrays my weakness, I whine, "Surely, you do not mean to leave me here?" *Just like Abraham has done on repeated occasions.* Regret follows quickly. These words signal weakness not strength. Submission, not authority. A slightly senile woman instead of a prophetess. Tears gather in my eyes, yet another sign of being unbearably vulnerable.

As if on cue, the rain becomes a deluge. Melchizedek spreads a damp blanket and sits down beside me. He lays the wool cloak Lilah gifted me over some rocks to dry. For a long moment, we watch the fire together and both warm our hands. Finally, he speaks, "This path is treacherous and unstable, especially in the rain. I could go ahead…"

Indignation floods my body, "Isn't it I who asked you to accompany me?" My throat seizes shut…. like I first experienced when others alluded to my barrenness. When I mistook dignity for being quiet and pretending it did not matter. Still, I speak to a man of God, a man who has offered me nothing but hospitality and kindness.

Before I can apologize, he intercedes gently, "Yes, it is so. My first inclination was to make you comfortable and let the next steps come. Please speak."

Thunder cracks nearby and I jump, jarring my hip. Cold seeps through the rock into the doeskin, and a damp wind pushes itself toward us. Yet where I sit now is largely dry, protected, safely encircled by light and heat radiating from the flames. I speak more to myself than to him, "Where is Isaac? Is he hunkered down in a cave as well? Does this storm grant me more time to find them, time I can redeem after a late start?"

Melchizedek radiates curiosity and compassion without condemnation. It is as if love has pushed out all fear.[11] He values me. *He does not discredit women.*

I reach for the stick he uses to stir the fire. Nudging the embers, I use it as he mentored me at our camp in the woods. Reading my intentions, he smiles and hands me a log he carried here on his faithful she-steed. Words now gush out like a spring pushing up after a long sleep. "I fear punishment. That Yahweh will take Isaac…I am not like you. My love invokes more fear instead of casting it out."

"Only a prophetess is so vigorously honest with herself," he says softly.

We sit silently again. And then I remember something Abraham told me. Fire not only burns, it cleanses. Perhaps within the burning in the wake of abandonment, there is cleansing.

He reaches over and gives my hand a squeeze.

"Thank you," I say. "Thank you for seeing me. But fear still chases me."

"What do you fear now?"

"I fear you going ahead of me, just like Abraham did. I fear men dismissing my fears as invalid. Isn't it possible Yahweh sent

[11] Love will never invoke fear. Perfect love expels fear, particularly the fear of *punishment*. The one who fears punishment has not been completed through love. 1 John 4:18

me after them? My son? My husband?" I quiet my voice into a petition. "And why is a woman's misstep judged as an emotional flight and a man's poor choice is lauded as boldness?"

"Ah yes, a prophetess reads the actions and motives of others before they know their own thoughts. She must then discern whether these are of the spirit or of the flesh.[12] You will find your way, bold one." He smiles at me and I see respect in his eyes. "My donkey has trod here often. Your friend's donkey is becoming anxious, a little uncertain. Rain makes the rocks beside the trail unstable and could cause a slide...."

"Does Yahweh only invite men to his appearing?" The words now fly out of my mouth unbidden as if they have lost their thorny protection. "Are only men able to gauge what is obedience and...what is lunacy?" I stop myself, afraid I will skid off the steep edge of a conversation I have longed for, but never had the courage to partake in.

"Sarah, you are highly esteemed. Your willingness to endanger yourself for your son draws Yahweh to you." He pauses for a moment, serene as one in deep contemplation. "When this time passes, he will need you."

Does he speak of Yahweh needing me, or Isaac needing me? Or perhaps Abraham? Before I can consider this riddle, a thought rises like smoke from the fire. Melchizedek believes I need to rest here. He will not take me beyond what my body can bear or on an unstable path. If I insist on accompanying him, he will wait until it is safer. Then neither of us will influence Abraham's decision. And, although Zerah is ahead of us, he has made it clear he will not intervene.

"What of my injured ankle?" I say. "What if I need to make my way down, alone?"

"May I?" he asks, reaching for my ankle.

Just when I think he might pull on my big toe like Ephron,

[12] If you live your life animated by the flesh—*namely, your fallen, corrupt nature*—then your mind is focused on the matters of the flesh. But if you live your life animated by the Spirit—*namely, God's indwelling presence*—then your focus is on the work of the Spirit. Romans 8:5

instead he lays his hand on my right ankle and begins to pray.

"Eternal God, the only God, I intercede for Sarah, your prophetess and one called to mother the son of promise. I pray that you will restore strength to her ankle, as if it had never taken blows on her travels to meet you on Moriah."

"I am humbled by your prayer," I say, looking him in the eyes, as a daughter would look to her father. "What do you believe to be best? For Yahweh and Isaac?" I am not quite ready to consider Abraham in this.

Melchizedek hands me Abraham's staff.

I finger it and feel something I didn't notice earlier. There is a new carving. I turn it to the light. It is the word *hinini,* the very word Abraham said he told Yahweh we would leave our country, our family and our home to follow him to a country we did not yet know. Did he carve it the night he decided to bring him to Moriah?

Now his eyes look fiery, as if consumed by a higher purpose. "The crucible purifies silver, the furnace winnows out gold, but only Yahweh can discern the motives of a person's heart.[13] The test is not only for Abraham, it is yours…as a prophetess and a beloved of Yahweh."

Beloved of Yahweh? Is it possible he esteems me in spite of my fear, my charging out on a path my husband would never approve of, for having a love that struggles to trust?

"Will you discern your gift? Will the eye that sees danger overcome untruth?"[14] His bushy eyebrows soften as his eyes sparkle. "This is the gift of Yahweh's daughters."

He refuses to choose for me. He speaks in mysteries—mysteries my soul hears as a faint echo of what I know.

"I will rest while Yahweh heals my ankle." My words cut, the knife of sacrifice dividing my will and spirit. "Please go ahead of

[13] Silver is purified in the crucible, gold in the furnace, but motives of the heart are judged by the Eternal. Proverbs 17:3

[14] But the truth is that My departure will be a gift that will serve you well, because if I don't leave, the great Helper will not come to your aid. When I leave, I will send Him to you. John 16:7

me." Pulling back my shoulders, I draw all my courage, my right to decide—free will as Abram calls it. "But whatever tests come, please continue on to Abraham."

He bows his head and his lips move silently. Sensing a prayer, I bow my head respectfully. Every yes Melchizedek utters will remain.[15] As a high priest of God, a holy man, he will not go back on his word, unless Yahweh himself redirects his path.

Now more urgent, he raises his head and speaks again, "The Lord appears within the fire of sacrifice to protect that which fulfills his covenantal purpose. He chooses his witnesses with great care. May the angels of the Lord stand beside you as you confront what you fear."[16]

He gives me a benediction, one that is as terrible as it is beautiful. I repeat to myself his words, knowing I can use one of my gifts to quickly commit them to memory.

The Lord appears within sacrifice.

He chooses his guests with great care.

He will protect whatever or whoever fulfills his covenant.

He gives before he asks.

Angelic beings will help me confront my fears.

Awe mixed with fear washes over me. The test is far from over. I know this as certainly as I also know I must stand under it alone. Has my quest, however foolish it may appear, attracted the attention of Yahweh? *How can an old woman propose to know?*

I watch as he covers himself with a cape. Despite his damp clothing and dripping white hair, he looks regal, like a prince whose currency is peace. *Lord, may I learn this wayfaring peace, this mighty spiritual warfare.*[17] Both the donks are sheltering in the mouth of the cave. He mounts his steed. Yoorie's dark eyes burn with the reflection of fire. Melchizedek's beard glows in the low light. Turning toward me, he says, "You have been prepared

[15] Because our God is always faithful to His promises, our word to you was not both "yes" and "no"... 2 Corinthians 1:18

[16] He has prepared the sacrifice, and He has chosen His guests *with care.* On the day of the Eternal's sacrifice, this will happen *just as He describes.* Zephaniah 1:7b-8

[17] See John 16:33

for this." He glances at me knowingly, "Your womb was a holy temple reserved for a child of promise. And now the father's beloved prepares to seal the covenant."

Mystery upon mystery. Is it possible that I was barren for this very purpose...to bear a son of Yahweh's promise? I wrap my arms around my chest. *Is this why my breasts would not make milk for Ishmael, lest I confuse God's work with my own?* A tear works itself out of my left eye and drips down my cheek. The sages say that the first tear dropping from the left eye is sorrow clearing the way for gratitude. Melchizedek nudges the pure one forward with his feet. The last thing I see is the flash of her white tail, as they bear right toward Moriah.

Looking around my meager camp, I decide to make it a temporary place of respite. A cave of rest and ascent. *I will call this the Cave of Moriah.* Resting near the cave opening, Azaz seems content to stay. I will give him water and secure him before I sleep. Beside the fire, I line up what I need in case the fire falters. I put a rock beside my bedding, and on it, I place a flint in case I need to restart the fire. I take the logs that Melchizedek had brought up from the woods and place it beside the rock. I separate it into kindling and larger pieces. Suddenly I remember the two golden eagle feathers that helped me to decide to venture alone into the wilderness. I check Abraham's staff and they are still firmly attached.

Lightning cracks once more, over my head it seems, and Azaz brays frantically. Startled, I drop the torch and put my hands over my ears. Before I can get to the donkey, he skids out of the entrance of the cave.

"No!" I yell. "Stay with me!"

Quickly, I throw on Lilah's cape to go fetch him. Surely, he chases his new female companion. I take a few steps down the path, wait and yell into the rain, "Azaz, come!" *He will not hear me over this deluge.* "Azaz!" I yell again.

After I reenter the cave, I hear a loud noise, much like the noise of the flash flood in the canyon that stole two donkeys. I retreat deeper into the cave and crouch underneath a rock overhang, with my hands over my head. The trembling ground and violent clattering of rocks and rain mimics my thoughts. Just as Melchizedek feared…it is a landslide to the right of me, exactly where I stood moments earlier. A picture of Azaz tumbling down the side of the cliff being battered senseless by rocks flashes through my weary mind. Kneeling down on the albino skin, I begin to weep wildly, my head in my hands, my stomach lurching upwards. My loud cries of despair echo through the close quarters. Do I attract destruction?

Finally, when my tears cease, I hoist myself up to replenish the fire. I force myself to breathe. Seeing the rain has ceased, and the moon is casting light between the clouds, I step outside of the cave. The path to the right, to Moriah, is unpassable, at least for an old woman with no donkey. As I limp back into the cave, I tell myself, "All is not lost. Thank Yahweh, Melchizedek knows where I am." At that moment, I hear him reply in my ear… *Yahweh is your protector.*

With my thoughts full of the donkeys I've known and lost, the companions who have come and gone, I lay down and curl up on the blanket, pulling the covers over my head with just enough of a gap to keep an eye on the fire. I must survive to see my son again. Regret courses through my blood leaving a remnant of bitterness. The path is unpassable. It is unlikely that the donk will return to me. Terrified in my aloneness, I remain in my blanketed cocoon as the fire burns down, unwilling to give up my slim sense of protection. I begin to pray silently, words that hardly make sense. Utterings that Yahweh will need to decipher. I am broken.[19] A dreamless sleep overtakes my weary body quickly.

When I wake, the fire is only smoldering coals. While it is still dusky, the darkness is changing. Dawn is several hours away and with it perhaps my last chance to act. I will head to the left, down the path, to seek Yasmine, the only one who can help me onwards to Moriah. Yet, I struggle to remove a single covering. *A little more time.*

Suddenly, I hear the crunch of rocks from the cave entrance, sending a rush of blood through my limbs. I throw off the blankets, get on my knees and grab Abraham's staff, my only protection, to help me push to my feet. A voice resounds through the darkness.

"Mother," Isaac says.

[18] What sacrifice I can offer You is my broken spirit because a *broken spirit*, O God, a heart that honestly regrets the past, You won't detest. Psalm 51:17

He teaches me to fight so that my arms can bend a bronze bow. You have shielded me with Your salvation, supporting me with Your strong right hand, and it makes me strong.

Psalm 18:34-35

CHAPTER NINE
Battle Song

ISAAC STANDS BEFORE ME IN THE ENTRANCE of the cave of Moriah, dripping from the storm. My travel-battered heart opens like a night-blooming desert cactus. My son is alive. In the darkness, his features are muted, but a mother knows her son, the curve of his jaw, the way he holds his shoulders, where his fingertips touch his hips. Isaac's curly hair glistens with drops of water that shine in the firelight. He wears a brownish cape I don't recognize, perhaps the hide of an animal? His voice is the voice of Isaac. Relief, raw longing and reverence wash over me. The fire is between us, so my body instinctively seeks to move around it to see him better. Isaac holds his hand up in protest. I stop, mouthing a silent please. *Isaac, let me draw you deeper into the cave where it is dry so that I can hold you, feel the life in you and hear our hearts beat in unison.*

"Mother, you must not come closer. Do not touch me." His voice drips with resignation.

"Isaac, I understand," I say gently. "You need space."

"I don't trust you…or Father anymore."

"Son, how did you find me?"

"Melchizedek, the so-called priest king. He alerted me of

your presence." He rolls his eyes like he did as a child when he was asked to submit. "Why do you trust men who abandon you and leave you defenseless? In trusting them you abandon me." Then he pauses and takes aim, "Hagar would not have allowed this."

His words bring to mind the dream where Isaac called Hagar mother, and called me Hagar.

He scowls. "Can you imagine what it is like to be tied on an altar by your own father?"

A tear twists a path down my cheek. *Oh, my dear Abraham, did you count this cost?*

I push away the wetness, stand my ground quietly, considering my boy—what he needs, how to help him. I've never seen him so withdrawn, so insolent. With anger twisting his face, I hardly recognize him. Although he refuses touch, I still have my voice. What can I say? Both light and darkness dance on my son's face. Isaac takes a step into the cave and puts his hands on his hips, a stance of authority, revealing his clothing. Do I see blood or just the flames leaping between us? Doubt seeks entrance, but I push it away. My son needs me.

"Son, are you hurt? If you are, please let me tend to you. I have a healing ointment that King Melchizedek made himself."

"You must not touch me, and your king's ointment will not help me," he utters, this time with anger in his voice. "I am no longer of this faith, of this family."

Hurt, I speed up my words. "Whatever your father did, he believed he was honoring Yahweh." When I see Isaac's face crumple, I push on. "Surely, your father will make this right. No doubt, he has an explanation. Yahweh would never seek your harm. You are the son of promise."

I softly sigh. Who am I to urge him to trust when my doubt

has driven me here, on a mother's wish that she had power to intervene?

"My father sacrificed me...for his One God."

My breath catches in my throat.

"Where is Abraham...your father? Why are you here alone?"

Isaac shrugs and sighs, as if my inquiry is beneath him.

I offer vulnerability as a peace offering. "Son, I too have questions. I followed the morning after you left. I snuck out of camp prepared to travel through the night if needed. I would have been with you sooner, but so much has transpired. Yahweh sent helpers to help me...find you." Caring witnesses flash before me including Zerah and his sister Yasmine, Ephron and his wife Lilah, and Melchizedek the King of Salem. Surely, all of them were sent to bring me to this moment.

Isaac stands silent, stoic. I hear the piercing cry of a hawk as she circles outside the cave. When he was a boy, Isaac learned to imitate the hawk's cry, "Awk, awk, awk." I remember Isaac exclaiming, "He says his own name, mother."

"Do you hear the hawk?" I say, grateful for a diversion from the cold silence. "Does she also seek her young in the night?"

"Are you listening?" he says gruffly. It strikes me that his voice is different. More like a man and less like a boy with fourteen years of living. More angry and less of the boyish joy I am accustomed to. All that has transpired has changed him.

"Please son, let me hold you," I utter. "Come sit by the fire with me. I love you, my one and only son."

He takes one half-step closer to me, lifting both palms in the air, fingertips pointing upwards. Another warning. Something red is splattered across his chest. The blood of the sacrifice he and his father made together? Although he holds himself stiffly, he seems strong in body. He made his way here after all.

"What happened son? Tell me about the sacrifice.... How can I help you?" Then I pause, thinking.... *How did you make it past the landslide?*

"Can you help someone who has laid under a pointed knife?" he asks coldly. "Can you breathe hope back into one from whom life was stolen? Can you enter the realm between this world and the next?"

"What matters is that you are here now. It is not too late." I am confused. It seems Moriah has embedded an arrow tip in my son's heart.[1] Impulsively I ask, "Did your father intend you as the sacrifice?" A vision comes unbidden.

I am the one tied to an altar and Abraham lifts a knife, with a holy fire in his eyes. Since terror has seized my voice, I beg with my eyes, plead for my life. One glance at his set chin tells me it is useless. His eyes are steely, determined. Terror, resignation and resentment come as the knife flinches, ready to make its plunge toward my heart.

Isaac calls me out of the vision, as if he shared it. "You as good as killed me, mother. You knew Father's blind faith. You could have come more quickly. You could have rescued me. You could have offered yourself to be the one." He shakes his head, disowning any remaining affection for me. "You cast out Ishmael, my brother, and Hagar, my second mother."

I hang my head in shame. He is correct.

"You let me go innocently like an ox being readied for slaughter."[2] He sighs. "Yes, he put me on the altar."

I reel in the accusation that presses hard on all my fears. My hands are shaking, and I ball them into fists, lest he see my hurt.

"Where is your father?"

"Why should I care?" he says, coldness in his voice. "I will never serve your so-called God, even if I still had the opportunity."

"My dear son," I say, my heart beating quickly, "I have made

[1] Or "get rid of every arrow tip in us." The implication is that we are carrying an arrow tip inside, a wound that weighs us down and keeps us from running our race with freedom." Hebrews 12:1 fn (TPT)

[2] And in the face of such oppression and suffering—silence. Not a word of protest, *not a finger raised to stop it.* Like a sheep to a shearing, like a lamb to be slaughtered, he went—oh so quietly, oh so willingly. Isaiah 53:7

many mistakes. Your father has done things he now regrets. We live with consequences from our actions, but the opportunity to serve Yahweh never leaves. There is still joy to be found. The promise still remains."

He laughs, a mocking chortle. "Do you think your regret absolves you from responsibility?"

"Isaac. My Isaac."

Suddenly rage contorts his face. "Don't you understand. Your Isaac is dead. Father sacrificed him. . . ." He sighs. "You can't touch me since the living cannot touch those crossing into Sheol."

I fall to my knees in shock and disbelief. "You are dead?" I say. "A spirit?" Again, I bow my head. I am guilty. Sweat is racing down my back. My mind cannot accept what my son is telling me. Finally, I whisper, "What do you want from me?"

"If you love me, join me now. Throw yourself off of the path. No one will know that it was not an accident. Then we can beee together foreverrrrrr."

The cadence in his voice reminds me of the snake I saw much earlier in this journey. Yet, my mother's heart refuses to doubt him. Just earlier, I told myself that I would give my life for him. Would my death honor him? Do I love him so much that I would go to live in the land of the dead? I whisper, "You would have me go where you are?"

Isaac's voice suddenly turns soft, drawn out like a vulture's cry, "You would beeeee with meeeee, motherrrr."

Oh, how I have longed to hear him say that simple word. Mother. All his other words fade away. Through fifty years of barrenness I longed, hoped, bargained for, and ultimately threw my handmaid at my husband for a chance to be called mother. *Mother* is why I am here in a cave, by myself, terrified. Is what he asks so difficult for a mother already full of years? Another vision swirls into the cave, almost as if commanded, to taunt me. . . .

I stand on the edge of the cliff, looking into the darkness. My heart slams against my chest. I slide my feet closer and closer to the edge. Rocks skitter over the edge. My feet refuse to move further. Isaac walks to me, takes my hand. "Don't worry mother, we will do it together. On the count of three. One…two…." Feeling the premature tug on my arms we both jump, but when I look beside me I don't see my son. "Isaac! I come to you," I scream as I fall to my demise.

I lay my hand on my chest to calm myself.

Isaac motions for me to follow him. My feet cannot help themselves. They shuffle after him, but keeping a safe distance from the edge, with Abram's staff securing my stance. Instead of being beside me, Isaac now stands five lengths away, balancing precariously on one of the rocks of the slide.

"Son, that is not safe!"

In a sky shut tight by the storm, the clouds now part to reveal a full moon. I see the narrow treacherous path, and the height of the cliff on which I stand. My knees tremble when I see how far I would plunge to my passing. Am I now the lamb moving toward slaughter? Driven by one obsessive thought…to be with my son? *Am I grain being sent to the threshing floor?*[3] A wind pushes my right side, making me feel unstable, like I could easily fall. My head swims, dizzy from the height and a son who is seeming less and less like my son.

Isaac's lips turn slightly upward with a mocking in his eyes. "The burial pit is now my father. The worms under the earth are my mother.[4] And now you will join me."

"Who are you?" I say, feeling a threat in his words. I move closer to him and suddenly see him fully. His skin is perfectly smooth, but Isaac's isn't. Isaac has a scar over his right eyebrow, one he came to believe makes him more rugged, like his brother Ishmael.

"You aren't my son! No, you are not Isaac!"

A bat interrupts, soaring over me and round and round my

[3] You shall come to your grave in ripe old age as a shock of grain comes up to the threshing floor in its season. Job 5:26 (RSV)

[4] If I hope only to live in the land of the dead, if I prepare for myself a bed in the darkness, If I speak to my *burial* pit, calling it "Father," and to the worms *in the earth*, calling them "Mother" and "Sister," Then where will I find my hope? And who will see it?" Job 17:13-14

head, like it has the power to uproot me, jolt me over the edge to my death.

"Help me, Yahweh," I say aloud.

The words of Melchizedek roll over me like a cleansing stream. "The test is not only for Abraham, it is yours…as a prophetess and a beloved of Yahweh." Remembering his kind eyes and empathetic stance, the fear slows down to where I can think. I move backwards into the cave, my eyes going between the apparition of Isaac, and the cave floor behind me where a rock could trip me.

Undeterred, the bat follows me, landing on the cave floor in front of the fire, in between me and the path. The vile creature spreads his wings wide, opens his mouth so wide that I see his teeth, all the way into his throat. He hisses a threat. I feel his anger at the failed entreaty.

I scream at the bat, "You have no power over me. You dislike that I do not act out my own death? Death does not belong to you. Yahweh reigns over death."

On an impulse, I lean over, pick up the white albino deer's hide and throw it at him.

A shriek echoes through the cave. In a high-pitched whine, I think I hear the devil's retort, "This isn't overrrrrr."

Was the bat real? I walk over, kneel down and flick the cloak like a wet garment, and to my shock, a bat flies out from under it and out of the cave. Even though it did not bite me, I check myself carefully for wounds. Bats carry a disease that can steal life. *The bat was not an apparition.*

I walk over to the entrance and look to the right and then to the left. No Isaac. No bat.

Feeling assured they are gone, I turn back toward my fire. My knees give way and I stumble, falling face down onto the stone floor of the Cave of Moriah. Blackness covers me.

[5] Since we, the children, are all creatures of flesh and blood, Jesus took on flesh and blood, so that by dying He could destroy the one who held power over death—the devil— and destroy the fear of death that has always held people captive. Hebrews 2:14-15

Suddenly I begin to rise, out of my body, up quickly toward the high ceiling, lighter than air. I look down on my body flat on the floor of the cave, unmoving. Having left my body, I am now able to see in the dark…like a bat. I hear cackles. Evil is all around me, carrying me upwards. *Shedim,* my mind tells me, the demons said to attend child sacrifice, demons in serpent bodies. A musky, offensive smell wafts around me, the smell of the Pharaoh the night he sought to assault me.

"Yahweh save me!"

As suddenly as I left my body, I am again face down on the cave floor. I will live to tell of this.

I roll over gingerly and test each part of my body. Each part moves slightly, but I am left with a heaviness, like I am under a pile of rocks. As if sand and soil weigh me down. *The way it must feel to be buried…*even though it seems that evil has fled for a more opportune time.[6] I cough until it seems I have no more air, and then I greedily slurp in a breath. *Evil tried to convince me that Isaac is dead. To get me to either kill myself or risk my life by continuing alone after Abraham.*

Then a thought comes that offers sweet comfort. *Whatever is happening on Moriah cannot invalidate the promise Yahweh swore to Abraham.*

Again, I hear the words of Melchizedek…. "Will you discern your gift? Will the eye that sees danger overcome untruth?" And then his benediction, "May the angels of the Lord stand beside you as you confront what you fear."

I fear Isaac's premature death.

I fear being barren once again.

I fear Yahweh might take what he has given.

I fear that Abraham has, once again, betrayed me.

Each of these are untruths to be overcome. Isaac is alive. I will

[6] The devil had no more temptations to offer that day, so he left Jesus, preparing to return at some other opportune time. Luke 4:13

never be childless again. *Yahweh's purpose will become clear. Abraham seeks to protect me.*

I say aloud to whatever angels may be nearby or even *shedim* still plotting and scheming to undo me, "Yahweh's purpose will become clear. I trust him as my shield and protector." Like a heavenly *so be it,* a mysterious peace descends from above, fluttering around my weary mind like the dove that finally returned to Noah. "Abram's test was whether he would go up to Moriah. Mine is whether I will go down. I want to return home."

At the moment, turning back is more than my battered body can bear. So I obey when sleep tugs at me. I crawl over and get the deer hide, knowing its purity cannot be stolen by evil. I get Lilah's cloak and wrap it tightly around me, and then choosing to trust the angels who must be nearby, I drift into a deep, dreamless state, as if slumber is the dividing line between death and life.

★ ★ ★

Daylight streams in from the cave's entrance and kisses my shoulder. In the place between sleep and wakefulness, I see angels inviting me to be a guest at a sacrifice made at the top of a mountain. A loud voice says, "Yahweh heard your entreaty. Take a seat of honor at God's table." When I sit at the table, there is a saddlebag, made for carrying valuables on a camel. A voice says, "Open it and enjoy the treasures that are left behind from battle." When I open it, I find a handcrafted copper dove. Its wings are coated in silver and its feathers shimmer with gold dust.[7]

A hawk squawks nearby and I startle, sad that the vision must end. Glancing outside, the position of the sun announces it is near the noon hour. Once again, underneath me is the white albino deer hide. My aged mind races. Where am I? Will my son once again come and tempt me? Are there angels nearby?

[7] "Kings who lead the armies are on the run! They are on the run! And the woman who stays at home *is ready, too,* ready to enjoy the treasures *that they've left behind!*" When they lay down among the campfires *and open the saddlebags, imagine what they'll find—a beautiful* dove, its wings covered with silver, its feathers a shimmering gold. Psalm 68:12-13

Looking around me all becomes clear. I went to sleep in the Cave of Moriah, with a sheer drop-off outside, a path that Isaac's apparition tempted me to jump off. *Evil masquerading as my son.*[8] Shaking off the remnants of sleep, I realize where I am. The wadi rock shelter, above where the flood came through carrying away the donkeys— Maya, Isaac's donkey, and Hamor the Nephilim donk. I sit up and stretch, completely mystified.

Did Zerah come back to the Cave of Moriah? Did he carry me all the way here?

Standing up to stretch, I note that my body seems lighter, less achy. I twist my injured foot, and my ankle allows it without complaint. I look down at my pallet and thrill to see fresh clothing, goat milk soap and a soft cloth for washing. There is a basin of water nearby. *Did Amah chase after me and prepare to serve me? Have the men at our camp deciphered my actions and waited nearby to whisk me home? Did Lilah intuit I would be here, where I last saw my beloved Maya?*

I see my supplies are with me from the Cave of Moriah. The flint rests on a stone. Next to it the healing ointment I depend on. Sticks are sorted and prepared for a fire. Lilah's cape lies neatly over another larger rock. Fresh food and water are nearby. I did not come here alone.

I walk over and check through the entrance. Seeing no one is in sight, I decide to quickly bathe with the goat soap and water, cleaning my face, arms and legs and washing my hair. A comb hiding behind the basin of water works the tangles out of my hair. Braiding it wet, I tie my gray-streaked hair with the cord that holds the kindling. The clothing is made of soft cotton with a matching cape and fits me loosely. I tie the purple belt around my waist. The tunic is the color of the sky, but the softness is extravagant. I imagine Amah's joy when I gift this clothing to

[8] No wonder they are *so good at it.* Satan himself poses as a messenger of heavenly light, so why should we expect less from his servants—*plodding over the earth,* pretending to be ministers of righteousness—but in the end, they'll get what's coming to them. 2 Corinthians 11:14-15

her. *It is my turn to serve.* My treasure is the wisdom that lingers after a terrible attack.

When I am finished bathing, I use the same cloth to clean the camel skin covers for my sandals. I take a long drink of water, and gratefully consume the dried meat and fruit. Mystery has accompanied me on every part of this journey, and now the riddle has reached far beyond my ability to understand. Am I still Sarah, wife of Abraham, a prophetess with 105 years of living? Were the shedim who carried me out of my body remnants of my childhood idol worship, the day I spent in the temple? Were they angry that my parents offered me, and that I was rescued from the temple worshippers consuming me as objects of their worship?

Moving outside the rock shelter, I warm myself in the sun. The desert heat feels like a warm embrace after so much rain. Impulsively, I unbraid my long hair to let it dry, musing how Abraham still delights in my long, still-thick tresses. As the minutes pass, snatches of memory come of how I moved from the mountain cave on the path to Moriah to here, the remembrance as sweet and fleeting as falling stars, one after another.

Warm, soft hands grasp my elbows.

Gentle words like an unwritten melody ring within my ears.

A warm current, like that of a river, carries me with no jarring, bumps or fear.

Water is poured into my dried lips and streams gently down my throat.

My weary body is laid on a comfortable pad, with warm, dry blankets.

A voice softly sings over me, like the voice of an angel.[9]

When my hair is dry, I once more comb it, gathering strands of hair from the left and pulling it over to the right, to create a

[9] The Eternal your God is standing right here among you, and He is the champion who will rescue you. He will joyfully celebrate over you; He will rest in His *love for you;* He will joyfully sing because of you *like a new husband.* Zephaniah 3:17

single loose braid, just as my mother taught me to do as a young woman. Later I will braid it fully for travel. Memories of the woman I loved before the pagan religion stole her warms me. Her playing a game with me of hiding and seeking among the trees at Mamre. *Mother, at 105 years, I still carry you with me. I pray you found a way to seek the one true God.*

Yasmine said she would get me clean clothing. Did she or Zerah carry me here? I go back inside to gather what little I have. In the corner, I see a tent, folded up for carrying with me. Outside I hear the sound of many feet. I recognize the sound. *Abraham's men.*

I take a deep breath and then steady myself as I walk outside to meet my fate.

But instead of the men from our camp, it is King Abimelech with ten of his soldiers, and his royal stallions. *Wasn't my last stay in your harem enough?* My heart races and I try to duck back into the cave unseen. Uninvited memories race through my mind. Nakedness. Vulnerability. Loss of privacy. The leering of foreign men. Then I hear his voice, lilted and seemingly concerned....

"Sarah, I see you are here. Does Abraham allow his wife to travel unguarded? Thank Yahweh that we found you."

I am startled by his calling on the name of the one God. Startled, but unconvinced.

Remember dignity Sarah. Putting Lilah's wool cape over my shoulders, I step outside, holding my head high with my husband's walking stick in my right hand, regretting my hair being on display for his enjoyment. My head swims like I might faint. The sun is too warm for this garment, but I cannot bear the thought of him seeing me without it. His men stand waiting for their King's command to scurry up the rocks with their weapons. When this happens, they will enter the cave and know with surety that I am unaccompanied.

"Sarah, your beauty remains beyond comparison. Your hair shines like burnished copper in the sun," the King says impertinently, like a young boy finding hidden sweets. His voice is smooth as oil, long practiced by manipulating a legion of women to do as he pleases. Yet in his words is a hidden sword.[10] "May I ask why you are here…alone?"

I look off to my left and right, as if searching for my party and then make my voice pointed. "Yes, it is Yahweh who delivers." I glare at him, willing him to remember how Yahweh intervened last time I was in his courts. "May I ask what brings you this long distance?"

"Why, kings and prophets long to know what transpires when Yahweh comes down to earth.[11] What else would have a woman alone in the wilderness…unprotected?"

We are now in a gambit with a high cost to the victor. He continues, "I heard a rumor that your husband has been at Moriah. Surely you wouldn't have chased after him, would you? This part of the wilderness is known for its sudden floods."

"Our affairs are not yours to judge," I say with all the boldness I can muster. "I am waiting for my escort to return from scouting."

King Abimelech laughs, "An escort? Unless your escort returns, we must insist on bringing you back to safety. After all, I couldn't abandon a woman who has shared intimacy with me."

My heart jumps in disgust. "This is not true," I say firmly. "We were not intimate."

"You worry about my men hearing? They are sworn to secrecy. They would never tell what they've seen in my harem."

He seeks to reduce me to a harlot. I look at the men and see their unsuccessful attempts to hide their sneers.

[10] Oh, how his *pleasant* voice is smoother than butter, while his heart is enchanted by war. Oh, how his words are smoother than oil, and yet each is a sword drawn *in his hand.* Psalm 55:21

[11] You just need to know with every fiber of your being that the Eternal, and no one else, is God up in heaven and down here on the earth. Deuteronomy 4:39

"Perhaps this can be our little secret, you and I, if you stay with me, more permanently, in a royal position. Since your husband broke faith once again. Like he did when he went after my livestock and riches through his own great deceit." When I hesitate, he presses on, "Yes, Abraham knew what he wanted before I took you. Now it is your turn to have power, influence and wealth." He clears his voice. "There will be no requirements of you. Only your wisdom."

Broken faith. Deceit. Power, influence, wealth. These words open up a heart wound that has just started healing. Abraham went on his quest without even informing me. His leaving with Isaac opened a rift, a crack. I can run away from our problems or sit with the unknowing, letting love fortify my resolve. An attack is always built on illusion, like Isaac's ghost. Magical thinking. Anything that Abimelech offers me will cost me my dignity.

"I will wait," I say. "Here."

"A prophetess, I hear? Such a woman would be a treasured asset to any kingdom, but one it seems your husband has not discerned." Abimelech continues. "And where has your escort gone?"

He will not let me escape his clutches easily. Is this another of the trials Melchizedek hinted at when he said there were tests to come? Shaking beneath my cloak, I reason that he can only tempt me to the extent I participate. I will stand eye to eye with this mountain lion. "My escort searches for two donkeys who were lost here days earlier."

"Ah, so you have been on a journey. If I may be so bold, it seems you ran after Abraham and now you run away from him. I do not believe he would want me to leave you here alone."

I sigh, asking Yahweh to guide me to words that cannot be easily manipulated.

"We can wait for a time," Abimelech says with a mocking bow. "Then we will all need to vacate because dark clouds are on the horizon."

I glance up at a clear, azure sky. At the edge of the horizon, there is one small cloud, the size of a hand.[12]

"You choose. You can come with all of us back to my home. Or I will personally escort you, by myself, back to your own camp." He smirks. "You can reward me with your affections."

He dares to hint at intimacy? At 105 years of age? I nod my head as if I am confused and weak. "Give me time…to prepare to travel with your party." With that, I go back into the cave, hoist off the wool cloak and oh so slowly braid my hair more tightly for travel, again using the cord from the firewood. I will never walk with Abimelech alone. I drag the tent close to the entrance in case Yahweh provides a way of escape.[13] I am more wilderness-ready than Abimelech imagines. On an impulse, I creep to the rock shelter's entrance hoping against hope they have moved on. Instead two of his captains sit on one of the lower stones. I am now under guard.

Yahweh, help me remember who I am, where I am going, where I come from.[14]

Kneeling on the white doeskin, I begin to pray, first softly to myself and then words weaving together into a song. Prayer has been said to move mountains, so perhaps it can remove a seductive king. I will continue until he insists I come out.

As desert enemies offer false peace,
Does favor promise temptation's release?
Will you bring an escape only I can see?
Only you know, Yahweh. You know.

[12] See Isaiah 48:19

[13] Any temptation you face will be nothing new. But God is faithful, and he will not let you be tempted beyond what you can handle. But he always provides a way of escape so that you will be able to endure and keep moving forward. 1 Corinthians 10:13.

[14] See John 13:3-4.

Is waiting better than priceless jewels?
Though desires sting like fiery fuel?
Will arrow wounds find sweet relief?
Only you know, Yahweh. You know.

Shall my end come at a ripe old age?
After I've offered my gift as a sage?
Still seen mysteries and beheld grace.
Only you know, Yahweh. You know.

Shall my tent stakes be widely spread?[15]
Will my fold find holy ground to tread?
See my offspring become a scarlet thread?
It is your promise, Yahweh. You know.

"Sarah, it is time." King Abimelech's voice resounds like he commands an army. I shudder. The canyon amplifies noise, so it feels like he is in this hole with me. "Please prepare yourself. I will come up to the cave to escort you down soon. You can ride behind me on my royal stallion."

The thought of being pressed up against a vulgar king, being jolted again and again against his body, repulses me. I put on my cape once more as a layer of protection and pick up a skin of water and the remaining food. I must distract him.

"If you want to speak privately, I can come into the cave," Abimelech says.

A donkey whinnies in the distance. I step outside to make an excuse, when I see Yasmine coming around the bend with two donkeys, Hamor, the Nephilim donkey, and Isaac's cherished donkey Maya.

"Maya! Hamor!" I exclaim in utter joy and relief. "Yasmine."

[15] Eternal One: Sing, childless woman, you who have never given birth….Enlarge your house. You are going to need a bigger place; don't underestimate the amount of room that you'll need. So build, build, build. You will increase in every direction to *fill the world.* Isaiah 54:1-3

I take off my cape to carefully navigate down the rocks, unsure whether my knees and ankles will make it. I set my face like a rock.[16] The King nods at one of his men who scurries upwards to help me safely come down the rocks. He reaches out his hands for my cape, and I reluctantly hand it to him. He drapes the cape over his left arm and extends his right hand. Letting him clasp my hand is not my preference, but I remember that he is a person, not so unlike us. I imagine him as someone who struggles to find his compass. I smile my thanks.

I move quickly toward Yasmine, and she nods toward Maya, already blanketed and harnessed so that I can ride her safely. She helps me onto the donk, walks over to the guardsman holding my cape and extends her open hand. Mesmerized by this fierce, tall, redheaded woman, he quickly hands it over.

While King Abimelech is distracted, I lean over and give Maya a tearful embrace. I whisper into her ear, "You have returned to me and to Isaac sweet donkey."

Skipping lightly up the rocks leading up to the rock shelter, Yasmine reappears with the tent and other supplies, and then moves quickly back down to Hamor, strapping them on his back. She turns to face King Abimelech.

"Thanks be to Yahweh!" Her eyes flame like the sun causing King Abimelech to avert his gaze. "Yahweh himself protects Sarah, prophetess and clan leader, wife of Abraham, the great chieftain." Her countenance is fierce, undaunted majesty.

Does Yahweh see me first as prophetess and clan leader before he sees me as Abraham's wife?

Yasmine moves Hamor closer to Maya and me, revealing a sword in a sheath attached to her Nephilim donkey. Gold glints on Yasmine's chest. Her deep purple linen vest is embroidered with thread beaten out of real gold. Such a garment is costly

[16] Because the Lord, the Eternal, helps me I will not be disgraced; so, I set my face like a rock, confident that I will not be ashamed. Isaiah 50:7

and heavy to wear. She is dressed for battle. She speaks again to King Abimelech. "Sarah walks by a compass you do not know." She smiles with unbridled strength, "Perhaps, you might do what kings do best….run after your next conquest."

A shiver runs down my spine…*so bold.* Did Yasmine hear what Abimelech said to me about first running after Abraham and then running away from him? *It would be impossible to hear around the curve where she emerged from.*

Abimelech is stunned. "Two women? One masquerading as a soldier?" he says with a nervous laugh. He glances at his men, and they put their spears in front of them. A warning.

Yasmine grasps the ornate hilt of her sword, ready to draw it, while keeping eye contact with Abimelech. Hamor, the Nephilim donkey growls and paws the ground, reading the danger. His narrowed eyes are fixed on Abimelech. It's been said that one Nephilim donkey can fight off 300 oxen. Although I should be afraid, I marvel at the standoff. Yasmine is what we call chayil, acquainted with battle.[17]

How does Abimelech reason? Selfishly, no doubt. It seems I can decipher his thoughts as they flash across his countenance.

Yahweh interceded the last time I took her into my care.

My men and I suffered before Yahweh released us through Abraham's prayer.

She walked away with my livestock and gold.

"I will allow it." Abimelech finally says haughtily, although I see fear in the edges of his eyes. He snaps his fingers and the guardsmen step back on either side to allow us a path through their party. The King throws a barb before we leave. "We are on toward Moriah to meet with the great clan leader, Abraham, and talk about his wandering wife Sarah and her, errr…, soldier, a red-haired woman."

[17] Who can find an aishes chayil (a woman of valor, an excellent wife Prov 12:4)? For her worth is far above rubies. Proverbs 31:10 (OJB). Strongs Greek defines chayil as a "force, whether or men or other resources…. valiant, virtuous, war, worthy.

He mocks a mighty follower of Yahweh. The most direct path to Moriah is blocked by a landslide, but since he appears to know all, I will leave that to them. Warned by Melchizedek, Abraham will return by a different route.

The men fall back, as we walk our donkeys directly through their royal regalia, their boasts, insinuations and taunts, and their oppressive harem system that devalues and destroys women. Yasmine winks at me, a smile beginning at her lips. I am heading home, where Yahweh is respected and dignity is valued.

A new battle is likely ahead. How will my charge into the wilderness with strangers, who are now devoted friends, be received by my husband? By my clan? How will Abraham and I navigate the muddy waters that now threaten to separate us? And what of my son, Isaac? By faith I see his return, but fear does not let go of the heart easily. I glance over at my glowing companion, and she throws me an easy smile, the sword safely sheathed and strapped onto Hamor. So many questions. I long to ask her about Zerah and so much more.

How did you find the donkeys, alive and unhurt?

What happened when you walked into town from Ephron's cave?

How did you know Abimelech would attack?

Were you nearby when the bat hissed and the evil spirit masqueraded as Isaac?

How did you become *chayil*?

In truth, my mind is weary. And so, aged and story-hungry as I am, I decide to ask nothing. Only you know, Yahweh. Only you know.

I will make sure your descendants are as many as the stars of the heavens and the grains of sand on the shores. I reaffirm My earlier promises…"

Genesis 22:17

CHAPTER TEN
Song of Sand

RIDING ON HAMOR WITH MAYA BESIDE US, I travel toward camp. Away from the wadi where the donkeys were both lost and found, and where Abimelech intruded. Away from where Yasmine and I camped last night, the hill smelling of cedar where the Pharaoh owl swooped down on a mouse. I lean over and whisper to Hamor… "Today, you will see your new home on the outskirts of our camp…with Maya." He shakes his head, seeming to be pleased.

Although our desert camp is temporary in its very nature, it is an abode adorned by Yahweh's presence for as long as our clan stays.[1] Picturing our sprawling desert village makes me smile. Our transition from living in our spacious stone home and gated compound in Ur to a semi-nomadic existence was jarring. Many times, I had to fight the impulse to complain. Now, after sojourning from the wadi rock shelter, to Ephron's cave, to the Cave of Moriah, our leather, camel hide, felt and wool tents with soft rugs covering the floors feel like a luxury. I will even welcome the pungent smell of animals that drifts through camp, depending on the winds. After all, meat, cheese, milk and skins come from our short-horned cattle, oxen, sheep, donkeys, goats

[1] *Your teachings are true;* Your decrees sure. Sacredness adorns Your house, O Eternal One, forevermore. Psalm 93:5

and camels who graze in the fields surrounding our enclosure.

Achy from my travels, I will ask for water to bathe, drawn and heated by my handmaids from one of our three wells. How I wish the hot springs off of Ephron's property were nearer. Choosing to believe Isaac will return, I imagine Abraham, Isaac and I traveling half a day from our encampment to the small oasis that has trickling water, springs, and numerous palm trees. One of Isaac's favorite places in this barren landscape. To the human eye, there is little vegetation near our camp to feed our large flocks, but the livestock hungrily jerk out the small plants that root underneath the desert soil. Going home means I may be far from my new friends, Zerah and Yasmine, Lilah and Ephron and Melchizedek. But I will send messengers to invite them to partake of our hospitality, including staying in our five-tent enclave for traveling guests. These have been placed on the side of our village where the hills provide a wind block, sheltering our guests from the sharp winds and occasional storms.

It is not a city like Ur with a canal system and running water, but it is ours.

Yes, the word *home* whispers comfort, but also anxiety at how I will be received. Yasmine left me this morning after I requested to travel the last part of the path on my own. She surprised me with her insistence that I take Hamor the Nephilim donkey as a gift.

"Hamor was given by Yahweh to watch over you. And Maya needs him." The authority and love in Yasmine's voice said that arguing was futile.

At the campsite early this morning, Yasmine used a rope to make it easier for me to mount the Nephilim donkey. As the donkey carries me, I rehearse the steps backwards she taught me in case I need to dismount. *Hold tightly to the rope around Hamor's neck. Swing your right leg over the donkey. Slowly lower yourself down.*

I glance at Maya. Beneath her dark, nonjudgmental eyes, I see exhaustion. *Ah, another way we share a fellowship of pain.* Last night at the campsite, I found some yarrow and sage which I mixed with the oats Yasmine brought, hoping these might cure my donkey's dullness. As if she knows my thoughts, Maya shakes her head at me and brays. I glance at her legs, slender fetlocks and hocks, knees and shanks. Compared to a camel, her legs are graceful, some might say, even charming. Yet these legs allow her to bear loads that are unimaginable.[2] *Yes, Maya, I see your vigor.*

I stroke Hamor as my way of asking him to go easy with me. His slow, steady pace reminds me to trust my decision to come down before seeing—for myself—that Isaac is still alive. Slowness also allows me to tend the tiny trembling flame of remembrance…all that happened on my journey.

Although I am disappointed I did not make it to the mount of sacrifice, two men of God went on ahead of me, Zerah and Melchizedek. Isn't this enough? Other reasons line up in my thinking like soldiers saluting my choice.

Yahweh does take away life in order to give it back.

Surely Yahweh told Abraham to *offer* Isaac, not to slaughter him.

Child sacrifice is a futile attempt to appease gods who are not gods.

Yahweh has tenderly cared for me this entire journey. Would he do less for an innocent boy?

Hamor the Nephilim donkey stops for a moment, jerking me momentarily back to the present. Maya stops as well, taking the opportunity to eat some weeds by the wayside. Hamor looks around, unsure, and then walks over by Maya to munch.

[2] Andy Merrifield, *The Wisdom of Donkeys: Finding Tranquility in a Chaotic World.*

Sometimes, I forget how willful donkeys can be. Moving one donkey along can be hard enough, but two? Using the rope around Hamor's neck, I lower myself slowly off of his back, sighing in relief when my feet touch the ground, and then tie them to a nearby tree. I sit down with the packet of goat cheese and dried meat Yasmine prepared for me, as well as the skin of milk. I lean against a slender tree for shade and rest.

While I join the donkeys in a time of refreshment, wonder wraps itself around me like Lilah's wool cape, now draped over the donkey's neck, heavy and full of untold stories. Are these mysteries to be shared or only silently savored, lest Abraham and whoever else that hears proclaim me senile or incompetent, the worst fears of an old woman?[3]

After evil incited me to kill myself through a vicious lie, I am surprised to find that I hold Isaac more lightly, allowing room for his own story.[4] Is there a larger purpose I have yet to see?

The sensation of leaving my body during the attack is still as clear as the unstirred water of a spring-fed pond—I rose up quickly with no real sense of motion as if carried by an invisible force, saw my body below me face down on the floor of the cave, heard the whispers of evil Shedim, cried out to Yahweh for deliverance, and immediately found myself back within my body.

Unlike a dream, that time out of my body still circulates in my bloodstream and thrums in my head. Yes, evil took aim at mind, body, emotions and soul. I let each attack come forward in my thinking, and then ask Yahweh to cast it to the wind.

The vision of being pulled off of my donkey and dragged into the forest.

Being told to jump by the ghostly imposter of Isaac.

The bat hissing at me with its sharp teeth.

Being lifted from my body by demons.

[3] ...and I think you will agree that the mystery of godliness is great: He was revealed in the flesh, proven right in the Spirit; He was seen by the heavenly messengers, preached to outsider nations. He was believed in the world, taken *up to the heavens* in glory. 1 Timothy 3:16

[4] Each person has his or her own burden to bear *and story to write.* Galatians 6:5

Did Yasmine come and carry me down the path to Moriah all the way to the wadi rock shelter where we waited out the flash flood? What surprises me most is that I did not ask. The words *divine intervention* come to mind, or as we once explained to Isaac, *Yahweh entering our story.* But is it Abraham's story, Isaac's story or Sarah's story? Then I hear with clarity, as if Melchizedek still accompanies me. "The true story belongs to Yahweh alone."

I picture a tiny shoot cultivated by the Eternal, throwing out roots further than the heart can see.[5] A promise must start as a tiny seed, one that could easily be trampled or disregarded. After it grows into a tree, mother birds build nests in the branches, so that their kind may fill the earth.[6]

I think back to my encounter with King Abimelech just the day before, in the very place where the flash flood took place. All was different after Yasmine confronted iniquity that masquerades as power. As Yasmine and I made our way away from the encounter with Abimelech toward the hill where the Pharaoh owl dropped onto the mouse, our words were few. Sensing my need for space, she rode ahead. With her gleaming vest and flaming hair, she exuded light as if Yahweh used her passion as the kindling for a holy fire.[7]

As we sat at the fire last night, Yasmine took off her beautiful vest with threads of pure gold. Then we both undid our braided hair, like sisters would do together. Finally, we set about the needed tasks together as equals, smiling at our companionship and gratitude for each other. But before we retired, her mood turned serious.

"Sarah, you seem heavy in your thoughts."

"Yes," I said. "Women look for their worth in their relationships, just as I have looked for worth in Isaac, instead of Yahweh." I sigh. "What is my purpose? It burns in one moment

[5] Then, oh then, a tiny shoot cultivated and nurtured by the Eternal will emerge *new and green, promising* beauty and glory. Isaiah 4:2

[6] Mustard seeds are minute, tiny—but the seeds grow into trees. Flocks of birds can come and build their nests in the branches. Matthew 13:32

[7] Because this is the way they speak, I am going to turn My words in your mouth into a fire. A *fire* that will consume these people; they are nothing but kindling for *My fury.* Jeremiah 5:14

like a fire and flees in the next like smoke. This leaves me unsure what to believe. Why does following Yahweh bring such chaos?"

Yasmine nodded. "Chaos ensues when the demon princes are threatened by the pure of heart. They despise the blessing of Yahweh, one they cannot receive. Every time righteousness prevails, their time grows shorter."

Suddenly I felt clearer. "Melchizedek is a prince of peace. Demon princes are imposters."

Yasmine wrapped her arms around her knees, warming herself by the fire. "Chaos was used by Yahweh to create all that is beautiful. But evil is threatened by those who see the unseen…"

"Like a prophetess," I said.

Her voice became even firmer, yet merciful. "Yes, as a prophetess, these powers seek to stop your seeing, prevent your claiming your gift, stop you from alerting others to spiritual realities. Evil would exploit your vulnerability by temporarily satisfying fleshly desires."[8]

"Abimelech," I replied. "Isaac, the bat, and the *shedim*."

Yasmine shook her head to loosen her glowing tresses, a gesture all women know as an act of freedom. "Yahweh's plan cannot be thwarted by any power or evil principality. During your attack you were accompanied by angels."

"The unseen," I whisper. "I wondered."

"Then you were carried to safety so that your feet did not hit a rock." She pauses, choosing her words carefully. "For a time, Yahweh allowed evil to press heavy on your shoulders, in order to disarm it, show his victory over it."[9]

Breathing in peace, I prayed silently…. *Yahweh, please instruct me in the warfare of righteousness.*

"From the beginning evil has wanted to undo women. No other part of creation can nourish an entirely new individual

[8] They're *snakes* slithering into the houses of vulnerable women, women gaudy with sin, to seduce them. *These reptiles can* capture them because these women are weak and easily swayed by their desires. 2 Timothy 3:6

[9] He disarmed those who once ruled over us—those who had overpowered us. *Like captives of war,* He put them on display to the world to show His victory over them *by means of the cross.* Colossians 2:15

who holds the spirit and breath of Yahweh. You were attacked as one who carried the son of promise."

"Like Eve?" I said.

She nodded solemnly. "I fear that women will always be in the Evil One's sights."

Before we slept, I asked if I could wash her feet and she nodded, her eyes tender. I took a basin of warm water, goat's soap, and the healing ointment. Following the example of Melchizedek washing my feet, I attended to her, slowly and tenderly, giving each toe, each curve of each instep careful attention. The sweet odor of the black cottonwood salve, goat's soap and the herbs I added wafted around us. It seemed such a small thank you but such a great intimacy. Our sages say that pride changed angels into demons, and hospitality turns mere humans into ministering angels. Now I have seen for myself that dignity is often found on one's knees.

The possibilities embedded in Yasmine's words seem endless. It may take my remaining years to decipher them. Suddenly Melchizedek's words come back to me...."When the intersection of Heaven and Earth occurs, Yahweh draws together all that are his."[10]

Yasmine told me she would leave in the early hours, so I decided to do the same. I am impatient to be moving back toward camp, to see if my son is already there, waiting. Untying the donkeys and keeping a hold of both ropes, I look at Hamor and realize I didn't count the cost of having to mount him again. If I were to fall, who would find me? Do I still have the strength to pull myself up? Maya lifts her snout and whinnies softly. Maya is lower to the ground, but Hamor has a better saddle. I was chosen for this...the warfare of Yahweh. If I can wage warfare in a cave,

[10] ...a plan that will climax when the time is right as *He returns to create order and unity*—both in heaven and on earth—when all things are brought together under the Anointed's *royal rule*. Ephesians 1:10

I certainly can lift myself onto a Nephilim donkey. Following Yasmine's instructions, I pull myself up onto the saddle with ease. When I nudge Hamor, he moves again. I sigh in relief.

A gust of wind pulls at my garments and swirls dirt around the donkey's feet. Maya and Hamor both lift their snouts in unison and sniff the air, determining whether there is a threat. Now I have two donkey protectors instead of just one. Yasmine's words swirl around me as well. When I asked whether the bat, Isaac and *shedim* were examples of evil pushing back, she agreed. *Did she already know all I had suffered?* Yasmine knew the attack could never undermine the promise. But even more intriguing were her last words to me before she departed. I asked, "Will I see you again?" She replied, "The wind stirs around us with a will of its own; we hear it and see its work, but we do not understand its origin or where it will go."[11]

The words come back to me that Yahweh said to Abraham, his promise of many descendants coming through Isaac. The last time he gave it, the wording was different. Our descendants would not only be as many as the stars in the Heavens, but also as many as the sand on the shores. Were the stars in the Heavens the covenant promise for Isaac, and the sand on the shores for Ishmael? I remember Ishmael's plaintive cry when he learned that Isaac would now inherit the promise, "What will be left for me father?"

A song begins to form in my mind, a song of sand. I laugh to myself. Am I becoming a traveling minstrel who chooses to sing her songs to donkeys? Still the words flow as smooth as honey. The words are so simple, a child could know them. Perhaps even a man-child born of a handmaid to a patriarch.

Song of sand, treasure sweet
Bearing fruit for all to eat

[11] See John 3:8

Given by the one Most High
To all, counted in his sight[12]

Song of sand, promise true
Plans of love for me and you
Whether you are far or near
Yahweh leans in with his ear

Song of sand, covenant new
Promise you are still in view
Trusting Yahweh for rebirth
Thoughts that touch all on earth

Song of sand, Ishmael's song
Peace that overcomes all wrong
Knowing you are in his plan
Yahweh writing in the sand[13]

Moved and cut by my self-protective ways toward one of the sons of the promise, I give Hamor a push with my feet to keep moving. All the thinking has wearied me. I pat Hamor's neck, wrap the rope around my hand, and close my eyes, repeatedly nodding my head and then waking.

I come back into full awareness when the path begins to slant downward. We are now on the path with the drop-off, the only part of this solitary journey I have dreaded. If my memory is clear, this is where the snake first appeared and the Pharaoh owl almost knocked me off of a donkey. My heart feels agitated like it would rip apart bone and flesh to leap out.

Ten feet ahead of us, a sand cat suddenly prances into the middle of the trail, around six handspans tall. He is so close I can

[12] Your people would have *multiplied* to become like the grains of sand, and your children would be like grains of wheat. And they would be forever in My mind and My presence. Isaiah 49:19

[13] Moses says in the law that we are to kill such women by stoning. What do You say about it?.... Jesus bent over and wrote something in the dirt with His finger. John 8:5-6

smell him. Bold red streaks run across his cheeks and his fur is blotchy and matted around his nose. His eyes are wild. I discern hunger.

Just when I think of enticing him to leave by throwing the rest of my dried meat, I gasp. Coming around a curve in the path is my husband on a donkey. Both wild joy and fear rush over me.

Abraham is alone. *Where is Isaac?*

The two of us have now hemmed the cat in. Abraham raises a hand, and puts his finger over his lips, instructing me to be still and quiet.

"Hooo–wah," he yells out in what I guess to be a call of an owl. "Hooo–wah!"

I take in a breath trying to prevent panic from radiating into my hands, disturbing the donkeys. The mangy cat turns and hisses at Abraham, as Abraham moves his donkey forward.

I put my hand on Abraham's staff tied on the side of Hamor.

Suddenly an owl swoops overhead and drops onto the cat like he is a mere mouse, dragging him toward the edge. The owl releases him and the cat crashes through some brush and disappears.

Hamor whinnies and Maya shakes her head. Both seem only slightly perturbed that their territory has been violated. I am shaken. As Abraham and I look at each other, both stunned, my mind seeks to process his arrival back at camp before me. Now it is all so clear....

Abraham was a day ahead of me on the trails.

The flash flood in the wadi stole our donkeys.

Zerah carried me from the wadi rock shelter to Ephron's cave.

Ephron and Lilah ministered to me.

Melchizedek built a fire and washed my feet.

Hamor bolted back to where Zerah found Abraham's staff.

Melchizedek left me in the cave of Moriah.

Of course, Abraham returned home before me.

My husband gets off his donkey and slowly bridges the gap between us. I take in his gray wavy hair, large eyebrows and dark brown eyes brimming with kindness. He catches me as I maneuver off of Hamor, and we embrace. I slide my head into the soft spot between his shoulder and chest to remind myself of the special place that is only mine.

"You smell good," he says, reminding me of the sweet-smelling healing ointment I rubbed into Yasmine's feet.

Whispering into his neck, my voice husky, I ask, "How did you know where I would be?"

"Melchizedek," he says simply, as we step back from each other grasping each other's hands. "He found us preparing to leave after the sacrifice."

"The sacrifice?" I ask wearily.

"In the end, a ram that God provided in the thicket."[14]

In his words *in the end,* I hear more to be told, words that may not come easily. From my time with Yasmine, I've learned to be still and wait. My head suddenly fills with a foggy mist. I feel faint.

"Yahweh provides," I say, no longer thinking just about Abraham and Isaac, but also of my own journey.

Giving my hands a final squeeze, Abraham walks over to take a good look at Hamor. "I must admit the donkey surprises me. A Nephilim, I see."

I smile, happy to have something of value to offer. "Yes, a generous gift from those who ministered to me."

I note to myself that the few words we do say sprout up out of layers of undisclosed meaning, like the ground underneath a

[14] Abraham glanced up and saw a ram behind him with its horns caught in the thicket. He went over, dislodged the ram, and offered it up as a burnt offering in the place of his son. Genesis 22:13

tree. Once, as part of Isaac's schooling, we decided to dig beside a cedar. A foot's length underneath the surface mat of decomposing needles, leaves, small roots and other bramble surrounding the tree, was a type of soil so smooth and black, Isaac wanted to taste it. "Mother, it is making me hungry! Will you make some bean paste for our bread?" I remember replying, "Isaac, the tree likes to eat just as much as you do!"

How Abraham and I will send out new roots, I do not know.

Abraham smiles and reaches over to touch my hair. From all our years together he knows how I long to go straight into the depths of a matter. But it is best to allow a man time to find the words he needs. I will harness my words.[15] When I speak too quickly, I sometimes find myself adrift on my own impetuousness, instead of being rooted in Yahweh's wisdom.

"Would you like to ride on Hamor? My friend Yasmine made a rope to make him easier to mount. I could sit on Maya."

"Yes, I think I would."

Once we are each on a donkey, we move forward side by side, Abraham's donkey now trailing behind on a rope. Maya sighs, content to be carrying me once again.

"Were you surprised that I followed you?" I ask, knowing that since he saw Melchizedek, he may know more of my story than I know of his.

"I was surprised you made it so far. Yet from the morning we left, it was a cost I had to count. You were never far from my thoughts." He tugs at his beard. "Melchizedek did not tell me much. Just that you were below blocked by a landslide, and that you were protected. I need not try to go after you." Abraham chuckles. "I would say in the fierceness of his eyes that he was giving me an injunction."

"I have experienced that," I smile. "There was another way

[15] Listen, open your ears, harness your desire to speak, and don't get worked up into a rage so easily, my brothers and sisters. Human anger *is a futile exercise that* will never produce God's kind of justice *in this world.*
James 1:19-20

down the mountain?"

"Yes, Melchizedek showed us a path on the back side of the mountain that carried us around to the front. It was steeper at points and even rockier but eventually we found our way back to the more traveled path."

Abraham points upward and I look up to see the same owl that pushed the sand cat off the edge of the cliff. His large wings cast a shadow but also remind me of the risks of the wilderness. Picturing my husband and son on a trail more treacherous than the one I experienced sends a shudder down my back.

Abraham speaks. "Melchizedek said something intriguing... that just as I had my test on Moriah, you had a test to go through as well."[16]

"Yes, it seemed Yahweh tested me moment by moment and then refreshed me every morning. The Most High prevailed."[17]

"I felt the same way," Abraham says. I see in his eyes a new kind of respect, born out of two people each having their own battle, yet somehow fighting for the same thing.

The breeze tosses the trees. Branches rustle as the wind takes off the old to make room for the new. The smell of pine clears my nose and opens my senses. After being so cold on the mountain, the sun now inserts itself through the boughs of trees. It is both hot and windy, a sign that a storm could be brewing.

"Sarah," Abraham continues, "There is so much to tell and so much to hear."

"Yes," I say, wondering where to begin. Another gust of wind charges across the path sideways, blowing the sheep's wool cloak off of Maya. "Lilah's cloak!" I exclaim.

Abraham pulls Hamor to a stop, quickly lowers himself off, and, keeping a hand on the two ropes holding the donkeys, manages to maneuver himself to the edge of the path, where he

[16] After a period of time, God decided to put Abraham to the test. Eternal One: Abraham! Abraham: I am right here. Genesis 22:1

[17] You examine them morning by morning; You test them moment by moment. Job 7:18

scoops up the cloak. "Would you like me to tie it to Hamor?" he asks gently.

"Please," I say, relieved we did not lose a cloak or spook another donkey in the wind.

"Who is Lilah?" Abraham says as we start again toward camp.

"She and her husband Ephron own a high-ceilinged cave, set in a hillside, near Hebron. They ministered to me after I fell off of Hamor and hurt my ankle." I continue, knowing my husband has no context for these happenings. "She is a believer in the Most High God. Her husband Ephron is a healer. We had a lively conversation about the risk of believing."

Before Abraham can ask more, the wind picks up as we turn onto the final stretch into our camp, this time hurling dirt to and fro.

"A sandstorm may be coming," Abraham says, concerned. They often come on the heels of a thunderstorm.

"Perhaps we should hurry. Isaac still dreads sandstorms," I say, my thoughts still never far from my son. "Remember when Isaac was five, how he hid from a sandstorm in the nurse's tent under a blanket, while we were searching frantically? By the time we found him, I was weeping, but he cried out, 'I am a donkey. If I don't see the dust, I won't be afraid.'" Glancing at my husband, I realize he has not said a word about Isaac. "Where is our son?"

"After the sacrifice, Isaac wanted to celebrate his entry into manhood by staying a night alone on the mountain. He said he had much to ponder. He reminds me of you, my love."

I gulp, remembering my horrible attack in the cave by the apparition, bat and the shedim. Panic creeps into my voice. "You left without him? He will navigate the steep path on his own?"

"Since I hoped to get back to camp before you, Eliezer offered to stay near him."

I hold back the words that want to come.... *Eliezer isn't his father. Don't you think I have worried enough? Are you sure we can trust him with our son? After all, he is third in line for your inheritance.*

Hamor shakes his head as if he feels my fear.

"Eliezer vowed to protect him with his life. Since we adopted him, before Hagar bore Ishmael and you bore Isaac, he is legally a part of our family."[18]

Telling myself that the attack comes in many forms, I pull my emotions back. "I expect that our son will come down from the mountain changed, more self-reliant."

Abraham nods, relieved. "The mountain called and Isaac's spirit heard."

The donkeys turn the corner as we finally near our camp. In the distance a single traveler on a donkey appears. When my aged eyes are finally able to focus, I see Amah's husband coming toward us. We bring the donkeys to a halt, and Abraham uses Yasmine's rope to dismount Hamor.

"Joshua, thank you for coming to us."

"Master, there is a sandstorm in the distance. It seems to be heading for our camp."

Abraham nods, suddenly serious. "Let us go to the overlook and see the direction the storm is moving."

While we move the donkeys forward, I ask, "Abraham, when do you expect Isaac to come?"

"Rest assured my ezer, Eliezer will not bring him when there is risk."

The three of us take the four donkeys to the desert-facing side of our camp, then up on the knoll. In the distance, a huge orange cloud lifts up. In the cloud I see orange pillars that hold up several giant, stormy rings of dark, spinning clouds. Abraham muses aloud, "He instructs the clouds in the skies and swings

[18] Abram: Eternal Lord, what could You *possibly* give to me *that would make that much of a difference in my life?* After all, I am still childless, and Eliezer of Damascus stands to inherit all I own. Genesis 15:2

open Heaven's doors."[19]

I reply with the words Yahweh gave my husband, the words that brought Ishmael to my heart and a song to my lips, "Your descendants will be as many as the stars of the heavens and the grains of sand on the shores." I nod my head at the threatening cloud, "Is this evil's attempt to secure the last word? Would he throw sand at us to mock the covenant promise?"

Joshua answers in the way so common to men, answering my fear with fact. "Extreme temperature changes thrust dust into the air. The greater the temperature change, the greater the wind." He puts his hands on his hips, reminding me of Ephron looking over his field. "It's been said that a dune of sand can produce its own wind."

Abraham whispers, "I have missed you my ezer." Then he turns to Joshua. "You and I should secure the donkeys. But first, could you see my wife back to our tent? Then bring Maya and meet me at the donkey enclosure?"

Before we turn to leave, Abram unties Lilah's wool cape, hands it to me, and then asks, "Sarah, can you prepare by yourself?"

"Amah will help her," Joshua says. I note the lift of his chin when he mentions her name. He is proud of his wife.

My thoughts spin like the dust, but I know Abraham is now focused away from me. *And I missed you, the chieftain who needs my seeing of danger more than you know.* I lean over and touch the golden oak walking stick Abraham carved himself. My husband will be excited to see this, but not now.

"I may take shelter with the animals." Abraham says as he turns Hamor and his other donkey toward the other side of our camp.

Riding Maya, Joshua and I walk the donkeys slowly toward the north end of camp, where Abraham and my camel skin and

[19] Nevertheless, He gave instructions to the clouds in the sky and swung open heaven's doors; He showered them with manna to soothe their *hungry* bellies and provided them with the bread of heaven. Psalm 78:23–24

goat hair tent is carefully situated so that it receives the least harm. Seeing the cloud, I would like to move faster, but Maya is winded.

"Amah is a great help to me," I venture.

"Yes, she feels privileged to serve you." He smiles, "The Nephilim donkey is a sight to see."

Picturing their daughter fills me with anticipation. "I can't wait for Nomi to meet him."

When we get to my tent, although the sun is high overhead, exhaustion overcomes me. I slide off of Maya easily, but Joshua helps me untie Abraham's staff. He takes the food, water and Lilah's cape off of the donkey as well, handing them to his wife who is waiting.

At last stepping again into my tent, I am greeted by colorful, linen tapestries from our journeys to Ur, Haran, Mesopotamia, Gerar and Egypt. Although these are a timeline of our marriage, I have the sure sense our best years are still to come.

"Welcome home mistress," Amah says slyly as my conspirator for this journey. She whispers, "I wanted to come with Joshua to greet you. He has promised secrecy about your journey."

"Please, call me Sarah," I reply, seeing that she has brought in blankets, water, milk, food, a small basin of water and a soft cloth so that I can wash my face, hands and feet.

"Where is your daughter, Nomi?"

"Ruchama is keeping her with her family. And Nomi is excited to be with the children." She looks into my eyes and then glances downward. "Would you like me to stay with you… Sarah?"

My name rolls awkwardly off of her tongue. In the past, I would have assumed she would take care of me. Even took it for granted. Instead I choose to reveal myself. "Amah, while I was gone, I thought of you. Yes, I longed for all the ways you served me. But there was more."

Amah listens, mystified.

"On this journey, I found myself with two strong women who taught me how to serve in equality." Waiting until she lifts her eyes to mine, I continue. "Could we forge something new? Differing gifts from Yahweh, but equal friends?"[20]

"You never treated me with disrespect," she says. "But I would like to learn from you. About Yahweh, and mothering, and yes, the eye that sees the danger."

"And I from you," I say with a smile, my spirit fluttering like a lone bird that suddenly hears one of her own calling.

Hearing the wind roar, Amah says, "It seems the decision has been made for us."

Together, we tie the tent door tight and collapse on the soft pillows in relief. Branches and bramble tumble over the top of my tent, but mercifully do not puncture it. Suddenly, I remember the broken stone in my pocket that I found on top of Ephron's cave. My own words come back to me… *sometimes life has a way of breaking you open.* I pull out the stone and hold it in my palm for Amah to see. "I found this stone when I was with a new friend talking about pain. Now I understand I need other women to step into the broken places with me."

I am nervous, but roll onto my side, leaning on my left elbow so that I can see her better. "I have withheld the wounded parts of me. I lost sight of your gifts and mine." Her eyes reflect both curiosity and friendship. "I long for pain and joy to flow between us."

"I am willing," she says humbly, as the light lowers inside the tent. "If you will step into my broken places with me." A

[20] Now there are many kinds of *grace* gifts, but they are all from the same Spirit. There are many different ways to serve, but *they're all directed by* the same Lord. 1 Corinthians 12:4-5

deafening wind follows.

In just a few words, Amah has reminded me that friendship cannot run one way. It must be mutual. I invited Amah into my life, and now she has returned the invitation.

Amah pushes her voice above the sound of the wind, "Surely Abraham and Joshua shelter near the animals."

Isaac still is not here. A tear runs down my cheek. I sit up and Amah hands me the soft cloth to dab my eyes. "Isaac and Eliezer are still far from our camp. Abraham gave our son permission to spend the night alone, watched over by Eliezer…to celebrate the successful sacrifice."

Amah nods. "Like all boys, Isaac sees his manhood on the horizon, and he welcomes it."

"Ah, yes," I say. "When Abraham saw the sandstorm, he said that *Yahweh rides upon the clouds.* Did Yahweh not create sand to move in this way? Did Yahweh not know the risks of sending a boy of fourteen years into the wilderness?"

Amah nods, intent on my words. Her eyes are full of questions about my sojourn into the wilderness that with time I know now I will answer. She offers a remedy for my fear. "When Nomi is afraid, we sometimes sing together."

"Would you like to hear a song I wrote today to ward off fear? I came up with it thinking of Ishmael, our son through Hagar." When I was sleepy on the donkey, I rehearsed the words again and again until they were a part of me.

She nods, acknowledging the name she almost never hears from me…*Ishmael.* I begin to sing softly and Amah leans toward me to hear, her head almost on my shoulder.

Song of sand, treasure sweet
Bearing fruit for all to eat

Given by the One Most High
To all, counted in his sight

Song of sand, promise true
Plans of love for me and you
Whether you are far or near
Yahweh leans in with his ear

Song of sand, covenant new
Promise you are still in view
Trusting Yahweh for rebirth
Thoughts that touch all on earth

Song of sand, Ishmael's song
Peace that overcomes all wrong
Knowing you are in his plan
Yahweh writing in the sand

"Sarah," Amah says, her eyes sparkling. "Ishmael will surely be encouraged." We both stand up, and I sing the song again, this time with Amah, and I instigate a dance with our hands and feet interpreting the stanzas. Afterwards, we collapse on the pillows.

"I have long served the one God," I confide. "But on this journey, I have come to know Yahweh personally, like a man and wife, only more mysterious, more secure."

She reaches over and shyly touches my arm.

We both listen carefully. Yes, the noise outside is gone. The storm was mercifully brief. After a dust storm passes, we wait for the sound of the shofar before we come out of our tents. This allows the dust to move through the air and find its new home.

"I love this quiet after a storm," Amah says.

"Amah, I have something for you," I say. In the corner, I pull out the soft blue and green garments I was given by Yasmine. "I thought you might enjoy wearing these for the next feast. Perhaps Ruchama could wash them for you." Hearing my own words, I realize I have never laundered clothing. "Or you could teach me how."

With that, we both begin to laugh. The laughter of women of different stations but of similar hearts, knowing that burdens are not meant to be carried alone. A vision comes of a circle of women, all teaching each other the ways of Yahweh and crying, then laughing until our troubles recede.

The horn of a ram, the shofar is blown, a symbol of conquest over whatever threatens, or life begun again. We also blow it to recognize the new moon.

"I should go to Nomi," Amah says, standing up and holding the new clothing to her chest. "She will be looking for me."

Finally alone, I prepare for Abraham. Using a flint, I light some incense imported from the east that is scented with berries, roots and resins. It will repel the insects that rode on the wind. I wash my face one more time, my hands and my feet. I slip into a loose linen dress made from flax and dyed with lilac from the myrtle tree, and an undyed linen cloak that is simple but comfortable. I shake out the pillow and blankets, sneezing from the fresh dust. Then I use a small broom to sweep the floor, although Abraham will not return for hours. He will walk the entire camp to encourage our tribe. There will be wells to check to ensure the covering didn't blow off, filling them with sand.

I lie down in our bed, intending to close my eyes for a time. I hear men conversing outside our tent and then the voice of Joshua.

"Sarah, may I have a word with you?

"Of course." I sit up, not yet willing to show myself, my eyes heavy.

"There is a visitor here and he insists he has to see you. He says it is urgent."

When I open the tent door, shock swirls around me like a veil of sand.

There will come a time in the last days when the mountain where the Eternal's house stands will become the highest, most magnificent—grander than any of the mountains around it. And all the nations *of the world* will run there, *wanting to see it, feel it, fully experience it.*

Isaiah 2:2

CHAPTER ELEVEN
Mountain Song

OPENING THE TENT DOOR, I SEE A YOUNG man grasphing a woven cloak around him. He has sand on his whiskered face, sand in his reddish-brown hair, sand on his clothing. He is taller, more weather worn and much more muscular, but I know him immediately. "Ishmael?"

"Yes, it is I. . . ." I see his lips begin to form the word mother, but he stops himself. In the moment of me catching my breath, he mumbles, "My feet brought me through the desert and mountains, all the way here," obviously unsure whether he will be accepted or once again cast out. His voice is raspy like he inhaled some of the sand.

Thoughts swirl around me making me slightly dizzy.

His bow in my terebinth tree chest.

The sand song I wrote for him.

Isaac's persistence in asking about him.

I look at Ishmael, taking him in. "You came with the sand?"

"That cloud was a raging beast that wanted to eat everything in its path," he croaks. "I have been thinking of visiting for some time. I would travel closer to your camp and then further away. Of course, the day I would decide to come all the way, a sandstorm would blow in."

Joshua stands by, protective. I nod to him as a signal that he can leave us alone. "He is Abraham's son Ishmael…and mine as well. This is his home."

"Very well," Joshua says. "Welcome home Ishmael. I am Joshua and I will be at your service."

"Joshua, can you prepare the finest tent we have available for our son and whatever he needs to refresh himself?" *Yahweh, may peace rest on my son and make him whole.*[1]

He nods at me, "I will be nearby if you need me."

Smiling at Ishmael, I motion to the folding olivewood chairs we like to sit in at dawn. "Please rest for a moment."

Although I will not put this burden on him, his words linger… your camp. Suddenly, I feel the silent sting of my words…*this is his home.* It might have been truer to say, "Although I was the one who shunned you, now I want you to accept this as home." *Yahweh, teach me to forgive myself, so that I may accept this boy, now a man.*

"Where did you shelter from the sandstorm?"

He sits with his knee moving up and down, as if it might spring into action and take him away from me. Now looking straight ahead, his tongue loosens and his voice returns. "With the animals on the perimeter of your camp, beside a camel who clearly recognized me. Imagine that, after all this time! Sensing I needed protection, she positioned herself on the ground beside me and I covered myself with the large blanket tied on her back. Although she could close her nostrils and her two lashed upper eyelids, I needed shelter."

"The she-camel you named Gamal?"[2] Guilt has burned the camel's name into my memory—the very one we offered to Hagar when we cast her and her son out. An offer she refused. I

[1] **Messenger:** Do not be afraid, you who are highly regarded by *God.* May peace rest on you and *make you whole*; be strong; be brave. At his words, I grew even stronger. **Daniel:** Please continue, my lord, for your words have given me strength. Daniel 10:19

[2] Gamal means to treat a person well.

quickly add, "You have always loved the camels, especially when you traveled with your father into the desert."

"Ah yes, Gamal, the independent one.... The desert is punishing but also merciful." Ishmael nods at the sand piled up around each tent and continues. "Shifting gray sands that turn gold near sunset. I remember Gamal bouncing along, always smiling, hardly ever complaining. How we would stop and get off to walk the camels downhill, lest we tumble over their heads. From a long distance, a camel appears to be walking on the water." He pauses, suddenly uncomfortable. "Yes, Gamal had a mind of her own, sometimes refusing to conform to my wishes. I liked that about her."

"I've always thought the desert is like a great breath, slowly inhaling and then exhaling. Perhaps the One God breathing on me."

"The desert can also steal all you have," he says flatly, breaking loose any remaining illusions that peace will come easy. His words bring to mind the story the traveler told of the Egyptian handmaid's son being abandoned under a bush to die, like a fallen husk of wheat tossed by an open wind.[3] The vision cuts me like a knife of sacrifice, exposing my idolatry born of barrenness.

"I'm so sorry my son," I say, knowing the words are not enough and that I have not earned the right to say them. "I would like to hear your story...when you are ready."

He looks down at his sandy knees, his eyebrows knit close together, and nods, as if any other response would be more painful than he could bear. The younger Ishmael would leave at this point. Yet somehow, this Ishmael, the one who became a man before he was ready, stays. He is quiet, without words, perhaps untrusting of his own anger.

Since I know his lingering to be a great mercy, I offer a token

[3] For those who focus on sin, the story is different. They are like the fallen husk of wheat, tossed by an open wind, *left deserted and alone.* Psalm 1:4

of peace. "Would you stay for just a little longer? I can get you some water to drink."[4]

Before he responds, I go inside the tent to get a skin full of cool water, a way to anoint him in the name of Yahweh. When I come back outside, he still sits stiffly in one of the olivewood chairs. I hand him the skin of water. He drinks quickly, water dribbling down his cheeks and into his beard, forgetting himself for a moment.

"When you were by the animal pens, did you notice the new Nephilim donkey?"

"Yes," he says, his voice cool, as he hands back the empty skin. "I went by to check on Maya and saw him. He may rival a few of the smaller camels."

I talk fast, seeking to outpace his bouncing knee. "Then surely you will have a good hand with him. His name is Hamor. He was swept away in a flood with Maya, Isaac's donkey, and I feared they wouldn't make it."

A shadow passes over Ishmael's face.

"I thought it was my fault…all of it." Suddenly, I realize Ishmael could easily hear my words as an attempt to secure his pity, rather than my desire to show him my weakness.

He clasps his hands tightly, with his elbows resting on his knees. Steely determination glints in his eyes. "I am covered in sand and know these storms." He looks around and stands up, "There is much to do."

The sun appears through the clouds and I see small particles of sand floating in the air, seeking their new abode. Ishmael is not ready to light here, yet the wind brought him. "Your father ran toward the animal pens with the donkeys. He will be glad to see you."

"Sarah, don't move," Ishmael says urgently.

[4] The truth of the matter is this: anyone who gives you a cup of cool water to drink because you carry the name of your Anointed One will be rewarded. Mark 9:41

Leaning over and grabbing a small branch that blew in, he reaches over and brushes something off of my garment, close to my neck. Spotting it on the ground, he steps on it with his sandaled feet and twists his foot back and forth to kill it.

"What was it?" I say, my soul once again shocked.

"A yellow scorpion," he says. "They can kill a small child."

Looking down, I see my hands are shaking. Another test.

"Son, you saved me."

"But who will save me?"

His words surprise me. It seems as if the wind not only brought a scorpion, it also blew in a man with a tender spot hidden among all the walls he has erected.

As he turns to leave, I touch his arm and he jumps. "Wait!" I go back inside the tent to take the soft cloth I used to wash my face and use the soap to clean it for Ishmael. I immerse it in the basin of warm water and wring it out. Coming back outside, I hand it to Ishmael. "You might like to refresh yourself."

Ishmael uses the cloth to wipe the sand off of his face and then hands it back.

Looking above our tents, the sky is now azure with white billowing clouds. "I will see you a little later?"

"Yes, I will stay at least through the night."

"Look for your father near the animal pens. If he isn't there, ask any of the men. Son, I am so glad you came."

As quickly as he came, Ishmael disappears, as if he was a desert illusion that walked on the water to make his way to me. We have a saying...wisdom has two sides, mercy and justice.[5] Ishmael has seen mostly justice from us. But there is hope. He asked for me first, before Abraham. Does he see me as the gatekeeper for this family?

Back in our tent, I go into the terebinth tree chest to retrieve

[5] ...although you can't expect to be shown mercy if you refuse to show mercy. *But hear this:* mercy always wins against judgment! *Thank God!* James 2:13

Ishmael's bow. Sitting down and leaning against the chest, I once again touch the bow's smooth arms, remembering how quick a study Ishmael was in archery. How proud he was to have a skill. But, also, how dangerous it seemed in his hands with a small boy, his brother, running after him, ever wanting to be more like him.

Yahweh, please remove the arrows that have sunk deeper into Ishmael's spirit and the poison that remains.

This I know. Ishmael has suffered from being driven out of this camp and now he will be treated in the spirit of Melchizedek. *Yahweh, is sand a baptism and Ishmael arriving covered in it evidence of new life?* I smile to myself. Gamal the she-camel knew how to welcome a long-lost friend.

The afternoon passes quickly, and the light begins to shift, lighting up our camp in shades of gold. Abraham comes by with Joshua to tell me he has seen Ishmael and that the men are going to work together to clean out a well that lost its cover during the sandstorm. I want to ask a myriad of questions, but instead I smile and nod my approval. Amah comes by and together, along with her daughter Nomi, we go to inspect the men doing the work. It seems a true wonder to see Abraham and Ishmael, working side by side with Joshua. Side by side is how men repair bonds. I watch how the men move their hands. With hands on their hips, they establish dominance. They slap each other's shoulders to convey emotion.

When Amah goes back to her own tent, I stroll to the edge of camp, seeking the path I left on to find my son. I smile, remembering Zerah standing with a torch and a huge donkey, his eyes full of what was yet to come. The donkeys who carried me along the long journey pass through my thoughts—Maya, Azaz and Hamor—and the donkey who carried a king, Yoorie.

The chances of Isaac returning soon are dimming quickly. Fear again returns, a foe not easily defeated. Fear incited Abraham to put me in a harem.[6] A conviction comes. Whatever we cannot share causes us to retreat. I am no longer willing to bear my fear alone.

By the time I return to our tent, my shoulders are weary. I see that Amah has prepared a simple meal for our family to partake of later. Fresh linens are laid on our bed. The basin of water has been replenished and warmed by the fire. There is a fresh cloth for washing. Sitting on a soft tapestry floor pillow, I slowly use the cloth to wash off all the new sand and grime. I unbraid my hair and comb it, enjoying the sensation of working through each strand, shaking it out as if Yasmine is still with me. I take a long drink of water and pledge to Yahweh never to take the women who provide these things for granted. Beside our food, there is a vessel of liquid. I sniff it. It is similar to the barley beer I enjoyed at the campsite with Yasmine. I drink it slowly, enjoying the warmth it brings from my throat into my chest.

I lie down, one pillow under my head, another pressed to my chest and a third between my legs. *Ah, the accommodations an old woman's body needs.* My arms and legs still feel heavy, but my heart feels lighter. I breathe the breath of the desert, picturing us as a family and clan, when we traversed the unknown for the first time. The sand dunes were so high and daunting, they seemed like mountains.

So much has passed and so much is to come. The wind comes through one last time making a sound like the whirring of many wings. Do I hear the noise of a river? Sleep comes quickly and with it another vision.

A mountain rises high above all the other mountains. On top of the mountain is a city that gleams in the light, as if it is made of gemstones.

[6] **Abraham:** *I did it for my own protection.* I did it because I thought this was not a God-fearing place, and I was afraid you would surely kill me to possess my wife. Genesis 20:11

Gleaming warriors, both men and women, use their trumpets to sound a call.[7] *People of every color, size, and age gather to see the mountain. Instinctively, I know it to be the house of Yahweh. Zerah stands in the doorway, greeting each person who enters. Across his chest is a golden sash.*[8] *Abraham walks up from behind me and takes my hand. Isaac walks from the other side and takes my other hand. Before we walk toward the entrance, I look far to the right and see a woman and man. Could it be Hagar and Ishmael? No, it is Lilah and Ephron. I am overjoyed to see a child in their arms. I look far to my left and see Melchizedek, standing with his doe-white curved staff, his hair blowing in the wind. I want to move forward with my husband and the child of my womb, but I am unwilling to move until I locate Hagar and Ishmael. Suddenly, I realize I am first to be called, before Abraham, before Isaac and Ishmael, before my friends, to the Maker of all that has been made. Everything goes dark, except for a single beacon of light showing me the way.*

Rolling over, I slowly urge my eyes to open but they resist. Finally, they flutter open to see the darkness is real, except for a lantern casting a small amount of light into the tent. Somehow, I have slept into the evening. I glance at the food Amah left and see a portion for me. Undoubtedly, Abram and Ishmael had their fill. I roll over sleepily, jealous that I have lost some of the few moments I might have with Ishmael. I quickly put on a light cloak for the evening chill and slip on my sandals. Outside I hear men's voices.

Yes, there is Abraham's voice, and Ishmael's. Is there a third voice? I walk outside as my spirit thrums in anticipation. Could it be Isaac? Sitting around a blazing inferno leaping into the air, I see the three who have come to define me: Abraham, Isaac and Ishmael. As bright embers float into the air like fireflies, my

[7] O land abuzz with the whirring of wings, *far away* past the Ethiopian rivers.... All citizens of the world, every last inhabitant of the earth, *pay attention!* When you see a signal raised on the mountains, look! When the trumpets sound *the alarm*, listen! Isaiah 18:1, 3

[8] See Revelation 1:13

thoughts join them. *What words have I missed?* As if Yasmine is beside me, I hear her. "Remember Sarah, it is better if the bond they share begins to transcend you."

Abraham, Ishmael and Isaac laugh together as the fire crackles, so much so that they do not yet see me. *When did you and Eliezer return, my son?* I hold myself back from running to my one son, thereby favoring him over the other. Isaac was gone for eight days, Ishmael for eleven years.

Under the cover of darkness, I breathe in the three of them. Now that both boys are more grown, I see Abraham in both of them, just in different ways. In the firelight, I see that Isaac has his father's bushy eyebrows and strong chin. Isaac possesses his father's heart for Yahweh. Ishmael carries the rugged character of Abraham. Even in the low light, I can see that Ishmael's knee is again quivering up and down impatiently, much like his father's. If an enemy threatened, Ishmael would not hesitate to charge into the desert in the darkness on a camel with his bow and arrows.

Both boys also carry traits of their mothers. Ishmael has Hagar's skin, the color of fertile earth, her high Egyptian forehead, dark flashing eyes and more reserved stance. Isaac has my sensitivity and ability to see what is unseen. Like me, he has copper streaks in his dark brown hair, high cheekbones and his eyes crinkle when he smiles.

Still desiring to be unseen, I hang back, unable to hear but able to read the way they move. Isaac leans in toward his father, anxious not to miss a word. Ishmael crosses his arms and leans back like he cannot reveal his desire for his father to notice him, love him. Both boys are sons of Abraham. From time to time, they sneak secret brotherly glances at each other, quick intakes to be sure they share flesh and blood.

Ah, family in all of its misery and mystery.

I move near as I dare for a silent prayer. *Yahweh, I have seen how love can overcome years of misgivings, errors and doubts. Please teach me to love each of these that you have given me.*[9] *Help me to repair what I have broken.*

Finally seeing me, Abraham stands up in respect. Is this a sign of something new?

"Mother," Isaac exclaims and walks over. He holds himself back from running into my arms, glancing over his shoulder at his brother. "It is good to see you." He embraces me lightly, whispering in my ear, "There is so much to tell."

I reach up and touch the scar above his eyebrow, thanking Yahweh silently that it never left him. "Yes, there are stories to be told."

"Come sit with us," Abraham says.

I glance at Ishmael and he nods, as close to affirmation as he can give. As I walk by him, I lightly squeeze his shoulder and he does not prickle. Hope grows out of the smallest seeds.[10]

"Mother, Father tells us you made a journey of your own," Isaac begins innocently, no doubt hoping for a good story.

"I also told him that was only yours to share." Abraham looks me in the eyes, nodding his willingness to let the boys hear at the same time he does.

My mind reels with what Ishmael and Isaac should or shouldn't hear. Then I hear the faint whisper of the voice I've learned to listen to, "Is it your story to tell? Or is it mine?"

"It is yours, Yahweh," I whisper before I walk over to sit by my husband.

All three of my boys look at me expectantly, but my eyes are on Yahweh.

"Before I tell you about my travels, I want you to know that

[9] Most of all, love each other steadily and unselfishly, because love makes up for many faults. 1 Peter 4:8

[10] The kingdom of God is like a mustard seed, the tiniest seed you can sow. Mark 4:31

Ishmael saved me today."

Ishmael is surprised, most likely supposing like anything else he had done, it didn't matter.

"We were sitting and talking outside the tent, when he noticed something on the front of my garment. Ishmael, what did you see?

"A yellow scorpion," Ishmael says. "The deadly kind. We call them death stalkers."

Isaac's eyes grow wide. "What did you do Ishmael?"

"I asked mother to stay still..."

"Without telling me a death stalker was on me," I add. "No doubt, I would have jumped, and it would have run up my neck and stung me." I shiver at the thought.

"I saw a branch that the wind blew in. I picked it up and brushed the creature off of her. Those scorpions are not easy to kill because they flatten themselves when they feel danger. I stepped on it with my sandal and turned my foot back and forth until I saw for myself it had perished."

Abraham and Isaac look at Ishmael with pride making his face glow with the warmth of recognition. I see part of our family's shame going up in flame and smoke.

"Well done," says Abraham.

Isaac turns to me. "Now for your story."

I rub my hands together, letting the fiery pit tinder my spirit. Looking at Ishmael, I begin. "After Abraham and Isaac left in the early morning without me knowing, I felt abandoned and angry. So angry, I kicked clothing across our tent. I feared the worst. My mind was flooded with visions of Isaac being bound and laid on an altar to be sacrificed."

Ishmael speaks to Abraham, now angry. "Did you do this? Bind Isaac and put him on an altar of sacrifice?"

Abraham nods at Isaac, encouraging his words.

"Yes, Father did," Isaac says simply. "With my consent. But first let us hear your story, Mother."

Ishmael looks at him with new respect. "It is good to hear that one other person in this family knows how I feel."

In the moment of silence that follows, none of us know what to say.

"Please continue your story, Sarah," Abraham says softly, his eyes sad in the firelight.

"When I set out to leave with Maya, loaded with provisions, I thought I would travel alone. But at the edge of camp, there was a mysterious man. Zerah, he called himself." I glance at Abraham, "Do you know of him?"

"I know of no such man," he quips.

"He said he knew you and that he came to serve you. Him and his sister Yasmine. They brought a Nephilim donkey."

Ishmael says, "The donkey you call Hamor?"

"Yes, the donkey you met, Ishmael."

"I have not heard of Zerah or Yasmine, but tell us more," Abraham says.

"Both of them walked and talked with a life-giving spirit. They ended up guiding me, preparing meals, and helping me see Yahweh through their kindness. At night, Zerah would put on the skin of a white deer and charge up into the mountains to seek you, Abraham. After guiding me all day, he ran all night. He would not promise to intervene, but at least hoped to find you." I lean back, unsure what to tell next. "Yasmine was mighty but tender, a woman warrior who taught me how to boldly confront evil."

"Angels?" Isaac says, rubbing his hands together in delight.

Ishmael leans forward and inserts himself. "My mother and

I were taken care of in the desert when she thought I might perish, after you cast us out. An angel came, and she named him, The God Who Sees Me.[11] She now refuses to worship any other God. I am not so easily convinced."

I take in a breath. *Does Hagar now seek the God Most High, Yahweh?*

Isaac now speaks up, "Mother went on a journey without Father. Ishmael almost died in the desert. And I was tied up on a rock of sacrifice."

I stand and stretch and walk over to the wood ready for the fire. And then think better of it. "I was going to help feed the fire, but the scorpion has spooked me." Now standing, I ask boldly, "Abram, what happened on Moriah?"

We all look at Abraham. He looks at each of us one by one, as if laying claim to those who are his. Sensing he is waiting for me, I walk back to my seat and get comfortable.

Abraham's voice is solemn. "I was called by Yahweh to sacrifice Isaac. I wrestled against the calling, wondering if my following of the One God was preposterous, misinformed. Even as we went toward Moriah, I kept waiting for Yahweh to speak again. Tell me I had misunderstood. That it was all a mistake."

"What happened Father? Ishmael says softly.

I draw in a breath, moved by the simple word, Father.

"Yahweh was silent."

Ishmael makes a noise of disgust and crosses his arms.

"As Isaac said, he put himself on the altar and let me bind him."

"As you would bind an animal," Ishmael says. "Why do you follow this god?"

Isaac now goes and gets a log, shakes the sand off of it and places it on the fire.

[11] Hagar: I'm going to call You the God of Seeing because in this place I have seen the One who watches over me. Genesis 16:13b

"I raised the knife but then what felt like a hand, held my arm back. A strong hand. I heard a rush of wings and a voice in my right ear saying, "This is not Isaac's to do. This is mine."

"Father was weeping," Isaac says simply. "He threw the knife far from us."

Ishmael again inserts himself. "Did you bring the knife home?"

"I could not touch it again," Abraham says, his voice cracking with emotion.

Seeing his father's emotion, Isaac continues the story. "He untied me and then a ram appeared in a thicket right by us, snagged by his horns. Together we made the sacrifice."

"Did you see anything?" I ask. "Were you frightened?"

Ishmael is now leaning toward Isaac, as if he doesn't want to miss a word. "You are only fourteen."

"Almost fifteen," Isaac says to Ishmael, as if that makes a difference, and then turns to my question. "Just a glimpse. But I knew I would be spared, even if the knife did enter me. The person who held back father's arm calmed me with the love in his eyes. Strangely, I felt safe."

Ishmael rises, placing his hands on his hips. With smoke wafting around his head and his clothing somewhat sandy, he speaks. "Now you have taken me beyond all belief with your stories." He yawns and stretches his arms wide, perhaps to shove away what doesn't rest well with him. "You have entertained me enough for one night."

Isaac begins to chuckle, and Ishmael joins him. Abraham and I cannot help ourselves but joining, our family's laughter cooling the tension like water has been poured on the fire. The hilarity feels healing, like proof that our flaws and mistakes may someday be redeemable.

Once more, I am given words which feel like miracles in and

of themselves. "Ishmael, I would very much like it if you would bring Hagar here. I would like to see her and make amends for all that has passed."

Abraham puts a few new logs on the fire and nudges them into position with a stick. No doubt, he is surprised, but he supports my wishes. "Yes son, we would like to see her."

Impulsively, Isaac stands and throws himself into his brother's arms. At first Ishmael is stunned, unsure. But then he slowly puts his arms around his brother and pats his back a few times. The embrace is awkward, but it is sure. "Ishmael, I am glad you came. Please stay."

"My mother is waiting a distance away to hear whether she is welcome here. If she was not welcome, then I had decided I would not come back. I will leave in the morning. She said to tell you we will return at the turn of the moon. I will leave before dawn tomorrow."

"Son, the camel I offered when you left." Abraham pauses, "When we forced you to leave."

"Gamal," I say, knowing in advance what Abram will offer.

"Take him as your own, now that you two have found each other again."

"Thank you, Father, Mother."

Abraham speaks up once more. "I will have Joshua load Gamal with provisions tonight, so that you will be well taken care of in your time away.

"Isaac, you have my word that I will return," Ishmael says and then, like the smoke lifting off of the fire, quickly walks away to find his tent. A tear drips down my cheek. One day seems far too short, but I must let Ishmael do what is right in his eyes.

Now that the three of us remain at the fire—Isaac, Abraham

and me—we all take a few moments of silence, each with our own thoughts. In the distance, I hear the howl of wolves and the song of an owl. Remembering the sand cat that came up on the trail, I pray silently, *Lord give Ishmael safety as he travels, just as you did Isaac and Eliezer.*

I turn toward Isaac, my son of the promise, "Son, were you ever scared?"

Isaac pauses as the fire spits and pops, the flames appearing to dance across his face. "Yes, I was terrified when I realized Father's intentions. When I asked him where the animal would come from for the sacrifice, and he said that God would provide the animal for the sacrifice, I saw tears in his eyes. I knew then. As we walked in silence, I felt like I could not breathe. I started to panic, thinking of ways to escape. Finally, I remembered something you told me."

"What was that son?"

"That Yahweh inserts himself into our lives. And that when he intervenes, he will not rest until things are set right. I did not think it right that I should die to fulfill a covenant promise that Yahweh promised would be fulfilled through me. Yahweh would not make me do what I believe to be wrong."

Abraham exhales, as if he can finally breathe. Still, there is more to be said.

"Isaac, can I ask one more question."

"Of course, Mother."

"What did you see when you were bound on the altar?"

Isaac thinks for a minute. "I saw a tall man with wavy hair. His eyes were kind and brimming with all that is true. He had a white cape tied around his shoulder. And he had a scar in the palm of his right hand, just like the one above my eyebrow."

"Zerah," I gasp so softly, it seems that neither Abraham nor

Isaac hear me. I had forgotten the scar, but now remember it clearly. "Zerah held back his arm." A silent prophecy comes. *When it is his time, Zerah will not escape the fires of sacrifice. Instead he will welcome it, scorning its shame.*

"I am glad Ishmael was here to hear about Moriah," Isaac says, his words brimming with both sadness and gladness.

"I wrote a song about Ishmael."

"I am afraid he won't return," Isaac sighs. "Would you sing the song for us?"

I begin to sing, projecting my voice over the fire, so that Isaac can hear, or even Ishmael in case he lingers in the shadows in order to hear what we have said after he left.

Song of sand, treasure sweet
Bearing fruit for all to eat
Given by the One Most High
To all, counted in his sight

Song of sand, promise true
Plans of love for me and you
Whether you are far or near
Yahweh leans in with his ear

Song of sand, covenant new
Promise you are still in view
Trusting Yahweh for rebirth
Thoughts that touch all on earth

Song of sand, Ishmael's song
Peace that overcomes all wrong
Knowing you are in his plan

Yahweh writing in the sand
The singing brings more inspiration and a new verse comes.

Song of sand, family lore
Witness to God's open door
Mystery calls from deep to deep
As we laugh and when we weep

After the song, Isaac comes to me and perches himself on my knees, wrapping his arms around my neck. I know moments like these will not come often and so I breathe it in, let the smoke burn it into my memory. Then he stands up and yawns. "I have traveled a long way today."

"I look forward to hearing about your night alone," I say, as Isaac sleepily makes his way toward his own tent.

Both sons have had enough of stories of angels and men. Then it occurs to me that Isaac will not go to his tent with his brother in the camp. No, he will seek out Ishmael.

Now alone, Abraham and I stand up and embrace. He says, "I am proud of you, my ezer. I sense there is much more story to be heard."

"Can we sit a little longer?"

"Yahweh is good," Abraham says. He has said this many times, but this time I hear a man who took his son to the altar, weeping all the while.

Courage floods through me, as tears wash my cheeks. "Yahweh's word is yes. Because he only speaks the truth, his promise is true, trusted."

"So wise," Abraham mutters. "A prophetess indeed."

I want to move forward, yet first I must look back. "The day the angels came to our camp, to tell us the time was near for me to bear a child. When I baked so much bread."

Abraham looks at me intrigued, his raised eyebrows an invitation to continue.

"We rejoiced in his promise." I gather my courage and push myself to tell him more. "Yet, shortly after that, you gave me to be in a king's harem for the second time. You gave me to Abimelech, calling me your sister. This brought back the pain and humiliation of Egypt. After that, I wondered if you had nullified the promise through unbelief."

We sit quietly, the fire singing its tune, demanding more fuel to keep up its dance. Abraham ignores it, deep in thought. Finally, he speaks. "I thought it was the only way to save us." He sighs and then conviction comes into his eyes. He waves his hands at the flames in front of us. "I put you into the fire, believing you would not be burned. It is as if I tied you up and put you on an altar of my own accord. I can see why it would be difficult to trust me. I left in the early morning with Isaac to do a sacrifice I was not willing to talk about. I knew if I told you, I would not go."

"You left without me knowing." I repeat, surprising myself. "I had quite a fit in our tent, kicking around blankets. I pictured myself beating you in the chest with my hands, like a mute swan whose offspring has been threatened."

Fearing I have been too bold, I look at him and see tears streaming down his cheeks. In the firelight, the tears appear to be made of fire. Tears I have longed for but could not call forth.

Abraham speaks, "Can you forgive me?"

I reach out and touch Abram's hand. As I learned from Melchizedek and from the cave on the hills of Moriah, there is no shame in admitting our missteps. "It is done. Whatever there is to forgive I have forgiven."

"Tell me the story of being in the harem of Pharaoh." This is how Abraham shows that he understands the great price of forgiving.

As the fire burns down into hot coals, I tell him the memory that came to me at the springs by Ephron's cave. The nudity. The beauty treatments. The king's banquet with the snake. The seductive dances and the way the King pawed at me. Being taken to the Pharaoh's chambers where I would likely be raped.

At times, Abram's face flashes with rage and indignation. When he hears of God rescuing me just before I was sexually assaulted, he puts his head in his hands.

Finally, I tell him of the attack in the cave of Moriah, the apparition of Isaac, the bat, the shedim and being carried to the wadi stone covering.

"My wife, the ezer and mighty warrior," Abraham says.

We sit for a time in the growing darkness, at peace with each other and Yahweh. When the fire goes completely out, I point above us. Like a beacon, hosts of stars declare the covenant promise of God.

"My Sarai," Abram says tenderly. "I put aside the 1000 pieces of silver that Abimelech gave in restitution and set it apart for you to use as you see fit. After all, it is yours."

In my heart, a vision for the silver springs forth, one I am not ready to tell. "Abraham, I just realized something. The donkeys Pharaoh gave us after I was in the harem? They parented Maya. Yahweh brought something good from what evil used to hurt us."

But there is more. I see my husband, bound to this ground by his humanity. Instead of only seeing weakness, I see a man who faithfully followed *hinini* to its most extreme ends. I see a father who saw beyond what is bruised and bent, to a candle that refuses to go out.[12] Though he faced pressure beyond what any father could bear, he climbed Yahweh's mountain to pledge his allegiance to the Most High.

Melchizedek's words come back again, "Who wouldn't want to witness the dividing line of Heaven and Earth?"

And so, tears rolling down my cheeks, I bow before my husband to give him the honor his heart longs for, but which he knows he does not deserve. Although I desire it, this sacrifice may be costly. Touching his feet and thinking the time will come when I wash them just as Melchizedek washed mine, I whisper,

"I honor you as lord."[13]

[12] What is bruised and bent, he will not break; he will not blow out a smoldering candle. *Rather, he* will faithfully *turn his attention to* doing justice. Isaiah 42:3

[13] Consider how Sarah, *our mother,* obeyed *her husband,* Abraham, and called him "lord," and you will be her daughters as long as you boldly do what is right without fear *and without anxiety.* 1 Peter 3:6

One person can't grant salvation to
another or make a payment
to the True God for another.
Redeeming a life is costly;
no premium is enough, ever enough…

Psalm 49:7-8

CHAPTER TWELVE
Redemption Song

IT HAS BEEN TWENTY-EIGHT DAYS SINCE Ishmael left to go to his mother. Laying on my right side, I roll over in bed to find my husband already gone. Apprehension rushes in, an early morning frenzy that has visited repeatedly ever since the day I returned to our camp. *Where is Abraham? Has another hinini come? Did he take Isaac?*

Two days after Ishmael left, I panicked and quickly moved outside the tent where Abraham was sitting in the chair meditating. My husband was gentle. He acknowledged my distress came from his decision and then let me give it words.

The morning when I awoke to find both you and Isaac, gone.

The afternoon I realized you were going to offer Isaac.

The evening where my fear turned into a fit of rage.

From my experiences with Melchizedek, Yasmine, Ephron and Lilah, and then being attacked alone in the Cave of Moriah, I have practice with this new form of spiritual warfare.

I speak aloud, "Fear, do you have something new to tell me today?" Is this the familiar dread, leftover from events now pressed into my bones?

With no answer to my own questions, I say, "Be still," and the anxiety lessens.

Now fully awake, I see the early morning light peeking through the tent's open doorway. As I pull back the covers, my hands tremble. Fear still remains. In two days, the new moon will come and with that, our eyes will be on the horizon for Ishmael and Hagar. Although I initiated this the day Ishmael blew in with the sandstorm, my heart still holds trepidation. By the time we awoke the next morning as the sun came up, Ishmael was gone. I was disappointed that we did not see him off. Isaac said he tarried into the darkest hours with Ishmael, enjoying a fire that they built together. Whenever he hears me doubt their appearance at the new moon, Isaac insists, "At least Ishmael will come. He promised me."

As any mother, I have been tempted to ask Isaac for the tender parts of his and Ishmael's conversation—to a mother's soul better than the fat of a sheep's tale, a delicacy. After inquiring of Yahweh, I decided it was best to leave their story, just that, theirs. He did volunteer, "We have few shared memories since I was so young when he left. There was much to learn about each other. We agreed to build something new."

Isaac, like me, has experienced lingering terror from the moments where he thought his father would kill him, before he reasoned his way to a place of submission. In his nightmares, the knife of sacrifice entered his chest. He woke up in a sweat, unsure whether he was dead or alive. For two weeks, he slept at the foot of our bed. I taught him how to confront his fears and for now, he says the nightmares have fled. Seven days ago, he declared he was ready to be back in his own tent. I was sad to see him go, but pleased he is finding peace.

To this day, I am astounded that Yahweh led us to divulge so much to Ishmael about all that transpired on Moriah. I fear we will face ridicule from Hagar, although I seek to trust her son's assurance that she is loyal to the God Who Sees Me. Choosing peace must be a lofty form of spiritual warfare, a type of *chayil.*[1] *Yahweh, give me the words to respond with mercy, no matter what she says.*

I stand up and stretch my back to ease the aches in my hips that also come in the early morning. The accumulated stress of Moriah plus the anticipation of Hagar's arrival...I tell myself. It has not been uncommon for me to sleep until the sun is high above me. Now I feel stronger than I did before everything that took place.

A few days ago, I finally found the courage to tell Isaac about the two harems, just as I rehearsed when I was riding Azaz. When I asked if he had questions, my son of promise put his head in his hands, saying, "I'm sorry Mother. I'm so sorry."

The next day he shyly approached and told me that he enjoyed the thought of me aging backwards. "Could that happen again, Mother?" In his eyes, I saw his plea for me to stay with him longer, not to abandon him when he still needs me.

Urged on by Isaac and by faith, I see twenty more years ahead. Time to raise my son and prepare him to marry some time after his thirtieth year. Like me, my husband seems to have found a new vigor. He has overseen the addition of permanent tents within our camp for Ishmael and Hagar, with touches of Egypt, in case they decide to stay. Sometimes, in the reaches of the night, my soul nags me that there is more to know about my husband's relationship with Hagar.

Seeing that I am awake, Abram walks into the tent with mischief in his eyes, lightening my heart. "I have a surprise for you," he says. My husband awakens the playful part of me.

"It has been twenty-eight days since Ishmael left," I say. "Did Hagar and Ishmael arrive?"

[1] Peace I leave with you; My [perfect] peace I give to you; not as the world gives do I give to you. Do not let your heart be troubled, nor let it be afraid. [Let My perfect peace calm you in every circumstance and give you courage and strength for every challenge.] John 14:27 (AMP)

"They will come with the new moon," he says, without a trace of doubt. Oh, the man of faith Yahweh has given me. He sees things that are not and calls them into existence before they appear.[2]

"Another *hinini*?" I say, the words escaping my lips unplanned.

He smiles. "I will surely tell you if another hinini comes. I have planned a trip for us."

"Today? What have you planned?" Immediately, I wish he had consulted me.

"A sojourn to the oasis at En Gedi. I hear the springs are flowing and the wilderness has awoken."

"Does Isaac know yet?"

"He and Eliezer are taking a day trip to explore the ways that trees and plants support each other." He strokes his beard. "'We will explore how their roots intertwine,' I think he said."

"Isaac is saying no to En Gedi? To glimpse the sandstone cliffs, dip in the springs and see the Red Sea from a distance?"

"I told him the two of us would travel there together another time."

"Would we journey alone?" I keep my words tentative because I now uphold my right to choose. As a prophetess, I must learn how to protect Yahweh's gift to me.

"Joshua and Amah will follow an hour behind us with food for the evening. We will spend the night in tents and return in the morning."

Looking into my husband's eager eyes, I see that he values time alone with me.

"Yes," I say. "After I change into clothing for travel, I will be ready." There is an urgency because, as all nomads know, sojourning the desert in the early morning is wise.

Abraham claps his hands in boyish anticipation and leaves to

[2] As it is *recorded in the Scriptures,* "I have appointed you the father of many nations. In the presence of the God who creates out of nothing and holds the power to bring to life what is dead, Abraham believed *and so became our father.* Romans 4:17

get the camels.

After I change into layers of linen for the dessert, I open the terebinth tree chest and pull out Lilah's wool cape, and on impulse the camel skin cloak. Both aren't necessary, but today they will come. After I close the chest, I pick up Ishmael's bow where it is still nestled beside the bed. Again, I don't know why, but it calls me. If Ishmael chooses not to come back, I will take this one last trip with him in spirit.

Riding our camel together, with another walking beside us, we now move through the desert, where time does not exist. The first hours of our trip to En Gedi find us alone in our thoughts. The natural colors, the closeness and the breeze rippling through our loose linen garments make us one with the sandy flatlands. Even at over a hundred years of age, I enjoy being rocked softly by the slow gait on the camels. It is here that each finds their own truth. A bird trills nearby, awakening my senses. I realize that as Abraham and I breathe in unison, the far-off horizons of rock and sand create a feeling of intimacy. Although there is always risk in the desert, it empties the soul, preparing it to receive. Perhaps here, I will open up to being more fully possessed by Yahweh. In him, I have come to find delight.[3] I picture Yahweh as a desert mountain, Lord of both wisdom and suffering. Ishmael's words also come back to me about the desert, and I look around me, trying to see as Ishmael sees. He still lingers at the edges of my thoughts, praying he will keep his promise to Isaac to return.

When we begin the approach to En Gedi, I lean into my husband. "Thank you for bringing me here. I forget the enchantment of this place."

"Yes, when we are in harmony with it, the desert trades in peace."

[3] *Imagine* the wilderness whooping for joy, the desert's unbridled happiness with its spring flowers. *It will happen!* The deserts will come alive *with new growth budding* and blooming, singing and celebrating with sheer delight. Isaiah 35:1-2a (AMP)

"When we left Ur, it took many months, perhaps even years to understand. And in some ways, I am yet to understand. There are times when I only see the risk."

"Ah, wisdom has already risen from the earth and descended from the sky, my wise one."

"I told you all that happened at the two harems. Thank you for making it safe."

'Of course," he says.

"Where were you when I was in the harems?" I realize my words sound thin, even awkward, but I know no other way to ask. My suffering has taught me to be more patient. He needs time to sort through what he wants to share.

"At Pharaoh's palace, I could not rest knowing you were there. Early every morning, I went to the gates to beseech Yahweh on your behalf. When I asked the gatekeepers about you, they said you were being treated with special honor, but that I could not see you that day. 'Later,' they said again and again. And every day I was tempted to curse myself for my helplessness to reach you."

A tumbleweed of anxiety lodges in my stomach. "When I inquired whether you, my brother, had visited, I was told politely that you had not."

His back tightens. He was disrespected and deceived. "I thought of charging in with all my fighting men and freeing you myself. But Yahweh was silent. As perplexing as it was, it seemed prudent to wait. Now I wonder."

I use my travel cape to wipe the sweat off of my forehead. The sun is throwing down heat which bounces off the sand. Yes, as Ishmael alluded to, the desert can also forsake you. I lean back and picture the breezes of En Gedi. Then I remember the proverb, a truthful answer is like a kiss on the lips. "The payment Pharaoh gave us in livestock, people and gold will never be enough. It was a bribe to keep the Most High from harming him, hidden under an illusion of generosity."[4]

"Pharaoh heaped wrong upon wrong."[5] His back stiffens with contained rage.

Now more mindful of Yahweh and my husband, I search for faith. "Since it was Yahweh that struck him and his entire household with illness, perhaps it was also Yahweh who compelled him to give so much." I reach up and put my fingers through his hair, an affectionate gesture I know he enjoys. "I do not blame you anymore, Abram."

"Look there! Sarah." He points off to the left where there are small patches of verdant green with pockets of flowers that only appear for a short time every spring.[6] Does he, like me, see this as a reminder of our growth? He continues, "Abimelech's guards misled me in the same way. Almost as if he and Pharaoh planned it together as a perverse battle against us."

"Yes," I say. "Pharaoh *and* Abimelech heaped wrong upon wrong. It seems that although evil provokes suffering, it is also predictable."

"Yahweh, may you restore us gently as this camel carries us. Teach us contentment in the deserts of knowing you and in the oasis of experiencing you." Abram's prayer is so sweet that it makes my love for him swell.

"Amah and I have started a small circle of women from our camp who meet together to share burdens and to talk of what it means to know Yahweh intimately. Each of the women have also expressed a desire to learn to read and write. I said that I will help them."

Even being behind my husband on the camel, I sense his change of mood. His narrow focus allows these sudden shifts.

[4] See Deuteronomy 10:17

[5] "You shall not give a false report; you shall not join hands with the wicked to be a malicious witness." Exodus 23:1 (AMP)

[6] All life is like the grass. All of its grace and beauty fades like the *wild* flowers in a field…nothing lasts except the word of our God. It will stand forever. Isaiah 40:6-8

"That is good to hear. May I ask which women you speak of?"

"Amah and Ruchama, along with Heba and Salma,[7] two Egyptian women that King Abimelech gave us from his household." I smile, "This reminds me that Maya was the offspring of two of the donkeys that the King gave us."

Abram nods his head. "I talked with Joshua before we left. I asked if we could grow together in the knowledge of Yahweh. He was receptive. My wife, now I imitate your faith."

Joy renders me speechless.

He continues, "I wonder how many animals we depend on now came from those two kings. God took what they intended for our harm…"

"and brought good." I add. For once, I do not feel the need to add the words, *even though I suffered terribly.* He has shown me that he understands this.

I surprise him by wrapping my arms tight around him and he jumps, surprised. He is usually the one who sneaks up behind me and suddenly pulls me tight. I begin to laugh, and Abraham joins me. This cleansing exchange of joy is an invitation into intimacy. Laughter aligns us with the brightness of the sun peeking through the clouds and the cooling waters that lie ahead.

When we reach the oasis, my heart thrills at the sight. Abraham coaxes the camel down to his knees, so that we can dismount. Here there is plenteous shade, a spring that bubbles up from the ground into a turquoise pool, and grasses and flowers that we don't usually see. Birds flit from tree to tree riding on the cool breeze. Sometimes we even see ibex. My neck is stiff, but nothing that the healing waters cannot resolve.

I know there is still a conversation to be had before Hagar

[7] Heba means "a generous gift from God." Salma means "she who generates peace."

comes. I need my faithful husband's truth to dissolve the fear. But it seems unfair to ask Abraham to speak of these things after we discussed the harems. How does a woman ask intimate questions she longs to be answered, without threatening her own peace or pushing her husband away?[8]

We sit down on a rock, take off our sandals, and roll our clothing up to our knees, happy to be alone. Dipping our feet into the cold water is pure bliss. I take off my headscarf, and my linen robe. Abram leans down and scoops up some water in his hand which he uses to splash me. I do the same with my foot.

"Ah, the bliss of Yahweh's creation of oneness," I tease. "Even for old people like us." We are damp, but our hearts are light.[9]

Abram steps down into the water and lies down. He motions for me to join him. Looking at his extended hand and smiling eyes, I cannot refuse him. Gingerly, I lower myself into the water, beside him. There, lying in blissful coolness while holding hands, we see white clouds crossing the sky, covering and then uncovering the sun. Whispers of the fragrance of henna float around us. I wish I could hold this moment still, prevent it from passing.

When we finally come out of the water back onto the rocks, we are both thirsty. Abraham retrieves a skin of water and we both take a long drink. When we are satiated, his smile reminds me of the man I knew before we married. He leans over and kisses me tenderly. Some might consider our romance chaste, but the thrill still remains.

"Sweet Sarai," he smiles, a shadow passing over his face like the sun has gone under a cloud. "How do you feel about Hagar coming? It was moving to hear you invite her through Ishmael."

Again, my husband surprises me.

"What was she like, Abram?"

[8] The Eternal *is ready to* share His wisdom *with us*, for His words bring true knowledge and insight.... Proverbs 2:6

[9] My love is like a fragrant bouquet of henna blossoms from the vineyards of Engedi. Song of Solomon 1:14

Seeing the softness in my eyes, my husband relaxes.

"Hagar...." A lump in my throat seeks to block the words. "As a woman, as the mother of your child."

He will not tell me intimate details. We agreed long ago this must not happen. I breathe in through my nose and push the breath down through my chest. Silently, thinking of the women in the harems I pray, *Yahweh, please allow me to hear without judgment. Let your aroma kiss my words.*[10]

The prayer is such a small offering, something new flutters in my stomach, almost like the first whispers of pregnancy.

"She was...." he starts, no doubt wondering whether the beauty of this trip will be lost.

"It is well," I say. "Please continue."

"She was a paradox, an enigma, a puzzle...." Again, he pauses to parse his words, measure them against his experience, and, perhaps, to my probable reaction.

I wince silently. Many men desire such puzzles. I look into his eyes and shake off my fear, "Yes, to me as well."

"The night you sent her to me, I agonized whether to accept her for your sake or dismiss her. She came as a servant. Her eyes declared she had no right to be there."

I nod. A new possibility swirls around me, one I had never considered.

"Yet she would not be pitied. She lifted her chin, looked around the tent, and planted her feet. I would have to come to her. She would not throw herself at me."

I take in a quick breath. So different from my vision of her dance of seduction, that over time became as real to me as the insults she threw at me at the least provocation. My mind quickly circles back to the harems where Abraham deposited me, where I witnessed the dances I inscribed to Hagar. Then I sigh. She

[10] ...and through us He spreads the beautiful fragrance of His knowledge to every corner of the earth. 2 Corinthians 2:14

used my fears against me. It was all she had.

I took a deep breath and then nod once more. I reach down into the cool water and splash my face and then watch as a little green bee-eater lights on a bush near us. I hear a desert lark warbling. *I am safe.*

When he speaks, his voice is low and hoarse. "Suddenly, I saw the frightened woman-child we met in Egypt. I saw the child who grew up knowing nothing but sexual slavery and oppression. And I saw the woman who did what she had been taught, but what she never wanted."

"It was so unfair of me," I whisper. He reaches over and squeezes my hand.

"I understand," he says. "I too considered the possibility of fathering a child through her." He looks up to the azure sky for strength. "I could not give you what you always wanted…a child. This might still be accomplished. Through Hagar."

Abram touches my unbound hair. "Surely to desire a child is the most sacred of prayers. I am sorry I left you to bear the responsibility alone."

He would not have me carry this alone. But he also desires something from me, words only I can give, but words that cost me everything—all my excuses, all my resentments and fears. But I am not ready. There is still more to be heard.

I nod once more, determined to let the conversation run its course. Even if it undoes me.

"On the night you sent her to me, I rose and came to her. She cast her eyes downward. I motioned to the cushions and said, 'Please, sit."

My heart starts to flutter. I wonder if he remembers our agreement.

"She said…," he draws a breath, steadying himself, "Sarah

wants this.'"

I suddenly see myself. The woman who bartered her dignity to be a mother. The woman who convinced herself that Hagar was just a womb, a vessel to deliver *my* child into my waiting arms. My request rendered her less than human. I think of carrying Isaac, the way our heartbeats became one as my blood nourished him. I asked the impossible of Hagar. She made the only choice she felt she had, to concede, but also to insist on her rights as the true mother of this man child.

"I am so sorry," I say. I put my head in my hands and allow the tears to flow freely. Abraham moves closer so that our shoulders touch. Feeling his invitation to be close, I put my head into his shoulder for a moment. Then I speak my shame, "Such a mess."

I glance at my husband and then reach over and wipe a tear from his grizzled cheek. He catches my eyes and in them I see a love more resilient than our wanderings. I feel his grace.

"We decided together," Abraham says.

"Did you love her?"

Pain flashes across his face, but still he speaks. "I felt tenderness for her as the woman who offered us her womb. I was intimate with her, yet I could never give her my heart, because it was already bound to you. Once she was pregnant, I largely left her alone. This stung her. Perhaps this is why she was so harsh with you. For that I blame myself."

I sigh. Now it is my turn to absolve. "You were in an impossible position and you found a way to give dignity to me…and her."

"Yahweh told me to listen to you. To let Hagar go," he says.

"And now it seems he might bring her back to us," I say. "I am scared, Abram. Not just of her, what she might do or say. I am frightened that I won't be enough for this. What if I say something that drives them both away, forever?"

"Sarai, she hurt you as much as you hurt her. If she leaves, it will be her choice for her reasons. It will not be yours to bear."

My spiritual vision clears. Yahweh did not punish me by asking Abraham to offer our son. No, he invited us into a bigger plan that would expand into the generations. Perhaps, in some mysterious way, Hagar played a part in this divine drama. My heart circles back to the dream that began this journey. The day I became Hagar, and Hagar became me. The day I was cast into the desert with Ishmael and watched my husband and my son abandon me. The day my son, Isaac, called Hagar mother. Surely this dream was a premonition of what was to come, given far in advance so that in this moment it could bring empathy. I whisper, "Lord, I am not enough, but you are enough."

Surrender is followed by sorrow. Decisions and deeds that can never be undone. Remembering how a spring continually provides water that is new, I pray, *Lord may I show her and all who serve us something different. May I display your mercy.* I glance at Abram, wanting to share this moment. "Abram, surely Yahweh remembered Hagar. Remember the traveler's story of Hagar?"

"He is the God Who Sees Me," he says.

I add, "May Yahweh be praised. He is the God who sees Hagar."

Abraham sighs with the relief of a man who has survived his greatest fear, plunging into the mired depths with the one he loves and somehow emerging with his shame cast away.

I look at him and smile. "May we treat them as Yahweh wills. Then I add the words he has longed for, "as family." This is what he has wanted from me; I offer it because it is right. Not because I am entirely ready.

We both stand up, and Abram steps toward me, his arms spread open wide. Part of me wants to push away. Instead, I step

[11] He observes every soul from His divine residence. Psalm 33:14

into his arms where I am enveloped by his strength, his manness. The long-dormant attraction stirs in my stomach. This is the man I love. The man I, by faith, called lord. This is the great chieftain and humble follower of the One God. Together, with our son Isaac, the boy who hastened his journey to becoming a man while strapped to an altar, Yahweh will increase us to be like the stars, speaking his blessing. Surely this was worth all the pain, all our missteps, all our falling short.

"I love you Abram," I whisper into his neck, as I plant a timid kiss.

When we step back, he scans the distance, "Look!"

Three camels move towards us, their hooves kicking up swirls of sand. We expected two. It seems more time has passed than we expected. One of the beasts carries Joshua and Amah, and another is loaded with supplies. "Amah must have been carried away with the cooking," I jest. The third camel is further back, still blurry in the bright light.

As quickly as we were soaked, the sun has now completely dried our garments. I put back on my robe and we make ourselves more presentable. I comb out my hair, braid it and we put our sandals back on. And then we sit back on the rock for one last time of solitude.

"Abram," I say. "I know what I want to do with the silver that Abimelech gave us for my pain in his harem.

"Yes my love?"

"I want to secure papyrus and quills. I know it is rare and quite valuable. But I want enough to write down my journey toward Moriah. And enough to use to teach the women. Perhaps five hundred or more sheets."

"It may take years to find a vendor who can supply that much, or a craftsperson to make it for us, one sheet at a time. But we will persevere," he says. He smiles. "This is an honorable way to use the silver. I knew you would find a worthy cause."

When I look up, yes, there are three camels. On one are Amah and Joshua. Trailing behind is a camel loaded with supplies. A short way behind them is a third camel carrying Ishmael and Hagar.

Joshua and Amah arrive first. In their eyes, I see a question of whether they made the right decision to bring our guests who arrived early.

Abraham immediately puts them at ease, "Joshua, Amah, thank you for bringing them along. We didn't expect them for at least another two days."

They look at each other relieved. Amah says, "We were not quite ready for them, and all the food we had prepared was on the camel. We knew you would worry if we didn't come. So it seemed best to invite them." Seeing the third camel moving nearer, she adds, "We showed them their new permanent tents on the other side of the camp from yours, so that they could freshen up to come with us to En Gedi. They seemed both relieved and unsure."

Joshua speaks up. "And, I brought two extra travel tents for them to use here at the oasis and other provisions. That is why we have taken longer than you expected."

"That gave us time we needed," Abram says, his voice full of grace.

Turning toward Hagar and Ishmael, I smile shyly and wave a welcome. Abraham takes my right hand with his left, and also raises a hand in greeting. This is the moment I have wondered about and dreaded, yet in a place I could have never expected.

Yahweh, you would have us reunite at a desert oasis, without Isaac?

They walk Gamal close to us, and then dismount. I note both how tender Ishmael is with his mother, and how strong she seems.

We walk up to them. I hesitantly reach out my hands to Hagar. She looks at Ishmael, and then lays her hands on mine barely touching. I squeeze her hands softly. "I am so grateful you came."

Abraham lays a loose arm over Ishmael's shoulders and Ishmael does not refuse him.

In my surprise to see them here, words have fled me. But it seems that the desert is the only place we could have met. The place where they suffered upon being cast out. Where Hagar met the God Who Sees Me. The place they had to navigate to make a new home with the silver Abraham gave them. The desert has no favorites.

"You made us a dwelling place in your camp?" Hagar says. "I was surprised."

"Yes," I say. "I hope you were pleased with your tents. Abraham took special care in the preparations."

She nods and I smile, neither of us sure what to say.

Seeing their opportunity, Joshua and Amah walk over. Joshua hands Hagar a skin of water and she accepts, taking a long drink. He nods at me. "Should, Amah and I set up camp here at the oasis before we attend to the food?"

"Please and thank you," I say.

Ishmael exclaims, "I will help you."

As the three of them busy themselves, Abraham and I are alone with Hagar. We are a three-sided union of pain. Two women who have borne children through one clan leader, a man of Yahweh.

Hagar looks with eyes of yearning at the spring water, excited to see it. So, the three of us amble over to the larger rocks where we can sit by the water. Yahweh brought us to a place both beautiful and calming. Words finally come to me. "Hagar, we brought you away from your home in Egypt, thinking we could rescue you from the Pharaoh who hurt me, perhaps even redeem you. Instead, we put you in an impossible position. You endured this trial. Today, you give us the grace of your return. Trusting us with your presence." I choke up. "Cutting off part of our family was not the answer. Trying to redeem another comes at a high cost. I hurt you."

My husband excuses himself to help the other men, and we both nod. We need this time alone.

We sit in silence. Hagar takes off her sandals and dips a toe, then both feet into the water. "Ahhh, so refreshing," she says.

"It is pleasant to get all the way in," I say. "And watch the clouds overhead."

Hagar plunges into her truth. "I find myself desiring your god, but it seems I grope for him in the darkness…[12] You call him Yahweh. I call him El Roi, the God Who Sees Me. In our wanderings, men have pursued me, even though I have a child. But I knew too much to be lured by lust and false promises."

I reach over to give her hand another squeeze, and she pulls her hand away. Desiring our God is more than enough, a place to begin. "What made you decide to come?"

"For a long time, Ishmael has wanted to return. But my heart has been slow…to let go."

"Yes, letting go has been my struggle as well. Not as much toward you, as toward myself."

"I longed for the gentleness of this family, for the spirit that moves it forward. At times, I even missed you, Sarah. Ishmael came home and said you and Abraham were different, kinder."

[12] This God made us in all our diversity from one original person, allowing each culture to have its own time to develop, giving each its own place to live and thrive in its distinct ways. *His purpose in all this was* that people *of every culture and religion* would search for this ultimate God, grope for Him *in the darkness, as it were,* hoping to find Him. Yet, in truth, God is not far from any of us. Acts 17:26-27

Her words remind me how unkind I was. I am no longer her mistress and I thank Yahweh she speaks in a way that asks for dignity. "We would be encouraged if you would stay. Isaac will be crushed to know Ishmael was here without his presence."

"We will see," she says. And in this moment, these three small words seem like a starting point from the God who teaches us to see.

"Sarah," she says.

"Yes, Hagar."

"I hear you went into the wilderness after Isaac and Abraham because he was ready to sacrifice Isaac on an altar in order to please Yahweh."

Again, I have no words. I nod.

"I would like to hear of that journey," Hagar says. "I understand the difficulty." She sighs deeply and wipes her eyes with her sleeve. "Not too long before Ishmael came to you, a man started harassing me. I knew what he wanted. With time, he found me alone and tried to force himself on me. I kicked and yelled and bit him. He punched me in the face. He did not succeed, but my trust for men was shattered. Then I remembered Abraham...and you."

"So devastating," I say. "You will be safe here."

"I know," she says. "I know."

Ishmael wanders back to check on his mother, and I excuse myself to see how I can help. Give them time to relax and enjoy the water.

Joshua and Amah have set up a tent for them far enough away, under a bank of trees, to allow them a little privacy. When Amah begins to pull out the food, I gasp. She has replicated the food I received from both Yasmine and Lilah—lamb with wild mint, wild greens with olive oil as well as fig, lentils and broad beans with aromatic spices. I reach over to embrace her for her kindness. Together we lay out blankets, while the men clear out the area where we usually build a fire. Seeing the weariness in my eyes, Amah leads me to a blanket and pillows under a palm tree where I can rest. She nods toward Hagar, "After they explore the springs, I will talk with her, if she likes."

Riding a camel requires a type of strength and I know an afternoon nap will help me through the evening. When I sit on the blanket, before I can lie down, Abraham comes by with his staff, fingering the feathers. "How could I have missed this?" he says. "There are now four feathers on my walking stick. Where did the other two come from?"

I smile. "Yahweh provides."

Seeing my tiredness, he says, "A story for another time."

By the time I wake up, Hagar and Amah are deep in conversation, saying words I long to hear, but trust that Yahweh has provided for the two of them. The meal is ready and spread out, and in preparation for the quickly dropping sun, a fire has been started.

We eat a feast of the One God. The conversation is light-hearted. Laughter rings from time to time. Joshua and Amah have won over Hagar. In her interactions with them, I see a woman I do not fully know. I entertain all of them with stories from my journey. The owl who fell on the mouse. How Zerah wore a cape and ran all night to redeem what I saw as unredeemable. The way Yasmine uncovered my gift of prophecy. Lilah and Ephron ministering to me. Melchizedek washing my feet. Riding by myself on a Nephilim donkey. The evil one posing as Isaac. Again, I wave my hands in the air, and use my voice, knowing this is the gift I have to give.

After the fire is out, and the conversation is silent, Abraham and Ishmael stand up to retreat to another place, where they can build a smaller fire and talk. From Ishmael's face, I guess that he and his father need more resolution. *Yahweh, please guide their conversation.*

"Ishmael, may I talk to Abraham for just a moment?"

He nods his approval, obviously curious.

I walk Abraham to where the camels stand and untie Ishmael's childhood bow. "May this guide you and remind you that Ishmael still needs you." He opens his mouth wide in surprise and tears come to his eyes, as he rubs the smooth arms.

"Your son awaits you," I say.

Laying in the tent by myself that evening, I hear a voice outside calling my name. Picking up my lit lantern, I step outside to see Hagar, wrapped in a thin cloak, shivering and nervously shifting from foot to foot.

"I think I would like to stay for a time," she says. "If you will have me and Ishmael."

"Nothing would make me gladder," I reply, feeling the pain of giving freely. "You must have numerous stories to tell. I would like to hear them."

Suddenly I remember the two capes. "I have something for you," I say. Pulling back the heavy tent flap designed to protect us from desert winds, I tenderly choose the golden-brown lamb's wool cape that carried me through the wilderness, through attack, through all of my fears. Somehow, I am certain that Lilah will agree with my decision.

Tears come to her eyes when I extend it. "Lilah gave it to me, and it protected me when I was frightened. Now I feel sure her heart would be glad if you had it to keep as your own."

"Are you sure?"

I nod, no longer able to speak. This time she reaches out a hand and squeezes mine.

We have been back in camp for ten full days since En Gedi, meaning forty days have passed since my journey. Forty days of recognition. Forty days of mourning. Forty days of Yahweh surprising us. Ten days of being with Ishmael and Hagar. They are so settled into the rhythms of our settlement, I think they might stay. Ishmael works daily with the camels and helps the men. Hagar cooks Egyptian delicacies and has a deft hand repairing clothing. They seem content.

Our women's circle is meeting today, at Amah's request. She has asked me to prepare something, a word from Yahweh. Wishing I already had papyrus and ink, which Abraham has already sent inquiries about, I count on my memory. We will meet in the afternoon, a time of resting from tasks, in my tent. Amah desires for me to mentor her in how to lead such a time.

Opening the terebinth tree chest, I pull out the stone I found on the top of Ephron's cave, remembering my words to Ephron, "Sometimes life breaks you open." With clarity, I know Yahweh wants me to speak to loss, how it wraps itself around the soul but breaks us open to something new. I light the incense made of berries roots and resins, filling the tent with a musky scent.

Before the group starts, Amah stops by with some Egyptian delicacies that Hagar has prepared. My mouth waters in anticipation. Ruchama stops by with floor pillows from their tents. Not too much later, the women begin arriving, first Heba and Selma, then Ruchama and Amah. Shyly, Hagar leans into the tent, and we all motion for her to come in. She seems uncomfortable, like she might flee at any moment.

After everyone is settled in their place, Amah speaks. "We have a special visitor today."

We all look toward the tent's opening, curious.

Lilah walks in, her silver hair nestled around her head like a crown.

"Lilah," I say as we embrace.

She whispers in my ear, "Amah told me about the cloak, and I praise Yahweh you gave it to Hagar."

"How did you know to come on this day?"

She glances at Amah. "A certain person sent a messenger."

Amah laughs, "Since you are well known in Hebron, it wasn't too difficult."

My heart lifts. "Is Ephron here as well?"

"He is with your husband and is anxious to see you. It seems he has decided that he likes the One God and can no longer pretend there are multiple gods."

I look at Hagar and smile. She will do well to speak with him.

In the hours our circle of women spends together, healing and good food abounds. After Amah prays, I tell of the Pharaoh and the night I was brought to him to be consumed. I explain how loss embeds itself into the soul, an arrowhead that cannot be easily removed. And remembering Ephron, I share how if we are full of spiritual water, a strike of lightning cannot burn us. We pass the cut rock with the sparkling crystals around, and each share one of our scars, a proof of our loss. Each of us listen with curiosity, knowing that love is best shown in presence.

Amah tells her story of witnessing her parent's sexual acts as they worshipped a goddess. How it skewed her growing up. Lilah shares about losing a child and losing their donkey Azaz. I am momentarily stunned, receiving confirmation that my worst fears are true. But the vulnerability of all the women lightens the load, reminding both Lilah and I that we are not alone.

Heba and Salma are hesitant, unsure. But in the group's loving embrace, they open up about them both being stolen from a caravan, forced into a harem, and then being judged for their skin color. Salma still longs for a husband but wonders if Yahweh hears her pleas. Heba's husband was killed by a robber after she was abducted. Ruchama tells of her many years of barrenness and the continued loss that comes with hope. The only one left is Hagar, and she looks down, and moves her head from side to side. No, she is not ready.

"Hagar, coming was enough," I say, knowing Amah is better suited to help her than I. "And the food you provided was a delight."

"You must teach me how to prepare this," Amah says, smiling at Hagar.

Hagar lifts her head. "Thank you." She looks around the circle. "You are all brave."

After the pink rock has been passed, I hand it to Lilah, "For you my friend, for showing me how women use their gifts to minister to each other."

She holds it up to the light, and we all smile as it glistens. A token of hope.

Before we close, I look around the circle, seeing our differences and our mutual yearning for One God who somehow takes all the pain, and weaves it into something beautiful. Then I remember the song I sang before I understood loss. A song that suggested that loss could only be healed if I knew the ending. I decide to sing it one last time for the women, and then let it be put to rest, until I inscribe it on the papyri that my husband will secure from Egypt.

To sing is to mourn.
To mourn is to accept.
But redemption comes
From Yahweh alone.

Born of idol worship.
Seeker of one God
Singer of Eve's song
Ezer to my husband.

As I sing, I wonder
Is it my song or yours?
Or so one, we cannot
Tell the difference.

This I do know.
Abram sang to me
Sarai the seeker
Bearer of prophecy.

Yet I became to him
Unable to deliver
Barren of a child
Denying his blessing.

All that remains
Is a song of Yahweh
Only I can sing
Only he can witness.

Then I wonder,
Is it my song or yours?
Or so one, we cannot
Tell the difference.

Despair brought chaos
Another birthing
The son of unrequited
desires and unbelief.

Now my true son
Born from a revived
Womb, carries me,
Into my hidden fears.

How do I obey
When Yahweh asks
Me to sing a song
Without an ending?

How can a husband
Be called my lord
Who risks the gift
For an unlikely faith?

Then I understood
It is my song and yours
Now so one, we cannot
Tell the difference.

There are some—indeed many—
women who do well *in every way,*
but of all of them only you are truly excellent.

Proverbs 31:29

Epilogue
Abraham's Tribute to Sarah the Prophetess

THIS MORNING, AS THE SUN CASTS AWAY shadow with its golden light, I take up Sarah's quill and the remainder of the papyrus she purchased with King Abimelech's silver. Poised on one of the olivewood chairs in front of the folding table I built for her, I begin to write. As ink flows onto the same papyrus that Sarah cherished, I remember her words of awe, "This paper is worth a king's ransom." Looking down on her papyrus, I picture my wife sitting by a fire she proudly built with her own hands, recording the story of all that transpired in her journey. In this way, before she died, she claimed back all that was lost. I pray that in the writing of these words, I might hold on to what is lost. *Yahweh, help me pay tribute to my wife.*

How could twenty-two years have passed since Moriah? How do I even begin to explain the impact of a godly woman who faithfully used her later years to disseminate the knowledge of Yahweh? A woman who leaned into being a prophetess in the years when many lay back in indulgence or rest? My Yiskah, who reminded us all that weakness can be the gateway through which glory comes.

This part of her story started after Moriah, after seeing Ishmael and then Hagar come to our camp, after starting the circle of women that would grow and multiply. It began with 1,000 silver shekels that I had stored away for Sarah given by King Abimelech to make amends. He knew not what he was saying when he exclaimed, "Now you are completely vindicated."[1]

Why did it take me so long to give her the shekels? Perhaps, I put too much weight on my ability to determine the times and places. All that I know is that Moriah changed both of us, bringing light into the dark corners of our faith. After Moriah the morning star rose in my heart.[2]

Sarah's request for papyrus stretched my faith. Yes, another way Yahweh would have to make something out of something that was not. I knew it could take a craftsperson a day to create one smooth sheet out of the aquatic sedge reed that grows by the Nile River. It was uncommon for people other than kings or Pharaohs to possess this pithy paper in large quantities. Most often, five to a hundred sheets were joined together to create a scroll. Sarah wanted single sheets that would easily fit on the small table I built. She credited the search for papyrus as finally turning her hair gray. But her gray hair was a crown of glory, cascading around her shoulder with rays of light.[3]

Without doubt, the recording of her journey *was* opposed by evil. The first shipment was lost to a sandstorm. Another time her promised papyrus burned in a mysterious fire. Sarah and I were incredulous at how many shipments were suddenly diverted or simply disappeared. It took a year to receive the first ten sheets. Five years to receive the first hundred. And twenty years in all to receive the five hundred she requested.

But Sarah remained undaunted, saying again and again, "All in Yahweh's timing. The Eternal does not see time as we do."

[1] See Genesis 20:16

[2] You would do well to pay close attention to this word; it is like a light that shines for you in the darkness of night until the day dawns when the morning star rises in your own hearts. 2 Peter 1:19

[3] See Psalm 71:18

To be honest, I wondered whether writing this manuscript was the purpose my wife sought. But once again, wisdom proved her right. As a prophetess of Yahweh, she taught from a storeroom deep within, helping the band of learners in our clan to expand.

Women and men came forward asking to learn to read and write. Literacy began to lose some of its dependence on the traveling minstrels. A living spring became available to the thirsty, thanks to Sarah's seeing of the unseen. After life emerged from her once barren womb, she knew nothing to be too difficult for the Eternal One.[4]

Yes, Sarah, vindication is yours.

Recording these words was no small conquest. Knowing her eyes were weakening, she taught Amah to read and then write. Inspired, Joshua also allowed me to teach him. When the strain of late-night writing in the low light took its toll, Amah took up the quill and continued the work. There were a few nights when Joshua stood in for his wife, slowly and carefully penning Sarah's words. Children would stop by at night, begging for just a morsel of Sarah's adventures. How excited they were when she indulged them.

How Sarah kept going, I do not know. Except, somehow, she saw the writing as rest. Her way to pause, a type of holy lingering around all that Yahweh did.[5] She also said she sensed Yasmine nearby, giving her words.

At night I liked to linger nearby to hear Sarah speak the words to be inscribed. This journey started because Sarah listened the night I agonized in prayer over a calling I could not understand to offer our son Isaac on an altar. Sarah was tested in her own way. But we also came to understand the thinness of the dividing line between heaven and earth. When others didn't understand what this meant, Sarah's explanation was profound. Although

[4] See Genesis 18:14

[5] On the seventh day—with the canvas *of the cosmos* completed—God paused from His labor and rested. Thus God blessed day seven and made it special—*an open time for pause and restoration, a sacred zone of Sabbath-keeping,* because God rested from all the work He had done in creation that day. Genesis 2:2-3

these words of hers are not recorded, this is my memory of them:

"At Moriah, heaven came down to meet earth and the curtain that normally separates the two was opened. What happened on Moriah was sacred. Yahweh took away what divides him from us. This is why couriers of all that is good were nearby, like Zerah, Yasmine and Melchizedek. But it is also why skirmishes broke out, like the attack of the bat, Isaac's apparition and King Abimelech's clumsy attempt at seduction. Evil was seeking a way to oppose Yahweh's eternal plan."

To this day, often late at night, I sit and read Sarah's manuscript by the fire, yes, one I tend carefully with my own hands. Sometimes, Isaac joins me. When I do this, by faith I hear the rise and fall of Sarah's voice, see her hands swaying in time, and watch as her facial expressions shift from sadness to joy, to terror, to mourning, then always to peace. In this way, she lingers nearby.

Now I understand that each of our separate journeys are but one story. A story of a family, raw and human, rich with history and ripe with pain. It is a story of angels and a God-man who held back my arm when I grasped the knife of sacrifice, perhaps the same one who proclaimed Sarah's miraculous pregnancy with our son. Although I shall not know until I am on the other side of the dividing line, I like to think it is the man she knew as Zerah. How I wish I had more than the few words spoken as I held the knife over our son, "This is not Isaac's to do, this is mine." Through suffering, Yahweh crushed and reshaped us into a different vessel more to his liking.[6]

On the top of Moriah, Isaac touched heaven and saw a heavenly courier face to face. Although it left him remembering the terror of being bound like an animal, it has emboldened him as a follower of Yahweh.

Recently, Isaac and I traveled to the Cave of Moriah at his

[6] And *as I watched,* the clay vessel in his hands became flawed *and unusable.* So the potter started again with the same clay. He *crushed and squeezed* and shaped it into another vessel that was to his liking. Jeremiah 18:4

request. On the way, after inhaling the aroma of pine and savoring the song of birds, we sang the Song of Sojourn as Sarah taught us. We spent the night in the cave and read from her story all that transpired. That night, a storm came through. An ominous dark cloud was followed by hail, and then far into the moonless night, the sky rumbled its displeasure. Neither of us could sleep, knowing the fierce attack that was suffered there. We worshiped and prayed. Later, Isaac told me that he had hoped to see Zerah there. All I could say was, "By faith, my son."

Isaac has so much of Sarah in him, her intellect, her boldness, and her sure sense of right and wrong. Missing her is almost more than he can bear. Although Maya is now old herself, some forty-five years with patches of different shades of gray all over her haunches, she can comfort Isaac in ways no one else can. His mourning will take time, as his fierce devotion to his mother has always burned brightly.

Very soon I will fulfill Sarah's other wish by sending Eliezer back to our people to find a wife for Isaac.[7] I pray he can find a woman like his mother, a *chayil.*

Ishmael also carries Sarah's image. He likes to oppose my thoughts with her honesty. "Why, mother Sarah said...." Whether he will find Yahweh, I cannot say. But a man can hope against hope that this honesty is teaching him to confront evil. Every time he visits or lingers here, I rehearse Sarah's words to him, reminding myself that mercy overcomes judgment. Sarah showed this same wisdom the day she bowed before me and called me lord. Knowing by then the extent of her suffering in the harems, I was humbled. Sarah saw in me what I am just now fully claiming in myself. Sarah called me the man of faith. But faith is perfected by Yahweh.[8] If I am the father of faith, Sarah is the mother. She carried faith in the womb of her mind and

[7] Genesis 24:2-58

[8] Now stay focused on Jesus, who designed and perfected our faith. Hebrews 12:2

heart and released it when the travails of its birth were complete.

It has now been six months since Sarah's earthly sojourn ended. She lived a full life of 127 years. On the day of her passing, she left gently, in her sleep, with a slight smile on her face, having completed life's sojourn. By faith I see my wife singing and dancing with Zerah and Azaz before the gates of the eternal city. One of Sarah's requests was to be buried in the cave of Machpelah where Ephron and Lilah ministered to her, a cave she aptly named, "Ephron's Cave." As Sarah suggested, I used the remainder of Abimelech's money to secure the cave.

After Sarah's passing, Isaac and Ishmael presided over her burial together. Hagar could not bring herself to come, but Ishmael tells me that she mourned with loud cries. It was a sight to see, our two son's unified desire to honor their mother—about the only belief they both have wholeheartedly shared. Afterwards, unable to process his grief with us, Ishmael rode off on Gamal the camel with Hamor trailing on a rope, the Nephilim donkey Sarah gifted him before she died.[9] Ishmael is a mighty archer and visionary, nursing the hope of building a city. I will honor Sarah's admonition to keep pursuing Ishmael, just as Yahweh keeps pursuing us. In my staying near, he might see the Eternal Father that stays near.

In part due to Sarah, Ephron has become a mighty man of Yahweh. To this day, he loves to tell how her vulnerable words, on the day she appeared in his cave, changed the way he saw. How he found a God who welcomed his weakness and loved him in his grief. Ephron is becoming a teacher of men and the man Lilah always saw him to be. They are raising their son to know Yahweh.

Sarah pulled me aside a few months before she died with a request. "After I leave to be with Yahweh, I think it would

[9] Look, all of you are flawed in so many ways, yet in spite of all your faults, you know how to give good gifts to your children. How much more will your Father in heaven give the Holy Spirit to all who ask! Luke 11:13

be fitting for you to invite Hagar back into the circle of the family." When I looked into her eyes, she added, "As your wife." Although I thought this was for the boys, my wife indicated there was more. "Hagar has been chaste in her pursuit of Yahweh. Now she can be chaste within the warm embrace of another."

Hagar desires a Hebrew name to honor her faith in Yahweh. On the day we wed, she will become Keturah, meaning incense.[10] She chose the name herself, thinking of the incense Sarah would burn when the women met together and how it slowly opened her soul to her own losses.

As for Sarah's manuscript, I had a camel's skin bag made by a local craftsman to hold it. Just when I thought the miracles had ceased, a traveling merchant offered to sell me a copper dove he had fashioned. When he pulled it out of his bag, it was exactly how I pictured the one Sarah described in her dream. Next week, I will set off to the cave to bury her manuscript, along with this tribute, her camel skin cloak and the dove. After I read these words to Isaac (he said he would not forgive me if I neglected this), and read them to Sarah at her burial site, I will entrust the camel's bag into the dark earth far in the back of the cave, deep as my aged hands can dig.

Although I hesitate to bury what means so much to so many, it was her wish. *Hinini.*

For now I mourn, but in Yahweh's timing I will see Sarah again. And together we will witness from afar as Yahweh's promise multiplies from generation to generation. On that day, our waking dreams of Yahweh's covenant promise will become our day to day walk. Since Sarah was a type of minstrel, it seems right to spin words together into what might qualify as a song, or at least a tale. Although I do not have Sarah's gift, I offer these words.

[10] Abraham had taken another wife, whose name was Keturah. She bore him Zimran, Jokshan, Medan, Midian, Ishbak and Shuah. Genesis 25:1-2

Song of Sarah
Prophetess song
Warrior for good
Chayil against wrong

Song of Sarah
Faithful and true
Mother and friend
Courier of the new

Song of Sarah
Partner of mine
Sojourned beside me
In covenant sublime

Song of Sarah
Singer of hymns
Vulnerable words
That cleanse within

Song of Sarah
Still shines bright
Heaven's messenger
Yahweh's bearer of light

Questions for Discussion

Prayer Song

1. The Wallace Stevens quote that begins the book says, "And not to have is the beginning of desire. To have what is not is its ancient cycle." Read Proverbs 13:12. What unfulfilled desire still causes spiritual tension as you long to "have what is not?"
2. In her beginning song (before the introduction), Sarah says, "How do I obey when Yahweh asks me to sing a song without an ending?" How do her words predict the nature of faith for all of us?
3. The intensity of Abraham's prayer strikes Sarah as being unusual, even worrisome. What did you learn about Abraham from Sarah's eavesdropping? What did you learn about Sarah?
4. In the introduction Sarah describes her gift of being an *ezer* (the eye that sees the danger) as both a burden to her husband and a gift from Yahweh. How is being a Godly *ezer* different from meddling?
5. Sarah longs for Abraham to come beside her and open up about his prayer. Why does Sarah struggle to express her truest need to her husband?

Chapter One — Barren Song

1. In Sarah's dream she imagines herself becoming Hagar and Hagar becoming her. Sarah is quick to explain their differences, but what do they have in common? Why is empathy difficult for both of them?
2. Sarah describes the "gaping canyon of life circumstances" between her and her maids. How do their differences tend to divide them?
3. What signs are there that Sarah and Abraham might see following Yahweh differently? What does Sarah value? How is that different from what Abraham values?
4. Sarah says that being in two harems has left "an emotional limp that endures." What signs do you already see that Sarah's past trauma still lingers?
5. Sarah puts together the clues in her dream and intuits that Abraham might be planning to offer Isaac to Yahweh. Considering their long history, do you find her reaction in or out of proportion to what is happening to her?
6. Sarah says there is a greater risk than thieves, robbers and predators—Yahweh himself. Read the last paragraph of the chapter out loud. How does following God seem like a threat to Sarah? Have you ever felt this way?

Chapter Two - Donkey's Song

1. Why does Sarah go to such length to describe her relationship with her donkey, Maya? What might the donkey represent to her?
2. What reasons does Sarah give for refusing to be passive? What life circumstances will she have to push past in order to be an active participant in her own family's story?
3. Sarah remembers the weaning party that took place when Isaac was three years old. Why do you think this memory comes now? How might it help explain Sarah's struggle to trust?
4. Sarah also shares the memory of the visitor to their camp who unknowingly brought the story of Hagar and Ishmael. What does this scene tell you about Sarah and Abraham's relationship?
5. Is Sarah's plan to follow Abraham and Isaac into the wilderness wise or foolish? What unfulfilled desire might be driving her forward?

Chapter Three - Song of Sojourn

1. Sarah sets forth with two God-fearing guides—Zerah and Yasmine, a brother and sister. How do Yasmine and Zerah show hospitality? What could this tell Sarah about Yahweh?
2. Sarah describes laughing when she heard she would have a son at her old age. She also describes her and her husband's "wild joy" over having Isaac, whose name means *"son of my laughter."* How does laughter help her access difficult emotions and painful memories?
3. Sarah says that she is going on this quest, "in faith, yet I am full of doubt." How do faith and doubt both serve as important motivations in Sarah's story? How might this apply to you?
4. Sarah shares how Abraham knows his song and trusts both the dark and bright strains. In contrast, Sarah senses her smallness in a universe full of stars, and wonders if she still has a song to sing. How are their perspectives different?
5. In the song of sojourn that Yasmine teaches Sarah, each stanza begins with a different word: song – verse – prayer – shout – whisper. What does this tell you about prayer? Why is singing so comforting to Sarah?

Chapter Four - Owl's Song

1. Sarah says to Yasmine, "This whole ludicrous journey is because of this, this…wild, moody God who falls out of the sky to terrorize us with his callings." Does Sarah see God's unpredictability as a threat or a calling? Read Ecclesiastes 11:5. How do we try to domesticate God's wildness?
2. As a single woman, Yasmine says, *"Yahweh put the desire into woman for a man, a partner, by creating Eve with part of Adam's rib. But since Yahweh breathed himself into women, our desire for him is even stronger."* What story do your desires tell you about your relationship with Yahweh?
3. The snake calls Sarah, "sweet barren one." Why was it important for Sarah to identify where the attack was coming from? Why does Satan want us to think we are always at fault?
4. Sarah prayed for safety for her beloved donkey, Maya. How could the flash flood create a spiritual crisis for Sarah? How have unanswered prayers influenced how you see God?
5. At the end of chapter four, Sarah says, "sorrow rushes over me, full of mud, sticks and rocks, ready to…push me into crevices where I do not want to go. What deeply rooted pain might Sarah be called to face?

Chapter Five - Spring Song

1. Sitting outside the cave by herself, Sarah prays... "My soul is downcast within me. Your calling has swept over me. Do I forget your promise?" What promises of Yahweh might Sarah forget when she is downcast?
2. In this chapter, we discover that Yasmine can also run through the night, like her brother Zerah. Talking to Sarah, Zerah says, "You might think of us as couriers." As couriers, what do Zerah and Yasmine carry? Why might this be significant?
3. Sarah sings a song about Maya, the donkey she lost in the wadi. Why was this loss so crushing? Why is it important to honor and mourn animals who serve us well?
4. Sarah has a dream with an angelic staircase (like the patriarch Jacob's dream in Genesis 28:10-17). In it Abraham wrestles against Yahweh's injunction to give Isaac, and even wrestles with an angel. How might this form a bridge between her and her husband?
5. At the springs, Sarah has a traumatic flashback of her experience in Pharaoh's harem. How might it help her to let the memory surface? What might Yahweh want her to know?

Chapter Six - Ephron's Song

1. When Sarah explains her sorrow over losing Maya, she says of Ephron, "I am thankful he doesn't offer well-trodden words that minimize pain." What kind of words hurt someone in pain instead of helping them?
2. Through Ephron and Lilah, Sarah experiences hospitality as an essential way travelers survive. What is most surprising to Sarah about being on the receiving end of hospitality? How does she minister to them?
3. Sarah chose to talk to Ephron on top of the hill instead of staying with Lilah. How does her vulnerability serve as a bridge between her and Ephron?
4. How are Sarah's interactions different with Lilah? What might have been Yahweh's purpose in bringing the three of them together?
5. At the end of the chapter, Sarah discovers that Ephron and Lilah left their treasured donkey Azaz for her. How does giving such a valuable gift impact Sarah's heart? What confidence does it give her?

Chapter Seven - Melchizedek's Song

1. Sarah describes *hinini* it as meaning, "I am here. I understand the call. I am enough for it. I will not desert you." How is Sarah, in her own way, living out *hinini*?
2. Knowing that, "stories of heartache soften in the telling," Sarah rehearses how she will explain her harem experience to Isaac, including how she aged backwards. What good impact could this have on her son?
3. Sarah says, "Would Yahweh say that all this turmoil is a call to forgive?" What does Sarah need to forgive? Why is it so difficult to admit we need to forgive?
4. Melchizedek washes Sarah's feet, humbling her. As she says, "To refuse the washing would be to refuse the companionship of a king and the ministering of Yahweh." Read John 13:8. How do Melchizedek's words and actions point ahead to Jesus?
5. After telling her story of early abuse. Sarah says of Melchizedek, "He must understand how stubborn of a hold an untold story has in the heart." How does Sarah's early life still impact her at 105 years old? How does something in your childhood still impact you today?

Chapter Eight - Wayfaring Song

1. How does pain "slice Sarah open" to the mystery of Yahweh's moving? Can you think of one pain that is having a similar effect in your life?
2. Twice Sarah finds herself at where the two paths meet. The second time, she asks, *"Does Yahweh drive me to this place of decision again and again?"* What decision is Sarah finding so hard to make? How do you relate?
3. When Melchizedek's donkey Poorie returns after running away, Sarah says "For a few sacred moments, our faces glisten with joy. The nasty attack in the woods shimmies away in defeat." Read James 1:2 How is evil defeated through joy?
4. Sarah says, "I am not like you. My love invokes more fear instead of casting it out." Melchizedek replies, "Only a prophetess is so vigorously honest with herself." What does Melchizedek want her to see about herself?
5. Melchizedek leaves, Zimrah the donkey bolts, and a landslide occurs. Sarah prays, "I am broken." Does admitting her brokenness weaken or strengthen her?

Chapter Nine - Battle Song

1. Why does the evil one appear as an apparition of Isaac? What fears and loves of Sarah's does he try to manipulate?
2. Isaac's apparition tries to get Sarah to take her own life in order to join him. What are some self-destructive responses that are tempting when shame visits?
3. How do the words of Melchizedek provide a way out for Sarah, "Will the eye that sees danger overcome untruth?" How does rehearsing what she really fears help clarify her thinking and help her to take a stand?
4. Sarah says, "Abram's test was whether he would go up to Moriah. Mine is whether I will go down." Were you disappointed she didn't continue all the way to Abraham and Isaac? What does this decision predict about her journey forward?
5. Back at the wadi rock shelter, Sarah is surprised when King Abimelech appears for yet one more standoff. How are women uniquely equipped for spiritual warfare? In what ways do you see *chayil* in your own life?

Chapter Ten - Song of Sand

1. Sarah has been reunited with her donkey Maya and then receives Hamor the Nephilim donkey as a gift from Yasmine. As the story of the donkeys comes full circle, why were they so vital to Sarah's journey? How are they involved in God's redemption of her pain?
2. Finally, traveling by herself, Sarah processes why she turned back, saying, "reasons line up like soldiers saluting my choice." How do you see her faith becoming clearer? Would you have turned back from Moriah or made a different decision?
3. As she rides, Sarah tells us about the time she spent with Yasmine the night before. There they discuss the meaning of Sarah's gift of being a prophetess. Why is this gift so uniquely feminine?
4. Abraham meets Sarah on the path, where together they scare away a sand cat. How do they each extend grace? What new thing might be coming in their relationship?
5. Sarah asks Amah, her handmaid, if they can be equal friends with different roles, saying, "I long for pain and joy to flow between us." Amah says, "I am willing. If you will step into my broken places with me." How might this open the door for both Amah and Sarah to grow?

Chapter Eleven - Mountain Song

1. When Ishmael appears, Sarah talks to him for the first time since he was cast away. What vulnerabilities do each bring to the conversation? How does Sarah use what she learned from her guides to show him he is seen and heard?
2. Why is it so important for Sarah to minister to Ishmael in a physical way (water to drink, and a wet cloth to wash his face)? Read Matthew 10:42 and John 4:14. How does physical water open the possibility of their relationship being cleansed?
3. Sarah has a vision of a mountain. How has Sarah's understanding of Yahweh's plans expanded through her journey?
4. When Abraham invites Sarah to speak at the campfire where both Isaac and Ishmael are present, she chooses to first tell the story of the yellow scorpion. How could their campfire conversation serve as a model for a blended family?
5. How did hearing the story of Moriah impact Ishmael? What motivates Sarah to ask him to invite Hagar to visit them?
6. Talking about Sarah's experience with Pharoah, Abraham says, "I put you into the fire, believing you would not be burned. It is as if I tied you up and put you on an altar of my own accord." How do these words reassure Sarah?

Chapter Twelve - Redemption Song

1. Twenty-eight days after Ishmael left to go to Hagar, Sarah has an early morning anxiety attack. Isaac is left with fears that had him sleeping in their tent for a time. What tools is Sarah able to impart to her son?
2. Abraham surprises Sarah with a trip to En Gedi, an oasis near the Red Sea. On their camel ride, Sarah is now ready to hear her husband's part of the harem story. Why is this important? How does calling out wrongs empower us?
3. Sarah asks, "How does a woman ask intimate questions she longs to be answered, without threatening her own peace or pushing her husband away?" How does Abraham and Sarah's faith allow them to have a difficult conversation about Hagar?
4. Abraham and Sarah are surprised by the appearance of Ishmael and Hagar, but decide to welcome them. How do they model biblical hospitality in both their actions and their conversations?
5. Sarah finally has the conversation she longs for with Hagar. What do you see as key moments in their interactions? How does Sarah make room for Hagar's hesitancy and fear?
6. The women's circle includes Hagar and two Egyptian women who were gifted by King Abimelech, as well as unexpected appearance by Lilah. How does Sarah lead them in a way that allows for pain to be traded? How is grace present?

Epilogue - Abraham's Tribute to Sarah the Prophetess

1. Abraham says, "Moriah changed both of us, bringing light into the dark corners of our faith." What dark corners of their faith did it bring light to? Why does Yahweh bring to light what we instinctively want to hide?
2. Amah becomes a mighty woman in their clan, prepared to carry on Sarah's work. How are women uniquely able to equip other women? What might the gift of being a prophetess entail?
3. Abraham now sees that each of their separate journeys (his, Sarah's, Isaac's, Ishmael's and Hagar's) are but one story that belongs to Yahweh. Is there a common thread among their journeys?
4. Abraham mentions the day that Sarah bowed before him and called him lord, using it as an example of how mercy overcomes judgment. Read 1 Peter 3:6. How has your view of this scripture changed over the reading of this story?
5. Before her death, Sarah requested that the manuscript be buried with her. What cultural considerations might have been at play?
6. Abraham says, "If I am the father of faith, then Sarah is the mother." How does Sarah serve as a role model for biblical womanhood?

Consider how Sarah, *our mother,* obeyed her husband, Abraham, and called him "lord," and you will be her daughters as long as you boldly do what is right without fear *and without anxiety.*

1 Peter 3:6

At one point, the women sang as they danced and celebrated....

1 Samuel 18:7

Afterword

From the Author, Robin Weidner

RECENTLY, I WAS READING YET ONE MORE Hebrew Commentary online on the stories of Genesis. In it, after considering Abraham and Sarah's story of harems, Hagar's saga, and a son bound to an altar, the author says something like...*I'm sure we are breathing a sigh of relief to be done with this terrifying and bewildering part of the scriptures.* Within my five-year journey of writing Sarah's Song, I have read many books about Abraham, Sarah and Hagar. The fiction I read usually stopped short of Moriah and didn't consider the traumatic impact of the harem experiences. When I decided to pen fictional accounts of the three "every woman" of the Bible, Eve, Sarah and Mary, I knew Sarah's story would start and end with Moriah. In her journey, it made sense that she would be triggered back into past traumatic memories like the ones she no doubt experienced in two different harems.

You may wonder why I took on such an ambitious project, including merging fiction with non-fiction. To be honest, the story of Sarah hasn't always inspired my trust. All that transpired between her and Hagar can be difficult reading, especially for someone whose father was unfaithful to her mother, and whose husband was unfaithful to her (more in a moment). The idea of multiple wives was triggering. Plus, in the conservative church I was converted into at age seventeen, Sarah was held up as an example of fascinating womanhood. She obeyed her husband and called him Lord (1 Peter 3:6 above). Over the years, I've heard culturally-sensitive explanations, that in New Testament times, calling a husband lord was not the same as calling Jesus Lord.[1] In Genesis 23, the same word is used by Ephron when Abraham is bargaining for his cave to bury his wife Sarah.

> My lord, listen to me. The property is worth 10 pounds of silver. Surely that is an amount we can agree on. So go, and bury your dead *in peace.* Genesis 23:15

The word lord was not only used by women toward men, but also in other conversations such as Ephron with Abraham. The word lord was a term of respect, but not referring to one-person-over-another submission. It is also interesting that in the story of Sarah and Abraham in Genesis, we don't ever hear Sarah call Abraham lord. Perhaps Peter was depending on oral history, the way stories were passed down and eventually recorded. Yes, I have always believed Sarah showed Abraham this great respect, but I yearned for more. For instance, how did she call Abraham lord and obey him, after he (seemingly):

> Told lies/half-truths that led to the indignations and likely sexual abuse of two harems.
> Allowed Sarah to wrestle alone with her barrenness and her handmaid as her only hope.
> Sat by passively, when Hagar began abusing her.
> Bound her long-awaited, miraculously born son to an altar, ready to lower the knife of sacrifice.

[1] Eddie L. Hyatt, "Did Sarah Call Abraham LORD, Lord or lord?" From the website, "God's Word to Women. http://godswordtowomen.blogspot.com/2012/08/did-sarah-call-abraham-lord-lord-or-lord.html

The writing of *Sarah's Song* suddenly began to give me a renewed perspective. We ascribe people with respect who have shown their trustworthiness through their sacrificial actions and true humility. Obedience is a free will gift given in response to earned trust. With context, the scene in *Sarah's Song* when Sarah kneels before Abraham and calls him lord moves me.

1 Peter 3:6 goes on to say that we are Sarah's daughters when we "boldly do what is right without fear and without anxiety." Although others count on me as someone who boldly does what is right, I can't say I easily do it without any fear or anxiety to work through first. Anxiety is a demon that I have fought hard. I expect it will always find a way to creep in, considering the amount of trauma I had in my early years—sexual abuse, my father's alcoholism and verbal abuse, marrying a sexual addict bringing twenty years of on and off sexual sin into our relationship. Wanting to understand the insecurity and fear that seemed to chase me at every corner, I began to write healing books. Eventually, in our own recovery journey (now spanning over twenty years), Dave and I launched a non-profit devoted to sexual purity called *Purity Restored Ministries* (www.purityrestored.com). Seeing the need for more training, I became a Certified Trauma Professional and Life Coach.

With a new focus, the vision for *Sarah's Song* still endured. Writing it would require God the potter reshaping me into a vessel, prepared for once again facing evil head on. And, yes, during this writing, the Satanic skirmishes (similar to the ones I experienced in the writing of *Eve's Song*) seemed to escalate. Terrible dreams and visions came, multiple venomous spider bites occured, and two bikes, including my treasured red "recovery bike," were cut off of our car and stolen. This took place during a writing session in a California coffee shop where I was working on Sarah's journey back home from the cave of Moriah. As my husband said, "They stole our steeds."

I could have never predicted that the most intensive parts of writing this book would span (on and off) through five years. It turned out that I would need my own journey towards my own kind of Moriah, to even know how to pen this story. Most of the attack scenes in this book are from my own experiences (including the bat and the out-of-body-experience).

The personal impact of writing this book has been astonishing. Sarah has become a type of biblical best friend, someone who I lean on to understand myself. I am now proud to be her daughter and somehow, in my own faltering way, to walk in her steps. When I am tempted to draw back in fear, rely on performance to earn approval, or even hide my imperfection, I remember Sarah. In moments of testing, instead of moving away from the women God has given me, I lean in towards them. When I need to engage in complicated conversations with close or extended family members, I remember how Sarah found a way to love Ishmael and Hagar. How she made space for them to have their own journey, while acknowledging that their experiences were part of a bigger story—God's story. Yahweh has taught me a gentle boldness, even when I am afraid. And now, nearing retirement age, I find in Sarah a vision for living out biblical womanhood until I stand on the top of the mountain, welcomed by Jesus himself into the eternal kingdom.

Most of all, the writing of *Sarah's Song* reinforced my long-time belief that the dividing line between heaven and earth is so much thinner than we imagine. During this time period, I have had the privilege of escorting dear friends and relatives from life to death. These experiences were sacred and moving. Yes, this book has gifted me with a different understanding of all that transpired on Moriah. And, it has strengthened my conviction that women are invited, welcomed and needed at the high places and the low places where God chooses to show himself.

You would not hold this book as it is without the women who walked with me through this journey. All told, there were thirty of us that processed the first draft of this book together. On Sunday afternoons we met online in two different groups to share insights and trade pain. They helped to carry me through ongoing attacks, as I ushered them through their own healing journeys. The circle of women God brought me was breathtaking and represented different cultures, backgrounds, ages and life stages. Their passion for the healing story within *Sarah's Song* was moving. A special thank you to: Amie Acuna, Christine Arsenault, Tania Ball, Jordan Brilhante, Kelly Dingmann, Teri Frederick, Mary Freeman, Pam Matthew George, Laura Hattendorf, Letasha Howe, Bianca Johnson, Jermiah A. Jones, Nicoleta Koha, Adam Levy, Gale Littlefield, Chrep Meitner, Diane Marie Mitchell, McKayla Owen, Dominique Patterson, Bobbie Winters, Michelle Santa, Robin Wadsworth, Janice Wright and Kathy Xu. To all who read chapters and sent encouragement, thank you! I also want to thank all of the women and men I have had the privilege of coaching over the last three years. Your vulnerability has been a bright light.

This story has been refined by three high-level editors who went through the book multiple times, asking me hard questions and offering their own responses to this story. Thank you to Thyra Root for her unflinching determination that I stay true to ancient Israel and true to the characters. Maxine Heath came later and poured herself into ironing out any inconsistencies. With Thyra in her twenties and Maxine a senior like me, I felt they bookended this work perfectly! And a special thank you to my husband Dave, who often had me laughing with his comedic take on needed changes. Truly Dave made a huge contribution by ensuring men could read this book as well as women. In the biblical sense, Dave, I joyfully consider you worthy of being called lord.

Beyond that, I leaned on the learning of others in so many ways. Jewish midrash opened up possibilities I wouldn't have considered, like the idea that Satan sent an apparition of Isaac to tempt Sarah. I have also read feministic perspectives on both Hagar and Sarah, books that cover both the Muslim and Christian responses to this Bible story, commentaries, desert stories, a book on donkeys, treatises from Jewish Old Testament scholars and as many fiction and nonfiction books as I could find on Abraham and Sarah. Often during sermons, I found myself with a whole new take on a concept within these pages. God has richly provided.

Recently I sat with a respected Bible scholar and friend of mine. When I explained the premise of *Sarah's Song,* he asked many questions. Then he settled back into his chair, and said, "It sounds like you are writing a modern midrash of your own." These words of affirmation gave me the boost of confidence that my often-accused soul needed. I am also grateful for my college experiences at Freed-Hardeman College and Harding University, where I was usually the only female in high-level biblical classes and certainly the only woman who regularly went to the preacher's club. I came out just short of having enough Bible hours for a second major (my first major being in Social Work).

Most of all, I thank Yahweh God, the Eternal One, God Most High and most of all the God Who Sees Me. I pray you find him in your own way through this book. I hope this journey reminds you that it is never too late to find a healing circle of your own.

Oh, the stories that will be told on the other side, as we each add our songs to the story that has always been God's alone. No doubt, the women will sing, dance and celebrate together. I would be honored if you would like to share your story. You can reach me at rwcopywriting@comcast.net.

—Robin Weidner

Booklist

Here is a partial list of books I read during the writing of this book, whose truths may be somehow reflected in *Sarah's Song*.

Abraham: A Journey to the Heart of Three Faiths
Bruce Feiler

Abraham and Sarah
J. SerVaas Williams

Born to Run
Christopher McDougal

Forming: A Work of Grace
David Takle

Genesis: Translation and Commentary
Robert Atler

Hagar: God's Beloved Stranger
Hester Thomsen

Hagar the Egyptian: The Lost Tradition of the Matriarchs
Savina J. Teubal

Inheriting Abraham: The Legacy of the Patriarch in Judaism, Christianity & Islam
Jon D. Levenson

The Beginning of Desire: Reflections on Genesis
Avivah Gottlieb Zornberg

The Gift of the Jews, How a Tribe of Desert Nomads Changed the Way Everyone Feels and Thinks
Thomas Cahill

The Holy Longing: The Search for a Christian Spirituality
Ronald Rolheiser

The Murmuring Deep: Reflections on the Biblical Unconscious
Avivah Gottlieb Zornberg

The Shattered Lantern: Rediscovering a Felt Presence of God
Ronald Rolheiser

The Solace of Fierce Landscapes: Exploring Desert and Mountain Spirituality
Belden C. Lane

The Soul of Desire: Discovering the Neuroscience of Longing, Beauty and Community
Curt Thompson

The Wisdom of Donkeys: Finding Tranquility in a Chaotic World
Andy Merrifield

Where God was Born: A Journey by Land to the Roots of Religion
Bruce Feiler

Who Ate Lunch with Abraham: The Appearances of God as a Man in Hebrew Scriptures
Asher Intrater

Healing Circle

Sarah's Song is a book that begs to be read and discussed with others. By choosing a regular time, and following a few basic guidelines, you can enjoy the kind of circle Sarah establishes in the book. Before *Sarah's Song* was released, it went through two online book groups. Here is what we found creates a deep, meaningful, relationship building group:

1. **Consider reading aloud:** If you are leading the group, choose what passages you would like volunteers to read aloud. Also offer for participants to share quotes or paragraphs they found especially meaningful. As you process, look for Holy Spirit moments to….

    - Go deeper—Most of us skip words when we read silently. In *Sarah's Song,* reading aloud will uncover many layers of meaning.

    - Hear and see—Encourage readers to mark passages that are meaningful, and read them again aloud.

    - Take time to process—When you hear emotion in someone else's voice, ask yourself, "How do I relate?" Take risks to open up and others will follow.

2. **Let the discussion breathe**—Pause often for discussion, asking questions like, "What stood out to you? Do you agree or disagree? How do you relate to this?

3. **Use the study guide**—At the end of the group, ask each person to choose one or two questions to journal on. At the start of the next group, ask, "Who would like to share?"

4. **Take advantage of the footnotes**—Remind readers that the footnoted scriptures are in The Voice translation, giving readers an accurate yet emotionally intelligent understanding.

5. **Set some guidelines**—In Sarah's group, Hagar didn't want to share at her first meeting. Sarah and the other members made it safe for her to listen quietly.

   Your guidelines (read aloud each meeting) might include:

   - Safe Haven—This is a confidential group. What is shared here, stays here.

   - Sharing—When someone shares, we will simply say, "Thank you for sharing." This is not a space to fix someone or propose solutions to their pain. We are here to safely process our losses, our spiritual battles and victories.

   - Support—We will keep our sharing brief to make room for others. We all commit to opening our hearts to God and each other.

   - Spirit—We anticipate hearing the Holy Spirit speaking and will celebrate his moving.

I would love to hear from your healing circle! Send your stories, response and questions to rwcopywriting@comcast.net. And yes, these will be kept confidential.

About the Author

Robin Weidner is also the author of *Eve's Song, Secure in Heart, Grace Calls: Spiritual recovery after abandonment, addiction or abuse,* and with David Weidner, *Pure the Journey, and Recovering Hearts: A gentle path to healing betrayal. Grace Calls* won the gold medal in the 2019 Illumination International Book Awards (Self-Help). Robin speaks in the United States and abroad on insecurity, trauma recovery, spiritual recovery, marriage and sexual integrity. Their non-profit organization, Purity Restored Ministries, touches individuals around the world. Robin and Dave have three adult children and two grandchildren.

Robin is a Certified Trauma Professional and Life Coach. She coaches individuals in spiritual recovery, healing trauma, and creative recovery, and with Dave coaches marriages recovering from betrayal. After studying Social Work at Freed-Hardeman, Harding University and New Mexico State University, Robin finally capped her BS from Western Illinois University (concentrating in English Literature).

Living in Idaho, Robin enjoys stand-up paddle boarding, hiking, camping and bike riding. Robin is known for her risk-taking vulnerability, gentle approach to difficult topics and use of healing humor. For information on coaching or bringing Robin (or Dave and Robin) in to speak, you can reach her at rwcopywriting@comcast.net.

Bible versions used in *Sarah's Song*

Scripture quotations taken from the Amplified® Bible (AMP), Copyright © 2015 by The Lockman Foundation. Used by permission. www.lockman.org

Scripture quotations marked "ESV" are from the ESV Bible® (The Holy Bible, English Standard Version®), copyright © 2001 by Crossway Bibles, a publishing ministry of Good News Publishers. Used by permission. All rights reserved. http://www.crossway.org

Scripture quotations marked "MSG" or "The Message" are taken from The Message. Copyright 1993, 1994, 1995, 1996, 2000, 2001, 2002. Used by permission of NavPress Publishing Group.

Scripture quotations marked (NIV) are taken from the Holy Bible, New International Version®, NIV®. Copyright © 1973, 1978, 1984, 2011 by Biblica, Inc.™ Used by permission. All rights reserved.

Scripture quotations marked (NLT) are taken from the Holy Bible, New Living Translation, copyright © 1996, 2004, 2007 by Tyndale House Foundation. Used by permission of Tyndale House Publishers, Inc., Carol Stream, Illinois 60188. All rights reserved. http://www.newlivingtranslation.com/

Scripture quotations marked NLV are taken from the New Life Version, copyright © 1969 and 2003. Used by permission of Barbour Publishing, Inc., Uhrichsville, Ohio 44683. All rights reserved.

Scripture quotations marked OJB are taken from The Orthodox Jewish Bible. Copyright 20 by AFI International. 1,248 pages.

Scripture quotations [RSV] are from Revised Standard Version of the Bible, copyright © 1946, 1952, and 1971 National Council of the Churches of Christ in the United States of America. Used by permission. All rights reserved worldwide.

Scripture quotations marked TPT are from The Passion Translation®. Copyright © 2017, 2018, 2020 by Passion & Fire Ministries, Inc. Used by permission. All rights reserved. ThePassionTranslation.com.

Additional Books by Robin Weidner

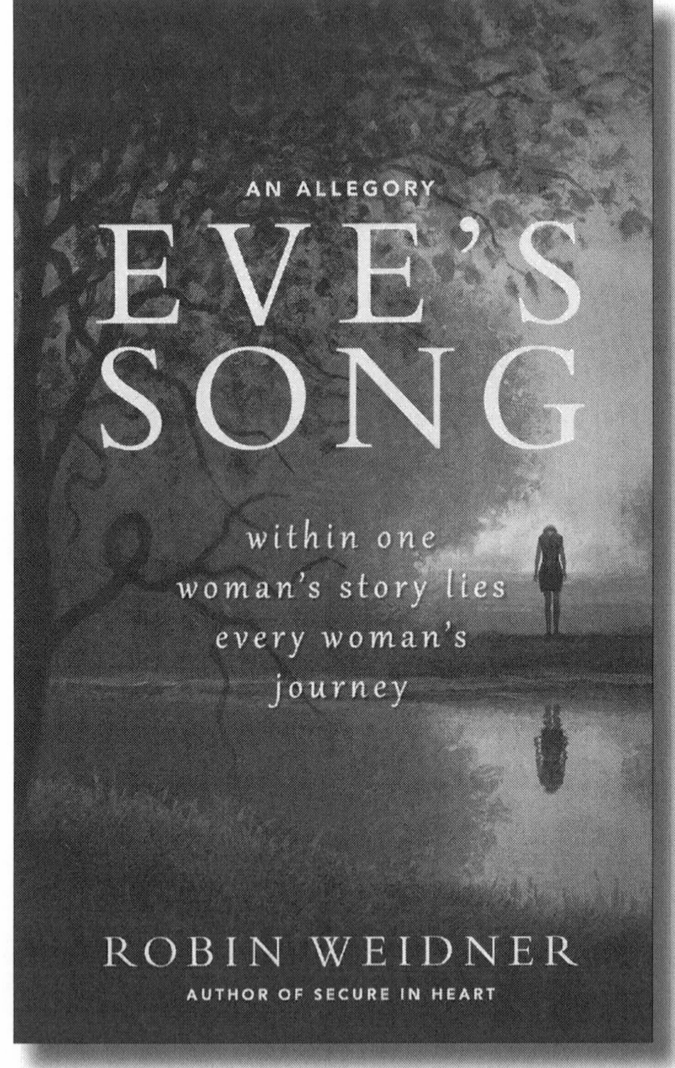

Additional Books by Robin Weidner

Books by Dave and Robin Weidner

Books by Dave and Robin Weidner

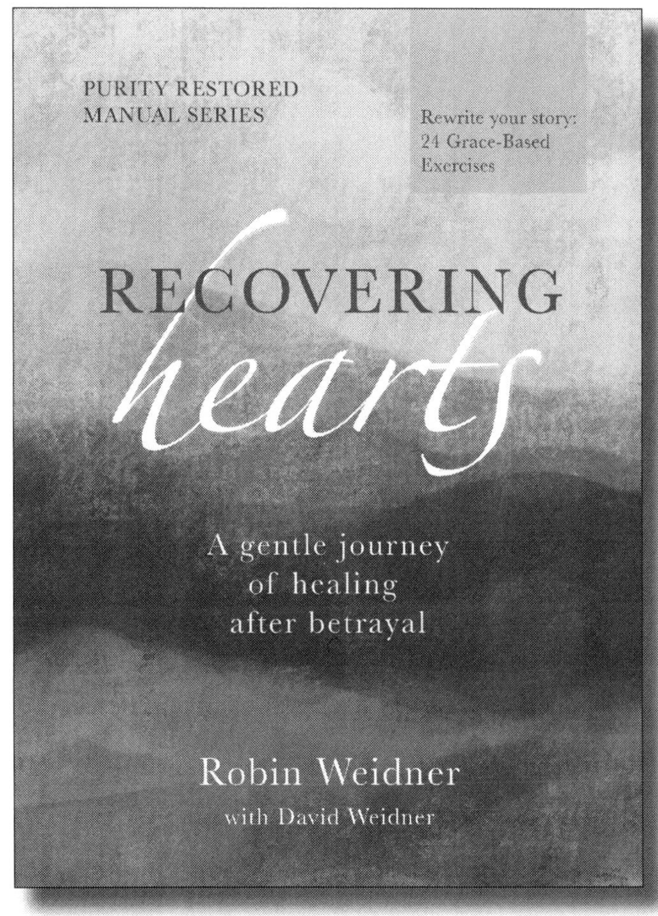

Libros en español de Robin Weidner

Libros en español de Dave y Robin Weidner

Available at www.purityrestored.com

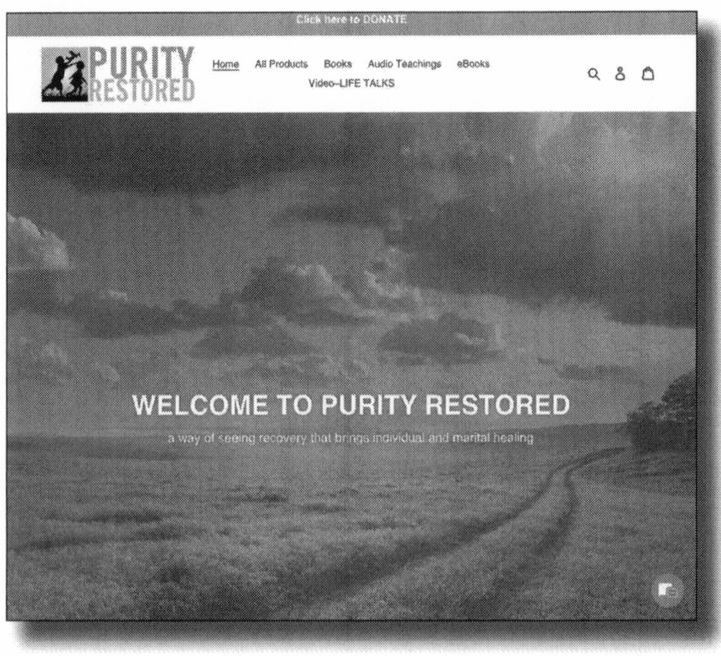

Made in the USA
Coppell, TX
28 November 2022

87297327R00187